Cover Design by Airicka's Mystical Creations
Editor: Sara Johnson

Staccato Publishing
Zimmerman, MN

First Paperback Edition: March 2012
Second Edition: December 2012
Third Edition: June 2013

ISBN: 978-1-940202-52-5

Printed in the USA

Secrets
by HK Savage

Chapter 1

"Nice Claire." Tonya Andrews leaned against the bathroom mirror to admire the culmination of her labors from the blur of the past few days.

I nodded dumbly, staring at the reflection of the woman I barely recognized in the mirror. My wavy, dark brown hair was pulled back in a sleek updo, ornamented simply with a clip hidden but for a strand of delicate pearls. The makeup Tonya had painstakingly been applying for the last half hour made me flawless in a way I had only believed possible for the celebrity set.

If I thought the hair and makeup were amazing, the dress was the true showstopper. It was a simple white satin gown cut in a slender A-line. The neckline went straight across the bust with delicate lace shoulders and sleeves. The effect was ethereal and did well to hide my numerous and recently accumulated scars, one of the few negative side effects to having vampires and werecats for friends. And enemies.

It had been James' idea to surprise my parents with a trip to Paris for their twenty-fifth anniversary. Tonight we arranged for them to take a romantic sunset cruise on a private yacht down the Seine. Unbeknownst to them, we would be joining them for a surprise wedding that they would be overjoyed to share.

Before James had come in to my life and helped me learn to block the emotions of those around me, my unwanted "gift" of empathy had kept me from being close to my parents, or anyone else for that matter. But now I had begun to develop a close relationship with both of my parents, Doug and Jeanette Martin.

"Tonya," I struggled not to be overly effusive with my gratitude for the normally distant eldest sister of my best friend Stephen. "Thank you so much for everything you've done. You are a magicican."

Wiggling her fingers, uncharacteristically playful, Tonya winked. "Maybe I'm not the only one who can transform."

Oh yeah, Stephen and his family were all werecats and could change shape at will, which made them quite a formidable family. I was understandably nervous when, at first, the girls, Tonya and Tara, hadn't exactly taken to me. Say what you'd like about cattiness, it was no joke when the cat was a several hundred pound mountain lioness.

"Am I interrupting a Hallmark moment?" Spinning on my heel I saw a shorter male version of Tonya grinning at me from the doorway beside his sister.

"Stephen!" I squealed and ran to embrace him enthusiastically. "How did you get here? I thought you couldn't leave the country."

He was laughing, eyes twinkling as he kissed my forehead. "Damn Claire, you *are* getting stronger. If any more of James leaks through you're going to be able to kick my ass."

I felt my bubble threatening to burst as Stephen reminded me of the rare psychic bond I shared with my soon to be husband and vampire, James Thomas. No one had experienced a bond such as ours for over three hundred years, so we were considered a curiosity by the few who knew about it. The bond bridging our sympathetic psychic abilities lent us telepathic powers that had proved life saving. Unfortunately, it was also blurring the lines between our natures and I'd been losing control of myself a lot because of it. I was afraid I was going to be lost to it completely all too soon.

Stephen saw the shadow cross my face. "Hey, Tonya will kill me if I make you cry and mess up your makeup." He snuck a look at Tonya who, by her expression, was in full agreement.

Never one to be serious for long, Stephen threw an arm around his sister and kissed her on the cheek. "Will you make me just as beautiful on my big day?"

Tonya rolled her eyes and wheeled out of the room. "I'm going to check on something, somewhere. You two behave; I don't have enough time to fix her back up."

With my newly acquired super hearing I heard the door close as she left our suite at the Four Seasons.

Dark mood successfully pushed aside, I grabbed Stephen's hand and led him past the huge bedroom and out onto the terrace overlooking the Eiffel Tower and the streets of Paris below. The sun hung low in the sky, making it hard to ignore the January chill in the air. Fortunately for my parents, the yacht was enclosed. The weather didn't affect James or the Andrews, or me so much anymore.

Refusing to dwell on my slippery slide into the supernatural today, I twirled happily and held my arms out to indicate the cityscape beyond us, stopping to shoot him a coy over the shoulder pose. "What do you think? Romantic, no?"

Stephen took in our amazing view of the city's lights illuminating the historic buildings below. "I'm glad I could be here for your big day." His expression darkened. "It's just for the night; I have to get back tomorrow or I'll be missed."

Stephen was being investigated as a "person of interest" in the disappearance of his former boyfriend, Brian. He wasn't the reason Brian had disappeared, but how does one explain to the police detective that his missing person had actually been killed while working for a vampire?

9

"Has anything changed? The body hasn't turned up has it?" No one knew what had happened to Brian's body and we were all waiting for the case to take a more serious turn should it inconveniently make an appearance.

"No, nothing's changed but I can't help but feel like the Detective knows something and he's just waiting for me to slip. He might be a problem." Stephen's brow furrowed as he eyed the skyline, avoiding eye contact.

I put my hand on his arm. "You know that's how they're supposed to be. That's how he gets you to crack and confess the crime, right? Just like one of those awful 'Law and Order' shows Tara doesn't want us to know she watches."

Stephen wrinkled his nose. "I don't know *how* she can stomach those. They've come out with about ten different series and they're all the same. Now she's even got Omar watching them."

Omar was a freshly turned vampire who was only twelve human years old and quite taken with Tara. She was the closest thing to a mom Omar had ever had and she relished the role.

"It should be considered child abuse making him watch that drivel." We both laughed. It had been too long since we had been able to hang out just the two of us. I didn't realize how much I missed just being with him. "You didn't tell me. How did you get here? I heard they were keeping an eye on you."

His eyes flashed deviously. "You're going to love this. Tara brought Omar over, he and I changed clothes and I snuck out. We're close enough to the same build, no one thought anything of it. I used a backup passport to fly out, and here I am." My confusion was obvious, he explained, "We always keep an extra set or two just in case."

I could only imagine what "just in case" meant, but if the last six months were any indication, I might want to get myself another set as soon as possible.

"Apparently, you talk in your sleep and Mr. Wonderful heard how badly you missed your best friend."

I gave him a look to evidence my displeasure, thinking he was renewing the animosity he'd shown for James a few times this winter.

Stephen held up his hands in mock surrender. "I don't mean anything by it. I'm just saying; he is Mr. Wonderful, right? Otherwise we wouldn't be here."

"Well, *I* think so." Sensing his hesitation, I was stern. "You *are* going to be nice or you can stay behind." I didn't want to think of tonight without him but I didn't want to fight with him, either.

"Of course I'm coming and I'll be nice. You need witnesses to make this thing legal, right?" His expression grew serious. "Are you sure you want to do this?"

Quick to lose patience lately, I frowned at him. "Stephen, I'm in love with him," I started.

He looked down and shook his head. "I don't mean the marriage. What I mean is this whole thing. Once you're in bed with them, they're never going to let you go."

He was talking about my new position working with newly turned vampires for their ruling body known as "the Court." James' old partner had been killed and, because of our special connection, the Court offered the job to me. My first assignment had been to work with Omar and just two days ago I had received my first paycheck. It was better money than I hoped to earn my first year out of college. Of course, when you consider that I was putting my mortal life on the line, I guess I had earned it.

"You're right," I acknowledged his concerns. "They're scary and I'm not sure whether they are all on our side, but it's James' job. He needs help and it's actually something *I* can do for *him*. Besides," I added wistfully, "it feels good to have my ability do some good."

"If that's what you want. In for a penny, in for a pound, right?" Stephen put an understanding hand on my shoulder and changed directions again. He could be very flighty. I loved that about him. "Hey, I was thinking maybe you and I could go out for lunch tomorrow before I have to leave. You know, one on one time before I lose you forever." He shoved his lower lip out in a mock pout.

I hesitated before answering, running through tomorrow's schedule in my head. We were hoping to take my parents out to dinner.

Stephen rolled his eyes, misreading the direction of my thoughts. "Don't worry, I'll have you back in time for your evening activities. I have a plane to catch, remember. More than a day or so and I think my constant police companions go into withdrawal. Did I tell you I think one of them has a crush on me?"

Giggling, I grinned at him. The consummate flirt, he never took anything too seriously. It was a lifestyle choice he had made a long time ago. I couldn't help but feel bad for him. The first time in a long time he had found someone he wanted to be with and he had turned out to be a traitor. Stephen was living with the aftershocks of his mistake daily with the help of the Minneapolis Police Department.

Hugging him again, I was reiterating how happy I was that he was there when a knock at the door interrupted us. Unsurprised, Stephen told me to wait wordlessly, holding up one finger. For a second I was nervous at his secrecy and held my breath until I came in off of the terrace to see a room service cart wheel into the room with a magnum of French champagne and two flutes.

I started to say no when Stephen grabbed the bottle to pop the cork. "I'm not supposed to drink. It makes it hard to keep myself straight."

The look Stephen gave me told me what he thought of that idea. The cork released with a sigh.

"Miranda said so herself. I'm not supposed to drink and I have to take better care of myself or I'm going to get James or myself hurt."

Miranda was one of the three members of the Court. She had taken a personal interest in James and myself, being the only other person still in existence who had ever been involved in a bond such as ours.

Stephen poured two flutes and held one out to me.

I put my hands stubbornly behind my back.

"It's your wedding day, toast with your best friend. James is going to be all over you for the next," he looked up searchingly for the right word, "forever." He gave me his most charming smile. "You'll be safe. If you don't believe me I'll swim behind the boat and make sure no one gets near you."

Snorting, I reached out to take one of the flutes. "You don't have to do that. I know cats hate to be wet."

We touched glasses and as I took a sip, Stephen frowned. "Claire, James and I have had our differences over the years but he's a great guy and I'm happy you two have each other." He added with a wink, "I just wish he had a brother."

We were back on the terrace and nearly to the bottom of our glasses when I heard a small cough from the doorway. Turning, I saw the man who was going to be my husband within a matter of hours, watching me. Even after being together constantly for the past four months, I still had trouble keeping myself under control when he was in the room. Now, seeing him in his black suit, I felt my pulse take flight.

Stephen tipped his head to James. "Congratulations, James. You've got a great girl here."

"I agree." He reluctantly tore his eyes from me to answer Stephen. "Thank you for coming. Having you here means a lot to both of us."

Stephen grinned, "I wouldn't have missed it." He winked at me, giddy to be away from his police escort and maybe a little from the champagne. I felt it; my shields were not one hundred percent after the drink. "I'm always looking for an excuse to come to Paris." Downing the last of his drink, Stephen reached over to hug me. "You're beautiful. Enjoy your last moments of freedom and I'll see you on the boat." He kissed my cheek and gave me a squeeze.

Stephen shook James' hand and leaned in to give him a somber warning. "You take care of her. It's a hard life you've signed her up for and you know it."

James' response was equally solemn. "I would never put her in danger if I didn't think I could take care of her. You know that or you would not have released me from my oath of protection. *I* still take that responsibility very seriously."

Stephen's shoulders were set and I could tell from his profile that his hackles were up.

I stepped in to prevent the fight I felt coming. "I appreciate your concern but might I remind you I've proven I can take care of myself?" I looked at Stephen and took one of his hands in mine. "This is my life and I choose to live it with him, doing this work." I kissed him on the cheek and laid a hand on it. "Just be happy for me Stephen, please."

Stephen hardened for a second studying my resolve before breaking into a smile. Cavalier Stephen was back, "Okay Claire, but don't you two go getting too wild before the big occasion. If you mess up that hair Tonya will have your head."

Stephen showed himself out leaving James and I alone. I felt awkward for the first time since we had met and wasn't sure what to do. Fortunately, I didn't have to wait long and the decision was made for me. Within approximately five seconds of the door closing, James was within arm's reach where he stood looking me over.

Blushing and feeling increasingly uncomfortable, I broke the silence. "Is there something wrong? I hope not, because Tonya spent a lot of time on me. It doesn't get any better than this." My hands nervously smoothed the front of my dress while I watched them.

James smiled and I saw his fangs were halfway out in his excitement. "Claire, you are breathtaking."

I blushed again, feeling like a kid on her first date. His soft growl brought me back.

"Now I am just wondering how upset Tonya would really be if I delivered you slightly tousled." I felt my lower half warm with the thought and glanced at the clock, visible over his shoulder to check if we had time. James wrapped his arms around my back and I felt his teeth graze my earlobe before he tracked down to my collarbone. It was one of my weaknesses and he knew it. His wicked chuckle vibrated against my ribcage, eliciting a soft sigh from my lips. "I promise to be careful."

Groaning, I had to push back the urge to yank off my dress right there. "We really do need to go if we're going to make the boat."

Another growl, this one from frustration. Inwardly I smiled. It was good to know I could inflame him as he did me. When your lover has been experiencing life for over one hundred and fifty years and you've never been with anyone but him, it can be more than a little intimidating.

Reticently he let go to take my hand, and indicated with an incline of his head that we should move on. We dressed in outerwear for appearances, he in his black wool coat and I wore a white brocaded wrap over my shoulders.

The cab ride to the landing was short and I paid no mind to the cabbie's banter or the historic scenery whipping past our windows. My mind was a blur of racing thoughts. My parents were going to be so surprised. I couldn't wait to see their faces. We had only just gotten engaged at Christmas and the last time I'd spoken to my mother I told her we hadn't set a date yet.

Feeling his gaze on me, I glanced at James. What I saw there was private and, not wanting the cabbie to intrude, I found the place in my head where our bond resided, lightly fluttering at it.

I saw James' eyes crinkle when he felt my "call." We were getting more fluid at this. We'd been practicing.

Instead of speaking, he sent me a memory of a woman with dark brown hair and familiar gray blue eyes. She was standing in front of an oval mirror. I saw the reflection of a quilt covered bed behind her. Her slender frame was draped in an old fashioned gown, off the shoulders with her hair piled on top of her head, a few tendrils pulled down around her face softened her already delicate features. Movement behind her caught my eye and I watched a man in a dark suit approach from behind her, he held a hat and gloves in his hands. He tossed the gloves into the hat and handed them both to someone behind him before walking up to put his arms around her waist resting his chin on her shoulder. She turned to face him and he kissed her tenderly.

Letting go of his wife, his father took back his hat and pulled his gloves out to give James a playful swat on the top of his head.

My eyes were drawn to the reflection of the small person holding the hat in the doorway. I felt the tears prick my eyes as I realized I was seeing a young James watching his parents. It must have been right before his mother got sick. She was bedridden when he was very young.

His big eyes were bluer then. His wavy, light brown locks swirled into his eyes and he grinned at his father. It was the same grin I'd fallen in love with.

I felt my heart nearly burst with sadness for the little boy who would soon lose his mother to illness, his father to alcoholism, and his siblings as they were sent off one by one when his father found the responsibility too much.

I never thought I would find what they had, especially after I was turned. I wanted you to see them like I remember them. Reaching up, I pulled his face down to me and kissed him softly.

Chapter 2

My parents were standing in the open area at the front of the cabin, staring at the lights of the city when we walked in behind them with our party who had joined us at the dock. The round table was set for eight and the lights sparkled on the crystal and silver. Soft music played in the background and an arrangement of white roses stood in the center, the single scarlet ribbon surrounding the vase matched Tonya's dress perfectly.

I wasn't surprised. She had arranged all the details aside from the yacht. She had done such a fabulous job, I didn't know how I was going to thank her enough for all of this.

The captain came in from the rear of the boat and smiled conspiratorially when he saw us. James gave a slight nod and the captain made the announcement.

"Well, now that we're all here I think we can get underway."

Mom turned and saw us first. "Claire!" Her hands flew to her mouth and Dad turned around. He took in our party, my dress, James' suit, and thankfully, I saw his lips curve into a smile. I'd been fairly certain they would approve, yet I had been a little anxious until right at that moment.

"Claire, James. What a nice surprise." Dad's unaffected demeanor was the product of a military career that had prepared him for nearly any situation. He had proven impossible to rattle over the years.

"Oh, I'm so happy you're here." Mom hugged me. "Is this what I think it is?" She looked askance at James over my shoulder. "Is this it?" She pulled away enough to look at my face for confirmation.

I nodded, all of a sudden unable to speak, my own eyes wet.

With a squeal, she pulled me in tight again.

Dad shook hands with James and I heard the catch in his throat as he spoke, "Good to have you in the family James."

Initial shock over with, I remembered my manners and extricated myself from Mom. "Mom, Dad, I'd like to introduce you to some of our friends; Henry Campbell and Stephen and Tonya Andrews."

We were making connections for my parents, pointing out how we knew everyone when the captain interrupted and a crewman emerged from below with a bottle in one hand, wire rack with a handle full of champagne flutes in the other.

"Some champagne before the ceremony. We can begin once we are underway."

Henry picked up glasses as they were filled, handing the first to James, the next to me. "I would like to propose a toast to the happy couple."

Henry wasn't normally one to express himself, I perked up, eager to hear what he had to say.

Glasses were raised as Henry's easy voice carried through the cabin. "I have known James a long time. We have traveled the world and seen amazing things both good and bad." He paused. "But nothing has ever held him like the bond he shares with Claire. May it last an eternity."

I couldn't help but smile at the double meaning and be moved at the same time. James' arm tightened around me at Henry's mention of eternity and the one nagging question that had recently sprung up in our relationship, my mortality, itched at the edge of both our minds.

Before I could spend too much time thinking about it, the rest of the party raised their glasses and drank. Henry and

James even sipped at their glasses for the sake of appearances. Conversation ensued and I was lost in the social demands of the occasion.

I only took a few tiny sips of champagne, remembering Miranda's warning that alcohol made me weak. I was going to need my strength to get through tonight without becoming an emotional basket case.

The music changed to Pachelbel and I watched the captain take his place at the front of the cabin windows.

"James, Claire, please join me and we can begin."

Ch. 3

After the ceremony we sat down to a dinner most of us enjoyed. The others would eat later. And as tradition would dictate, everyone enjoyed a piece of cake afterward. Henry and James nibbled a little bit for appearances. Stephen snapped off a few pictures with a fancy looking camera as our unofficial photographer for the evening.

When the yacht returned to the dock, we gathered to say our good byes. My parents insisting we let them put together a family reception for us when we returned home.

Mom put her arms out as she said good bye to Henry and I stared in disbelief as she hugged the ancient and powerful vampire. "You have to come too, Henry. You're the closest thing James has to family and I just can't wait to get to know you better."

Henry was a gentleman and hugged my mother back, shaking my Dad's hand. "I would be honored, Jeanette."

He nodded at my Dad and looked him directly in the eye.
For the first time in my life, I saw my dad lose his composure. Instantly, he looked shaken and Henry blinked, releasing him from whatever had started to take hold of Dad.

Freed, Dad's gaze shifted to me and I saw his confusion. He turned to James beside me and stared. Cold dread settled in my stomach as I watched suspicion spark in my father's eyes.

"So pleased to have met you both." Stephen stepped between my dad and me to shake his hand. Being polite, my dad finished saying his goodbyes to our wedding party. I held my breath when it was our turn.

Dad shook James' hand, doubt returning to his eyes. "Be good to her." He looked like there was more he wanted to say yet he refrained.

James was unfazed by Dad's change in tone. "Doug, I made a promise today that I intend to keep. I will take care of her forever." I felt the stirrings of anger beneath his calm façade.

Tonya swung in and hugged Dad cutting short the tense moment. Dad couldn't help but be distracted by the six foot tall, sexy creature clinging to him. Wow, did I owe Tonya.

We parted at the dock and Henry accompanied the Andrews clan to their hotel where they were going to continue their merriment. James and I took a cab back to our hotel to celebrate our union in private.

Ch. 4

The chill in the night air was crisp and smelled fresh. I loved the smell of winter. According to the locals, it was an unseasonably warm January here in Paris, forties and fifties for the most part and no snow. James and I were standing on the terrace in our room watching the lights below us, waiting for the Eiffel Tower to light up. They were not constant, but illuminated hourly and we were coming close. Watching the traffic below, contemplating everything that had changed for me, I sighed.

His arm lay behind my shoulders, holding me close. "Are you happy?"

"I am." I answered softly leaning into him. "Dad felt something when he looked at Henry, didn't he? I've never seen Dad even close to scared but he looked it tonight."

James' lips were tight and his eyes dark, telling me he was anxious as well. "Yes, I think it would be wise of us to limit your parents' exposure to Henry. Your mother seems oblivious but your father is more observant." He tried to joke, "That must be where you get it."

"Aren't you worried? Dad might start watching *you* more closely as well. You saw the way he looked at you."

"I'm sorry, Claire." His remorse was sincere. "It eventually happens whenever we're around a human for too long."

"So much for bringing my two worlds together." I couldn't help feeling a pang of loss.

His lips brushed my forehead. "It's hard to live a double life. It only grows more difficult with time when everyone else ages. That is one of the many reasons my kind doesn't often dally long term with yours."

I shook myself from the negative direction of my thoughts. "What am I complaining about? I have two wonderful families and I have you. I'm not going to feel sorry for myself that we can't have everyone get together more than once or twice a year."

"I love you, Mrs. Thomas," he muttered against my lips.

I felt myself flush at his mention of my new name. With a start, I remembered something. "Stay there, I'll be right back." I trotted in to retrieve something I'd been hiding in my luggage.

Feeling slightly embarrassed, I looked down at the gift I'd picked up this week with Tonya.

"What is that?" James frowned, uncomfortable to be receiving and not giving the gift.

I shrugged, "We aren't a very traditional couple so I figured I could pick and choose which traditions I keep." Glancing down at the little box, I worried it wasn't enough. "I like this one."

"By my standards we are a very traditional couple, Claire." It was my turn to be skeptical.

"Really, we are. When I was raised, a man took care of his wife, protected her. My parents worked side by side every day of their lives until she was too sick to help anymore. We're the same."

Closing the gap between us, I took his hand with my free one and felt the band of gold now resting there. "I like working with you and being with you, but you have to be honest with me if it starts to get to you. Some couples are rarely together and we're the opposite, we're rarely apart. I don't want it to get to be too much." I peeked up at him through my lashes. "I know you've been alone a long time."

He kissed me gently. "You don't have to worry about me getting tired of your company, I assure you."

I placed the box in his hand and he looked down at it. He tried to hide his awkwardness yet it was still there, in my head as well as in front of my eyes.

I found it endearing. Considering he became a vampire at the age of twenty over one hundred, fifty years ago, he certainly had the potential to be ungrateful. The fact that he was the polar opposite was sort of sweet.

James' long, pale fingers untied the silver bow and tore off the white paper to reveal the simple black box. His eyes were midnight when he glanced up at me. When he opened the box, he stared within for so long I feared he didn't care for the contents.

"Do you like them?" Suddenly uncertain, I started to doubt my choice. They had seemed like such a natural choice when I had bought them, now I wasn't so sure.

Tonya and I had been walking back from the dress shop yesterday and I saw them in a jeweler's window; a pair of cufflinks. They were my exact eye color, light brown with shades of green. I had thought back to the opal necklace James had given me, saying it reminded him of us, always changing but always together. The check had just come in from the Court and I took pride in having my own money. Impulsively, I bought them for a small fortune.

Now, as I watched him stare, I worried he didn't like them. They weren't diamonds or gold, and silver was out of the question since that could kill a vampire. Finally he startled me with an unusually rough voice.

"They're beautiful, Love. Thank you."

I touched the opal around my neck and met his eyes. "They seemed right."

He continued to stare at me, his eyes dark and face unreadable as he slipped the box into his suit pocket. James put his hands on my shoulders, thumbs stroking my flesh before sliding them down to my hands. "There is another tradition I'd like to keep."

When his lips moved, I saw his fangs again. He was excited and, knowing what tradition he was referring to, I felt my body respond.

My physical reactions never escaped his notice. In a superhuman flash, my legs went out from under me and I was swept into our room. He slowed down to set me gently in front of the bed. James' hands reached around to unzip my dress and I watched his eyes blacken as he slid my dress down my body.

His mouth found mine and I felt his tender kiss grow more insistent, my hands went from tie to shirt laying his skin bare to my touch and he shivered in pleasure when I pulled the fabric from his shoulders. James' arms slid around my body and pulled me close, his hands pulling me harder against him.

Lifting me up to lay me on the tall four post bed, James kissed my lips, then my face. He lay down beside me, taking the time to kiss the scars left by the myriad encounters with vampires. I gasped as his tongue swirled across the sunburst scar above my heart where one had nearly chewed through my chest when I offered my blood to save James.

"I will do everything in my power to keep anyone from hurting you Claire." I felt the intensity of his resolve, "I swear it."

I ran my fingers through his hair, grabbing it tightly in my hands to bring his face up to mine. When he felt me get aggressive he growled and let me guide him. Everything else was forgotten as we made love as husband and wife for the first time.

Ch. 5

The aroma of breakfast pulled me from my dreams. After our busy night, my stomach greeted the smell with a hearty growl.

The chuckle beside me made me smile before I even opened my eyes. When I did, I saw James grinning crookedly at me from where he lay beside me. He reached over to push back my hair from my face and kissed my nose. "Come have something to eat."

Imagining what I must look like, I rolled to press my face into my pillow. "Give me just a minute. I'll be right in there." I went in the bathroom to put up my hair and take care of my needs.

"James, it smells amazing. Join me?" I indicated the chair opposite me as I sat.

He sat and I saw he had already been having his own breakfast. He favored covered travel mugs to hold the donor blood he drank in place of feeding directly from the source. I appreciated him making his feeding unobtrusive. There was just something about watching a man drink a cup of blood. Oddly, it didn't bother me when it was in a wine glass, though. Chalk it up to my ability to make my perception fit the situation. How else does one explain not being completely freaked out by living in a supernatural world?

My breakfast was one found on a normal menu. French toast made from a type of bread called brioche, served with warm maple syrup and applewood smoked bacon. He poured a cup of tea for me with cream and sugar as I took a bite of my French toast.

"Mmm," I moaned in pleasure, closing my eyes. "It's wonderful. I wish this could last forever."

"It can," he spoke quietly.

I opened my eyes and looked at him, "No it can't. I'm meeting Stephen in just a few hours for lunch and then we need to start thinking about going home. Classes start for me in less than two weeks."

"Are you sure you're going back?" he asked, reminding me of a previous conversation.

I had been intentionally avoiding having to make this decision. Working for the Court was going to require that we travel and the majority of our assignments would be in Edinburgh, the seat of the Court's power. Henry and James had suggested that I consider online classes or transferring to the University of Edinburgh to continue my studies. James had even taken me on a tour of the University on our last trip to Scotland.

I took a bite of bacon and chewed it slowly, savoring its perfect combination of smoky, salted meatiness. Not sure what to say, I bit off another chunk.

Immortals are very patient on the whole and James was no different. He busied himself watching me eat and taking the occasional sip of his own meal.

After a few more bites, I still didn't know what I wanted to say. James finally broke the silence.

"Claire, you will have a very long life; longer than most. You can choose to continue school through several different avenues, but the traditional avenue you've been pursuing is no longer going to be feasible. There is no shame in taking a few years off college to go to work; no one will question it."

He was right of course. I knew I couldn't keep pretending to be a normal college student. Our bond had given me many of his benefits, including a life that would outlast that of an ordinary human. He wasn't the only one who would have to explain away his endless youth in a few years.

My worlds were splitting further apart and there was no way I could deny it, no matter how hard I tried. The time to begin making decisions was forcing itself upon me. I worried my human family would think me a drop-out and a failure, that they would think less of me. They would blame James. How could I add more lies to the growing list of falsehoods I already had to keep up?

Breakfast no longer held much appeal. I had to choke down the last swallow of chewed meat, now bitter on my tongue. "James, how do you propose I explain to my parents what my job might be? I'll be gone for weeks at a time and taking off with little notice." Forcing a tight smile, I pointed out, "The 'I'm a travel writer' excuse is already taken."

"If you need to come up with a cover story, I think I might be able to help you." He rubbed his hands, watching them instead of me. "I spoke to my editor and he likes the idea of us traveling together, getting the couples' take on trips."

Tipping my head, I gave him a severe look.

He held up his hands, "What? He came up with it on his own. I did nothing to sway him. Besides he liked the combined perspective from our trip to Edinburgh, he says it's a good angle."

I didn't feel the relief I knew I should have. He was right, of course. There was no shame in telling my parents I was going to take a break from school and go to work. They would be excited that it was a job that let me travel and I could even take classes online for a while. It was a win-win situation. Right? So why did it still feel wrong?

"Okay, I'll think about it. I can call the school tomorrow and see what it would take to switch to online courses and lower my class load. We can take a little longer to tell my parents, but not much. They'll be expecting me to be back at school soon and the bills *do* go to their house. They'll figure it out pretty quickly." My mind was spinning through all the details I would need to hammer out to sell the lie.

A slow smile spread across his face and he set down his mug. "Actually, I believe we need to talk to the school about where to send your bills. Your life has changed now and your parents are no longer responsible for you."

"Oh my gosh, I didn't even think of that. I'm working now and I can pay for myself. They're going to be relieved even if they don't want to admit it."

In my excitement, I didn't notice the smile fleeing James' lips.

"I was referring to the fact that you are my wife. *I* am responsible for you now. Your father is released from his obligation."

I bristled. "I can take care of myself. You're my husband, not my father and you're not *obligated* to do anything."

A wrinkle formed between his brows. "I know that you're capable of taking care of yourself, I'm not disagreeing with you. However, I *am* responsible for you. Husbands take care of their wives and I'm glad to do it. I love you."

"The man said to 'care for each other,' not be responsible for each other. That's a *big* difference." My blood was heating up as James continued to try to defend his point.

He put his hands on the table and stood up. "Claire, why are you getting upset when I say I want to take care of you? I have said that very thing from the start and you've never taken offense. What's different now? Where I come from, there is nothing insulting about being responsible for the care of one's spouse. You would care for me if I were sick." James' voice was rising and I watched his eyes darken as he struggled with his temper.

My own voice spiked in self-righteous anger, "This is not 1860 and I will not be a burden!" Somewhere in my head reason was being slapped away and my unjustified rage began to burn; my throat did as well.

James was still trying to maintain a civil conversation, but was not one to be pushed too far and I saw his fangs growing long as he fumed.

Jumping out of my chair, heedless of the crash it made when it flew, I continued my attack. "You haven't been married to me 24 hours and already you're taking away my school, my family and calling me an obligation. You're such a chauvinist!"

Spitting the insult, I stepped around the table edge and launched myself at him. My inherited speed and surprise got me through James' initial defenses fast enough he had time only to grab my wrists as they came up. I had struck him before and he knew I wouldn't stop at a minor slap.

I hissed through my clenched teeth; the burning heat in my throat became all I could think about. James was holding me close to his chest, my hands held tightly in front of my face. Without thinking where the urge came from, I lowered my mouth to his hand and bit down, feeling the flesh give under my teeth, exciting me enough to clamp down harder.

James had not been expecting it and instinctively released my wrists, pushing me away. He was strong. I was thrown backward and hit the floor hard, my arm swinging out behind me striking a table leg.

I lay unmoving where I landed. My hip hurt where the carpet had rubbed it raw and I had a sharp pain in my head. It must have hit something. But the worst of it was that in that moment, I wasn't sure if any of me was human anymore.

James' reaction was instant. His anger was gone. "Claire, are you all right?" His hands roamed over me to feel my body for broken bones. When he reached my left wrist, I yelped.

"I am so sorry." He continued to probe my limbs for damage but aside from knowing I was going to have serious bruises to contend with for a few days, there were no other injuries. "Claire, can you speak?" His panic was building, I could hear it in his voice.

I tried to answer but my brain was still jumbled from hitting the table. Instead, I tried to stand up. James put his hands under my arms and helped me to my feet.

Once I was standing I became aware there was blood in my mouth and felt a wave of nausea. It rapidly became clear that it wasn't going to pass and I stumbled past him to get to the bathroom. He could feel it and picked me up to get me there faster. Even with his help I barely made it in time to lose my breakfast.

After my stomach was empty, I felt my head clearing as well. I tried to speak, but my tongue was too thick. What could I say? I had been completely unable to control my body or mouth, overreacting to the extreme. Once again, our bond had blurred our natures and I had failed to control the impulsiveness of the vampire.

I rinsed my mouth in the sink and shut off the light on my way out of the bathroom, collapsing into an overstuffed armchair in the adjoined sitting room. I was grateful to have the physical pain of my arm to focus on. I couldn't bring myself to look at James.

"Claire, are you all right? Please speak to me." He put his hands on my shoulders, anxiously trying to make me look up at him.

Feeling the shame tighten my throat and the tears well up under my eyelids, I shook my head.

"Are you still angry?" I knew my rapidly changing behavior was keeping him on edge as well and I hated myself for not being stronger and better able to fight it. There was no denying it, the vampire nature was choking the human. It had nearly won.

"No, I'm just having trouble keeping a human and vampire in one body." My voice broke on the last word and I started getting up to leave the room. I wanted to go hide, mortified to have lost control of myself again.

Before I could get all the way out of my chair, he was kneeling in front of me, his hands on my knees. Not able to face him, I tried to push him away. I was becoming as helpless as I had been before I'd met him, when my empathy ruled my life.

He wouldn't allow me to flee. His arms hardened to steel and wrapped around me, holding me tight. "Claire," he tried to reason.

I struggled against him, trying to get away. I wanted to leave this room, to run from the hotel and out of the city itself. He didn't flinch or give in. My resolve and my strength were failing. I felt the hot tears start to stream down my face, losing control again as I dissolved into hysterics.

"Claire, please stop. This isn't you. *This is not you.*" His voice was tortured.

My body went limp in his arms and I tried to stop the tears. "James, what's happening to me?" I was blubbering. "I can't do this again. It almost drove me crazy before." I continued my descent into a messy emotional wreck. James flipped open his phone and talked fast.

"It's worse." He sounded so distressed I cried even harder. "Hurry."

He closed his phone and picked me up to sit down, setting me on his lap. I curled up and let him wrap a blanket around me. He was right, I was a burden.

Ch. 6

After my hysterics eased into a state of emptiness, I was left devoid of thought or emotion until there was a faint knock at the door. James got up, leaving me in the chair.

They kept their voices low as James led Henry into our room. I couldn't hear their footsteps as they entered, I never could. And then they were there, standing in front of me. James crouched down to look into my face, smoothing back my hair. I sat watching them, unmoving and mentally exhausted.

"Claire, stand up," Henry commanded and I couldn't resist him.

I pushed myself out of the chair and James stood beside me, not touching me, ready to catch me if I fell.

Henry's voice rang out again, "Look at me."

Even knowing what he was going to do, I couldn't resist. Our eyes locked and I felt the familiar shift in my perceptions as he rolled my mind, looking for whatever it was he wanted in my head.

After I don't know how long, I felt him release his hold on my psyche. My body started to fall when a familiar pair of hands caught me. James carried me back into the bedroom and lay me in the bed where we had been so obliviously happy only hours before. Fortunately I was too tired to have another meltdown just yet.

James kept his voice low. I listened objectively, as if it wasn't me they were discussing. "Is it getting worse or is she just tired from yesterday? I'm feeding almost constantly already, I don't know what else I can do."

Henry's voice was thoughtful. "Yesterday was unexpected; her father may prove challenging."

I couldn't help the noise I made in my throat. Thinking of what Henry could do to my dad made my stomach tie up in knots.

"It isn't an option." James was firm. "We'll find some other way to diffuse the situation *if* it even gets that far."

More persuasively, Henry continued, "We've talked about this. She cannot continue to live in both worlds much longer. She *is* growing worse; you must stop denying it. Humans cannot tolerate the sensory overload without complete breakdown. Why do you think most human servants end up insane and have to be put down? You should turn her now before it is too late. I warn you, not all of the mental damage will be repairable."

James didn't speak.

"Is that what you want?" Henry asked him pragmatically.

My heart broke at the anguish I heard in James' voice. "What would you have me do, Henry? I can't turn her or we'll both be monsters, and I can't be without her."

"Then this will be your world for as long as it lasts." It was quiet for a moment before Henry's voice came back. "Is this what you foresaw when you decided you had to have her, this intolerable suffering on both your parts? How long do you intend to let it go on? How long do you think the Court will allow it before taking matters into their own hands? We can only hide this for so long before they notice."

They lowered their voices and I heard nothing more. Eventually, the door closed again and I felt James return to lay in bed with me. He drew me to him, holding me against the firm line of his body.

I let him hold me against him and closed my eyes. In the darkness I created for myself, I felt his hesitation. He wanted to talk to me though he didn't know what to say.

Only our physical contact reinforced my shaky mental defenses, insulating me, and I began to reclaim control over myself. In a few minutes I was able to sit up. He watched me, keeping his hand on my leg to maintain my defenses for me.

Feeling ashamed of my frailty, I felt the urge to escape once again. So much intense interaction was not something I had much experience with and I was failing to handle it well in my condition. "I'm supposed to meet Stephen for lunch."

He didn't object when I got up and dressed, my back turned to him. The scarring on my body was something I tried to hide. Unfortunately, I couldn't help giving him a full view in the light of day now.

I knew James had a hard time seeing the results of my captivity. I felt it when he soundlessly came up behind me to stand inches away. Painfully aware of his presence, I felt the familiar pull, as always, when he was near me.

He didn't touch me with the exception of one finger I felt tracing the scars. His touch raised goose bumps on my body and I felt my physical need to be with him beginning to take over.

Fighting the impulse before it became too much, I stepped out of reach and arranged the sweater in my hands so that I could pull it down, hiding my body from his eyes. I turned, facing him.

"James, I heard you and Henry." He wasn't surprised. He knew better than anyone that my hearing was nearly as good as his own. "I can't continue to be a problem that constantly needs handling. I've seen how they all look at me when I'm

38

having 'an episode,'" I quoted Stephen. "I don't want to lose my mind, and I don't know if I can turn."

Something unidentifiable was playing behind his eyes. "You are not a problem for me or anyone else. Each one of us started as a human and each one of us had challenges with our respective transitions. Some merely have better recollections than others."

The calm façade slipped and I saw him wrestling to rein in his warring emotions as he asked, "Are you really considering being turned?"

It was such a multilayered answer, I didn't know if I could put it into words. Wanting to show him, yet not wanting to go through our bond where he could see too much, I held out my hands, palms up.

James looked down at them and back to me. He had used the same technique to train me months ago. Once he put his hands on top of mine, I let my shields come down enough that he could see what I was going to show him.

I was much more experienced now than I had been at the beginning and found it easy to pick the subject I wanted to let him examine. Staring at our hands, I brought forth my thoughts on becoming like him and I felt him start to unravel them.

The subject was complicated and how I felt about it was no simpler. My instincts rebelled against the thought of having to survive on someone's blood. Even if I didn't hunt for my food and went the route of Henry and James, taking only donor blood, I had felt the thirst through James. I knew its searing burn, so powerful it came before anything else. I knew it would fade with time, as would the hypersensitive emotional roller coaster I was currently riding, though it would always be there, never completely tamed.

Then I showed him what I feared the most. It was possible that if I turned we might lose the bond that connected us, that had drawn us together. I was afraid that if I turned, I would lose what made me special to him and in turn, lose him in time.

James quietly withdrew from my thoughts. I had begun to lower my hands when he took hold of them.

Not daring to look him in the eye as the intimacy of what we were doing was already hard to manage; I stopped resisting and let my hands rest in his. He relaxed his grip so that he loosely held me with our palms touching. James rarely lowered his shielding to me and I respected his privacy. That was why when he brought them down now I wasn't sure what to expect.

First he showed me a distant memory, it was fuzzy with the passage of time. It was the night he'd risen after being violently attacked and turned by accident. Henry had found him and stolen him away in the night before he could be tried for the murders he'd committed when he'd woken hungry and alone. His thoughts were unreadable, not so his feelings.

The thirst he'd felt burned ten times hotter than anything I'd felt; it had driven him mad enough to slaughter the doctor whose house he'd been brought to. And then there was the guilt that had rocked him when at last he'd banked the fire in his throat.

He'd been sitting in front of the oven, trying to warm himself, contemplating taking his own life when Henry had come in. As soon as Henry had come near, James felt a sense of peace wash over him.

Then he directed me toward a more recent memory. It was me, how he felt when he saw me. I felt his wanting. It had been so strong, he'd wanted me that very night; though he hadn't yet decided if it was for blood or sex, but it was powerful. Then in our very first training session he had seen into my mind, saw the loneliness that matched his. I felt the strength of the desire he felt when I first kissed him and the love that had grown from there, how much our bond meant to him.

He gave me a nudge telling me it was time to go. He would show me no more. With a sigh, I released his hands and felt my mind pull back, my shields settling back into place.

"Claire," the sound of his voice in the silence startled me. "Do you see what you mean to me? That you're a part of me? You make this livable."
"Is that what it's like for everyone?" I doubted I was strong enough to be a vampire if I had to go through that kind of enduring pain. These snippets were too much and they were only a taste.

"Everyone is different, but yes. It is essentially the same for us all. With time, and training, we learn to control ourselves and ignore the constant burning."

"Henry's effect on you, I feel that sometimes when he commands me. Is that an ability or just ancient vampire stuff?"

James continued to study me, deciding if I was back under control I supposed. "Henry's gift is unique in that he can get into anyone's mind. He can influence people, a power that has strengthened with age. I have never met his equal or anyone who could defy him."

"Wow, I'm glad he's on our side."

James' lips curved upward, it wasn't a friendly smile. "I think it is us who are on his side."

I tried to settle myself, but I couldn't think standing here with him; his nearness clouded my judgment. Being with him pushed out any sense of self-preservation.

"I have to go." I stepped around him to leave and he moved with me. Without thinking, I put my arm up to his chest to stop him. Biting my lip didn't entirely stop the sound that came out of my mouth as my fractured wrist twisted against his chest.

His hands came up to cradle my arm and he directed me back to the chair I had just vacated. I didn't object. "We need to take care of this first." He left me to use the phone beside the bed. It took me a moment to recognize why the cadence was off. He was speaking French, flawlessly.
When he came back I was gaping at him.

"What?"

"You speak French?"

"I was born in Quebec. My family was English, but a number of my neighbors were French. It was impossible not to learn it."

"Oh." I felt stupid for never having considered that.

"There is so much I don't know about you."

He sat on the arm of the chair. "Claire, nobody knows everything about anyone. That's how it is supposed to be. We must all have our little mysteries. The important question is how you feel. Do you believe there is anything about me that would change your feelings toward me?"

Thankfully that answer was the same as it had always been. "No."

"Then anything else is just noise."

The doorbell rang and James left the room. When he returned, he held gauze padding, some splinting materials and self-adhesive bandages in his hands.

Realizing what was happening I had an image of a permanently bent limb. "Are you qualified to set broken bones?"

Kneeling down in front of me, James looked evenly into my eyes from less than a foot away. I smelled his spicy vanilla smell as it wafted around him in his movements. The combination of the sight and smell of him was dizzying. He was muddling my mind so I wouldn't feel the pain.

I felt his hand against my chest pushing me back; I'd shifted forward in the chair and was leaning toward him.

"Try to be still."

In my half stunned stupor I asked the question I was afraid to before. "Do human servants really go insane?"

James' hands froze mid-wrap. "You heard everything then?"

"Yes."

His hands went on, methodically doing something he appeared well practiced at. Fortunately the bandaging was close to flesh colored, I didn't want to explain what I'd done.

"Human senses are easily overwhelmed and being exposed to vampires' senses often proves too much for them after a while." His speech was halting and clipped. He clearly didn't want to talk about it.

I looked down at my arm. He had done a good job as far as I could tell. It would hold my wrist straight for the day or two it would take for the bone to heal. The bruising would probably show up by lunch and be gone by bed. Fast healing was one of the positives of being marked by a vampire. Good thing too, considering I had needed it since becoming involved in their affairs.

"I have to go. Stephen's waiting," I reminded him, needing space to think.

He nodded and stood, giving me room to get up.

I threw on a light coat. "I'm just meeting him for lunch, I'll be back after. Okay?"

"That's fine. I have some things I need to take care of here in town." He hid his eyes from me, not wanting me to read something there.

Ch. 7

The crisp January air helped clear my head and I walked for a few blocks before pulling out my phone to call Stephen. We'd never figured out where and when to meet for lunch.

When Stephen picked up I could hear street noises in the background. "Hey Claire. Are you up for lunch or did you two get too wild last night?"

I laughed tightly at Stephen's teasing thinking he wasn't far off. "Yes, I'm starving." Never mind why my stomach was currently empty.

"Is everything okay?" Concern warmed his voice.

"Yeah, I'm just tired." I changed the subject. "Where and when? I don't know this town very well so I leave it up to you."

"There's a café down the street from you that has some of the best coffee I've had here in Paris. Sound good?"

It did and I said so. I walked down the street and sure enough, there was a little place with tables out front. They were all empty considering the temperature. I saw most were empty inside as well. Not surprising given it was early and Parisians ate late.

I took a table and ordered a coffee. I was sipping on it when Stephen walked in.

His skin was flushed from the chill and his gray coat buttoned up to his striped scarf. I hadn't realized it had grown colder overnight. I would have to pay better attention to people to make sure I was dressing appropriately for the weather now that I couldn't feel it very well.

Stephen must have been thinking the same thing. He lifted an eyebrow and pointed at my outerwear. "That wouldn't keep *me* warm and I run hotter than *your* kind." He sat down, unwinding his scarf from his neck. He was nearly done when I thoughtlessly took another sip and he saw my hand. Before he could comment, I held up the other hand.

"Let's chalk it up as an accident and leave it at that, please?"

He tightened his lips yet honored my request, saying no more about it. With a nod and a wave he motioned to the waiter that he wanted a coffee as well, throwing in a wink for good measure. The waiter smiled back and brought his coffee, brushing Stephen's hand with his own in the process. When the waiter had gone, I laughed at my friend.

"Don't you ever give it a rest?"

"What?" He grinned back. "I'm a people person."

That much was true. The werecats were especially touchy like their namesake animals.

"Have you had any dates lately?" I was curious if he was back in the dating game after his last debacle.

Eyeing his coffee, Stephen shook his head. "That's one of the things I wanted to meet with you about. I'm thinking of going away for a little while after this thing back home cools off."

I sucked in a breath, "What? Why?"

When he looked at me I caught a rare glimpse past his mask of fun loving playboy. There was a deep sadness in his hazel eyes and my heart ached for him. He hadn't talked much about what had happened when we were held captive and tortured because of the trap his boyfriend had lured us into.

Laying my hand on his, I felt the heat of his flesh penetrate mine. "Stephen, talk to me. What's going on?"

He withdrew his hand. "It's hard to be around all of you when you are all pairing off and I can't."

"What do you mean 'can't'? Stephen, it was just one guy. I'm sorry it didn't end well, but he fooled all of us. Don't let that one get you down."

He was fidgeting with his coffee, running his fingers around the mouth of the cup. His reply was so quiet, a normal human would have missed it. "It wasn't the one guy."

"How do you mean?"

He puffed up his cheeks and blew out hard. "There was someone else, a long time ago. He was someone from my life before. It ended badly."

Hearing him willing to talk about something of substance was rare, I waited with my hands on my cup.

"I'd left my home in my teen years when I realized I was different. It was even less popular then as you can imagine. The best place to go was a big city, to get lost in the crowds. We met and immediately were attracted to each other. It wasn't long before we were spending every day together."

Stephen stopped to take a sip. He took a minute, rolling the warm, fragrant liquid around in his mouth before he started speaking again. His eyes were distant and I knew he was seeing another time.

"We were together the day I was attacked. Frederick and I used to go on picnics to the country where we could be alone. We'd lost track of time, it got late and we were packing up to drive back to the city when I heard the cat." His telling sped up with the recalled fear. "He was closer to

47

the car and was able to make it in time. I wasn't as lucky. The cat attacked me. Frederick tried to help. He beat the animal off of me with a fallen tree limb.

Freddy drove me home and was able to clean up the wounds himself. He stayed with me through the first phase of the change. We thought I had rabies or an infection; my fever was high and I was delusional. The doctor didn't understand, either. He gave me an elixir that was basically whiskey and wouldn't have cured a cold.

When I changed for the first time, Freddy stayed. He wanted to help and tracked down a wise woman; the locals called her a witch. She told me how to handle it and what to expect. Afraid I might hurt him, I asked Freddy to leave but he wouldn't."

Stephen stopped. He'd gone pale. I sensed what was coming and I felt the weight of it pressing down with a nearly physical presence.

"We'd been warned that excitement could bring on the change in a young were, but I thought I could control it." He closed his eyes and I saw his throat working convulsively. When they opened again, I could see the grief he normally kept locked tightly away. He whispered what I had already guessed. "Things went too far one night and I lost control. I killed him."

I didn't know what to say. Again I reached across the table to touch his hand. This time he let me.

"I waited a long time to try to be physical with someone again. And never with anyone special, just in case. Until Brian. I thought he was different." He composed himself again, that part of him neatly tucked away once more. "Maybe it's best this way. Look at you and James, Troy and Heidi, Henry and Tonya. Everyone has all of these issues. It's like watching a soap opera. Troy has to hide who he is from Heidi, Henry and Tonya have this whole back and forth thing, you and James are 'merging,' I don't want to deal with it anymore."

"Wait, what? Henry and Tonya are in love? What about Tonya's interest in Donovan?"

Blinking in disbelief, he stared at me. "I didn't say she doesn't enjoy a fling now and again, but trust me, he doesn't mean anything. It's all for show; she does it to piss Henry off. That and the fact that she thinks if she can pretend for long enough, her feelings will magically disappear."

"Please don't go, Stephen. I need you, your family needs you." Tonya and Henry? I was floored.

"I said I wouldn't go until the investigation was closed. I need a break from here and from my family."

Before I could object, he held up his hand. "You have no idea what it's like to live with the same family and their squabbles for nearly a century. I need some fresh perspective. Maybe South America, I've never been to Argentina." He flashed a tired attempt at flirty, "I hear they still have cowboys."

Ch. 8

I said a miserable goodbye to Stephen, making him promise not to leave before I got home. Instead of walking straight back to the hotel I diverted, choosing to get lost amongst the crowd for a while. I was in the habit of lowering my shields for "sweeps" at regular intervals. During one of those intervals I felt something familiar. Vampire.

Instantly, I started scanning the crowds for anyone paying an unusual amount of attention to me. He wasn't trying very hard to be sneaky. I saw him half a block up when he ducked into a grocer.

Angry, I stalked up and into the shop and found him standing just inside the entrance, unrepentant. The diamond stud in his nose caught the glare of the overhead lights and radiated its own beam on the wall next to him.

"Iain, how have you been? What tears you away from our friends in Edinburgh?" He performed simple tasks for Miranda at the Court and also knew James from way back, continuing to carry out errands when requested. I wasn't sure which he was working for at the moment, although I suspected he was spying.

Iain smiled his snarky grin, running a hand through his artificially blackened hair while giving me a thorough once over. It wasn't false vanity. From what I'd seen, Iain looked like that at everyone. "Claire, what a pleasant surprise. What brings you to Paris?" His hand slid down to loop his thumb over the top of his black leather pants.

"I got married yesterday." Biting my tongue I barely remained civil. "You?"

He looked slightly amused. "Nothing as fancy as that. Say, have you seen James lately? I have a message I need to pass along."

I nodded, playing equally friendly. "I have. I can call him if you'd like."

A big, cocky grin broke out across Iain's face. "I'll do you one better, my car's out front."

When we stepped out, he didn't need to point out which car was his. I had seen this particular black Ferrari before in James' garage. I had teased him saying it was flashy and impractical. He'd agreed and sold it. Now I knew to whom.
"Nice car," I sneered smartly as Iain went around to the driver's side. It went against my better judgment getting in a car with him.

He didn't drop his own smirk. "Thanks, I was given this as a gift for services rendered, both past and future."

His comment gave me further pause as I got into the passenger side and buckled my seat belt. Once we were both in I got real.

"Why are you following me, Iain? Did James put you up to this?"

Iain was shaking his head, his smirk had gone as well. "No, Miranda has an assignment for the two of you."

"Oh." I felt the bottom drop out of my stomach and ignored his ulcer inducing driving in the crowded streets of Paris. It was a good thing our hotel was close.

Ch. 9

"How was lunch?" James asked as he came out of the bedroom, halting as soon as he sensed that I was not alone.

He glanced in confusion from Iain to me. "Iain, what are you doing here?"

"Miranda has work for us," I answered as I crossed the living room on my way to the back bathroom.

They waited for me to discuss the details. Upon my return Iain spoke up, "We have a report of a newbie with an ability who will require your guidance once we find her again."

James was all business, "Where?"

Iain smiled, "Back home for you two. Minneapolis."

James and I locked eyes across the room. He gave a barely perceptible shake of his head and I kept quiet.

"Do we know who turned her or any details?" James was obviously very interested in any vampire activity that took place in his home territory.

"No, we don't know who our culprit was. The smell isn't one anybody recognizes offhand. The newbie was found outside a vamp club I believe the two of you are familiar with, Glamour?" He smiled innocently at me, knowing my history with the club where Stephen and I had been kept for the worst five days of my life by a conspiracy spinning vampire named Bradley.

I swallowed hard. "Associates of Bradley's?"

Bradley was dead now, but the club was still open, being run by some mysterious parent company, Nightshade Holdings, LLC. We were trying to dig up more information to find out if the company had any connection with Bradley's intended war against humans. Nothing had turned up thus far.

"One might assume so." He wiggled his eyebrows. "I believe Miranda was hoping you two might be able to find out more. When we found her, her mind was raw. No one got much out of her before she slipped away."

"When are we expected?" James didn't sound pleased to have to cut short our honeymoon. We had hoped to spend at least a few more days in Paris.

Iain actually looked apologetic. "Miranda has a rush on this one. There's a lot of local law enforcement active in the area. This one was from the same campus another student disappeared from not too long ago."

James spoke for both of us. "Shit."

Ch. 10

The door closed behind Iain and we waited a few minutes, giving him ample time to get out of earshot.

"What do you think? It couldn't just be a coincidence, could it?" I knew better than to believe it, but I kind of wanted him to lie to me.

No such luck. "In my experience nothing is a coincidence."

James had altered my memory of the worst of my time with Bradley and his hired mercenary, Gaston. But I still remembered and bore the scars, some more visible than others. Shooting him a weak smile, I shuffled past James and crawled into the bed. It provided some small amount of comfort in its downy cocoon.

James came to lay with me, pulling me close. "I told you, I will never let them hurt you again and I meant it."

"There are some things even you can't do, James." I felt hollow inside and wiggled back against him, trying to burrow closer still as though he could somehow fill the void where my sense of security used to live.

When I awoke, it was growing dark. The clock read nearly six. It took a moment for me to realize what had caused me to stir. Lying together, I felt James' phone buzz in his pocket. He fished it out and flipped it open. We were close enough, I heard the caller. It was Stephen.

"We have a problem," he said simply. I could hear the panic underlying his forced composure.

"What's happened?" James was on alert. I felt his body go rigid.

"Brian's body was found this morning in Minnehaha Park."

Bradley's crew had dumped me in the same place; we should have thought of that. I caught Stephen's panic.

"Shallow grave. I'm not sure the condition of the body but it has been cold enough to preserve it, I would think. They're running DNA." He paused, "Detective Hanson made up his mind an hour ago. He's going to try to put the murder on me. He's building his case now." Stephen's ability let him read someone's intentions. It wasn't reading the future, it was reading the present. As soon as the Detective had made up his mind Stephen would have known about it.

"We're coming home tonight. I have us on the evening flight." James proceeded to fill him in on our new assignment.

"I don't think I can help with the other disappearance or they'll try to tie them together and mark me as a serial killer *if* they aren't already." Stephen sounded resigned.

"No, you're right. Don't go near this one. Claire and I will do what we can to find out who was behind it. I'll get someone else to dig further into the Nightshade business. I have someone at the paper that might be able to help."

"I'll see you when you get home." I was touched by his sincere apology. "Tell Claire I'm sorry you have to cut your honeymoon short."

James thanked him for the sentiment and assured him he would tell me before hanging up.

His hand went back to rest on my hip. I tried to ignore the racing thoughts that kept swirling around in my head. Our argument, my impending insanity, Stephen's loneliness and now persecution for a crime he didn't commit. And who was this mystery girl who had disappeared? Who had attacked her? How many more were working for Bradley's cause? His final words warned us there were others; it sounded like they were making their move.

Ch. 11

We were back in Minneapolis by ten p.m. local time. It was too late by human standards to go poking around anywhere and I was dead on my feet so we went straight home.

When we pulled into the garage, James came around to let me out. I had grown accustomed to his chivalry, except this time, he swept me up to carry me in his arms. Eyes wide in surprise, I looked to see him grinning broadly, flushed nearly to a human shade with a twinkle in his eye.

"A groom has to carry his bride across the threshold. It's one of the traditions *I* like."

Our wedding seemed forever ago already. I had my arms around his neck and kissed him before laying my head on his shoulder, a big dopey smile on my face. He carried me directly up to bed and barely got my shoes off before I ruined the romance of the moment and promptly fell asleep.

The next morning I woke alone. It was rare that he didn't lay with me while I slept. I still had the occasional nightmare and was always reassured by his presence. The wrapping on my arm felt tight and very delicately I unwrapped it, testing it by clenching my fist. It was stiff but the bone was healed. My enthusiasm wasn't what it should have been.

Voices were coming from downstairs. I recognized two of them, but not the third. James had undressed me while I slept, so I threw on a sweatshirt and jeans and headed down.

They heard my footsteps long before I came down. James stood across the room facing the couch where I recognized the back of Henry's head. The stranger sat beside him.

"Claire, I'd like you to meet Indira. She works with me at the paper." James had been watching me since I'd started down the stairs.

He motioned toward me and the woman stood and turned as I came around to James' side. She was exotic and beautiful with dark features and large almond shaped eyes, slight of build and shorter than me, maybe five feet at the most. She made me feel like a giant. She was a vampire, of course.

"Indira," James slid his arm around my waist, "meet Claire, my wife." He winked at me and I felt my face split into a gigantic grin. It was the first time he'd called me that.

Indira's green eyes were cool. "Claire." She inclined her head politely. "I have heard of you. You killed Bradley's man." She cracked the thinnest of smiles, "Thank you for that. He was a scourge on our people."

Uncomfortable with her bringing up the memory of the only life I had ever taken, I blushed. "You're welcome, I guess."

James gave me a squeeze and changed the subject. "Claire, we were just discussing Nightshade and the need for some help with fact finding. Indira is in our research department and a pro with our databases as well as those at the state and county records departments. She's going to take a look and see what she can turn up."

I turned back to Indira, "Isn't that dangerous? What if they figure out that you're investigating them?"

She smiled and her eyes flooded black. "I would welcome the opportunity to face any of those cowards. They are responsible for the death of my father."

"Your Father or your dad?" Vampires often referred to the one who turned them as a parent figure.

Indira clarified, "My creator Father. My blood Father died well over a century ago in a tribal war."

"Can I ask how you know Nightshade was responsible for your Father's death? I thought we didn't know who was behind the corporate face." I looked at each one of them, clearly not up to speed.

Henry cut in, "We do not know the identity of those behind the name, however, the corporate entity reinvents itself every generation or so, each incarnation being responsible for its own share of death, both vampire and human."

I nodded, understanding. "I'd like to help."

James forgot to breathe and I felt a tingle of fear through our bond. I refused to hide while they fought just because I was more fragile than they were. My left wrist twinged as a reminder me just how fragile.

Indira noticed me rubbing my arm. "Is it true?" she asked Henry. "Is it true she heals like we do?"

"She's right *here*." My irritation was quick to flash.

"I heard you were bold, I see that it is true." Again I saw the thin smile. She turned to James, "Why would you choose this one to mark? She is not subservient as a servant should be."

Henry interrupted before James could respond, "Mind your manners Indira. Claire is James' choice and you will respect the choices of your elders."

Her reaction surprised me. She dipped in deference to Henry and then to James, "Yes Sir."

"You have your work cut out for you." Henry moved to the door and opened it for her. "Call when you have something."

Recognizing her dismissal, Indira bowed again to Henry and walked out the front door. I had never seen Henry with any other vampires aside from members of the Court and James. I hadn't realized the power he must have as the head of the local coven. Or that James was second in command.

"Stephen is on his way over," James informed me. "He's going to fill us in on the investigation. Now that we're back the good detective is going to be paying us a visit. He'll want our statements about Brian and Stephen's relationship." He looked down his nose severely at me, "You'll need to work on yours since you are a terrible liar."

"If you're so worried about it, maybe you should tell the police I don't *need* to give a statement. Mess with their heads or something." I tried not to sound defensive.

Henry shook his head. He'd already considered that. "Too many will be involved in the case now that it is a homicide." Pursing his lips, he considered me. "Maybe we could see about a written statement."

Ch. 12

Stephen arrived a few minutes later, weary and strained, bags under his flat, hazel eyes. His hair was growing back out from when he buzzed it short and now it was sticking out like two inch, fluffy duck fuzz not yet ready to lie down.

"You look terrible. Has it gotten worse?" A lump rose in my throat at the thought of Stephen in jail.

"Nothing new. I don't think he's going to decide anything until they have the DNA results and it will still take a week or so to come back even if they rush it."

Henry spoke from the kitchen doorway. He had a glass of something red in his hand, another held out for James who stepped away from me to retrieve it. Fortunately he stayed by Henry while he drank it. Without a lid, I could smell it and preferred not to.

"Are you certain you're the only suspect?"

Stephen was frowning. "For the murder yes, but it looks like they're blaming some of the wounds on animals. There are fox and coyotes in the Park. The confusing thing is that they're trying to tie this one to something else, only I can't tell what. The detective is good at keeping himself locked up. I can only get glimpses."

"Stephen," I said, feeling the sadness of the inevitable settling in, trying to point out that it wasn't the end of the world for him if they did tie the death to him, "you can go away somewhere they can't find you; you have the documents to travel, right?"

Stephen dropped his eyes and stared at me. "Claire, they can't get my DNA."

"Why not?" I still didn't get it.

"Because it isn't human." James' voice was ominous.

"Oh." I hadn't thought of that. Exposure was a bigger deal than being accused of murder for a were. "So what are you going to do?"

He frowned and shook his head, eyes downcast. I glanced over at Henry and James and didn't see anything encouraging from their dark faces either.

I put a comforting hand on his arm and forced a smile, "You'll figure something out; I know it."

"Yeah," he laughed bitterly, "I can go up to Canada or back to Utah."

"I thought they could extradite you from Canada."

"I wouldn't go like this." He indicated his body.

My heart skipped a beat. "Stephen, you can't be changed for a long time, doesn't that make it harder to change back?"

"Yes, there are some complications. If we change to our beast for too long we risk losing more of our humanity; our physical features change as well. Some never come back."

I sucked air through my teeth. "There has to be another way." Looking at him, I was reminded of how his time being kept between forms while in captivity had made him taller, broader and added years to his appearance.

"I'm all ears," he said flatly.

Henry coughed and I looked up, he was giving James his empty glass. "Stephen, go upstairs. Detective Hanson and his partner are here. It is probably best if you aren't visible." He smoothed the front of his shirt.

In a blink Stephen was upstairs and I heard a door close gently. Less than a minute later, the doorbell rang. James emerged from the kitchen to answer the door pointing for me to stand by the couch. Henry was posed behind a chair in the dining room, completely at ease. I tried several poses finally settling on leaning a hand on the furniture back.

The door opened and James greeted the Detectives.

Ch. 13

"Mr. Thomas?"

"Yes. And you are Detective Hanson, I presume? I apologize for being unavailable previously. Claire and I were abroad."

"Yes, sir. This is my partner Detective Williams. May we come in?" the detective asked, not giving the impression "no" was an option.

"Please," James stepped back and waved him in, unperturbed.

Detective Hanson was a big man. He was tall, definitely over 6' and big boned. I would guess football had been his sport in school. Now he was at least forty and his muscle was being replaced with something softer. His dark hair belied his Scandinavian name although his straight nose, fair skin and piercing blue eyes were what I'd come to expect from one with his lineage.

He wore a dark blue suit with a French blue shirt. The black dress shoes on his feet were desperately in need of a polish, impossible to avoid this time of year in the slush and salt. Otherwise he struck me as being very conscientious of how he presented himself.

Detective Williams was a young, barely thirty, severely thin black man dressed smartly in a black suit, white shirt and black tie. He looked like FBI in training.

Detective Hanson stepped inside and politely wiped his feet on the rug. I immediately looked at his left hand. No ring, yet the habits remained. Detective Williams mimicked his superior's actions.

The Detectives' eyes scanned the occupants of the room. Hanson paused at Henry. I held my breath seeing him instinctively sensing the threat. I, on the other hand, barely warranted a glance by Hanson. Williams' gaze stayed with me.

Detective Hanson tore his gaze from Henry to face James. "You're the travel writer, right? Were you traveling on business?"

James smiled genuinely and came to stand behind me, hands resting possessively on my shoulders. It didn't bother me though I wondered if he'd noticed Williams' interest. "Claire and I were married in Paris, actually."

Detective Hanson pulled a notebook from his inner coat pocket and clicked a pen I hadn't seen him retrieve. He flipped the notebook open and glanced at it. He looked at me, "Would you be Claire Martin, then?" He turned his head, "Henry Campbell?" Pen poised, he worked to check off more people from his list of possible witnesses.

"Claire Thomas," I corrected him, liking the sound of it.
Detective Hanson gave me an indulgent smile. Williams' face didn't change, I wondered if he was following along at all.

Hanson took the lead. "As I'm sure your friend Mr. Andrews has informed you, we are investigating the murder of his friend Brian Peterson."

"Murder?" Henry feigned surprise. "I thought it was a missing person case."

Detective Hanson studied him carefully. "It was until yesterday. We found a body."

We all expressed our disbelief at that. I tried to keep my gasp and "oh no" simple and believable. Detective Williams was still ogling me, I wriggled uncomfortably.

"Mrs. Thomas, how well did you know Mr. Peterson?" Williams asked, his eyes boring into me.

The house felt ten degrees hotter and my heart hurt where it banged into my ribs. I saw Brian's face when he chased me down the street. The next time I saw him, on the floor of Stephen's cell below Bradley's nightclub, his dead bloodless face was frozen in a horrific mask. "Not well. I only met him at our Christmas party before he disappeared. We left for Europe shortly afterward."

Hanson was writing notes to himself, bobbing his head without looking at me. After what seemed an eternity, he blinked up at James.

"All three of you are going to have to come in to make statements. It's pretty standard, nothing to worry about. We do like them live and in person, though." It was obvious from his posturing there was no negotiating that one.

James was appropriately respectful. "Absolutely Detective. Claire and I can be there tomorrow morning if you would like."

I felt my hopes for a written statement deflating with a sad sigh.

Hanson nodded once and turned to Henry expectantly.

"I believe I have an opening in my schedule tomorrow morning as well."

"Why don't we have Mr. and Mrs. Thomas come in at nine and Mr. Campbell you can come in at ten." Hanson turned to us, "I assume that's alright with you?"

James bobbed his head agreeably and I did the same.

"Fine. Thank you for your time and I look forward to seeing you all tomorrow." Detective Hanson opened the door and Detective Williams followed him out with one last sweeping glance.

Seconds after the front door closed, one opened upstairs. I had forgotten about Stephen.

"Damn, Claire. We're going to have to drug you or you're going to have a panic attack right there in the station," he teased, but I heard the real doubt under his taunt.

I defended myself, "You said to stay as close to the truth as possible and that is exactly what I did. I didn't see him again until he disappeared."

Ignoring Stephen, James growled, "If that young Detective doesn't control himself he's going to walk with a limp."

I giggled nervously, trying to picture Detective Williams fighting off James and stopped immediately. It definitely would not be funny.

Henry held up a hand. "So far he is not interested in any of us." There was a hint of sympathy in the look he gave Stephen. "Other than you, of course."

"How can you tell?" I didn't know the extent of Henry's skills but was starting to believe he could do anything. Maybe even fly. Didn't Dracula fly? Mentally I put the book on my list of must reads.

"His heart rate remained steady when each of us spoke. Humans' bodies betray them when they are under stress or excited, which he would have been if he had thought he had something."

"Well, that may be the case today but it won't last unless we get Claire a story she can sell." Stephen eyed me dubiously.

"Truth or not, your body tells them you're hiding something. If your heart does what it did earlier while you're there, you'll sweat. If you have to do a polygraph you'll be in the chair next to me facing a judge."

It was useless trying to defend myself. Stephen had a point and I was fairly certain that if I got caught lying I could get in pretty big trouble, never mind what damage I could do to Stephen's defense.

"I don't lie like you guys do. Most people think that's a good thing."

"We aren't most people and lying is a necessary evil of our existence," James answered evenly. "We must lie or alter people's perceptions when necessary to avoid detection."

Hearing him speak so matter of fact about lying to the police and messing with people's heads, I saw an aspect of James that I hadn't before, the other side of the vampire. The physical side didn't bother me, I'd seen it and wasn't threatened, nightmarish as it might be. But he was being so cold, so calculating, not the white knight I had made him out to be.

Ch. 14

"I'm going upstairs. I need to practice my story." I fought the urge to stick out my tongue at Stephen and couldn't look at James. This vampire, so comfortable with lying and manipulating, wasn't the man I had just married. They were two different people in my mind and I wanted to keep them that way, but was finally seeing the impossibility of it and kicking myself for my naiveté.

Upstairs, I went to James' office. There I took a notebook and pencil out and sat down to write down what I knew of that night. Then I wrote down what I was *supposed* to know about Brian, not what I *actually* knew. With that information in mind, I tore off a second sheet and wrote out a simple story.

Brian and Stephen came to our house for a Christmas party the Friday before the holiday. We were introduced briefly. The two seemed fond of each other. Should I tell them Stephen and I fought, I wondered? No, keep it simple I reminded myself. The fewer details I gave them, the less likely I was to mess up.

We had fun, sang Christmas carols and I think they left a little after midnight. That was true. What would I say if the Detective asked if I had seen him afterward? Could I say no or should I say I ran into him on the street? He *had* been complimentary of Stephen. It just hadn't been honest.

I continued to wrestle with my story and think through all the different questions they were likely to ask until my stomach growled. Glancing up, I saw the clock on the desk said it was after one. I never had breakfast and now it was past lunch.

What would Miranda say? She would expect me to be following her orders of taking care of myself. I would put both James and myself at risk and, as much as she put the emphasis on James, I had to think she liked me a little. At least she saw value in me.

I'd been so caught up in the bond and what it was doing to us, I hadn't fully thought through what being with him would mean. Lying went beyond just telling my family why I looked young.

Anyone who noticed a discrepancy would have to be lied to, altered, or worse. For the weres and vampires to survive they required secrecy; both had governing bodies that demanded it under penalty of death. That was the one common thread of truth that even Hollywood got right, explaining why no human alive knew about either race. If they did, they knew better than to talk about it.

My head was swimming as I untangled my stiff legs and stood up to stretch. I went downstairs to rummage in the fridge, listening for company in the process. My hearing was good, although I often couldn't hear the vampires unless they wanted me to.

I couldn't hear or feel anyone on my way to the kitchen to forage. James was good about keeping fresh produce for me but we'd been out of town for so long I didn't know what we had on hand.

We had cream for tea, baby carrots and grapefruit juice. I checked the pantry. There was still no rhyme or reason to the organization. A vampire who doesn't eat just doesn't know how to separate out dry goods.

"Find anything good?" His voice startled me.

I jumped and was only partially successful in cutting off my shriek. "Don't sneak up on me like that." My hand flew to my chest, stopping my heart from driving its way through.

James was leaned back against the cabinets, hands up behind him resting on the countertop. My heart started again for a totally different reason. The faded jeans and solid navy cotton shirt complimented his build and coloring. He could've been an Eddie Bauer model minus the tan.

With an effort, I pushed back my desire. "There isn't much food in the house. I think I need to go to the store."

He stared at me, not commenting, not moving.

I wanted an excuse to get out for a while. "Can I take the car or do you need it for something?"

He reached into his pocket and fished out the keys. "Want some company?"

"I'm just going to the grocery store." I assured him, "I'll be safe."

James' face remained unreadable. "We've gotten cocky about your safety. We're going to have to rethink that with this latest attack at the club."

"I'll go back to having a constant shadow tomorrow but let me have my independence today." I sounded like I was begging and changed my tone. "I never get to be alone anymore. I used to be alone all the time and I miss it sometimes."

He tipped his chin down one time, slowly. He sensed my disquiet. Setting the keys on the counter, he pushed gracefully off and strode out of the kitchen.

I snatched up the keys. The thought of being out by myself was intoxicating. I was positively giddy as I pulled the black Audi onto the street.

Ch. 15

Grocery shopping was cathartic. For one thing, I had gotten a juice smoothie and a cheese stick at the store and my blood sugar was back to normal. By the time I pulled into the garage I was back to being happy and was looking forward to seeing James. I wanted to tell him about what I had bought, maybe cook dinner with him. He was a good cook and I looked forward to learning a few techniques. He was definitely better with a knife than I was.

I unloaded the car and put the groceries away with still no sign of James. Curious, I went looking for him. Maybe he was giving me the space I'd so badly needed when I'd last seen him.

The door to his office was cracked. I knocked softly. "Come in," he called quietly.

Easing the door open, I glanced around the room and saw him standing in his closet with a shoebox in his hands. He walked over to sit on the bed and I took a seat beside him.

"Are you cleaning?" I pointed at the contents, paper scraps in varying shades of yellowing.

He fingered one particularly old clipping. "It isn't a perfect way to exist, having to lie and deceive." He held up his hand when I started to object. "It bothers me as well but the alternative is not to exist at all." He let me think about that for a few seconds. "I wanted you to see some of the good I've done."

"Did you write these?" My eyes searched the top article to get the gist of it.

He shook his head. "No, these are things I've *done*." He spoke quickly, explaining himself. "I don't collect these to glorify myself, but to remind me of my humanity. Before I found you and you brought it back, I had thought I would come to a day when I had none left. These would be my only reminder."

My one apparent contribution through our psychic bond was that my human emotional range and conscience was bleeding over to him. More than anything, he feared being an unfeeling soul like so many of the ancients of his kind.

I didn't know what to say, instead reaching into the box. There were a number of good Samaritan articles: "Mystery Man Saves Boy from Burning Building," "Child Found After Boating Accident," "Good Samaritan Saves Woman from Car Accident," "Kidnapped Child Found Unharmed." They went on and on.

"These were all you?"

"If you're around long enough you end up being in the right place at the right time for some fluke rescues." He rolled his shoulders. "Finding people, that was arranged though." He pointed to an article about a boy lost in the mountains. "I heard about the child and went out after him. I returned him to the main road and muddled his mind so he thought he'd found the road on his own."

I looked up from the articles and my eyes scanned his handsome features, heavy with his reflections, before resting on his eyes, my barometer for his mood and honesty. They were smoky grey; he was at peace. He was telling the truth.

I reached up to his face to feel the familiar, cool flesh under my hand. "I love you and I'm proud to be your wife."

His eyes instantly burned to midnight and he set the box on the nightstand beside the bed freeing his hands to take hold of me. He stared at me to gauge my truthfulness and I felt him brush against my thoughts to be sure. There was no need to hide my feelings from him and I didn't. When he felt it, he leaned in to kiss me.

I ran my hands across his shoulders and up into his hair pulling myself closer. Feeling my want, his kiss grew more insistent and his hands ran down my back to grasp my hips with a squeeze that bordered on painful. Moaning, I climbed up and threw a leg over, wrapping my arms around his neck to press myself tightly against him. Our clothing came off and I shivered from the temporary chill of air above and cool body beneath until I grew warm from the way he moved against me.

Afterward, I lay cooling in James' arms. "Do you regret it?"

I ran a finger down his stomach. "I don't. There are things I don't like about how complicated it all is and not knowing who or what I'm going to be, but I don't regret it."

He sighed at the sensation and stroked my hair. "You do things to me no one has ever done before."

"I'm sure someone has done *that* to you before." I smiled up at him. "You don't have to play the virgin with me."

James laughed out loud. I loved that sound. "I don't mean physically, Love. You make me feel differently than I ever remember feeling. Even as a human."

I felt a warm liquidy glow inside my chest. "Well, I'm glad I could return the favor. I've certainly never felt like this before." I kissed his chest, "And I can honestly say no one has ever done *any* of what you did to me before."

He laughed again, this time more ominously, catching my chin and lifting it to his face. Kissing me he his hands ran down my back sending a shiver up my spine.

"Are you cold?"

"No."

"Good."

Later, we threw on clothes and got to fulfill my wish and cooked dinner together. After perusing the now replenished food stores, we had what we needed to make beef bourguignon, a French beef stew of sorts with copious amounts of red wine. The alcohol would burn off making it safe for me, but the flavor was much deeper than normal stew.

James manned the music and we had an eclectic mixture of alternative music with a few guilty pleasures from decades past thrown in.

He sipped his mug and poured a sparkling water with a twist of lemon for me while I practiced cubing beef. We were waiting for dinner to cook down when my phone rang.

Flipping it open, I saw that it was my mom. He gave the nod, he didn't care if I answered. Though convenient, cell phones could be incredibly intrusive.

"Hi Mom."

She picked up on my good mood right away. "How is married life honey? Are you still in Paris?"

"It's good. We had to come back; James had to work. We are doing great though, we're just cooking dinner right now."

We visited about their trip to Paris and how wonderful it was. Mom had me put James on the phone so that she could thank him again herself. He was a good sport about it and let her chat him up before handing her back.

"I was calling because I wanted to ask if you two mind if I have a party for you. You know how your Dad's family can be. They really like to get together and I worry if we don't have a reception for you we'll be black balled from the family events for the next decade."

I knew James could hear. I looked at him and shrugged, asking his opinion. Putting his hands on my waist he nuzzled the ear without the phone and whispered "yes" in a way that raised goose bumps down that entire side of my body.

"Nothing huge, okay?" I knew she wouldn't listen and once she invited a few, word would spread and it would be huge. Dad had a huge family and they loved to get together. Mom was an only and not good at reining in a rambunctious family, but I knew deep down she enjoyed the chaos. It was something she hadn't had growing up and liked having tastes of it on occasion.

We hung up and I tossed the phone aside to put my hands on his shoulders; his lips were doing things to my neck that made it hard to concentrate. "That's going to be a mess." I closed my eyes and sighed.

His low chuckle nearly buckled my knees. "You can handle vampires; this will be a breeze."

Ch. 16

The Minneapolis Police station was a beautiful building. Its grey limestone, green roofs and towers gave a historic feel to the relatively youthful city. I had heard the jails were below from my late uncle, an officer with the force until he'd been killed in the line of duty.

On the other side of the guard desk it looked like any other office with cubicles, boring grey carpet and a few conference rooms with glass walls. I would presume the transparency was for the sake of protection so there could be no accusations of inappropriate behavior or it could have just been to allow natural light to shine through to the interior rooms too; I couldn't be sure.

We asked the guard for Detective Hanson and were told to wait in a spacious tile floored foyer filled with the echoing cacophony of footsteps and voices. We stood for the five minutes or so until he came to get us; by then I was sufficiently disoriented from the loud noises and was staring longingly at the carpeted area with puffy upholstered half walls promising to muffle the noise and make it more bearable. James squeezed my hand in solidarity. I saw the faintest hint of tension around his eyes, he was feeling the strain as well. The detective led us back through the maze of cubicles into a hallway that looked older. Judging by the cinderblock walls and wire mesh running through the windows in the little rooms, we were in the interview area and not everyone who was brought here wanted to be.

James was led into the first room with Detective Hanson, Detective Williams joined us just in time to lead me into the second. I watched James tuck away his displeasure at the pairing. He remembered the Detective's leering. Squeezing his hand before we parted, I got him to meet my eyes. I winked at him and smiled. He smiled back, probably because I was terrible at winking, but my purpose was served. It broke the tension and I showed him I was okay.

Williams and I entered the small light green room tinted the color of mold by weak fluorescents and he waved me to the chair on the far side of the metal table. He took the seat opposite me. The recorder on the table and microphone reminded me this was going to be in the permanent file. In my head I ran through the story I had gone over last night repeatedly until I knew I had it cold.

Detective Williams asked if he could start the tape and I said that was fine. He did the introduction: who we were and the time and place before he directed his attention back to me.

"Claire Thomas, are you aware we are recording this interview?"

"Yes, Sir."

He flipped open his little black notebook. "Let's begin with you telling me about the first time you met Brian Peterson."

I went through my rehearsed story of all the facts from the night of the party.

"And did you see him after that?"

"No," I answered steadily, meeting his eyes and concentrating on breathing evenly. He stared at me. I stared back.

"How long were Stephen Andrews and Brian Peterson involved?"

"I'd heard he was dating someone a few weeks before but I hadn't met Brian until the night of the party. It was the only night I ever saw Brian." That was true. The other encounter I'd had was during the day.

We went on for a few more minutes. Detective Williams trying a few more approaches to see if my story had any holes. Seemingly satisfied, he announced he would be ending our interview and again gave the date, time and location.

When the machine switched off I started to stand.

"The Detective will be a little while with Mr. Thomas. He'll come get us when he's done." He indicated my chair and I sat back down, uncertain what else to do.

"Um, okay." I put my hands in my lap, trying not to fidget.

Williams' gaze was making me itch. I could feel his dark beady eyes on me even when I was studying my hands. I fought the urge to call out to James, telling myself I could do this.

"Newlywed, huh?" He didn't look all that interested, merely making small talk. I started to breathe again.

"Yes, we were married a few days ago." My shoulders relaxed.

"Paris? Must be doing pretty well to go to Paris to get married while you're in college." He let the insinuation hang.

I took the bait. "Yes, James has money. But if you think about it, by the time you have a wedding here and feed everyone it's a lot more expensive than flying a few people to Paris for a couple of days."

He nodded, noncommittal, "Why Paris? Do you speak French?"

"Only a little bit, James is fluent." Detective Williams was starting to seem like a normal guy, not a suspicious detective anymore. I unclasped my hands.

"Where'd he learn French? Did he live in France before?" Williams used his pen to scribble a crescent on his paper.

I shook my head. "No, he lived in Canada for a while."

"Canada?" he asked without looking up. His change in pitch was minor I barely heard it.

Alarm bells started ringing in my head.

"When did he live in Canada?" He was still scribbling on the pad, now there were trees below the crescent. It was just doodling while two people were talking, right?

I shook my head again, my mouth felt dry. "I don't remember, just that he said he lived there for a short time. Maybe after his parents died. He lived with a relative after that."

"Really? That would be hard losing both parents. Who took care of him?" More trees.

"I don't remember. He doesn't like to talk about it much." I decided to end the interview. "Do you think they're done yet? James and I had some things we needed to do today."

"No, Detective Hanson will peek in when he's ready." Detective Williams wouldn't make eye contact with me making me even more nervous.

I had one more idea to end this before I gave out any more information. I found our bond in my head and tickled it, knocking.

Immediately he responded, *"What is it?"*

"We need to be done." I knew he could sense my panic.

"What's the matter?" Detective Williams asked glancing up. Now he was eyeing me curiously. "You seem distracted."

"No," I fought to keep my voice even and my breathing close to normal. "I don't like being underground, it makes me nervous." Also true.

"Hmm. Well, if I shared that sentiment I would go crazy." He laughed, a sharp sound in the tiny room. "I'm in the bowels of this building more often than I care to admit. Research, processing, escorting prisoners, interviews; it seems like it all happens down here. Imagine if you had to be in jail? That would be really hard, huh?"

I stared at him, willing the door behind him to open. I tickled again.

Seconds later, there were two sharp pounds on our door just before it opened. The Detective's dark head peeked in as he growled, clearly annoyed. "We're all done. You?"

Williams was hesitant, seemingly unwilling to let me leave. I had the briefest flashback of Brian trying to keep me on the street for Bradley to come and collect me. Finally he turned and said that he was.

I tried to keep myself from jumping up and running out. It was a brisk exit, yet I was able to hold it to a walk. Upon reaching the hallway, I looked behind the Detective and saw James. Outwardly he was cool and relaxed, only I could feel the agitation vibrating on the edge of our connection. Williams followed me out and I saw James fight down the anger flooding him. His eyes went black for a heartbeat before he blinked them back to normal, he'd misread my distress call.

I wove around the detective, James held out his hand and I took it greedily. He tethered me to my reality and right now I needed it. I had been careless in my cockiness that I'd managed not to give anything away about Stephen, but now I worried I'd opened a can of worms for my husband.

He "knocked" in my head. *What did he do?*

I answered, working to keep my face neutral. I had to look at our hands while we followed the detectives. *Nothing, I gave my statement okay enough. Afterward we were talking, I told him you were from Canada. Is that going to give anything away?*

His response was untroubled and I felt his tension dissipating. *No problems there. No record of me in Canada for over a century. Anything before that can be pure happenstance; there weren't any pictures taken of me as an adult.*

I heaved a huge sigh, relieved. Detective Hanson glanced back, eyebrows raised. I smiled stiffly, opting for silence as my best strategy.

We moved efficiently through the building and were nearly to the dizzying lobby when I heard my name being called.

Turning, I saw my Aunt Sandi coming from the front entrance moving toward me rapidly. Concern creased her tanned face.

"Claire, what are you doing here?" She hustled the last few steps and reached out to hug me.

I let go after a quick hug and she glanced from my face to James' then turned to the detectives.

"What's going on here? Are you in some sort of trouble?" Normally I would have appreciated her concern, not so much today. I didn't want anyone in my family to know I was here and to start asking questions. Combined with Dad's budding suspicion of Henry and James, I wasn't sure it would end well for Dad.

Sandi had been married to Dad's younger brother, named Jim coincidentally. He'd been the police officer in the family and was killed while on duty about three years ago. She had kept his name, Martin.

Sandi was in her mid forties, her brown hair, growing more salt than pepper these last few years, was cut short in a bob. Dark brown eyes tending to be a little wide lent her an air of bewilderment that I'd always found disconcerting. Her shirt hung partially tucked into a denim skirt stretching over her belly, softening with age though still not large by modern measures.

Detective Hanson was glancing between Aunt Sandi and me. "How do you know Claire, Sandi?"

"She's my niece." Her eyes didn't move from my face. She was far too focused on me for comfort. "Claire, you didn't answer me. Why are you here?"

I tried to downplay it. "A friend of a friend disappeared. The detectives just wanted to talk to us and see what we knew." My eyes slid sideways to Hanson.

He was rubbing the back of his neck. "Martin. I should have checked that out."

The detective obviously had not made the family connection by our last names. It was an easy mistake, Martin was a very common name up here. Hanson surprised me by speaking openly to Sandi. "The Peterson case. These two had a party he and the boyfriend were at a few days before he went missing."

"The boy who was murdered." She was all business, a side of her I hadn't seen. She was so collected; nothing like the scatterbrained aunt we all knew was a little "off." Mom called her eccentric.

My mind caught up with me. "Aunt Sandi, what are *you* doing here?" Uncle Jim's case had been resolved last year and as far as I knew there was no other reason for her to be in the station.

Detective Williams spoke up, sounding pleased with himself. "Sandi consults for us on unusual cases. She has a unique perspective."

"That's enough, Williams." Detective Hanson's interruption was swift and echoed through the chamber.

Sandi's focus switched to James. She was staring at him, a crease in her brow.

"I'm sorry, Aunt Sandi, I forgot you weren't at Vanessa's wedding." My cousin had gotten married a few months ago and James had met most of my family at the event. "This is James Thomas."

I glanced at him and he appeared to be holding his breath. I wanted to ask but the conversation was taking too much of my focus to use our bond to talk with him privately.

She blanched, and then forced a shaky smile. "I couldn't make it, I was working. I heard something about a boyfriend."

Detective Williams piped up; he seemed to enjoy stirring the pot. "They're married. That's why we couldn't reach them. Apparently they went to Paris for a quickie wedding."

Hanson shot Williams a look. I didn't think the senior detective approved of his young partner's loose tongue.

Sandi's brows shot up, "That was fast. Wait, weren't your parents out there? You two gave them tickets for their anniversary or something? They were thrilled."

I nodded, breathing easier thinking we had finally bridged over to less dangerous ground. "Yeah, it was their 25th. We thought it would be fun to surprise them." I added quickly so that she wouldn't be upset, "They're going to throw a reception for us here so we'll all have a chance to celebrate together."

"Well, welcome to the family, James." Sandi stuck out her hand.

James was slow to take it. His expression was pained like he was sure it was going to hurt. Not far from it. When their hands met Sandi sucked in her breath and her entire body stiffened. Eyes wide, she goggled him.

Freaked out, I lowered my shields to try to feel her. When they dropped I felt the full shockwave of her reaction. She knew he was other than human, though not sure what. She was frightened and angry with him, thinking he had fooled me and intended to hurt me as well as some other source of rage I didn't get a chance to dig into.

Feeling my intrusion, she whirled on me, still holding his hand. I saw and felt her fury aimed at me.

"Sandi, are you okay?" Detective Hanson sounded worried, his hand reaching out to touch her shoulder.

She saw it and stepped backward, releasing James at the same time. "No." Sandi shook her head, clearly agitated. When she looked up at me, she was still wrestling for mastery of her features.

My heart was flying and my stomach started to churn. I wanted to say something to her, to stop her from saying anything to the police. She obviously had an ability or knew something about supernatural creatures. Either way, she could put us in mortal danger with the next words out of her mouth. Eyes wide, I shook my head at her, trying to signal her not to speak without getting caught by the Detectives now both on full alert.

Sandi recovered herself. "Claire, James," her voice was strained with her efforts, "I would like to catch up with you." She glared at James. "And to get to know you better. Would you like to come to dinner tonight?"

I smiled tightly. "We'd love to come."

The Detectives were uncertain what to do; Sandi's reaction was alarming yet they couldn't see any outward threat. They were watching the three of us, waiting for some further reaction when things got worse.

I watched Henry walk through the glass entrance doors behind Sandi. He was hard to ignore, handsome in his dark suit, gracefully striding across the lobby with virtually no sound from the hard soles of his shoes. Our tension did not escape his notice; he was assessing our moods when Sandi turned to follow my gaze.

Her eyes met his and I saw her panic ebbing, her shoulders released their tension and she locked in.

"Hello James, Claire," Henry spoke coolly.

"Detectives." His eyes returned to Sandi who remained riveted on him. "And you are?"

Sandi's voice was airy, "I'm Claire's Aunt, Sandi Martin."

"More of Claire's family, hmm?" Henry's hand flowed forward. "Henry Campbell, I'm a friend of the groom."

When their hands touched I could see an involuntary shudder run through her, barely perceptible as he held her eyes and controlled her reaction. Henry released her and took control of the conversation, effectively minimizing the damage.

"Detectives, I am here for my interview. I was hoping we could begin a few minutes early, I have another engagement this afternoon."

Detective Hanson was watching Henry warily as if he expected him to pull a gun. He knew something was happening but that it was beyond his scope of understanding was obvious. "Yeah, we've got a room set aside. We can start right away." He assessed Sandi's state, still pleasantly vacant, and put a hand on her again. "Sandi, are you going to be okay?"

His tenderness struck me as odd when he touched her and peered into her eyes. She nodded at him, a tiny wrinkle beginning to form in her brow again as if her ability to think for herself was slowly coming back.

Henry saw it too and began to walk deeper into the building. The detectives had no other choice but to follow him. Disagreeing wasn't something anyone saw as an option with a force like Henry.

"Aunt Sandi, can I walk you out?" I asked her once we were alone again.

She touched her forehead, blinking a few times attempting to clear her muddled thoughts. "No, I'm fine." She brought her focus back up to us, staring intently at James. "I will see you tonight at seven." She pointed at Henry's retreating back, "Do *not* bring him."

I nodded mutely and she turned on her heel, striding briskly out of the building, perfectly in control of her own thoughts once again.

Ch. 17

James and I followed suit, not speaking until we reached the car. After he shut my door he went around to his side, got in, and put his hands on the wheel. I saw his knuckles go white and heard the wheel groaning under the strain as he tightened his grip.

"What is she?" I asked him, not certain what I had just witnessed.

"She's a sensitive like me, only human so it isn't quite as strong, but it's enough to cause us problems." He spat the words, his voice tight as he fought down an anger borne from fear.

I was struggling to fight down the panic rising in my chest, threatening to cut off my air supply. As I hyperventilated, I started to see spots. James reached over and I felt his cool hand cover my own as I clutched my knees. My vision cleared and my breathing began to return to normal as his shielding wrapped me in a protective layer and I did my best to soothe him, seeing his eyes gradually return to normal.

He started the car and exited the ramp, gliding seamlessly into traffic. We were home within fifteen minutes. His hand never left me the entire ride. I was grateful for that.

Once inside, I put the kettle on. A hot cup of tea was my comfort food and I was desperately in need. James dipped into his own food, stored in an opaque back drawer of the fridge when we didn't have company.

After we were seated and relatively calm, we tried to analyze the situation. "Tell me what you know of your aunt." James asked first.

"Well," I began, "you know I wasn't really involved in many family events before. With my ability, all the family politicking and infighting was unbearable. But I do remember Sandi as being always on the fringe. Kind of like me. No one really knew her and Dad wasn't all that tight with his brother. Jim was the youngest, about ten years younger than Dad I think, and a police officer. He was killed three years ago." I tried to remember everything I knew about Sandi. "There was one time when I remembered hugging her and she felt more..." I struggled to find the right word to describe what I had felt. "It was a swirling mess. Like she was a bunch of people all mixed together."

James was nodding his head, seeing something I didn't. I waited for him to share.

"What you felt was how a *human* with sensitivity feels. She senses any strong personalities, abilities, and overwhelming feelings coming off of people. Until it's protected by shields, it can be as confusing and disabling as yours was." He was sympathetic. "She probably avoided social settings like you did before mastering your own abilities."

"But what's she doing with the police?" That bothered me more than her surprise ability. Her being there intimated a possible leak to the family and I didn't want them scrutinizing us too closely. It was too dangerous for everyone involved.

He was thoughtful, swirling his glass. I heard the liquid inside sloshing around and tried to think of coffee or some other benign drink, not the donor blood it actually held. "I don't know, but she was wearing a picture badge. She goes there often enough to warrant more than a visitor's pass." Looking at me he frowned, "You said her husband was an officer?"

"Mmm hmm." I swallowed the tea in my mouth. "Jim was a Detective. He was killed a few years ago in the line of duty. I heard it was a weird case but I don't know anything about it.

Like I said, I had limited involvement in the family dynamic."

We continued to discuss our options for what to tell Sandi tonight at dinner. I jumped when James' phone rang. Of course it was Henry.

"She didn't know." Henry wasted no time interrogating James. "She says they both avoided the crowds at family gatherings." James listened for a few minutes before it was his turn again. "We've been invited to dinner tonight at her house and were told specifically *not* to bring you. She clearly felt you altering her even if she couldn't stop it. She came out of it very quickly as well."

I hadn't thought about that. Sandi had known what Henry had done to her, which was why she singled him out as dangerous. That, and James had a point. It seemed to me when I had seen Henry alter someone's perceptions it lasted for quite a while. It had been in effect only when he was actively using his power over her. As soon as he let go, it had passed.

"She must be pretty strong," I muttered. "That would explain why she felt you through your shields."

Again, the crease in his brow, "Good point, Claire." He brought Henry into the fold. "She was strong enough to feel me through my shields. However, we don't know what it was she felt. It could have been my ability or my nature. I should hope it was the former." His expression was grave. "Yes, I know what that would require."

"No!" It came out without thinking. "Can't you mess with her memory or something if that's the case? You don't have to kill her. She didn't do anything wrong." I dropped my voice, pleading, "She's family."

90

I heard Henry's tone. James sighed, "If Henry's mind control is short lived, how long do you think erasing her memory would last?"

My tea was cold. I welcomed the excuse to walk away and heard James speak too low for me to hear.

When I came back from the kitchen James was off the phone. He was reclined on the couch, his own cup on the floor beside him. He patted his chest, my favorite pillow. I swallowed another swig of my temporarily hot tea and set it on the coffee table, taking him up on his offer.

We lay quietly, he stroked my hair and I closed my eyes. I tried to empty my mind. We wouldn't know what Sandi knew until dinner tonight. I told myself there was no point worrying now. I said as much and James agreed.

"We'll go to dinner tonight and find out what she knows. If she does not know what I am, we can explain that I am a sensitive like her. I saw her reaction when she felt you use yours; that will help."

"She can tell when we're using our abilities." A chilling thought pierced my consciousness. "Has she met Stephen yet?"

James' hand stopped moving on my hair. "I don't think so. He would have mentioned it; he wouldn't have missed it when she figured out he was like her." His hand resumed its motion, continuing to soothe away my nerves.

Relief warmed the chill that had settled into my bones. That was one hurdle avoided; if we could keep her clear of Stephen, that is. Now a potentially bigger hurdle was yet to present itself tonight. I needed a distraction.

"Let's do something," I suggested. "I can't sit here all afternoon thinking about tonight."

"What were you thinking?" His hand trailed down to my shoulder and started stroking my back suggestively.

I laughed. "Tempting, but we can't do that *all* afternoon."

"Can't we?" His chest vibrated with his chuckle.

"Not if you want me to stay awake at dinner."

His hand had stopped on my hip. Playfully he swatted it and started to sit up. "Then let's go." James smiled secretively, "I have something I've been meaning to do."

"Okay. Is there any sort of dress code?" One never knew with a vampire if a formal gown for a Court appearance was required or hiking boots to dump a body.

He made a show of eyeing me up and down. I felt my body react, flushing when I saw that he sensed it. James' eyes were darkening in response. "I think we should go while we still can."

Ch. 18

James' thing he'd been "meaning to do" was located at the Mercedes dealership in Wayzata. We pulled in and he shut off the car, turning to face me.

"Claire, as a wedding gift, I wanted to give you back something you lost." Removing his sunglasses, I watched the corner of his eyes tighten against the pain of the sun. "I know you've had to rely on me more than you're used to. Consider this the down payment on the return of your independence."

A suit clad salesman was approaching from the monument of glass housing the elite models in the showroom.

"Thank you," was all I said. I knew he could see that it wasn't the gift but what it meant that moved me. I reached out to take his hand and squeezed it.

I kissed him, getting excited by the prospect of having my first car that would be entirely mine. "Now this is *my* car, right? I can do what I want with it?"

He nodded.

"I can put girl bumper stickers all over it and a flower steering wheel cover on it?" I teased, trying my best to act girlie and giggly.

His face twitched irritably. He loved nice cars and I knew it would pain him to think of me defacing it that way.

I laughed, "I'm kidding."

James put his hand on the door making ready to meet the salesman now smiling at his window. I tried not to smile like an idiot as I stepped out to reclaim my freedom but failed. I didn't care.

Ch. 19

At ten after seven we were ringing the doorbell at Aunt Sandi's condo in Edina. I'd had to call Mom for the address since I hadn't been there before. Sandi had moved out of her house after Jim was killed. She had never had kids and didn't need the additional space or responsibility the house had required.

After assuring Mom I would say "hi" for her and getting roped into discussing our reception again, I started the process of figuring out what to wear. I wasn't sure what the dress code was for visiting an estranged relative who may or may not know that my husband is a supernatural creature who might have to destroy her if she did indeed know. I asked James.

"I would say go for business casual," He responded dryly to my inquiry.

Plopping down on the bed to watch him button his blue shirt, I sighed dramatically. "Do you think it would be too much to ask for us to have a week without the threat of someone dying?"

He finished buttoning and stood at the foot of the bed where my legs hung over the edge, his knees against mine. "There has definitely been a lot of activity these past few years. Bradley and his crew, Nightshade, division in the Court; it has all been building animosity among our kind as we creep toward a larger war. Let's hope we can find the root of this and destroy it so that we can be done once and for all. We can return to the relative peace we used to enjoy."

I was relieved. "So it isn't always like this? Danger and intrigue around every corner?"

He smiled and started tucking in his shirt. "No. We always have to be careful around humans and protect our secrets, but we don't usually have such widespread infighting." He furrowed his brow in thought.

"How long has Nightshade been a problem? Henry thought they've been around in different incarnations for a while. Decades, wasn't it?"

He patted my knee, "You'd better get dressed or we'll be late." James put on his watch and rolled up the sleeves of his shirt to mid forearm, his usual look. "Yes, there have been several different faces over the past hundred years or so that have come and gone. Each one stirring up trouble, killing those on both sides, threatening to expose us and start an all out war. The Court has been surprisingly lax in their discipline which leads Henry and me to believe at least one of them is in league with the other side."

I chose a black skirt and fitted light blue sweater. It was one of my favorites when paired with my black heeled boots. I dressed, feeling James' eyes on my back. I added a little shimmy to my hips for effect as I wiggled into my skirt. Turning, I saw his eyes burning black, his fangs partially extended.

"We don't have long."

It was only due to James' insanely dangerous driving, made only slightly less so by his vampire reflexes, that we made it when we did. James had been kind enough not to muss my hair too much which saved a few minutes, I laughed with guilty pleasure at the thought. It was good to be a newlywed.

Sandi answered the door in the same clothes she'd been wearing earlier, her hair disheveled as always. Her spooked eyes shifted nervously from James to me and back again. It was off putting, since I wasn't sure if she was listening to anything I was saying or having a seizure.

She stepped back from the door and asked us in. James graciously accepted her invitation. It allowed him to step into her home. Vampire rules said you had to be invited inside by the owner of the home. I didn't understand that one exactly, it had something to do with the dead crossing into the domain of the living.

Her small, one level condo was builder's beige inside with bare white walls. We could see all the common areas from the entryway. The rooms hardly looked lived in except for the tipping piles of paperwork on the floor in the corner of the living room. Otherwise she had a couch, chair and tv in the main room. Her dining room contained a square table with four chairs, very basic woods and designs.

I usually liked going into someone's home because I thought it was the best way to get a sense of who they were. There was nothing "Sandi" about this house. It felt like she'd rented a furnished condo.

There was, however, a good smell coming from the kitchen. It smelled like something my mom made in the winter. It made me think of home and family; I fought to remove myself sentimentally from what we were doing here. I needed to stay calm tonight so that I didn't leak anything or fall apart.

"Smells great, Aunt Sandi. It's familiar, what is it?" I shrugged off my coat.

She smiled distractedly, tension playing at her features. "It's pheasant Madeira, one of our family favorites." She hung my coat in the hall closet and turned to take James'.

I saw that he was careful to avoid touching her. "Pheasant was one of my mother's specialties. It brings back old memories."

"I didn't know that," I said softly. James didn't often speak of his human life.

Sandi looked curiously at James. "Where is your Mother?"

"Both of my parents are dead." His voice was carefully controlled.

Now that I knew I was going to have to start bending the truth to survive in my new life, I studied James when he did it, trying to see what he did to make it believable.

Sandi's curiosity showed in her eyes. She wanted as much on James as she could get. We were going to have to be very careful. "How did they die?"

"My mother died of tuberculosis, my father fell from the hay mow and broke his neck."

I'd never heard how his father died. I had assumed he had passed due to old age and alcohol. "I'm sorry."

Sandi dipped her head, not moving her eyes from James' face. "I'm sorry too. No child should be alone. Who took care of you?"

He didn't flinch. "I was staying with a friend of the family after my mother passed. I wasn't there when he died; nobody was."

She was watching us both carefully. I felt her interest shift to me. She sensed my weakness, I knew it. "Can I get you anything to drink?"

I nodded weakly, trying to smile. "Um, sure. Do you have any ginger ale?"

"No ginger ale, but I have Sprite."

"That would be fine, thanks."

"James?" she asked.

"I'll take water, thank you."

Sandi disappeared and we heard her clattering around in the kitchen. I wandered into the living room; James followed behind me. We sat beside one another on the couch. I wasn't sure what to do with my hands and settled for clasping and unclasping them in my lap. Fingers interlaced or on top of each other, I couldn't decide. Finally, Sandi returned with drinks and cheese and crackers on a tray.

We each took our drinks. I noticed Sandi had a large glass of white wine for herself. I politely took a smear of brie with a water cracker. James surprised me taking a small wedge of white cheddar. Sandi and I both watched him place it on his napkin. I wasn't sure if he could eat something if forced or what. Could a vampire digest?

She took a seat in the chair facing us. We all sat, watching each other for different reasons. I chewed my brie slathered cracker, it was really good. James' cheese remained undisturbed in the napkin he had in front of him on the coffee table with his water. Sandi didn't touch anything either. She was too busy being suspicious.

"James, do you go to Augsburg with Claire?"

"No, I work for the paper as a travel writer."

"Really? How interesting." She did not sound enthusiastic in her responses. "Then how did you two meet?"

The corner of James' mouth twitched. "At a party."

I fought the urge to snort. Some party it was. I was meeting weres for the first time and in walked two vampires. It was the night that changed everything for me.

"What was a grown man doing at a college party?" I saw the ever present wrinkle in the brow had deepened.

"It wasn't a frat party. It was more of a get together amongst friends," I interjected.

"Was one of those friends Stephen Andrews?"

There it was: the case, rearing its ugly head.

James fielded the question. "Actually yes, I've known the family for a long time and Claire met Stephen at school. Stephen's older brother and sister had just returned from an extended trip abroad and I wanted to see them." He turned to me, his eyes gentle. "We've been together ever since."

My body warmed at his reminder and I couldn't stop the dopey smile that spread across my face.

"And when exactly did you tell her you were a vampire?"

Ch. 20

The world around me stopped spinning and I felt James go still as stone. We all stared at each other for several heartbeats. Sandi's expression was serenely curious, as if she awaited the answer to an innocuous question like "what do you do in your free time."

James was the first to recover, asking her evenly, "How do you know about us?"

If her question surprised me, her response forever changed my perception of her as scatterbrained.

"Vampires killed my husband three years ago." She took a deep drink of her wine, a flame igniting behind her wild eyes. "I use my ability to work with Jim's old partner, Detective Hanson, and together we tracked down the humans they brainwashed. They eventually were able to confess that they had no recollection of what they'd done. We may have caught the one that pulled the trigger but not the one who put the gun in his hand." She blinked away the wetness in her eyes. "I've been working with Detective Hanson on cases with a similar element to them trying to find the ones responsible." She smiled unhappily, "They think I'm psychic."

I took a sip of my soda to wet my suddenly dry mouth before I found my voice. "Have you told anyone else what you know? James, if she doesn't tell anyone is she okay?" I couldn't hide the pleading in my voice.

He was shaking his head, visibly troubled.

"Knowing puts you in grave danger, Sandi. Does anyone else know it was vampires who killed your husband? What about the Detective?"

The fire went out of her eyes and her shoulders slumped. "No, no one knows it was anything but a bunch of punks that killed Jim." She laughed bitterly, "They think I'm crazy but credible. If I started talking about nightmarish monsters, they would toss me out on my ear and I'd never find out who killed Jim." She stuck her chin out, "I have to stay connected to the Detectives any way I can. They get reports of strange and unexplainable crimes and call me in. There's always the same feel to them and I know eventually one will lead me to the bastards who had Jim killed. They hide behind a business front but I know it's them. I know it's vampires who are behind Nightshade. I'll find them and I will have them brought to justice." Her face contorted with pain and rage, "And now here you are, casting *your* spell on my niece. Maybe you and your friend Henry are in on it. I should have you brought in as an accomplice in Brian's murder."

"We're hunting for Nightshade, too," I blurted out. "They're the ones behind Brian's murder."

"Claire." James' voice was sharp.

I looked at him. His eyes were getting darker as he grew angry with me for saying too much. I could be in danger if it ever got back to the Court that I shared anything with a human, he knew that. I put my hand on his arm, hard beneath my touch as he clenched his fists on his legs. "James, it's okay. No one has to be in trouble. She can obviously keep a secret." I tipped my head at her. "Plus, she can help us prove Stephen's innocent, don't you see?"

He remained motionless and I went on, trying to explain myself. I saw a solution and hoped I could get them to see it too.

I turned to face Sandi, who was watching us carefully. "You aren't supposed to know about vampires. They'd kill you if they knew you were aware of them."

Sandi's mouth hardened. "And how is it *you* know and are still here? Are you one of their servants?" She watched my reaction, "Yes, I know about those, and how they feed off of humans and control our minds. I know all of their tricks. I've become a bit of an expert in the last few years."

My husband spoke again, still trying to get an answer to his earlier question. "How many others know about vampires?"

Her eyes held a naked hatred now that she didn't feel the need to hide it. "I'm the only one who knows for sure. Williams is limited, he has no imagination. He thinks it's some sort of cult we're after."

I didn't miss her omission. "What about Detective Hanson? Does he know?"

She didn't exactly meet my eyes when she answered. "I don't think he does. He doesn't seem open to that sort of thing so I've never discussed it with him, but I really don't think so."

"Aunt Sandi, James and I connected when we first met. The connection is something we don't fully understand, just that it's special. They let me live with the understanding that I can't ever tell anyone and because I'm James' mate." I decided to leave out the part where I worked for them. "You can't tell anyone either or they'll find you." I hoped she understood how serious this was.

She didn't comment on my warning. Instead she remained focused on James. "Is this true? You monsters are organized into some sort of society? I thought it was just roving bands."

He bobbed his head once, his eyes trying to read her motives. "We have a social structure similar to your human royalty that has been in place since before the crusades. They work to enforce our laws and hold our secrecy in the highest

102

regard. We wish to maintain the balance between our two races. Not all of us want to kill humans." His tone had taken on a soothing cadence. I couldn't tell if he was trying to alter her perception or just calm her down.

I had to give her credit, she was listening. As much as she didn't want to, she *was* listening. She mulled over what we were saying. James was silent. I held my breath.

"Tell me what really happened to Brian Peterson."

I let out my breath in a gush. Smiling uncertainly, I shot a glance at James.

He closed his eyes and moved his head nearly imperceptibly.

"Brian was a servant for one of Nighshade's members, a really bad guy. He used Brian to get to us."

"Does 'us' include Henry as well?" she asked evenly.

I looked to James, not sure if I should give more than what she needed to hear. James nodded to her again.

"Thought so. He felt like one of you. I knew what he did to me, trying to make me forget what I saw in him. It doesn't work on me, not for long anyway." She narrowed her eyes. "You let him know I won't be manipulated."

"I will." James agreed. I thought I saw a hint of a smile on his lips. He liked her nerve. I hoped it would be enough to convince him to keep her as an ally instead of seeing her as a liability.

"Now, what about this bad guy?"

"Brian lured Stephen to Bradley," I dared to say his name feeling his ghost creep up on me, "and Bradley used Stephen to bring me to him. He wanted to get back at James and he thought he'd use me to do it."

James' teeth flashed. Sandi caught it and gasped.

"My connection to James brought him to us. Stephen's family, Henry, and James were able to get to us before it was too late." My scant account didn't escape her notice.

"Were you hurt?" Sandi's voice softened for the first time since our arrival.

I nodded, not wanting to go into too much detail. "Yes."

James rumbled low in his chest from beside me.

She glanced from one to the other, clearly sensing we were hiding something from her. "What happened to this Bradley guy?"

"Dead," James ground out.

"What do you know about Nighshade? It's all vampires, right?" She let the omission go.

"We think so. Bradley was a front man for the larger corporation. We haven't always had a name for them although their organization has plagued us for over a century, hiding behind a series of vampires acting on their behalf. They kill the ones we know about whenever our investigation leads us closer to their identities and we are again back at square one while they regroup. Some of us have committed ourselves to finding and destroying them regardless of how long it takes. Quite a few of our own have been destroyed in the process."

His honesty surprised me and he sensed it. "If she is going to help us she needs to know what she's up against. We're the closest we've been in a long time. Maybe the police have access to something we don't. I'm willing to try and see what we can find out by combining our resources."

My distress was only partially alleviated. I knew that if it didn't work out, Sandi's life was forfeit and possibly Detective Hanson's as well. That was a lot of blood on my hands if it came to that.

The timer on the oven went off, making me jump and startling Sandi from her pensive trance. Her eyes took on their normal wide look, whites showing. "I'll go check our dinner." She got up, smoothing her shirt pointlessly. "You two stay here."

"You don't want any help?" I asked her, starting to rise.

She shook her head. "No, I'd just as soon be alone if you don't mind."

I eased back down, reclining against the couch cushions behind me.

"It's going to be alright, Love. This might be exactly what we need to finally end the threat of war. We can get on with our lives."

I saw the flicker of hope in his eyes yet couldn't completely swallow my own worries. "But what if it doesn't work? What then? I can't stand by while my own aunt is killed."

His arm went around my shoulders, pulling me into his chest. "I will do everything in my power to stop that from happening. I promise you."

I drew peace from the cool stillness that was him for a few minutes, listening to Sandi clattering around in the kitchen. I didn't notice when it went quiet, then I heard her clear her throat from the doorway.

"Dinner," she announced coolly.

We all sat down, Sandi serving both of us in turn. She poured two glasses of red wine as well. She and I each took a bite of our meals. James sat at the table beside me, nothing in front of him. He didn't have to pretend anymore with Sandi. She watched him while she chewed and by the third bite, I saw her make up her mind.

"Okay. I can arrange for Detective Hanson to come alone and hear you out. I can't guarantee anything, except I can tell you he wants to catch these killers. They're responsible for a number of deaths and other crimes in the area. And that's just what we *know* about."

Confused, I asked her, "But I thought you said he didn't know about vampires and you weren't going to tell him."

Her eyes narrowed and her tone was uncharacteristically snide. "We'll just have to come up with a story we *can* tell him." She aimed a suspicious glance at James. "I'm sure you can manage something?"

"When would you like to do this meeting?" James asked her, ignoring her barbs.

"Are you available later tonight?" She asked me.

"We are if you can come to our house." I glanced at my watch. It read 7:43. "At midnight?"

"Yes, we'll both be there."

We ate and made minor small talk about family and vacations. Aunt Sandi, it turned out, was an experienced traveler and had been around the globe.

Despite her anger toward vampires, I was excited by the prospect of having a family member with whom I could share nearly everything in my life. She could be someone I could really enjoy if the few glimpses of the real Sandi I had seen tonight were any gauge at all. By nine-thirty, we were saying good-bye, agreeing to meet again in a few hours.

Ch. 21

James fed heavily as soon as we arrived home. We both waited in our own ways. James remained still, whereas I paced, straightening out any messes and looking for various chores to keep my hands if not my mind busy.

Henry arrived by 11:30. He was somewhat optimistic for the joining of forces. He had not been able to have someone infiltrate the police force as of yet. "This could be the missing piece of the puzzle that makes all the difference this time," he said.

I dared not ask him what he thought might happen to the other side should it not go well. For once his brutal honesty wasn't what I needed.

A few minutes past midnight I heard a car on the street. James was the first to the door and welcomed them in. The detective entered first, surveying the room and its occupants; Aunt Sandi was close behind him.

"So," the detective started once the door closed. " Sandi says you have something you can't share on the record?"

Henry answered politely, "Yes, a great number of things."

Sandi's lips tightened at the innuendo. She really didn't like Henry, that was abundantly clear. Hopefully she wanted Nightshade as much as we did so we could try to hold our shaky alliance together for long enough to finally capture them. I bore no illusions as to what would happen when we caught them. Sandi and the detective wanted to bring them to justice, only I didn't think vampire justice was what she had in mind. Although having seen the depths of her fury, I didn't anticipate our form would be a problem for her.

"Can I get anyone anything to drink, Detective Hanson?" I hadn't had many chances to play hostess in my new home yet. I held out hope that one day I would even get to without it being for a war council of sorts.

"Call me Earl when we're not at the station. Do you have scotch?" I looked to James for confirmation, aware I didn't know the full contents of the liquor cabinet. He nodded assent.

"Sandi?" Detective Hanson gave her hand a squeeze as she stood beside him.

She nodded. "I would have a glass of something red." Catching herself, she quickly added, "Wine, red wine." I had a quick flash of dread, maybe she *couldn't* keep a secret.

Henry looked amused. I didn't like how easily he was accepting her inclusion.

My return didn't disrupt the conversation. They were all deep in discussion, sharing what they knew of the Peterson case.

Sandi and Earl were sitting close together on the couch, Henry stood by Earl's end, James by the chair clearly reserved for me. I sat down to listen in after delivering the drinks to our guests. Earl was talking about what the police knew of Brian's death.

He was willing to believe Stephen wasn't the killer though he wouldn't say why exactly, just that he was willing to buy Stephen being framed by Nightshade. However, his willingness was based upon the assumption that we could come up with some more evidence. But, we had to be quick because if the DNA was back before we brought something else in to support our allegations, there wasn't much he could do to suppress it.

The detective mentioned the "animal marks" they had assumed to be post mortem were bite marks on the neck. It seemed the marks were not being tied to the deaths just yet. Obviously that was a secret better kept unless absolutely necessary.

James explained that he had someone at the paper investigating Nightshade and any mention of them in the business pages or in the government records listing new businesses, assumed names, licenses, and building permits.

Earl said he believed the people behind the corporate façade had to be well connected. They had been involved in various scandals he'd investigated in the last five years, which had been promptly covered up. The files were always lost or destroyed before anyone could investigate and when they had gotten too close three years ago, Jim was killed as a warning.

James explained that he assumed he would hear something by the end of the night or tomorrow from the source at the paper. He would call Earl immediately. Henry said that he would be following up with some of his contacts in the UK tomorrow. He intimated that Nightshade might have some ties there as well.

Our meeting broke up by two with everyone agreeing to touch base tomorrow evening. James handed out coats. Sandi hugged me and gave James a grudging handshake, barely looking at Henry. Earl shook everyone's hands equally and I watched his hand go to the small of Sandi's back to guide her on the way down the walk.

Henry was the last to go, telling James he would speak to Troy in the morning and fill him in on what was happening. He would have Troy speak to the clan so everyone was on the same page but they weren't to get cocky about Stephen being in the clear. We still had the possibility of DNA testing, an even greater threat that we had to divert. Plus, we were a member down; Tonya was still "helping" Donovan in Edinburgh.

I tried to imagine how hard that must be for Henry to feel how he did about Tonya and watch her go off and have affairs with other men. Tearing up, I hugged him good-bye thanking him again for helping my Aunt. He gave me a queer look before tolerantly smiling at me and bidding good night to James.

After the door closed James wrapped his arms around me and escorted me up to bed. Sleep was neither quick in coming nor restful.

Ch. 22

The next morning I woke up by nine and had some housekeeping to do. I had been putting it off as long as possible and I could deny it no longer. I called the Registrar's office at school to make an appointment.

"Do you want me to go with you?" he asked over breakfast, sensing my nerves. Not a surprise given my pulse increasing just at the thought of what I saw as a failure. I still didn't know how I was going to explain this to my parents. For now, I would put it off. I seemed to be doing a lot of that lately.

"No, I want to do it by myself." I took a last sip of my tea before I went upstairs to get dressed.

The only upside to the trip was that it let me drive my new car. It was liberating to be able to drive at my leisure and even stop for a coffee I didn't necessarily need. Parking in the student lot, I drew some envious stares, including one from a passing professor. I had to duck my head to hide my smile. Define failure, I asked myself.

Meeting with the Registrar was not as painful as I had thought. She was understanding that I had just gotten married and offered a great job traveling.

Because my reasoning was sound and I expressed a desire to continue my education, she sent me over to the Weekend College office. They had online and weekend options that would be easier to schedule a job around, the Academic Advisor explained. My mood had done a complete one eighty from what it had been when I'd left the house that morning.

My next stop was my dorm room. I had taken most of my clothes when I went to James' over the course of our break. All that remained were some books and stereo equipment which translated to an MP3 dock my father had proudly set up my first day on campus. Unhooking it, I reminisced to myself about all that had changed in such a short time. It was hard to believe it was my life and not some fantastic story.

Within two hours I was packed up and had carried out in three loads of all of my belongings. I arranged with the RA from my floor to sell the loft for my bed either to someone in the dorm or leave it for the next resident who would be taking over the room. The same went for my little futon I had so proudly bought to entertain my guests, both supernatural and not. I didn't need any of it now.

I ran back up to grab the last box and lock my door before turning in my keys and ran into Lindsey. Lindsey was a perpetually cheerful blonde, every bit a flake yet somehow hard to dislike.

She held out her arms. "Claire!" she squealed as she jogged up to grab me. "How have you been? I haven't seen you since finals. What have you been doing this month? A few of us stayed, who wants to go home?" Lindsey waggled her eyebrows, "Have you been spending much time with your man?"

I felt the big stupid smile creeping across my face. No one but family knew. I held up my hand.

"Oh my God! You're engaged? Wow! I'm so happy for you." She called out to the girls who had stepped out of her room at her screams. They all knew about James and we'd talked some in the halls and on campus. I'd gone to breakfast and various meals with them last semester, even taken a class or two with one of them. Trudy was her name I think, although I couldn't remember the third one's name. She was nice as I recalled.

Shaking my head, I spoke up loud enough to get Lindsey's attention. I had to say her name twice, raising my voice to a near yell. I forgot I had to speak louder with humans. I was around them so rarely now I had grown used to speaking softly.

"Lindsey," I finally got her back into my orbit and her friends as well. "Not engaged, married. We got married in Paris a few days ago. I'm just here getting the last of my things." Anything else I was going to say was lost in the following screams.

Lindsey spoke up, flapping her hands for the girls to quiet down. "What are you doing for lunch?" She rolled her eyes in excitement. "You *have* to let us take you out before you go. Consider it a belated bachelorette party."

I started to come up with an excuse for why I couldn't when I realized there *was* no good reason not to. That and I *wanted* to go to a girls' lunch. I'd never been to one before that wouldn't be painful for all the old reasons. Now I could shield. I liked these three and there was a Vietnamese place nearby I had wanted to try since coming to school here.

"Sure, what do you think of The Lotus?" I suggested.

The answer was a resounding yes.

We all walked together down to the front desk where I turned in my key.

"I have to put this last box in my car. Do you want me to drive?" It was pretty cold for a human to walk the half mile to the restaurant and I was proud to be able to offer.

"When did you get a car?" Trudy asked.

"Wedding present," I smiled, trying not to sound smug. Inwardly I swore to remain humble, even if I did enjoy a few of the perks as James put it. The tradeoffs were certainly working on my humility.

Everyone's curiosity piqued and all of us in high spirits, we went out to the parking lot. When I hit the locks and popped the trunk I heard their murmurs of approval and maybe a little jealousy.

"I didn't know James was hot *and* had money," Lindsey ooh'd. "Does he have a brother?"

Her question reminded me of the big family he'd been born to. They would be long gone by now, even their grandchildren would be dead. "No, he's an orphan." I kept it simple.

"Oh, sad," Lindsey cooed sincerely. "It's a good thing he found you."

Interestingly perceptive, I thought giving her an indulgent smile. *I* liked to think it was a good thing too.

We drove over to The Lotus. I called James on the way to let him know I was going to an impromptu lunch.

"With friends?" he asked guardedly. It was understandable with all the kidnapping and lying that had been going on that he might be a little worried.

"Yes, some girls from the dorm. I moved my stuff out and they insisted on taking me out for a celebratory lunch. You didn't have anything planned, did you?"

"Not until this evening." His tone lightened. "I have some things I can do at the office since you're out. Just call me if you end up going home early. I can always break away."

"Okay. I'll see you later then." Quietly and feeling incredibly lucky, I added, "I love you."

His throaty chuckle made me shiver, "I love you too."

My lunch dates were all giggling when I hung up and I felt my cheeks burn but I didn't care. I was on top of the world today and nothing could bring me down.

The restaurant was three stoplights and seven minutes away. It was a glass front unit with a neon lavender lotus flower in the window. Inside, the front counter which shared duties between the hostess station and take out order staging area had a plug in desk water fountain with layers of slate stone. It made a pleasant enough sound, although cliché in an Asian restaurant.

We all talked about our breaks and what we had been doing. They were, of course, most curious about my big news. It was fun to dish about the details of the impromptu wedding, the rushed run up to it and the last minute dress fittings. It didn't take long when I left out the murder and mayhem.

"So are you leaving school?" the third girl, Sheila, asked.
"No, I was meeting with Academic Advisors and Registrars and everything here today. I'm switching to Weekend College so I can travel for work."

"Work? Where?" Lindsay asked, shocked. "You have a job too?"

I sipped my tea, buying time and mentally kicking myself for bringing it up. I wasn't sure what I was going to say and without all the details worked out I feared I would stumble.

"Claire, where are you working that you're going to travel so much you can't go to school?" Lindsey asked, prodding. Her eyebrows shot up as an idea struck her. "Did you get a job with James at the paper?"

"I didn't know you knew where he worked." Her attentiveness caught me off guard. I hadn't honestly given her much credit as a reader, certainly not of something serious like a newspaper.

She looked offended. "I do read the paper, you know. The Travel section is my favorite, all those exotic locales and restaurant suggestions. I always think I'm going to do something on my next break but I never do." Popping the last section of her spring roll into her mouth, she mumbled around the mouthful, "I'm jealous."

Taking the life raft she was throwing, I nodded agreeing. "His editor thought the husband and wife team would be an interesting take and cater to our primary audience, married couples. It's cheaper for the paper too, one set of benefits you know." I grinned stiffly at them, hoping they wouldn't ask any more questions.

With a relieved sigh, I watched them all nod and move on. Sheila asked Lindsey about an upper classman she had been dating over break. Having seen how smoothly it seemed to work on the girls, I thought I could make a decent go of telling my parents provided I found out more from James since they were sure to ask more questions.

I drove the girls back to campus and dropped them at the school store. It was open for another half an hour and Lindsey wanted to buy a sweatshirt. Her little sister had stolen hers while she was home on break the first week and she just *had* to have a hoodie for her morning classes when she didn't want to get dressed.

Ch. 23

Just as I eased onto the freeway, my phone rang. It took three rings to find the Bluetooth button on the dashboard to put it on speakerphone. This car was safe which pleased James greatly. I didn't mind either. Why take chances?

I didn't recognize the number. "Hello?"

"Is this Claire?" Female and Scottish.

"Can I help you?"

"This is Davina. I'm Alan's daughter, from Helios Fountain in Edinburgh. You had my Da checking into a book for you and he's found it."

Helios Fountain was a bookstore in Edinburgh owned by a witch and his daughter. When I'd visited, he had given me an amulet to protect me from vampires, not knowing I *wanted* to be bothered by my vampire. He had, however, let us know someone's human servant had come in and bought a book on psychic bonds. We figured it was too coincidental not to be connected with the attacks on us while we were in the city. Alan was going to get the book for us.

"Hey, Davina, thanks. So are you sending it?"

"No, we found it at one of *your* local bookstores. It's called Mystic Books on Lake Street in Minneapolis. Do you know it?"

I didn't, though it would give me a chance to try out my GPS. "I can find it. Is it on hold or do I need to know the title?"

"We've put it on hold. Just go in and ask for it under Thomas."

"Thanks Davina. I'll go right now."

I pulled over and got my owners manual out of the glove box to figure out my GPS. It was relatively easy. I got the directions pulled up and merged back into traffic. The bookstore wasn't far and I was there in a flash.

Typical South Minneapolis traffic situation, there wasn't a nearby parking lot so I had to park about four blocks away and walk down a flight of concrete and iron stairs before walking around the front of the building. I was glad I wasn't temperature sensitive anymore or I would have been freezing by the time I opened the door.

Mystic Books was an alternative bookstore; that meant it smelled like sage, had an apothecary supply on the back wall, racks of candles, crystals and then the books. There was a mix of books for real practitioners and those aimed at the gothic types who wanted to pursue alternative religions and spiritualities without understanding the reality behind any of it. I couldn't be too hard on them, though. Before I knew the truth about supernatural creatures, I had dug through some of the same books looking for answers.

I approached the tall man putting labels on a pile of stone ashtrays at the counter. He was very pale, had long black hair and was wearing a concert shirt for some band I had never heard of involving puppets and meat.

"Hi, I think you have a book on hold for me. It's under Thomas."

His red eyes took a few seconds to focus on me. I was guessing pot was part of his daily diet. "Let me go in back and look." His words were sluggish, nearly too much so to make out. It had to be something much stronger than pot or he'd smoked a ton of it.

While I waited, I looked around at the various necklaces. None were like my amulet. I wished I had remembered to bring it. I wanted a chain for it so that I could wear it as a necklace when I wasn't going to be around James or Henry. It's protection might prove necessary someday.

"Found it." Mush mouth called out. He shuffled his way back to the counter.

I wandered back there myself and saw he had the book already in a bag and rung up. I paid and walked out of the store. Once on the street, I pulled out the antique looking leather bound book. It was obviously used, and my guess was, probably no longer in print. Alan's store had had lots of those.

Flipping to the table of contents, I found what I was looking for. "Psychic Connections" was on page 334. How convenient. I stopped walking and started to read.

The book said they were rare and usually only between kindred spirits, except in the rarest of cases. Meaning human to human or dog to dog would be the most likely pairing. Once a bond was forged, it could only be severed by death.

I put the book back in the bag and started walking again, staring at my shoes on the ice and listening to the crunching of the salt under my soles. The book said a bond could be severed only by death. What did that mean for my turning into one of them? That was a physical death yet the mind survived. Would our connection? I was eager to discuss it with Henry and James.

Taking out my phone, I concentrated on dialing James. He answered on the first ring. Vampires were so fast when they wanted to be.

"Hello Love, are you home already?" I smiled at the sound of his voice.

"I got a call from Davina. You remember Alan's daughter from Helios? She said they had the book we were looking for at a shop here in Minneapolis. I just picked it up and read the section on psychic connections. It says they can only be broken if one of us dies. Do you think turning constitutes death or can the connection live in my head if it comes to that?"

"I'd like to avoid it entirely, if at all possible." His initial response was not as jubilant as my own. "How did she get your number? We gave her mine."

"You're always so suspicious. Did you hear what I said? That could be a good thing if we have to look at me turning, not that I want to either." In my head I could hear Henry's caution to James that eventually I would *have* to turn or go mad. That he was continuing to deny that was bordering on the ridiculous. "James, you can't pretend we aren't going to have to face this," I started.

He sidelined me, "Claire, my suspicions aren't ill placed. Alan is trustworthy but we know nothing of his daughter. If you will recall, she was irresponsible. Always losing her keys and laying with men Alan doesn't approve of. I am merely saying we should use caution with her." He backed off, probably hearing how harsh he was being and offered a concession. "I'm going to get out of here. Why don't you meet me at home; we can look at it together."

Right as he said the last, I reached my car and stopped. Leaned against it were two vampires. I could see them in the fading sunlight.

One was very young and, I was guessing from the way her mind was buzzing and banging into mine, just turned. I could see the wildness in her eyes. She was my age; I think I'd found the girl we'd come back to help. It was surprising she could be out in the sun so young. James said that like thirst, it burned the most as a newly turned vampire before slowly fading.

Glancing up I saw that the sun had gone down and only its last glow was keeping full dark at bay. I'd been reading for longer than I'd thought, and in the dark. My eyes were better too. There wasn't time to be excited or upset about that little discovery.

The other was a man turned in his late twenties. He was a shorter Asian man with his long hair pulled back behind him. I recognized him.

My heart skipped a beat and I struggled to find my voice. It took two tries to get out more than his name. "James, I think I found the female who disappeared on us. She's on my car." I paused, my voice low as though they wouldn't hear me. "She's with one of Bradley's crew."

"Can you run?"

"That was my plan. They're going to be faster." I couldn't depend on them needing to remain secretive if no one could see us. Looking around, I hoped for people or streetlights.

"Hello again, Claire. Why don't you come talk to us?" The man's slippery voice made my skin crawl.

James heard him and his frustrated growl came rumbling through the phone.

The vampires heard him too and I watched a cruel smile cross the male's face. His teeth were growing. The female was already fully vamped out. The man's hand on her shoulder was all that restrained her. Her only thoughts would be for blood, which I had. It would be worse than normal with her being out in daylight. Even fading, it was taxing her body and taking a huge toll.

I started backward slowly. "I was at Mystic Books on Lake Street. There are two of them. I'll try to call you if I can. Do you understand?" I knew he would understand that I didn't mean on my phone.

His words were clipped, spoken through tight lips and a clenched jaw. It was easy to picture him trying to fight down his own panic while I heard him moving through doors, the sound of glass breaking came through the line. "Buy as much time as you can and stay away from her as long as you are able."

I tried to speak again and failed, my voice was stuck behind the lump in my throat.

"I *will* protect you Claire. I promised."

I didn't point out the obvious, that he was most likely going to be too late, before tucking my phone away. I heard only the snow crunching beneath my shoes. The two were starting forward silently, following at a comparable pace. Turning, I picked up speed and headed back out to the street behind me, I needed witnesses as soon as possible. It was a few more feet down the stairs and I would be in the open. I pondered whether yelling would help or hurt my cause.

Drawing attention might rush their plan and speed the process, or it might bring good Samaritans. I didn't want to get anyone else hurt though and these two didn't seem the sort to care whether a few innocents were harmed.

I broke onto the street, already in a jog. The vampires were walking briskly behind me. They weren't in a rush to catch up. I was determined to use their patience to my advantage. The first store I passed was an auto parts store; it was deserted. I needed more people than that, a crowd would be perfect.

There was a well attended café two stores up and I ducked in. The hostess was at her station and seated me immediately. From where I sat, I watched the two walk in after me. The female's eyes were roaming over the other patrons scattered about. I was hopeful she would keep her companion occupied with controlling her around all these humans.

Now that I had found a place to wait in relative safety, I turned my focus inward. I found our bond immediately, I had the strong feeling that he'd been waiting for me. My menu had the café's name. I let it run through my head, feeding him the address off the menu as well. He sent back that he was in the car, on his way, and to try to stay as long as possible.

The waitress brought me a hot jasmine tea and left me to peruse the menu. My eyes flicked up to survey the crowd every few seconds. The female vampire was tucked tightly against the male in a booth. He was most likely holding on to her so that she didn't frenzy. It couldn't last, they both looked ready to blow.

Ch. 24

I finished my first cup of tea and heard the bell at the front door chime. A breath I didn't know I'd been holding went out in a sigh. James walked in scanning the interior. His eyes landed on me and I saw how hard it was for him to hold himself to a human walk as he came to slide into the same side of the booth with me.

He took my hand and squeezed it. I flashed him a tight smile and leaned into him. His arm around my shoulders made me feel victorious. It didn't matter that they were still waiting for us to leave, I felt invincible with James at my side.

"I'm glad you got here fast. I don't think I'd be able to stay much longer. Things are looking a little tense."

He looked over at our fan club and nodded. "Is that the toy Gina used to keep around?" Gina was one of Bradley's crew, now dead.

"Yes." I hadn't realized James had never met him.

"Was I right? Is that the girl?"

"She fits the description." He scented the air. "She smells new."

"What do you think we should do? We can't stay here without putting lots of people at risk." My eyes remained on the female's crazed eyes growing steadily wilder. Her fangs were altering her profile. I could see them when she would champ her teeth, like she was tasting flesh between them already.

James was quiet. "You're right. We don't have much time." He glanced outside through the windows. "It's dark. Let's move."

He put a twenty on the table, paying for my tea ten times over and we stood to leave. We took our time putting on our coats, taking turns watching the vampires until we walked out the door.

They hadn't shown signs of leaving until we were out on the street. James was able to hear them and told me of their progress, "They're out on the street." We were three stores past the restaurant.

We hadn't gone one more when James caught the street sign and made a triumphant noise in his throat. "There are some condemned houses in this neighborhood coming up, the city's buying them up to put in some sort of new housing. If we can make it inside one of them, we can dispatch these two out of sight." A truck roared by on the overpass half a block over; noise wouldn't be an issue.

I was glad the moon was nearly full or I would have been seriously challenged to see anything beyond my feet. As it was, my visibility would be greatly diminished compared to the others doing battle. They could see very well in the dark with their enhanced sight, mine was good, though far from equal.

We sped up, James guiding me with his hand on my elbow. The first boarded up house we saw was a tired Victorian with dark paint peeling from the porch railings and gingerbread around the screen door. There was a light on in the house to its immediate left. We didn't stop.

It felt like any minute I would feel a cold hand on my shoulder, clutching me in its grip. I felt my body itching with the touch I knew surely was coming. We jogged around the back of the next abandoned building that used to be a home and James easily tore the boards off the back door. He tore the door off as well and ushered me inside.

There were tiny slivers of light around the boarded up windows on the upper floors coming in from the moon and powerful halogens on the freeway. I tried the light switch in vain and heard James snort bitterly.

"Sorry Claire, we can't have it all." His nerves made his voice tight and his joke fell flat.

I was glad I couldn't see him. I didn't want to see him scared. I didn't want him to see me scared. Before I could ask if we could call for backup, they were on us.

The female screeched like a banshee as, unleashed, she hit the door opening. She crouched and focused on me, I could hear her clacking her teeth. Her target was clear. I felt the fear coiled tightly in my stomach.

James moved in front of me, preparing to defend, and the male stepped inside the door to crouch opposite the frenzied female. I felt James hesitate, deciding which to go after first, which one posed the greater threat. The male would be stronger and a more experienced fighter yet the female would have the unpredictability of frenzy on her side.

The male took the choice of the matter away from us; standing back as the female came forward first.

She launched herself at me, trying to rush around James, but he was fast. I hadn't seen him go full speed before.

At once terrible and awesome, he was incredible. He caught her around the neck and threw her sideways into the wooden stairs, smashing through the banister. She was back up before I could draw a breath. Again she came at me and he threw her backward. It happened three more times before she seemed to calm down enough to learn.

She tried a different tactic, diverting at the last second, feinting left. When James realized his mistake it was too late.

She spun back to the right and grabbed my arm. I screamed and thought about channeling some of her rage back on her, but without knowing her focus I could potentially make her more dangerous to me. So instead, I hit her with my free hand, feeling a sick satisfaction as her cheek collapsed under my fist and she shrieked in anger and pain.

James snapped back to my side and tore her hand off my arm. I heard several bones in her arm crunch with the pressure. She roared in frustration and I saw the male launch himself into the melee.

He did have more experience, displaying it with his blitz attack. He was very good at reading the female's intentions and each time she would come at us from the left, he would come from the right, and when she came from the right, he took the left. James was fighting valiantly.

Tireless as a vampire was, I knew eventually he would make a mistake. It was inevitable. I used the seconds available to flip open my phone and dial Henry's number. He heard the hisses and snapping teeth and wasted no time getting our location. Henry said he would be here in a few minutes and hung up.

I was wondering what else I could do and looked around my guarded position against the wall near the bottom of the stairs. A few feet to my right, my adjusting eyes made out several pieces of broken rail from the wooden banister. It would work to paralyze a vampire if I could get it into the body; a challenge considering it wasn't sharp though the end was relatively narrow. I would have to shove hard to get through their tough skin.

No sooner had I made my decision than James had thrust the female back and the male lunged at him. Throwing myself, hands out in front of me in a dive, I skidded into the makeshift stakes. Taking one in each hand, I was repositioning one when I felt something heavy land on top of me, pressing me flat into the floor.

Something hard shoved into my side from below, I felt it pierce the skin and I gasped. My left hand was still holding a stake and I swung it out to my side to try to clear the vampire on top of me when she struck me again.

The scream tore from my throat as she bit down on my neck from behind, tearing the flesh like a dog. Her hair was covering my face so any chance I had of seeing was gone while her body held me pinned to the ground. Her free hand shot out to grab my fingers holding the stake and she crushed them in one squeeze. The weapon fell from my useless hand.

The feeling of her sucking out my life was agonizing. I had been bitten several times, but never by a young vampire in a mad frenzy. She wasn't just biting; she was tearing and chewing, destroying purely for the sake of destruction.

The ruckus in front of me grew louder. I thought I heard more crunching and tearing sounds come from their direction and I said a silent prayer that it was not James who was losing body parts.

She continued to feed and I was rapidly losing my ability to fight. My struggles grew weaker and still she fed. I couldn't speak. I heard the air bubbling from the hole in my neck when I tried.

With my vision fading and my body finally blissfully numb to the pain, the weight was pulled off me and I heard the tearing sound again as James removed her head, mercifully ending her punishing feeding.

My body was rolled over and I caught James' profile illuminated by a sliver of moonlight from a window behind him. Glowing pale white, he cradled me in his arms on the floor.

"Claire, my love," his choked voice was tormented. "I've failed you." He stroked my cheek. "I didn't keep my promise."

I tried to speak only to hear gurgling. His eyes were dark. I couldn't tell more than that in the dim light. I struggled to concentrate on him in my head, to talk to him there. It was hard, I was so weak but he felt it and opened up from his side, holding onto our connection.

It isn't your fault. I should have done what you said and stayed put. If I would have listened to you none of this would have happened. I've been such a fool, so headstrong. My snort came out as a wet cough.

I felt his anger at himself. Being in his head, he couldn't shield from me as well. I felt the direction of his thoughts before he could push them back where he hoped I wouldn't see.

James, we can't avoid it anymore. You have to decide or I'm going to die.

"No." He spoke out loud, shaking his head.

James, please? It isn't what either of us truly wants, but I know I could go through anything with you beside me. Can't you consider having me with you forever? His unwillingness stung worse even than the burning pain of my ruined flesh.

He was in turmoil and he could not hide it in his head, or in his voice. "Can't you see? If I turn you, I've doomed you to the same eventual insanity as I face. You gave me my humanity, but I would willingly give that up if it would save you." His voice cracked. "No, Claire, if we're both monsters, I will be responsible for your madness. How can you ask me to do that?" James' voice broke, lowering in defeat. "I can't be the one who takes your life, and your sanity." Leaning down, he kissed my forehead tenderly. "I love you, Claire."

A throat cleared behind us, his voice giving him an identity. "James, she will not make it to the hospital. I am afraid your moment is upon you."

Henry knelt down beside me to speak, surprisingly tender. "Claire, can you hear me?"

"She can," James answered for me. "She can't speak but I can hear her."

Henry was one of the few who knew what that meant. I saw his silhouette incline his head once. "Have you offered her a choice other than death?"

James made a strangled noise. "She says she wants to be turned."

Henry heard his Second's anguish. "Then the problem is yours, not hers?"

"I can't do it." He stroked my cheek with the back of his hand. I couldn't stand to hear the heartache I was putting him through. Nor was I ready to let go while there was a way for me to stay with the man I loved.

James, speak to Henry for me please. I felt my life ebbing, they were becoming more blurred and it was challenging to hold onto the thread of what they were saying. Stubbornly, I did.

"She wants me to tell you something," James whispered, his voice rough with pain as his senses surely told him my life was failing.

Henry waited, watching my face.

I'm ready. I know you two can help me through it.

James spoke the words, though I could feel his resistance.

131

Henry, I want you to do it. Please turn me before I die.

After James repeated the message, I spoke just to him. *James, do you remember what Miranda said in the beginning? She lost the love of her life because he wouldn't be turned. She said it was the worst mistake she ever made, not forcing him.* Dropping any illusion of self-respect, I pleaded with him. Desperate to remain with him however that had to happen. I'd meant it, I could face anything with him. Even madness. He heard my reasoning, holding my hand to his forehead, bringing it down to his lips. More directly, I attempted to sway him. *We can keep each other sane. We'll remind each other of our humanity every day. I'm not scared as long as you're with me. Say you'll keep me by your side, James. Please, I need you.*

Henry was watching James, I could tell from the direction of his chin. My sight was nearly gone with my dimming consciousness. My heart skipped in its weak rhythm and Henry spoke gently.

"We are going to lose her. The decision is yours, but I do have an opinion, if you wish to hear it."

"What should I do, Henry?"

"I prefer not to be a sire; only in a few cases have I intervened. This woman is special to you and to our kind. You lived with the risk of losing your humanity before. You will again no doubt. It is up to you whether you do it alone or with her by your side. If you truly want her, this is not a difficult choice. However, you must make it now, or say your good-byes."

My eyes failed me and I recognized my death. My last breath rattled in my chest, wheezing through my bloody throat, and my heart beat one last time. Our connection left me and I was suddenly alone. I whispered through it, not knowing if he heard before it was lost, *I love you James,* and the darkness took me.

Ch. 25

Something cool and wet pressed against my lips. It smelled of iron and I would have pulled away if I had any strength. Instead, I lay immobile while the blood dripped down on my lips, slowly filling my mouth.

My throat tried to swallow and failed, pushing the blood out of my mouth and down the sides of my face. It dripped into my ears. More blood ran into my mouth only this time, a hand gently stroked my ravaged throat, helping me to swallow.

Immediately I felt an impulse to swallow again, the blood filled my mouth fast. As each mouthful went down, my strength returned and the pain faded. All too quickly, I was being scooped up and carried out. The house grew hot around us as we left. I smelled the burning wood even if I couldn't see it.

I was carried hastily to the car, aware that James sat with me in the back seat, my head in his lap. I knew it was him from his smell and the feel of his hands. I would know him deaf and blind, he was as familiar to me as my own body.

The lights of the freeway flashed by us overhead, glowing bright through my closed lids. We stopped and I was carried into another house. It smelled like home and my notion was confirmed when James carried me upstairs to our room.

He stripped me in the bathroom and used a wet cloth to wipe the blood from my body before dressing me carefully as he would a child. After I was cleaned and dressed, he laid me in our bed and disappeared. I was exhausted though I knew that I would not sleep. I would never sleep again. Omar had told me that while I changed I wouldn't even be able to move, not until I "rose" at sundown as a vampire.

The hum of voices came to me from downstairs and I knew James and Henry were discussing this latest attack. I wondered in passing if anyone had picked up my book from the house before it was burned. I had dropped it in favor of having my hands free during the fight.

Davina. She was a bad guy. Who did she work for, Nightshade? It had to be. But why? She was a human and her father was friendly to us. I didn't envy whoever had to break the news to Alan that his little girl was in league with the baddies.

Eventually James came back into the bedroom. I had never heard him before unless he tried; this time I could hear his feet and the air around him as he moved. The bed shifted as he slid in behind me, his hand on my hip in its usual position. I heard him turn on his MP3, too low for me to have heard it any night before this one. The songs gave my mind something to work on while my body lay frozen.

The skin of my throat itched as it came together and the bones in my hand where they'd been crushed now reforming tingled and vibrated with all the activity going on under the skin.

As much as I wanted to talk to James, to have him to share my fears with, I was terrified to try our bond. I had died, my mind had gone for a time. It was possible the bond had gone with it.

At one point, his phone rang and he flipped it open. I heard Troy.

"Henry told us. We are trying to keep Stephen confined so that he doesn't go over there. He's not happy that it's happened and he wants to be with her. We have tried to remind him he won't be safe from her and it might bring the police to you too soon if he is acting suspicious."

James' reply was bitter. "I'm sorry Stephen is 'not happy' but she was dying. You could ask him if he would have preferred the alternative." Hearing that he was lashing out, he changed the subject. "Has Henry informed you of our meetings with the detective and his consultant?"

Troy said that he had.

"Stephen can thank me later. They will be a bigger problem for me now that Claire has been turned. They might even back off of him entirely and decide to come after me."

I hadn't considered Aunt Sandi's reaction or her influence with the police force. She had the power to make life very uncomfortable for all of us. To increase my frustration, I knew I wouldn't be able to talk to her safely for a while. She would *really* hate Henry if she saw me now, thirsting for her blood.

"I will be sure to mention it, James. Please call when she can accept visitors. I am sure Stephen will be eager to see her and Heidi is becoming difficult to keep away. She hasn't been able to give you both her wedding gift and she won't ship it."

James said that he would and ended the call.

Heidi was a good friend I worked with on campus at the library. She was dating Troy. It had only been since the Christmas party we threw at the house, but they had been virtually inseparable since then. Troy was an experienced enough were that he hadn't told her what he was yet, but the time was coming for them too.

We were laying together, curtains drawn when I began to feel heat growing in my body. It wasn't thirst, I knew through James what that felt like and it would be in my throat. This was all over, like I was being consumed by fire. I was afraid of what was happening. More afraid of finding our bond broken, I stayed silent, unable to know if he was calling to me through a severed connection.

The burning continued to build slowly and steadily for what must have been hours. Finally, it began to fade as gradually as it had come on. Incrementally the burning left my body until it was banked.

My relief was short lived. The heat was quickly replaced by the familiar burning in my throat. This one I knew. Only this was not like the thirst I had felt through James. This was much more intense, it was all consuming. My other thoughts were cast aside. I could only think of my burning throat and how I could ease it.

When the burning in my throat had driven me nearly mad, I opened my eyes. I glanced about the room, seeing it was black. Even the faint sunlight usually visible behind the curtains was nonexistent. I had risen.

Ch. 26

I wasn't sure if my voice would work, I was afraid to try it so instead I rolled over to face James. When I did, my breath caught in my throat out of habit.

My new enhanced vision made seeing him possible in the dim light from the rising moon. He was smiling his crooked smile at me. He only did that when he was being playful or he was nervous.

"Do you know where you are?"

I nodded, still afraid to speak.

"Do you understand what's happened?"

Again I nodded.

He hesitated, "Can you speak?"

"Yes." My voice sounded strong when I tested it, not the croak I was ready for. The surprise showed in my face and James' smile lost some of its tension.

"Then let's get you something to drink. Henry had extra brought over for you after..." He didn't finish, he was obviously still nervous about my mortality status changing.

I couldn't think about his anxiety or its exact cause. Right now the thought of food had me excited. A strange sensation, a faint vibration was coming from my mouth. Raising a hand to feel, I touched my fangs. They were coming out as my excitement grew.

"Come on," James led the way into the hall and down the stairs.

The new feel of my body was distracting as it moved its strong new muscles to sit up and then to stand. I heard him chuckle at my wonderment.

"It's fascinating, isn't it? That is my favorite part of helping the newly turned, watching them awake and discover that they are stronger than ever before. I think the women like it even more than the men."

We walked downstairs and went to the fridge. We had done this very same thing a hundred times, only this time what he got out was new for me. James removed a wine bottle from the top shelf, removed the cork and handed it to me.

"Would you like the bottle or a glass or should I put it in a covered mug like I drink it?"

I barely let him finish before snatching the bottle from his hand and putting it to my mouth. The metallic scent and thickness of the liquid would have made me gag yesterday, but today was a new day. It was delicious. My throat cooled as it slid down into my stomach.

The strange sensation as it hit my stomach made me pause. I wasn't getting full. I felt a movement under my flesh instead. Small pulses ran across my skin, underneath instead of on top. In confusion, I put down the half empty bottle and looked askance at James.

"Did you never wonder what our bodies do with the blood? How we can bleed when we are cut when we have no blood of our own?"

I had never thought about it. I assumed so much about him was magick that I didn't put much thought into the biology of being a vampire.

He continued on, giving a well-rehearsed lecture, one I was more interested in than any the schools had offered me. "The blood runs into our stomaches and goes in and what was once our circulatory system, which is stimulated into action by the electric impulses our nervous systems retain from being turned and becoming brain dead. They send blood pulsing through our veins. When we are hungry, it slows and when we are starving or go dormant, it stops."

The bottle returned to my lips, the pulses continued to move beneath my skin and now I found the process intriguing. The feel of it was stimulating. My body was coming alive, pulsing and ready to satisfy another need.

I put down the empty bottle on the counter and stepped forward putting me close enough to lay my hands on James' chest. The way his body felt under my fingertips was amazing. His body was still firm, yet now I was able to push into his muscles as I would have a human. I credited that to my new strength and the fact that now we were equals.

The thought gave me pause. "I'm a vampire."

Hesitation flickered across his face. He waited silent and unmoving for some anticipated reaction from me.

Looking down at my hands and turning them over in front of me, marveling at the pale smoothness that was now my skin, I said it again. "I'm a vampire." Suddenly I had an urge to look in the mirror. Faster than I thought possible I darted into the bathroom on the other side of the kitchen wall.

I turned on the light out of habit and was dazzled by its brilliance for a few seconds.

"That will fade quickly. Interior lights are easily managed," James spoke from behind me. He had matched my speed.

The face I saw was me and not. I had always thought of myself as average, nothing special. The woman staring back at me with black eyes and fangs had that softened, beautiful look in spite of the obvious vampire qualities now on display. All of my flaws had been washed away as though I had been airbrushed to near perfection. It was impressive.

It also struck me that I could possibly explain this face away to friends and family as makeup. It wouldn't necessarily alter how they saw me, other than the pale skin. Again I could argue makeup.

"You're still beautiful, Love." His face was close behind my shoulder, yet he hadn't reached for me since getting me out of bed.

Bed. That reminded me of the tingling skin and heightened senses I wanted to try out. Spinning quickly around I was suddenly facing James, our faces inches apart. Closing my eyes I took a deep sniff, the strong smell of him filled my senses. His eyes were dark blue turning to black when I opened mine and watched him responding to my interest.

I smiled in victory knowing he wouldn't argue. One of his eyebrows went up and I reached for his hand.

He swept me up and carried me into the living room. I didn't want to be carried and straightened, bucking my body from his arms.

Surprised, he stopped, facing me in the short hallway. I knew what I wanted and I didn't want to wait. Placing my hand against his chest, I tried out my strength by pushing. He was flat against the wall instantly, shock quickly replaced by heat.

I laughed wildly, feeling the energy my feeding had given me and threw myself at him. My hands tried to unbutton his shirt and were too slow for my tastes. I tore it from his body in my haste and inexperience. His pants followed suit.

My own pajamas he had put me in last night were off in shreds and he pushed me against the opposite wall. I stared into his black eyes, watching his expression as he lifted me up and wrapped my legs around him. It was with pure unadulterated pleasure that I threw my head back, realizing he was happy with my change if I was. He sensed my exuberance and matched it with his own.

Ch. 27

When we were lying entwined on the couch, I asked James what the other burning had been. The one I felt when I was turning. I knew it wasn't thirst.

"The sun. That is how it feels to us at first." He rubbed my arm gently when he felt me stiffen. "It will fade in time. Now you can understand why you can't go out in the daylight right away."

The limitations of my new life were few though significant. They would take some getting used to for sure. "How long does it usually take?"

"It depends. We're in the Northern Hemisphere and it's winter. You might be able to go out for short periods in a month or so. I wouldn't try a summer day for a few years at least," he explained.

"That long, huh?" I lay quietly as I processed my new laws for living.

I heard a ringing from behind us on the floor where James' pants lay. What was left of them. "You'd better get that."

There was always something happening so we usually grabbed our phones even if we were otherwise indisposed.

He slid out from underneath me and rolled over the back of the couch, neatly landing on his feet. I wondered if I could do that.

"Henry. Yes, she's awake and doing well." James winked at me. "What?" His mood changed to serious at once.

I sat up trying to hear Henry's side of the conversation. He was speaking so softly all I could make out was a low humming. If I was closer I knew I could hear. Moving to get up, I saw James hold out a finger to stay my intrusion. My temper flared and I felt my teeth growing. He noticed and hurriedly ended his call.

"Don't shush me." I growled around my awkward new teeth. "I'm your wife, not a child."

He did not look apologetic. "You have to trust that I will tell you anything that pertains to you or that I don't have to keep private."

"Private from me? What can I possibly not know about your life?" My quick temper was building.

James tried to placate me. He reached his hand out to touch my arm. "There are things that you will know soon but not yet. These are political scenarios which need to be played out, with more lives hanging in the balance than just our own. Henry and I are the only two who know the identities of all involved. Please trust that this is the safest way."

"Oh," While I understood cognitively, I was still having a hard time not being offended, rightfully or not. It wasn't like the Vice President of the United States told his wife everything. "Well, I'm going to get dressed. You can make whatever calls you need to, I'll be upstairs." Trying not to stomp, I went up to find something to wear. He did indeed flip his phone back open and I heard him make another call as I ascended the steps.

I had taken my time getting ready, marveling at the lightening of the scars on my body, the sheen my hair had taken on and the glow of my pale skin.

When I came back down, James had another bottle for me; this time I opted for a glass at a time. My thirst was down to a low grade burn.

"I have a brief errand to run. Could I get you to agree to stay in while I'm gone?" James looked a little nervous asking.

Trying to listen and keep my hypersensitive feelings from getting bruised, I asked jokingly, "Why, so I don't leave and go on a killing rampage?"

His expression was completely serious. "Actually, yes. You need to stay away from humans for now. Until we have a chance to work with you and your control. You are no different from any other newly turned vampire until we can confirm differently."

Obviously, I didn't want to harm anyone. "Okay."

James kissed me lightly and stepped out. I heard the garage door go up and his engine start. Wondering what to do with myself, I sipped at the only food I would ever taste again.

I was on my second glass, trying to settle my racing mind enough to read a non-violent, sure-to-stay-away-from-blood-and-guts book about hobbits when the front door jiggled.

I was up and out of the chair before I had a conscious thought, sweeping to the door in a second and sniffing to determine who or what was on the other side. I couldn't place the somewhat familiar smell, no surprise considering *everything* smelled different now. There were more nuances in everything I smelled, saw, and heard. Too bad I could no longer eat food, or maybe that was good. Different wasn't always better.

Remembering I wanted to find out who my visitor might be I whipped open the door, a nagging thought plagued me at the back of my mind. Some reason I shouldn't open the door. It was too late. As the door swung wide, it created a wind that swept something small off of the front stoop and into the room behind me. My eyes followed like a cat with a laser pointer. It was a card in an ivory envelope.

Swiveling my head back, I saw Heidi still crouched down in the act of placing a gift wrapped in silver and ivory paper on the mat.

"Claire?" She was obviously surprised to see me. "Troy said you weren't going to be home until late tonight. I thought I would leave this here for you." Heidi's eyes narrowed and she stared into my face trying to make sense of the changes she saw.

Worried she would see too much, I ducked my head. Smiling closed lipped, I looked up only briefly. "Thanks Heidi. That was very thoughtful. We've only just gotten home."

"Oh," she looked into the house past me, "am I interrupting?" She winked, "Newlywed business?"

I laughed at Heidi's gravitational pull to all things sexual. "No, James had to step out for a little while."

"Well, then there's no point leaving this out here." She picked up her gift and to my horror, walked into the house.

There was no polite way of turning her back, so I decided I would hold my breath and try to make this short. I was deliberating testing out the survival of the bond and calling James as I started to shut the door and something stopped it from the other side.

It was a hand, Troy's to be exact. He was glaring daggers at me. "Hey Claire, I thought you wouldn't be here." That wasn't true. He knew I would be; he thought James would be here as well, however, making this a very different situation.

I tried to convey my discomfort and apologize to him with my eyes. "Yeah, we got an earlier flight. James had to take care of some things at the office. We're going on that long assignment in a few days."

My eyes went to Heidi and I saw her watching me again, pensive while a faint smile remained on her lips. "I was walking past the door when I heard it move and thought I would check and see if it was another delivery." I forced a chuckle. "Wedding presents, you know."

He caught the hint about the trip. I would be hiding out for a while. He played along. "That's right. Where are you going again, Greece for a month?"

Confused about the destination, I stared at him until he bugged his hazel eyes out at me.

"Yes, Greece. We'll probably be a month or more if we piggyback it with another trip. We'll see what our editor says."

Heidi had been walking the package over to the dining room table during our exchange. Having placed it and recovered the card from the floor, she turned and joined in. "A month or more? What are you going to do about school? We start back up next week."

Pleased to finally have something I could tell the truth about, I replied. "I'm switching to weekends. I got a job with James at the paper and we're going to be traveling a lot giving the Twin Cities the husband and wife perspective." I gave a lame little laugh. "It will be easier to work my schedule around weekend and night classes." Definitely nights for a while I thought, remembering the burn of the sun.

"You're not working at the library any more are you?" She sounded hurt.

I hadn't considered that she would take my changes personally. "I'm sorry, Heidi. This all kind of came on so fast. I haven't had much time to think all of it through."

She looked at the house around her and held out her hands. "I guess you don't really need to work at all, huh?"

Irritated that she thought I would be sponging off my husband I reminded her sharply. "I *do* have a job you know. I make my own money too."

Heidi held up her hands, palms up. "I know, I'm just saying. You did all right for yourself." She smiled slyly, "Hot guy, money, nice house. You could have done worse, Claire."

Troy's throat clearing reminded us girls of his presence. Heidi flushed, "No offense Troy." She smiled genuinely. It was one rarely seen until recently. No pretenses. I saw beyond the piercings and dyed red tipped hair; she was beautiful and warm when she let her guard down.

"Heidi, I'm going to miss you." It came out without thinking. "While I'm abroad I mean, not working with you." I scrambled to recover.

She smiled again and threw herself at me, wrapping her arms around my neck. I wasn't ready and it took me completely by surprise, I breathed in from the shock. Her hair was in my nose as was the smell of her blood. I was painfully aware of the pulse in her neck inches from my face. My control flew out the window and I knew I had only seconds to extricate myself from her arms before I attacked.

She felt me hesitate and laughed. "Relax Claire, you need to learn how to let people hug you. It is normal human behavior you know." In a total Heidi move, she kissed my cheek.

The last thread of my control snapped and I tightened my arms around her body, holding her tight.

"I love you too, dear." Heidi laughed at me again, releasing her arms to move away.

I couldn't let her. My canines vibrated as they grew and I felt the need rising up in my body, my throat all at once on fire. Her pulse pounded in my ears and I was swimming in the smell of her.

My mouth opened and I barely grazed her neck with my fangs before a strong set of hands grabbed my arms, pulling me off of her. I turned toward Troy and snapped, angry at being denied. He released one arm long enough to level a powerful backhanded blow to my jaw.

Heidi screamed, "Troy what are you doing! Let her go!" Then her voice changed to confusion and panic. "I'm bleeding. Claire did you bite me?"

He'd spun me when he pulled me off, hiding my transformation. Troy was holding me tightly with my face against his chest while I continued to struggle to get to Heidi.

"Heidi, go get a glass of water or something. Claire is having a seizure." Troy ordered quickly, trying to control the situation.

She shot back at him, "Well why the hell did you hit her then? Shouldn't you put something in her mouth or something so she doesn't bite her tongue off?"

"Just go." He nearly shouted, adding a belated "please" as she stalked away.

Once Heidi left the room, Troy whispered hotly in my ear. "Get a hold of yourself or we are all going to have a lot of explaining to do." I heard the cold menace in his voice as he added, "Don't hurt her or James or no James, I *will* kill you."

With Heidi's scent being replaced by Troy's, I felt my senses returning. Troy, thankfully enough, didn't smell appetizing to me. Maybe I didn't like animal meat anymore. I felt a hysterical giggle bubble past my lips.

Troy stared hard at me, willing me to listen. "Can you pretend to faint? I can keep her away from you except you have to make yourself not move. Okay?"

His plan sounded easy enough. I straightened out my face and nodded. He watched me for a few seconds making up his own mind.

Carrying me over to the couch, Troy put me down. He laid the blanket over me and I turned my head toward the back cushions hiding my face and hopefully blocking as much of her smell as possible.

When Heidi returned to the living room with the water, Troy explained that I had "fainted" and that he was going to call James to let him know then put me upstairs.

"No," Heidi objected. "She should stay down here so we can keep an eye on her."

"Let's go wait in the dining room, give her some quiet." He suggested. I heard them walk away and two chairs slide on the rug.

Buttons were pushed and I heard the ringing. "James, it's Troy. I'm at your house." He paused. I could hear the hum of James' voice. I could tell he was agitated. "Listen, Heidi and I stopped by to drop off your gift thinking you weren't home yet."

I heard a few choice words from James, he was very loud in my ears.

Troy got up from the table lest Heidi hear as well. "Yes, you're welcome. Claire heard Heidi and let us in."

Another furious outburst from James' end.

"While we were here Claire had a seizure. She is resting now, I think she's fainted."

James was silent.

"We were going to stay with her until you could get back here. Are you close?"

His reply was too soft to hear but I heard Troy relay it to Heidi when he hung up.

"He's at the office. He's getting out of his meeting now and should be here in twenty minutes. Okay?"

"Sure, that's fine." Heidi's voice was uncertain.

"You don't think we should take her to the doctor or anything? I didn't know Claire had a problem with seizures."

"Yes, James mentioned it to me once before. Remember at the Christmas party when I was helping her around? She was having trouble that night too."

I had to admire Troy's quick thinking. He had been helping me to shield because I was weak from James' hunger and it had bled over. I'd tried to attack Tonya that night. I hoped those days were soon to be behind me. To have control over myself might almost make up for losing our bond, a fact I was too scared to test.

I listened in on their conversation with one part of my brain while I counted the minutes with another part. James "called" me after five minutes.

I've just gotten loose from my editor. I'm on my way. Are you okay?

If I'd been human I would have cried, it had survived! *I'm sorry, I was trying so hard but then she hugged me. She smelled so good, I lost control.*

We'll work on you when I get home. I have good news, you're officially hired.

How can he hire me without even meeting me?

I hope you don't mind, I liberated some of your writing samples you had lying around from school and he agreed to let you do a few pieces. He'll decide long term based on that. Interviewing isn't an option right now.

Right. I suppose I should thank you. My joy at having our connection was tempered by annoyance.

But?

But it's frustrating to feel like I have no control in my life. Again.

Claire, no one has ultimate control over their lives. We all make decisions based upon others' actions and decisions. You now have much more freedom than most humans. Money, immortality, love, you have it all in front of you. Let yourself enjoy it. In time it will be much easier.

It's easy to see how some vampires let it go to their heads. I feel so strong, invincible.

Our humanity is what separates us from those who we fight against. You will have to remember yourself so that you don't forget why we protect humans. I'm nearly there, hold on.

Just hurry, she's moving around a lot. I can smell her.

Ch. 28

"James, we're so glad you're here." Troy didn't have to fake his relief.

Heidi sounded worried. "She had some sort of seizure while I was hugging her and she accidentally bit me."

She came closer, her scent was dizzying. I held my breath again.

"See," she must have been exposing her neck to him. "Troy grabbed her and held her so she didn't hurt herself. Until she fainted that is."

James' face peered over the back of the couch and I opened my eyes once I smelled him. "Yes, I do see." His hand touched my jaw. "Did she hit her head on something during this seizure?" Eyes narrowing slightly, I saw him fighting to control himself.

My own eyes widened and I shook my head slightly, pleading wordlessly for him not to confront Troy.

I was rewarded with a gentle caress to my sore jaw, already healing but tender nonetheless.

Heidi was silent as Troy justified the blow three of us understood. "When she started to seize, her teeth clamped down on Heidi's neck and I reacted without thinking. I knew I had to get her off before she did any permanent damage." His explanation was wholly truthful if not a little misleading.

James thanked them graciously. "Thank you for staying. Troy, why don't you take Heidi home and tend to her injury."

A few more pleasantries and concerns for my well being were voiced and finally I heard the door shut. This time,

James threw the deadbolt blocking out any other uninvited guests.

"You can get up now." He sounded relieved.

Finally, I took a breath to speak. "How do you stand it?"

He relaxed as he wrapped his arms around me. "Eventually, you control yourself for so long it becomes second nature. It's merely impulse control."

I laughed uneasily, "Some impulse."

James kissed my head. "Speaking of impulse control. Are you ready?"

Realizing he meant to start working now, I nodded my head vigorously. "The sooner the better."

He pulled away and indicated I should sit. We sat next to each other on the couch.

"Do you remember how we worked on shielding? I held mine back while you built your own, then slowly let them down."

"I remember." It had been the single greatest discovery of my life, the beginning of my new life. "Is it like that?"

"It's like what we did with Omar, only you're Omar." Serious, his brow furrowed and he slid to the edge of his seat turning to face me.

I mirrored his movement so that our knees were inches from each other, careful not to touch. Watching his face, I waited for something to happen.

It did. He used our bond to push temptation at me. He took my memory of Heidi's scent and fed it back to me.

My stomach twisted and my fangs grew. I felt the desire for her blood just as strongly as when she was right in front of me. The burning flared up in my throat and I was on fire with the wanting of it.

"Control it," James commanded. His severity took me by surprise. He'd never used that tone with me.

He saw me flinch and softened his expression only slightly. "This is the single most important thing for a vampire to learn. Without it, you can go rogue and the Court will put you down." His brow pinched again, "Now concentrate and try." James' mouth twitched, "Please."

I grimaced as I was again hit with the blood lust he had found in me. We could find anything in each others' minds with our bond constantly connecting us as it did. Usually we were polite and respected each other's privacy, but this was a special circumstance.

I focused on Heidi as a friend and as a person, someone important to me. Once I saw her face, I was able to confine the thirst to a corner of my mind and push it back. It was still there but caged.

James smiled proudly. "That's great. You're doing well, Claire."

My eyes flashed to him and I saw that he was still focusing. "There's more?"

He lifted an eyebrow at me before frowning again. This time, he pulled up a memory of his own. At first I was struck by the era. The clothes of those involved dated it as near the turn of the century. The woman had high button shoes and a stiff collar marked the neck of the gentleman with her. Then I "stepped back" and saw the scene for more than a costume party.

The woman was dead. Her body was white and blue from loss of blood and a gory wound marred her neck obliterating part of her shoulder. The man beside her was barely breathing. A form attaching itself to his arm moved, catching my eye. It was a wild thing. Maybe it was a vampire, I couldn't tell, it was more animal than human hunched over the body. It was not just draining the blood, but putting its hands in it, worshipping it.

James came upon the scene and the scent of blood was overpowering. His body reacted instantly, his throat burned, fangs grew and he was drawn to the feast. However, I felt his disgust at the desecration and he fought down the urge.

For our purposes, he let me smell the blood fresh on the ground and in the air. I smelled the meat and felt the frenzy the other vampire was in as well as James' own desire. It was harder to fight because it was so much stronger, but I drew from my last success and pictured the humans alive and talking. She had pretty red lips and an upturned nose that would have twitched when she smiled. He was handsome and had a strong jaw, very masculine. Personalizing them helped and I was able to cage my thirst again.

"Don't get overconfident," he cautioned, " but I think you'll be a quick study, Love."

My attention came back to him here in this room and I sat back, exhausted. I rolled my shoulders and neck, easing the tension that had built up there as I concentrated.

"The most important thing to remember is that you need to feed a lot when you're young. You'll need to feed more than me. Now that you've turned, I've felt my need returning to normal."

Reaching out I put a hand on his arm. "I'm sorry it had to come to this."

"It wasn't your fault," his expression was bittersweet, "and how can I regret having you with me forever?" James' blue eyes brightened. "We have our connection, aren't you pleased?" He knew that had been one of my bigger concerns after the whole loss of family and friends thing.

"You've lost the most important thing about it, my humanity."

"Not the most important thing, Love." He tried to hide the depth of the loss except I saw the sadness and doubt settle on his face. "My humanity has been refreshed for the present and you and I will just have to remind each other." He smiled and put both hands on his thighs preparing to rise, swiftly changing the subject. "Snack?"

The burning flared up at his mention and I nodded.

We worked all night and before I knew it, I felt the familiar burning I had felt when I was turning. This time I knew what it was and was somewhat prepared for it, although it did not make it any easier to endure.

"The sun is coming up." I was sitting on the counter in the kitchen. He was standing in front of me. We had taken another break for refreshments.

James knew what I was feeling and rested his hand on my knee. "I'm sorry Claire, there is nothing to be done for that. It will fade relatively quickly with so little sun this time of year here. That's the best we can do. Distraction is your only comfort."

"What did you have in mind?" I had an idea.

"Do you play chess?" He raised an eyebrow.

"What?"

James' silky laughter rippled through my body. "Sex is a fantastic distraction, though not a good option when you're in pain. Chess is better, trust me." He stroked my arm, "I have trained many a vampire, none of which did I have sex with to distract them. Chess works just fine."

"Really? You didn't have sex with *any* of them?" I don't know why that surprised me.

Offended, he snorted. "No, I did not. Claire, how well do you know me? These women are not in control of themselves and I am charged with their care. To take advantage of that would be wrong."

I leaned back considering him, my head rested on the cupboards. "What?" He looked uncertain.

"I love that about you. You're completely unassuming." Clarifying, I added, "You're this spectacular person, super sexy, have had over one hundred and fifty years to let it go to your head, and you haven't." I reached out to put a hand against his cheek, "People just aren't like that."

"No," he gave a short laugh. "People aren't."

Rolling my eyes, I responded in kind. "Vampires aren't either. I'm just saying it's a no brainer why I'm in love with you."

He reached around my back and pulled me forward so that my legs were on either side of his waist. His face filled my sights and I wrestled with the desire rising up and the burning filling my being at the same time. In an uncharacteristically chauvinistic move, James slapped my butt and winked but not before I caught the darkening of his eyes.

"Let's go play some chess."

Ch. 29

Before we were two moves into our first game, James' phone rang. He looked at the display and took the call while still in his seat at the table.

"Yes, Henry."

"Have you forgotten about our agreement to touch base with the good detective and his assistant?" I heard Henry ask him.

"No, I have not. We've had our hands full here tonight."

"Oh?"

James smiled impishly at me before he responded. "I was out getting Claire a job and she tried to eat Heidi. Troy controlled things here." He frowned in thought before going on. "Her training has been going incredibly well, I would say she'll be safe to travel in a few days. I was thinking of telling our human investigators that we don't have anything new just yet but that Claire and I will be looking into some leads overseas. What do you think?"

"That is good news about Claire. I am sure you explained that although I am her sire, your unique relationship makes you a better mentor."

I had the distinct feeling Henry knew I could hear him and that was for my ears. Either way the message was clear. I would be James' responsibility, not Henry's. That took an incredible amount of trust from Henry considering if I messed up, he would be held accountable for my actions.

"Traveling overseas is a good idea to deflect attention off of you two for now. Sandi might suspect something but she has admitted she can't tell anyone at the police department. She values her connections there far more than she does her relationship with her niece. I'm sorry Claire, it is true." Henry didn't sound apologetic, only honest.

"That's all right Henry, I kind of figured that. We've never been close," I replied, unhurt.

"You should call Sandi tonight and give her an update as promised. Have you heard from Indira?"

"No, I was going to call her tonight and check in. She was supposed to meet me at the office but I was called away early and missed her." He stared at me, the corner of his mouth twitched. He was being awfully loose about my near miss.

I realized I could smack him now without breaking my hand and resolved to try it out soon. He had been downright giddy since I had been turned except for when we were training. It had weighed on him as much as me it seemed. His mood was infectious. Why shouldn't it be? Most of our worries were gone. I wouldn't go insane, we had kept our bond, he was happy with my turning as was I, and I was learning control much faster than anticipated thanks again to our unique connection.

The only deterrents were the limitations of the new lifestyle, though that too could be managed in time. It sounded like under a year could see me enjoying the outdoors and human company again with relatively low risk of catastrophe. That wasn't so long in my new scheme of things.

"Let me know if you hear anything from Indira. Are you playing chess?"

James' eyes crinkled. "I'm that predictable am I?"

Henry's voice was light and joking, a rarity these days. I pondered for the millionth time how he could pose as the head of the media center at the college. He said it was a strategic placement that allowed him to do research and keep a watchful eye over a group that was one of the most frequently targeted populations by vampires. "I wasn't sure about *this one*, but yes, chess is still a good distraction while the sun is up. Claire, be glad you didn't turn in July."

Our chess games were a joke. My family was bookish and we had never played many games so chess was relatively new to me. James had to keep explaining the moves each piece could make and he could easily strategize four moves ahead.

In our fifteenth or so game I had James in check, my knight about to take his king and his phone rang. I didn't need to look out the windows to see that the sun would be setting soon. I could feel the flames banking for the night and my body beginning to cool.

"James, this is Indira. I have found what we were looking for."

James sat up straight. "What did you find out?"

Her monologue was businesslike, no frills or personal interjections. "I found a reference to Nightshade Holdings based in London going back to 1904. They moved operations here to the States in the sixties and set up an office in New York first, then followed up with a second here in Minneapolis.

Go to your computer, I have scanned a picture I found of someone very familiar who was present at a building dedication at the first site in New York. I cannot speak for long, there are others here." There was a shuffle, maybe she'd turned her head, brushing the phone with a hand. "I hear someone coming, I must go."

"I understand. Thank you for your efforts, Indira. I'll go up and wait for the email now." They hung up and James got to his feet. "Should we go look?"

"You just don't want me to win one," I teased him, indicating the chessboard with a tip of my head.

"Would you like to take my king then before we head up?"

"Yes, I would." He moved a pawn quickly and without purpose. I didn't care. I picked up my knight, and took his king. Mock cheering and raising my fists in the air triumphant, I celebrated.

"Take a victory lap before we go up and check the computer. Go ahead, you've earned it." James was shaking his head and grinning at me.

"Thanks, I think I will." I did and it was sweet.

I danced up the stairs and into his office. The computer was on, he pulled up his email. I settled in and sat on the corner of the bed behind his chair to watch the screen over his shoulder. It was a laptop with a 17" screen so I could see it without any problems.

We waited quietly until we heard the message hit. Both of us were silent while he opened the attachment. It didn't take but a second to figure out who we were looking for in the picture.

It was a grainy newsprint photograph from five decades ago, yet there he was. Once my eyes picked him out as one of the four people at the dedication ceremony, it all fell together. It made perfect sense. He hated humans, he had wanted James and I dead the last time we had been at the Court. A Court member would be powerful enough to manage a legion of vampires with treasonous sentiments and to orchestrate a war between the two factions from behind the scenes.

"Oh my gosh. What can we do?" We couldn't kill Anton and who were the others in the picture? I couldn't tell if they were human or not.

James was staring at the men in the photograph. Without taking his eyes off of the monitor, he pulled out his phone and dialed. "I have a picture I'm sending you." It took less than a minute for Henry to receive the image and to be looking at the same faces we were.

"We will meet here tonight. Troy will have to recall Tonya from Edinburgh; she is in danger there." Henry couldn't command the Andrews clan, or they him, however they were compelled to help each other per the nature of their own bond. Cats were Henry's animal to call, meaning it was similar to a witch's familiar.

Either way, it was a two way street, their compulsion to obey each other; much the same as James and I had in our bond, though they couldn't communicate the way we could. That was uniquely ours as far as I knew.

I felt for Henry, knowing the woman he loved was in danger and not being able to do anything significant about it. I wondered how often that happened for them, I would imagine it was frequent.

"We can be there at six. Does that work for you?" James was staring intently at the screen, he hadn't even blinked since opening the file.

"Yes, I'll see you both here at six." Henry ended the call.

James didn't put his phone away, he redialed Indira. She didn't answer and he had to leave a message. "Indira, James. Call me back, I need to know if you found any captions or listings of names attached to this photograph."

I looked closer, I hadn't noticed initially but the photograph wasn't part of an article. It was merely an isolated image with nothing attached. The label on its edge in a plain font was "Dedication ceremony for Nightshade Holdings LLC, Manhattan, NY." The image showed a clean cut around the picture. I asked James what that meant, he knew more about how newspapers handled those sorts of things.

"The photographs used to be stored in paper files with the articles before we had digital storage. On occasion, a photograph was left out if the article was a small one and didn't have room. It looks like that was the case with this one, though it would typically be stored with a copy of the article." His brow wrinkled and his lips were tight. "I would like to know where she found this. I am guessing it wasn't in an ordinary file."

I felt a tingling of my nerves. Call it a premonition, I feared for Indira's safety. "Didn't Indira say she was worried about being heard on the phone? Do you think they've found her?"

"I've considered that. If we don't hear from her by the time we finish at Henry's I'll go to the office and check on her."

"I'm going to get a drink." Wandering downstairs I let my thoughts swirl. Would James and I be safe with Anton now that I was no longer human? Probably not. His man Bradley hadn't liked vampires who were friendly to humans any more than he liked humans, and I would assume his boss would share the sentiment.

The location of the bottle was not a mystery to me at this point. I could probably find it with my eyes closed. Laughing to myself, I realized that was true. I could find it by smell very easily. This time, however, I chose to use my eyes.

A sense of relief flooded me as I felt the last of the sun's burning fade away and the thirst ebbing as I fed. I sat at the dining room table, running my fingers around the edges of my glass, marveling at the sensations, when I heard James descend the stairs.

"Would you like to play another game?" he asked, not sounding any more up to it than I felt.

"I'd rather not," I answered honestly.

He sat opposite me and picked up his Queen. He studied the piece for a long time. I was lost in my own thoughts when his phone interrupted.

Startled, I jumped. "I hate that thing."

"Me too," James replied. "I remember when we didn't have phones. It was much more peaceful. It's saved lives though." Giving me that to think about, he answered. Immediately, we both sat up and were focused on the call. "We'll be right there," he said and hung up.

I had heard his editor's excited chatter on the other line and nodded dumbly, "They killed her. She was right."

James agreed, "The strange thing is that they tried to make it look like a break in and tossed *my* office. Since the paper is never really closed, it would take someone very bold or stupid to do that." He spared a glance at his watch. "If we hurry I might still be able to get a few clues the police can't."

Ch. 30

The offices for the Star Tribune were open and modern in their time. There was a lot of glass and shiny metal but once we were inside, it was much the same as any other office. Tons of cubicle mazes filled the center and offices lined the outlying walls of the structure.

James' cubicle was virtually naked. There had been a wire rack that obviously held the folders now papering the floor. The contents: article notes from trips, pictures, menus and assorted receipts were intermingled. I wouldn't know if anything was missing, so I stepped aside to allow James a full view.

James was acting disturbed and confused, everything he should be. Only I could feel that he was not overly upset about the office. He *was* very concerned about Indira's murder and felt responsible. The police were interviewing potential witnesses throughout the building and we knew it was a matter of minutes before the officer on this floor approached us.

"Where did they find her?" he asked his editor and my new boss.

The Editor, introduced to me as Phil Greenburg, was nearing hysterical and hadn't stopped pacing since our arrival. Phil was about 5'8," pasty and had the average build for a writer versus an athlete in his forties. He continually ran his hands through his heavily gelled, curly black hair, only stopping long enough to answer our questions before going back to pacing. His intense eyes behind his frameless glasses were small and black, beady even, making me think of a mole. I wondered which one saw the sun more often between him, James, and the mole.

"Phil," James' posturing changed and I heard him take on a commanding tone. "Calm down. I need to know where they found Indira. She was working on a story for me and I need to know if anyone else is in danger."

Namely us, I thought secretly.

James was planting the idea in Phil's head. Phil accepted it and slowed his pace. After one more lap up and back, he stopped and leaned heavily on James' cubicle wall.

"Indira was going out to her car. She took the stairs in the ramp, she always took the stairs. She must have caught them leaving, they got her in the stairwell between two and three." Phil was shaking his head, closing his eyes as if to erase the image that would never fully go away. "How could they burn her like that? I mean, how do you set fire to a human being?"

"Phil, you need to go home and rest. This will fade in your memory. The details of the scene will blur after you tell the police. It won't be so bad by morning. You'll see." Again he was commanding. It did seem the humane thing to do.

As if on cue, the officer approached our trio. "Mr. Greenburg I'd like to take your statement now." He glanced from James to me, "You too. This is your office, right," he searched his notepad. "Mr. Thomas?"

James pointed at his name plaque affixed to the fuzzy cubicle wall giving an anxious laugh. "That's me."

The officer put a hand on James' shoulder believing the human facade. With a final pat he turned back to Phil and indicated they would go to an office not far away. There wasn't a visible name plaque though I was guessing it was Phil's by the way he automatically walked around the desk to sit in the high backed leather office chair behind it.

Their interview took forever. It was at least forty minutes before the officer excused himself from Phil to approach us.

167

Officer Sandberg took down James' name and asked him about any articles he was working on, had worked on recently, anywhere he might have gone in the past six months or if he remembered seeing anything unusual in his travels. The travel reports Phil kept showed that James had done some local travel lately, which seemed to interest the officer the most. James claimed ignorance on all counts, even managing a nervous stutter or two and eventually Officer Sandberg ended the interview.

"How was she killed?" James asked the officer. "I heard she was going to her car. Are we safe?" He looked wide eyed at me.

The officer flipped back in his notebook confirming his facts. "She was in the stairwell going to her car and we think she surprised them coming or going," he repeated the same story Phil had related. "We believe she was stabbed before they burned her. The tapes are all blank so that's all we know." He shook his head, "The guard said he had gone out on rounds and didn't hear a thing until the fire alarm went off but by the time he got there it was too late. She was dead and the fire was already out."

The officer paled at the memory of the scene. To reassure us, he put on a brave face. "Whoever did it is probably gone but don't go anywhere alone for the time being."

The thought of knives and blood had me working hard to win the match with myself between bloodlust and human decency. James noticed and put his arm on mine. His shields were helping to give me extra protection, it wasn't enough. I could smell the officer, smell his blood, and I was having a hard time concentrating.

"Are we done Officer? I don't mean to be rude but my wife is finding it hard to be here." He gave the police officer the "man to man" look, "She worries about me," he confided to him.

Officer Sandberg spent a little longer looking at me before agreeing. I kept my eyes down. "Yeah, she doesn't look so good, she's awful pale. You'd better get her home. We'll call you if we need anything else." He reached into his back pocket and withdrew a business card. "Call me if you find anything is missing. Even if *you* don't see a connection, we might."

"I'll do that." James responded respectfully, sounding all the while like a very concerned citizen and employee.

Ushering me out, only partly for show, James had his arm around me until he deposited me in the passenger seat. Instead of getting in as well, he stuck his head in and announced, "I'll be right back."

"Where are you going?" I fought down the fear he was going to do something foolish like track the killer.

"I have to see the scene. There are a lot of things I can catch that they can't." He would smell vampire if we were right and if he recognized the scent, we would have our killer.

"What about the cameras?" I thought about what the officer had said. They would catch him on tape.

Unconcerned, he shook his head. "I can stand underneath it and move faster than it can track me getting in and out." He touched my arm, "Don't worry. I will only be a minute."

The door closed and I was alone. There weren't any other humans within my scent and I had fought down the urge to feed for the moment. I just hoped James would be back soon before it returned or someone happened by to renew the temptation.

It wasn't five minutes later and we were on the road. Now that I was not a human I had to admit driving fast didn't frighten me the way it used to, nor did it seem so out of control. My senses were much sharper. I could see the openings in traffic and my reflexes could handle the rapid shifting of positions of those around me. It didn't scare me though I still didn't like it.

I tried to relax into my seat, closing my eyes until James announced we were at Henry's. I had never been to Henry's house here in town, just his flat in Edinburgh. It turned out it wasn't all that different.

He lived in a condo downtown on the river. I wondered if he originated near water, he certainly gravitated toward it.

Stephen let us in, stepping back to let us enter. He stared down at the floor. "Don't be expecting a thank you," he mumbled sullenly.

James' response was tight. "And for what exactly are you not thanking me?"

"The police don't believe I was *directly* involved in Brian's disappearance or murder now and they've cancelled the DNA sample. They still have me lumped in with you as a person of interest. Detective Hanson's buying his partner's idea that we're all part of a cult or something." He walked away to plop himself down on the light colored leather couch without so much as a hello to me.

James reached for my hand. Stephen wasn't sure about me being involved in all the vampire doings and my turning would just involve me more and we both knew it. Too bad, I thought. It was either this or death and I *chose* this. My stubborn streak sustained me. I would not apologize for wanting to live.

The condo was large and elegant in an industrial sort of way; high ceilings and exposed ductwork typical of a warehouse loft, polished concrete floors and no walls but for a hallway to our left that led to bedrooms I was guessing. The floor to ceiling windows facing the river were framed by silk drapes matching the cream color of the other furnishings in the room. The kitchen to our right was stainless steel with dark granite countertops.

It was almost *exactly* like his other flat. I wondered if that sameness was a comfort for him with all that changed around him over the centuries.

Inside, I scanned the room to find Troy tinkering on Henry's piano, Tara sitting on a chaise, and Stephen sitting dejectedly on the couch. We hovered between Troy and Tara to wait. Omar was apparently sitting at home tonight. He was fascinated with the tv, probably safest for a young vampire for the time being. Henry emerged from the hallway, buttoning his shirtsleeves.

"Pleased you could make it." He met James' gaze evenly, his sarcasm audible.

"We had an emergency." James explained what had happened at the office.

Henry spun around, his eyes gone instantly black. "Troy, have you reached Tonya yet? I want her home *now*." He pushed his authority with the leader of the clan.

Stephen gave an exaggerated sigh, shaking his head. I thought about what he had told me in Paris about being tired of everyone having someone but him. I could see where that would get old after a few decades.

Troy was shaking his head troubled. "I have left several messages."

We talked over Anton's emergence as a member of Nightshade, bringing the clan up to speed on what we'd learned. Stephen came to offer a few suggestions and we were debating the wisdom of saying something to Miranda when Troy's phone rang.

He took it out and looked at the face. "Tonya."

Henry's eyebrows flicked up, unable to hide his interest. I glanced sideways at James and he pretended not to notice.

"How did it happen? Is he dead? Can you get to the airport? Don't worry, we'll figure something out. Sit tight." He gave a few more "mmm hmm's" and hung up. "Donovan's been killed," he updated us. "Punks on the street attacked them just an hour ago. She says they're not vampire, not human; maybe thralls."

Henry's posture changed, his body nearly hummed with tension. His fists clenched at his sides, teeth bared and his eyes caught fire.

Hand up to stop his outburst, Troy reasoned with Henry. "She's safe for now," he shook his head answering the question before he asked. "She can't get to the airport, they've got her on the run. She's scared Henry, go easy."

I didn't understand. James "knocked" and I answered.

Don't get involved in this. It's more complicated than you think. Tonya is, I felt his hesitation as he tried to put his exact thoughts into words, *she likes to be in control. Henry is more powerful and of a different nature. Our kind doesn't typically pair off with hers so it is complicated on many fronts.*

I had asked Henry once why he didn't have someone and he answered it had to be someone special; now I knew why. He had someone special already. The hint of a softer side took a tiny bit of the terrifying away from Henry's persona.

James switched gears. "Henry, have you spoken to our contact about the identities of the others in the picture?"

172

Henry said that he had and no more, not wanting to share too much in front of the rest of us. It was easier to respect their secrecy now that I knew people's safety was at stake. Besides, I was pretty sure I knew who it was. Iain's work at the Court and the "erranding" he did for both James and Miranda made me think that either he or he *and* Miranda were both working to root out the conspiracy from the top. Bradley had said the Court was divided on humans, apparently it was.

"I never liked that guy. He's a weasel." Tara went back to our prior conversation about Anton's involvement. Given her loyalty to Omar and Anton's willingness to have him killed, I could understand her animosity.

Stephen threw an arm over the back of the couch, rolling his head along the back cushions to see Henry. "Is there something we need to be doing? Otherwise, I had plans tonight."

Troy snapped at him, "Would you try not to act so put out when your family needs you?"

Jumping to his defense, I whirled on Troy. "Stephen does everything you ask."

Stephen sprang up from his seat, spitting with sudden rage. "I don't need *you* to fight my battles for me, Claire. Just because you're one of *them* now doesn't mean you can talk to us like you own us." He rose and stalked out of the room.

Unwilling to let his unfounded accusation go, I followed him down the hall. "You know I would never try to order you around." I lowered my voice as I approached.

At the sound of my pursuit, he stopped and spun sharply to face me.

"Stephen, how can you be so angry with me for having what you admit you want for yourself?" My approach both shocked and angered him, yet I pressed on frustrated with his insinuation. "If our positions were reversed, I would be happy for you. Didn't you accuse me of being selfish and only thinking of myself once? Now who's being selfish?"

I saw the impact my argument had as his face started to crumple before he caught it and snapped his sullen front back in place. Having seen behind his mask, it made sense. I moved still closer and put my hand on his arm, softening. "I'm sorry you lost him but you can't punish the rest of us for it. He knew the risks of staying with you. *He* wouldn't have wanted you to keep punishing yourself for an accident."

Stephen's hazel eyes welled up and I saw my argument hit its mark. His self-imposed emotional isolation was not just a result of fear, it was out of guilt as well. He whispered, "How can I try again when I might lose control? Do you know what it's like to be afraid you'll kill someone you love? I can never forgive myself." His voice broke off.

I thought of Heidi and my parents, "I'm starting to get an idea." I put my arms around him. Fortunately, like Troy, he didn't smell appetizing even though he had a pulse. "You have been punishing yourself for two lifetimes over an accident. Forgive yourself, if he loved you he would've. You know better than I do, forever is a long time to be alone."

Stephen hugged me tight. Whether he would take my words to heart or not, I couldn't be sure. I felt like we had leaped over a hurdle in our own friendship, at least.

Returning to the rest of them, we heard Tara asking, "So do you think any of us are in danger? Obviously this lady at the paper got close and was discovered. Whoever is here in the States knows James was connected to her. Should we go looking or wait for them to come to us? We could always go kill Anton," she suggested cheerfully.

Henry was pensive. "I have considered that."

I spun around to see if he was joking. He wasn't. Henry was very powerful, yet Anton was one of their rulers. Death was the penalty for treason.

"Don't you, we, have people for that? Someone in the Guard or another member of the Court?"

The Guard was the vampire's answer to law enforcement. James had been in the Guard during the early part of the century and left after he was forced to compromise his principles when it came to humans. The Guard was who the Court sent to execute Bradley after he was captured.

James answered my questions when it became apparent Henry was still thinking. "The Court cannot fight amongst themselves and the Guard can't attack a member of the Court unless he's already a prisoner. We must keep to the protocols or it would be anarchy and we would soon see our society fall."

"Then is there nothing we can do other than capture him ourselves? How can we get him away from the safety of the Court?"

"I appreciate your willingness to help Claire, but you would not stand a chance against Anton. He is old and very powerful."

In my head, I thought, "So are you." I wasn't worried about Henry so much in a fair fight. It was more likely Anton would cheat and then Henry wouldn't stand a chance.

You're right.

Ch. 31

My eyes shot to James' across the room. He had felt it too and I watched him as the meaning settled into his brain as well as my own. He had gotten into my head without any effort at all. We didn't need to focus to find each other, but could connect anytime; it was like having an open channel to each other through our shields. For the moment, I could only see the upside. It was exhilarating.

I wondered what Miranda would think of this new development. Thinking of her gave me an idea and impulsively I blurted it out. "What if we go to Edinburgh and take Anton by surprise? All we have to do is get some silver on him and any of us can kill him. None of us are bound by any rules like Miranda and Charles."

Henry and James exchanged a glance. I thought they were considering the wisdom of my suggestion. Or lack thereof, whichever the case might be. My ears were listening and so was my mind, attempting to use my ability to glean hidden details. It was no use against a heavily guarded crowd like this one.

James was shaking his head. "It isn't a possibility. How would we get the silver into the hall? None of us can handle it without thick gloves, not even you now." He let that sink in before going on. "Besides, the city is an important one for our kind. There are more vampires there than anywhere else in the Western Hemisphere and we do not know how many are loyal to him. Even if we could get to him, there is no guarantee we could get out."

"Let's not be so hasty to take him out," Troy announced from his perch on the piano bench. "We don't know who any of his compatriots are nor do we have any means by which we can find their identities other than an old photograph."

James nodded, picking up the torch. "Detective Hanson might be able to help us on that." We all sat up and paid attention, curious where this was going. James furrowed his brow, thinking through his idea as he spoke. "The Detective has access to state and Federal databases, doesn't he? We can give him the photograph and ask him to scan for facial recognition. Maybe he could check with Interpol as well, I'm not sure how their forces communicate."

"How do we explain the dated photograph?" Tara wanted to know.

Henry answered her, "We don't. Cut out the date, give him the photograph and tell him it is a lead and what we would like him to do. He's never seen Anton so the age won't bother him. He will agree, he wants this too."

James was in agreement. "I'll crop and scan him a copy tonight."

That decided, I floated an idea that had come to me while I lay frozen yesterday. I'd had nothing but time to think. "If we're going back, I'd like to contact Alan Brightmore at the bookstore. I don't believe he's in on this but if he tells Davina and she *is* mixed up with Anton's people, we can be sure she'll spread the news that we're back in the country. If we can follow her, we can maybe find out at least who is arranging all of these street attacks like the ones on James and me and now on Tonya and Donovan." My glance went automatically to Henry when I mentioned Tonya's name and he showed no outward reaction. "It might give us another lead to pursue," I finished uncertainly.

James nodded approvingly. I surveyed those around me and saw they were considering the idea and were probably going to agree. Proud, I bit my lip to keep from smiling like a fool.

"So, are we going to do this tonight?" Tara returned to the issue of immediate safety from our mysterious enemies. "*We* are probably safe for the next few hours, but what about you two?" She directed this last question to James and me. "She was working for you and they know it, look what they did to your office. That was a warning."

Henry agreed. "I am not waiting here. I will leave as soon as possible. Troy, call Tonya back and tell her I am coming. If she has to change and go up into the hills to be safe, so be it. It is rugged and there are places for a cat to hide. I can find her." He pulled out a phone with significantly more bells and whistles than mine and searched for flights. "There are two going out early tomorrow morning. One is at five, one at eight." He looked up from his phone and swept his eyes across the group. "Pick one, we'll see each other in Edinbugh." His decree was final. No one was going to argue.

Unable to get on the first flight as Henry did, James and I booked seats on the second and agreed it was a bad idea to go home. We found a hotel by the airport, paying in cash and signing in under a false name. When the door to our room was shut and locked I felt the burning beginning in my throat and knew I was in trouble.

"James, I'm hungry," I admitted anxiously.

His face was grim. "I was worried about that. We can't have someone bring anything and risk our position if they're followed. How hungry are you?"

Feeling the burn climbing up the back of my throat, intensifying, my eyes widened in fear, "Very."

"We do have an option, if you are willing." His eyes never left mine, gauging.

"No! I can't do that." My voice dropped to a whisper, "I can't kill anyone."

"You will not kill, I can make certain of that. We can find a donor and I can make certain she doesn't remember."

I started to agree, keenly aware of the building thirst driving me to distraction. Now that I had said it aloud, the burning was all I could think about.

There was no way to have me on an airplane safely for over six hours with a bunch of humans. Not like this. "So, how do we do this?" I wanted to know, trusting him to keep me from committing murder.

He had only fed from donated blood since I had known him and I had very limited insight into how they hunted. How *we* hunted. I'd never seen it done.

"We're near the airport. Our access to solitary travelers is limitless. We'll find one, I can Glamour her and after you feed we're done. It's really quite simple."

He made it sound easy and harmless and I trusted his experience. James would not let me hurt someone and I knew that he was strong enough to stop me if it came to that.

We got back into the car, agreed to try hunting. James drove to the "Arrivals" doors, sliding into a gap along the curb. He honed in on a young woman standing at the taxi stand. My hand shot out to touch his forearm, staying his exit. He eyed me curiously.

"Um, can it be a guy?" I asked nervously. I remembered how intimate it felt to be fed from and couldn't imagine doing that with another woman.

James considered me for a few seconds before his laughter reverberated inside the car. "If you prefer. Everyone has their favorite flavor." He froze, afraid he'd said too much.

I was glad he wasn't going to make a jealous stink about it, I was nervous enough already. "What is that, vampire humor?"

He only stared at me, waiting for what he knew I was going to ask. "What was *your* favorite flavor?"

"You."

I was embarrassed despite myself, even though I could tell he was avoiding telling me anything about his life before me. He leaned over to kiss me and I felt the beginnings of another hunger. We really were animalistic in the beginning, they hadn't lied about that. His lips curved around mine, "First things first."

The solution to my dilemma was a tall, thin young man wearing an old army jacket and jeans. His luggage was an army duffel bag with a Belgian flag stitched on the side. James eyed him as he approached the taxi stand. "Dinner," he mumbled to himself without looking at me and opened his door.

I watched him approach the young man, his hand extended. The young man took it, features confused, and when their skin touched, he stiffened. James' lips moved and Dinner's eyes took on a glazed look. James returned to the car, Dinner following obediently behind him. The familiar scrambled look of a Glamoured victim tainted his expression.

They both got in the car and James drove off. I wasn't sure what to do so I sat in the passenger seat and did nothing. Within minutes, the car stopped on a frontage road behind one of the runways. There was very little lighting and when James turned off the headlights I knew we were invisible from the roads.

The leather of his seat made a soft noise when James turned to face me. He studied me carefully, reading my every movement; his words were meant for Dinner. His voice took on the commanding tone I rarely had a chance to hear from him. It made my skin tingle. "Give her your arm."

Dinner did as he was told, his arm reached through the space between the front seats.

James' eyebrow flicked up. "Claire?"

I shrugged my shoulders at him. "I don't know what to do."

"Take his wrist." He pantomimed holding it up to his mouth and biting down.

I looked down at the pale wrist laying exposed to me. At first I wanted to reject it, saying I couldn't do it, and then I stopped. There it was in the blue line beneath the pale skin, his pulse. It drowned out everything else, lighting a fire in my brain. My fangs grew. There was no room left for conscious thought. I was pure animal.

Of their own volition, my hands reached out and wrapped around his arm. His sleeve pulled up as I raised his limb to my face and once I smelled his blood so close to me, I sank my fangs deep into his flesh. Dinner didn't move or struggle in the slightest. I let each beat of his heart push the blood into my mouth, swallowing reflexively.

My thirst had just begun to be sated when I felt a hand on my shoulder. Instincts still dictated my behavior. I pulled away from the intrusion without releasing my prize.

"Stop."

Ignoring him, I continued to drink.

James was more firm, "Claire, stop. You'll kill him."

Dinner's pulse was weakening and I had to suck to pull the blood to me.

"Claire, stop now." His command was impossible to disobey.

I felt myself setting down the wrist. James picked it up, licked it and sealed the wound, our eyes locked all the while.

James told him he had sold his blood for money, not unusual for someone his age. Then he started the car and we drove back to the airport. Dinner was deposited in the parking ramp across the street from the terminal, away from any witnesses who might have seen him get picked up.

We returned to the hotel, not talking until we were locked in for the night. "What a difference a day makes," was the cliché that kept running through my mind. I went in to the bathroom to wash my face and hands. I couldn't see any blood on me, though my skin itched where I swore I could feel it. Unable to wash away the grime on the inside, I scrubbed the outside twice.

I felt him behind me in the doorframe. Looking up, I saw his reflection watching me. I ran the towel over my eyes, obscuring my vision briefly. When I lowered it, he was right behind me, putting his arms around my waist and resting his chin on my shoulder.

He spoke to my reflection, "I had to make you stop. We couldn't afford the attention a body would draw, nor would you want it on your conscience." His own experience, killing fellow townspeople because he had no one to help him at first, put him in a position of authority on that and I didn't care to repeat the mistake he had.

"I know. It was just so hard. I understand now why you call it a 'need.' It's so much stronger than human hunger. It's like the need to breathe when you're underwater. I couldn't fight it."

"You will learn how to control your needs, we all did. Give yourself time." He squeezed my waist, the move pressing our bodies together.

"Speaking of needs," I winked at his reflection and watched his eyes darken with the force of his own ardor. "I'm not looking forward to flying in the daylight tomorrow. I sure could use a distraction."

Ch. 32

Going to the airport in the morning was a new rung of Hell. My body burned with the sunrise. I could feel its rays through the tinted windows of the car, through the walls of the airport, it was everywhere I went, every second. Yet, I had to try to remain outwardly calm and collected so we didn't raise the suspicions of airport security. James had his arm around me until we reached the security checkpoint.

Our connection became a lifeline, his soothing voice ran through my head. *Tell them you have a migraine if anyone asks why you look like you're sick.*

Is it that obvious?

Yes Love, it is.

We went through security without incident. Luck was with us and we had a crew of uninterested security staff who would not have cared if I was brandishing a bloody axe. The thought cheered me slightly, maybe on the way back that was an option. It might get us through the line faster.

By the time we made it through the terminal to the gate I was feeling faint, if that's possible. James directed me to a chair and pulled out a book for me. For the first time as a vampire I wished I could sleep. It would be a welcome escape from the physical torment I was cursed to endure.

The book was one of James' favorites he had been trying to get me to read. *Crime and Punshment*, he loved the dark Russian authors. It depicted a man's attempt to commit the perfect murder without being caught until his humanity gives him away.

The flight was uneventful and I finished my book somewhere over the Isle of Mann. Miraculously, the sun's burn began to cool in my system as we flew into the sunset.

By the time we landed, the burning in my flesh had eased only to be replaced by the fire in my throat.

"Does it ever not burn *somewhere*?" I asked as we walked out to the car rental agency. Romanticizing this was a farce, I wanted to give the world a real account of what it was like to be a vampire.

He stopped walking and kept his eyes over my head. "Are you sorry you chose this?"

I shook my head slowly. "No, I'm not sorry." I shrugged, "You all made it look so simple. Well, not simple, manageable. It never felt like that through you. It never occurred to me your control made it feel like that."

James was silent as he resumed our path. I followed a few steps behind, stopping when we reached our car. It shouldn't have surprised me that he'd rented a German luxury car.

"Well, this is a flavor we haven't driven yet," I joked as we put our bags in the trunk. James came over and opened my door for me. His chivalry had grown on me and I no longer tried to beat him to my door, even though I probably could now.

Once we were on the road, James called Henry. His phone went straight to voicemail so he tried Troy.

"Troy here."

"We are heading to the flat now. Is anyone else there yet?"

"Henry has headed up into the hills to find Tonya. The others are on the second flight, they should be here in an hour or so."

At the flat, we headed straight up and Troy let us in. He returned to his cooking, I smelled something Italian brewing on the stove and sidled over. My nose worked to discern the mixture of spices.

"Marinara sauce." He noticed the object of my scrutiny. "When they all get here, they'll be hungry. This is a family favorite." Troy took good care of his clan, they were lucky to have him.

I watched him cook, enjoying the process until the buzzer sounded an hour later. Stephen and Tara walked in, sniffing the air. Troy saw it and winked at me, smiling.

I could see what Heidi liked about him. His quiet strength and confidence were what she had always wanted in a man and yet Troy was much more. He was a natural leader with an enthusiasm and charisma I hadn't seen before she came into his world. She had brought him to life as he had her. I was hopeful they could make things work.

Feeling optimistic, I made a suggestion to Troy. "When we get home, let's all four go out. To a movie or something."

Troy's hand stirring the pot hesitated. "Maybe we should wait until we know you won't eat her."

Stephen belly laughed from the living room and Tara sniggered.

James dutifully defended me, "She won't take long Troy. Though I would recommend no close contact for the time being."

We all sat down together at the table. The Andrews ate pasta while James and I had something from Henry's personal blood supply in his fridge.

Tara was clearing the table and Troy sat down at the piano. We heard the door and everyone froze.

In walked Henry, Tonya following close behind.

Tara ran out of the kitchen. "Tonya, what a relief!" She threw her arms around her sister in a not oft seen display of affection.

Tonya was slow to respond, she had the look of a soldier returning from battle. Shell shock was the term that popped into my mind. She was dressed in Henry's overcoat.

Underneath the coat as she moved, I saw scratches and bruises on her arms and legs as well as some sticks and debris in her tousled hair. She was a far cry from the beauty I usually saw.

Troy and Stephen joined in the hugs, Tonya's expression didn't change but her arms came up to hug each one of her family members like an automaton.

Henry spoke for her. "Why don't we let Tonya rest?" He reached for her hand and she clutched at it, her tether reclaimed. Without another word, Henry led her down the hallway into one of the bedrooms. We could hear her tired shuffle the entire way.

He was gone for only a few minutes. We all milled around, on hold in his absence. A door closed quietly and Henry returned to us.

"She's been running all night. I caught one when I was tracking her." He grimaced. "He was a thrall mindlessly following orders, who commanded him I could not tell. It wasn't a smell I knew."

"Who messed her up? The ones who killed Donovan?" Stephen asked.

A low growl rumbled in Henry's chest. I'd never heard him growl before, I had a hard time not shivering from the chill it sent through me. "Yes, she said there were four who attacked. Also thralls. As humans they would have been nothing but punks, easily picked up with a little flash of money or a female's promise. Their identities tell us nothing about our foe. Tonya was able to kill two, but not before they killed him." That he didn't speak Donovan's name caught my ear, James' too. I saw his eyebrow flick up at Henry's omission; he kept his mind silent.

"She was able to flee after the initial altercation, which is when she called you." He glanced at Troy. "They were relentless, she was nearly spent when I found her. My only regret is that I was unable to kill the other one." His eyes were black and he exuded pure unadulterated menace. "We will find who is behind this and kill him slowly."

Being in the same room with him was intimidating even if wasn't me he was angry with. I believed with every fiber of my being that he was strong enough to fight whatever we were up against.

"Was there *nothing* familiar in the scent on the thrall you met, nothing of its creator? Were you able to interrogate it?" James asked Henry.

Henry was shaking his head, lips tight in frustration. "I did not recognize it and no, I did not have the opportunity to interrogate it before it was destroyed."

"So it couldn't have been Anton's, right?" I asked, shaking off the picture of Henry tearing apart another being. "You would have recognized his scent."

"Correct. It was someone new." He spoke to all of us, eyes passing over each one before resting on me.

"Claire, I think it is time to call Alan."

My phone was not up to the job, I held out my hand for James' phone. He started to hand it to me and stopped. Expectant, I looked at him.

"Davina thinks you're dead." That line was between his brows; he was thinking. "That you're alive should remain our little secret for now, don't you agree?"

I did and let him take back the phone, slightly deflated to have to play dead while they went forward with *my* idea.

"Could I speak with Alan please?" He put his hand over the mouthpiece while he waited for the desired party to come to the phone. "Davina" he mouthed, watching me.

"Perfect," Tara's satisfied smile did not bode well for Alan's daughter.

"Hello Alan," James' tone was light and conversational. "I'm curious if you've had any luck in tracking down the book I asked you about the last time we spoke."

I heard Alan reply he had indeed found the book, however, Davina had sold it by accident so he had not contacted James yet. He was back on the trail of one he had found with a book dealer in Amsterdam. He hoped to have it within the week.

I let out a breath I didn't realize I had been holding. Human habits die hard, I thought to myself. I had hoped Alan wasn't involved, I liked him. That he didn't appear affected by James' call spoke volumes.

Alan agreed to call James as soon as it came in and this time he would send it directly to our house. They disconnected and James returned his phone to his pocket before speaking.

"We need someone on the shop constantly. I would suggest we work in pairs in case of any trouble. I can take the first shift if anyone needs to sleep," James offered.

"No, I want to go and besides, she knows you and Claire." Tara's determination was apparent in her even tone.

James watched her for a moment before nodding. "All right, Tara can go first. Who will you take with you?"

"Stephen, I think." Tara's tone softened when she mentioned her sister. "Tonya may want Troy when she wakes." She darted a quick sideways glance at Henry.

Henry hid any reaction he might have had to the slight. "Come back at dawn, we will have another pair go out. If anything happens or she meets with anyone, call in. We can send out another pair to follow if need be."

Everyone agreed. Henry disappeared into his office, Troy and James played chess, and I flipped through a magazine. James and I had decided to hold off on any training while Tonya was laid up in the other room. We didn't want to disturb her should I have an adverse reaction and get loud.

Around midnight, we heard some activity down the hall and a shower turned on. "Tonya's up." Troy made a move to get up. "Henry is with her." James held up his hand to stop him.

Annoyance soured his expression for a second before he tucked it away. Tonya was not incorrect in her thinking that a match with Henry would not be entirely welcomed by her clan.

Voices were coming down the hall too low to make out their words. Tonya leaned into Henry when they came to the end of the hallway and into our view. Henry had his arm around her waist, holding her tightly against him. I recognized the possessive way he held her. It was how James positioned me, especially when he was worried for my safety.

Troy's displeasure was clear. Henry didn't miss it nor did he change his protective posturing. He was making a declaration. Troy and Henry were equals in their symbiotic relationship, though personally I believed Henry would win if it came to a fight.

A vampire was usually stronger than a were and Henry was an old one at that. Regardless of who would win between them, neither probably wanted to deal with the fallout from Tonya should one hurt the other.

Troy approached as Henry sat her on the couch. Henry moved off toward the kitchen. "Are you feeling better?"

Tonya had most of her normal color back and her injuries were fading fast, yet she still had a somewhat dazed look about her. I wondered what she had seen to affect her so. "Yes, I'll be even better once I eat something." The clicking of a burner being fired up on the stove confirmed dinner was on its way.

Tonya didn't feel like talking, but Troy pushed her anyway. "We need to know exactly what you saw. There could be others and now we have Tara and Stephen on the street. We need to think of their safety."

Seeing that he did not intend to back off, Tonya sighed heavily and leaned her head on her hands, elbows on her knees. Her voice was so soft a human would have missed it.

"We were coming out of a pub after dinner. Donovan had drunk his share of beer. We were nearly back to his flat when they struck. They had been waiting outside his building. They were faster and stronger than humans. Donovan was no match for them." Tonya's voice didn't change to indicate emotion, though she hurried through her story, eager to be to done with it.

"They had knives and bats. One of them knocked Donovan down and then went to work on him while he was on the ground. I couldn't help him. My hands were full with the other three. By the time I was able to kill two of them, the others had fled. I called you right away. They followed me up into the highlands. I tried to fight at first, but they were unstoppable. They weren't great fighters but they never grew tired. When they weren't fighting, they were chasing. By the time Henry found me I could barely stand. If it hadn't been for him, I would not have survived."

"Then I suppose I owe him my gratitude." Troy did not sound sincere.

A cupboard slammed in the kitchen. I looked and saw from the back that Henry's shoulders were stiff. I heard the clatter of a plate and the noises associated with meal preparation. We all sat quietly, absorbed in our own thoughts. James was silent in my head and I gave him privacy, I wanted my own as well.

Minutes later, Henry came out of the kitchen carrying a plate and glass of water. Tonya's affection for him was plain in her eyes and my heart ached for her, thinking what I would have done if someone had stood between James and me. I vowed to do what I could to bring them together, ignoring James' warning in my head.

Ch. 33

Troy's phone rang at dawn, it was Tara. "Davina went into a dance club, Faith on Cowgate. She went into one of the private rooms in the back. The crowd coming in and out was heavily vampire flavored but we didn't see anyone of a respectable age. We're guessing whoever we're looking for is still in there. We *are* starting to get more than a little interest from our targets. I think it might be time to change the guard."

I flashed my palm up quickly to signal I wanted to go. "I could wear a disguise or something," I offered. James started to object but Troy spoke up first.

"Davina is going to be more likely to notice if you are together. I think we should break up our pairs for this little adventure." He stared directly at Henry. "Henry why don't you go with Claire and I can go with James or Tonya later depending who is ready."

James started to argue, "Claire is young. We cannot risk her going into a nightclub full of humans and losing control. Dawn is breaking as well and she'll need help handling the sun. I prefer to stay with her."

Troy was ready for the objection, "Henry is her sire. He is older and more capable than you, in case you forgot. I am certain he can handle Claire if she steps out of line and I should think that this assignment will provide her with plenty of distraction from the sun's burning."

James was stuck. He couldn't argue with the logic and couldn't speak negatively of Henry. Instead, I felt the backlash of his anger as it roared across our connection and into my thoughts.

I was rethinking my newly acquired affection for Troy as I saw the ugly side of him. He was intolerant and jealous when it came to his sister. It didn't matter that he was behaving like any protective big brother with a slight case of prejudice, I was unhappy with his "Father knows best" routine.

With the constant tension and my current inability to deal with it effectively, I was getting so jumpy it was hard to stay inside my own skin. And now I felt the incessant burning coming on again. So when James' rage crossed over, flooding me, I snapped. My desire to sink my teeth into something, to take out my anger on someone got the better of me.

With a speed new to me, I leapt over the back of the couch and rushed toward where Troy was standing by the bookcase on the edge of the room. His eyes widened as he realized I was coming for him.

But when I was nearly within striking distance, Henry appeared in my path and caught me by the throat, stopping me in my tracks. I was still struggling, trying to reach my target, when Henry snapped at James, "Control yourself, James. You are going to get her killed."

At once I felt a warm, calming feeling wash over me as Henry turned his attention to me and spoke.

"You will control yourself in my presence." Sanity returned to my brain, letting me think again.

Troy was glowering at James, the source of my outburst.

"Yes James, I wouldn't be so worried about Claire's control if I were you. No one is going to get her in trouble but *you*."

James was locked down. I could feel nothing coming from him, I didn't need to, I could see the tension in his pinched shoulders and clenched jaw.

Feeling like a gigantic fool, I gave the excuse that I needed to dress to go out and retreated to one of the bedrooms to collect myself.

I changed into a fitted pair of black leggings, black sweater and ballet slippers a la 1960's Audrey and was sitting on the edge of the bed when I heard a light knock on the door.

"Come in." I spoke softly, expecting James.

Tonya opened the door instead. "Claire, can I talk to you?" Her voice was hesitant, not the usual strong one I was more familiar with.

"Sure." I scooted over on the bed.

She sat down and fidgeted with one of her nails. It was broken and had been peeled up, a blood blister visible below the cuticle. I hadn't noticed how long her fingers were. I wondered if she played piano like her brother Troy.

She interrupted my musings, "You are the only one who might understand since you aren't one of us."

Seeing my offense, she put her hand on mine then took it off immediately. Her eyes flashed up to mine and offered apologetically, "Sorry, I just wasn't expecting the cold."

"That's okay."

"My brother means well, he is just very protective of me because he was the one who changed me."

"What? Did he change all of you? Is that why you all look so much alike?"

"No. Not all of us, just me. We are all from the same region, Northern California, Idaho and down into Nevada. Those who changed us were all from related clans. That is why we all have similar physical traits after being changed."

Her voice grew stronger. "I told you I sought this life, that I wanted to be a changeling. That was true. I wasn't happy as a human. People gave me attention for my looks from a young age and instead of enjoying it, I cursed it. It was the same when my mother's husband started to notice me, punishing me for the temptation he felt."

I watched her face contort with the pain the memory still caused, shame leaked through her weakened defenses.

"When I heard the legends about creatures who could make me like them, strong, fast." She met my curious gaze confidently. "I wanted to be like them. I baited the woods out back for a week before he came for me. It was horrible being attacked, far more painful than I'd thought. But I knew he was going to let me live. I could feel he was holding himself back. He understood that I wanted to change."

"He didn't leave you after he attacked?" I'd thought they abandoned each other, that they were left to sort it out alone.

"No," she shook her head. "He dragged me under some brush and left me for the first night. That is when we're most likely to die. When he came for me the next night, I was feverish with the change already taking place in my body. He took me in and guided me through the first transition."

"Did you ever see your mom again?"

Her eyes softened. "After I was gone her husband took off. She sold the farm and moved into town. She had a good life working at the milliner's. I checked on her now and again without her knowing. I even bought a few of the hats she made."

196

"Guys always wanted you for your looks, is that why you keep things from getting serious?"

"It's just easier that way," she admitted back to fidgeting with her ruined manicure.

"Or is it because you're in love with someone else?" I plunged headfirst into it.

Her shoulders stiffened and her hands froze.

"Whatever you think you see is just friendship, nothing more."

"Oh come on." I rolled my eyes in exasperation. "Everyone sees it, especially Troy. That's why he's being such a jerk all of a sudden. I know you see it."

She caved easily, her emotions were too raw to hold back today. "Troy doesn't want to see me get hurt. It's an impossible situation."

I couldn't help but be encouraging, "You know he's in love with you, too. I thought I saw it in Austria except I wasn't sure, and then there was Donovan." I watched her reaction to the mention of his name very closely. She barely flinched. "Do you remember how Henry wouldn't let you be alone with him while he was here?"

"I needed him in Austria and he was kind. That is his responsibility; he sees himself as our protector after our last master." She frowned.

I had heard only the scantest of mention of their previous master. He had been cruel to the clan. Stephen bore terrible scars and refused to discuss it. It wouldn't surprise me if any of the others had been abused as well. "Henry is protective of you all, but it's more than that with you. If you had seen him when you were in danger you would believe me."

Tonya glanced up. "Really?"

"Yes," smiling, I filled her in, "he was trying to pretend it was just business getting you back here until you called. As soon as he found out what happened, he yelled at Troy and just about turned inside out. I've never seen him like that." I reached over and put my hand on hers to stop her fidgeting. "He was on the first flight and he went after you the second his plane landed. Haven't you noticed he hasn't left you since he brought you back? Even with Troy so unhappy."

James intruded, *Stop right there.*

The fact that he'd been listening made me mad. *Can't I have some privacy?*

You are interfering with something you know nothing about.

Oh, and you are an expert in relationships?

I do know something about relationships that cross species. Not so long ago I fell in love with a human and it wasn't easy for either of us.

I felt my irritation with him ease up a little. *Then how can you stand by when two people who love each other are so miserable for no good reason? We're talking about eternity alone. Doesn't that bother you?*

He ignored my argument. *I can explain later. Suffice it to say their Council and our Court would take issue with it.*

That's dumb, I replied childishly.

"Claire?" Tonya was staring at me annoyed. "Would you like to tell me if we are alone?" She guessed accurately the cause of my distraction.

Embarrassed, I was glad I could no longer blush. "Yes, we are. He was just trying to get my attention to let me know I need to leave soon. Henry's waiting."

She blinked at me, unconvinced. Though she had her doubts she did not argue.

"Are you in love with Henry?" I tuned in to her emotions for an honest read.

Her emotional upheaval was shocking. I felt her deep love for him as well as a fear of reprisal from family or her Council, I wasn't sure which.

"Yes, I am," Tonya whispered her shoulders drooped in defeat at her admission. It was the first time she'd said it aloud.

I reached over and hugged her. "Don't look so sad, this is a good thing." I withdrew and touched her hand. "If two people love each other, there has to be a way to make it work."

She smiled sadly. "I wish there was Claire." She hugged me back, "You are still so human."

Not sure what that meant, I stood and announced it was time to go. She rose as well and together we rejoined the family in the living room. Troy was reading a magazine though I saw him eye us both suspiciously over its top edge.

Seeing him so acting so superior, I felt my irritation instantly rising against him. He had a human girlfriend who had no idea what he was and was living a lie himself. I glared at him and opened my mouth only to be interrupted by a throat clearing. Before I could say something stupid, I grabbed my coat and blew a kiss at James. "Don't wait up." I winked and scurried out after Henry, already walking out the door.

What are you doing? His warning voice in my head nearly made me stumble down the steps.

I am doing what I'm told. Isn't that what you want?

You don't feel entirely like you. Are you feeling all right? Are you protecting yourself?

Properly chastised, I caught myself with my shields wide open. I brought them back up at once, mentally kicking myself for leaving them down. *Sorry, I was trying to...*

I know what you were trying to do. Now you're drunk on the false hope you just gave her in addition to stirring a pot best left alone.

Why can't they be together? What if someone had told you to leave me *alone?*

That isn't the same thing. Our kind are not allied with them except in the rarest of circumstances. She would become an outcast to all but her clan. He would lose face, possibly even losing the protection of the Court, leaving him open to attack from any opportunistic enemies. And believe me, he has a few.

I didn't realize there was real danger in it.

There is a whole world you don't understand yet, Claire. His tone softened, returned to normal. *I know you mean well, still you can't assume you know best. It wouldn't be a bad idea to just observe for a while.*

I bristled at the condescension I heard in his tone and, realizing he was right, felt foolish. *I'm not going to play mute.* I shot back, trying to save face, knowing I sounded stupid.

His temper flared and I started humming in my head to drown him out. His response was increased frustration to no avail. He could not reach me over my personal noise machine. I made a mental note that this did provide some amount of obstruction when necessary.

Henry stopped at the base of the stairs, catching me off guard. I glanced up at the last minute just before I crashed into him and saw his "human face," that of the kind man I'd first met. That seemed a lifetime ago, before I learned better.

"Claire, I trust you can keep yourself together today." It wasn't a question.

I tried to control the nerves I felt bunching up. I had managed to infuriate both Troy and James, now possibly Henry as well, all in a matter of minutes.

The good news was that I was too distracted from the sunrise and its ensuing burn to spend a lot of time worrying. Grudgingly, I admitted Troy had gotten that right.

"Yes, Henry. I certainly can." I was determined to make a good showing today. I had a lot to prove.

Ch. 34

"Faith" was in a renovated church in the middle of Old Town Edinburgh. Even though it was dawn, there was still a rather large group of wide awake party goers dancing and drinking to the ground shaking, tooth rattling techno music. Granted, humans probably didn't think it was that awful, but to me it was deafening.

Henry was very good at being unassuming and blending. I watched him walk past Stephen and Tara without so much as a glance. Knowing my own limitations, I studied my fingernails. Using him as my study I tried to mimic his casual stroll, following him up to the bar where he ordered us both a drink. Casting him a dubious glance, I doubted the wisdom of drinking as a vampire.

"We will not be drinking them. They will ask us to leave if we are not purchasing anything *and* not dancing." We had no trouble covering our conversation with the music.

The bartender, a friendly enough human named Donald according to his nametag, announced they would be closing soon. I shot a glance toward the back rooms trying to see if they were breaking up back there.

Henry thanked Donald and took both of our drinks in hand. Again I followed him, this time to a small table as near to the back rooms as we dared. Henry took the seat in the direct line of sight of the little room, whereas I was forced to glance over my shoulder whenever I wanted to take a peek at what was going on back there. Only a few times did I dare.

Henry shocked me by broaching a subject I hadn't intended to discuss with him after James' chastisement. "So Claire, I understand you fancy yourself a matchmaker."

If it could, my heart would have stopped. I wasn't sure how to answer.

It turned out my answer wasn't necessary. "I realize you are young and eager to make things happy for everyone. Let me remind you that there are some things you do not and cannot understand so easily. These intricate dances between the species take time to comprehend and much to maintain."

"I don't understand why you can't make it work. You both feel the same way about one another. So what if it isn't very popular? Our match wasn't and *we* made it work; they'll forget in time."

Henry's patient mask eroded as his displeasure bled through. "You think that immortals and near immortals will forget something 'in time'?" he mocked. "You have no idea the kind of unpleasantness that can occur with an 'unpopular' choice in mate. The only reason *you* lived was because James promised to go back to work for the Court." He watched my reaction. "Of course he did not tell you that; why would he tell you what your life cost him? Then they discovered you were useful to them, and now you've turned and are theirs as well." He laid his hands on the table. "The only way unconventional matches are allowed, dear girl, is by being of some use to those above, and I assure you I have no intention of giving the Court what they want of *me*."

His sudden stop told me not to ask what it was the Court wanted that he would not give. I could only imagine. Instead, I tried another angle. "Couldn't your alliances help you? What about Miranda? She of all people would understand wanting to be with another kind."

Miranda had been in love with a human and lost him, she admitted it nearly destroyed her. She had warned James and me of avoiding the same fate and now we had.

The heat now missing from him, Henry mumbled resignedly, "Women have not changed in a thousand years. Always meddling in affairs of the heart." He cut his eyes to me as he carefully tipped his glass below the bar, letting a small amount spill onto the floor. That explained why he had ordered martinis. They were clear and the glasses tipped easily. He raised the glass to his lips and faux drank it. Around the edge of his glass I heard him say, "I challenge the man who says if women ruled we would have no war. I would have to take arms purely out of principle."

I made the first wise decision of the day and held my tongue. Testing my subterfuge skills, I mimicked his actions with my glass. He noticed and I received a tiny flicker at the corner of his mouth as a reward. No one would have called it a smile, still I felt my spirits lift at his miniscule acknowledgement of my success. He was the closest thing James had to a father and I'd had a strong need to please him even before he'd become my Master.

Henry sat straighter and I watched him hone in on the back of the bar. "They are on the move. Our intended cannot be far behind those coming out now."

Fearing I would give us away by something so obvious as turning around and staring, I watched Henry closely. I tried to read him for any hint of what was happening beyond my field of vision. The frustration of reading a vampire was not lessened in the slightest by becoming one. I still couldn't read an impassive face. James was the only being I could truly understand, including humans, and that was only because I could cheat and read his mind.

Finally, Henry uttered below a human's hearing range, "Let's go." He stood and turned to leave. I hurried to follow. Donald the bartender waved and bid us good morning while he cleaned glasses.

We followed the party of five, as far as I could count, out the back doors and into the alley. My stomach tightened at the thought of entering an alley. They had not been friendly places for me of late. Sure enough, we exited the building and were immediately set upon by the three junior members of the party we had been following.

Henry growled in frustration and dispatched one, removing his head without hesitation. The corpse turned to ash within seconds. The other two were not very old and were deciding which one of us two was the lesser threat. I was the clear winner but Henry stepped in front of one, singling him out, and I turned to the one staring at me, a youngish punk with more piercings than a normal being could probably handle. He grinned wild eyed at me before reaching out and trying to grab me by the head. Clearly he had the intention of performing the same removal technique as Henry had on his friend.

The threat of being decapitated brought on my anger, which seemed to be a vampire's answer to adrenaline, letting me feel the full extent of my strength as it surged through my limbs. My hands wrapped around his neck, easily crushing his windpipe and then went through to break his spine behind it. In my head I heard James. He wasn't there right then, but I heard the echo of his former warning that I must remember my humanity or I would be in danger of becoming the monster our kind could be.

I backed away from the body in front of me. The punk was still on his feet, his head laying useless on his shoulder while he remained animated coming after me. Turning, I saw that Henry had finished his second opponent and now sat watching me to see what I would do. I was guessing he was not as concerned with his humanity. As much as he defended humans, he did not confuse himself with them.

The pierced punk touched me, an undead nightmare, his hard fingers tearing into me, trying to rip a hole in my body. It was a move not designed to kill but to inflict pain. The idea of being tortured reminded me of my captivity and the awful things Gaston had done to me. I felt an irrational rage cloud my mind. Before I knew what I was doing, I had his head in my hands and his body was already turning to dust. Seconds later, his head followed suit leaving me holding nothing as gravity and the breeze took it from me a little at a time and I stared aghast at what I had done.

My shock of horror was interrupted by Henry's quick order. "Well handled, Claire. Follow me, we must not lose the rest." He set off at a brisk pace.

I had no choice but to follow. I even welcomed his rapid pace, forcing me to concentrate on our march instead of what had just happened. At the same time, I found it helpful to be distracted from the sun's burning by my internal war with my humanity. I hoped not to be so sensitive when summer hit and daylight stretched to significantly stronger rays and longer days. At the moment, I was disillusioned with immortality and would have warned anyone against choosing it were I asked.

The two ahead of us came into view as we entered the main street. They were moving with mortal speed, seemingly unaware we still followed them. Speeding up, I came abreast of Henry and asked in a low murmur so as not to be overheard by any of the sparse humans sharing the streets with us in the early morning hours.

"Do you think they know we're behind them?" My eyes left their backs for only a second to see Henry's face though I wasn't certain why, his expression had yet to prove helpful in gauging either our level of danger or his mood.

"Yes, either they are trying to lose us or lure us." His gaze was appraising as he fixed his eyes upon me. "Can you handle it should we need to fight?"

Of course. How I handled myself moments ago when he watched me dispatch my opponent had been a test. As discomfiting as I found that, Henry's clinical assessments of my performance was necessary to gauge whether or not I would get any of our party killed out of ignorance or idiocy, both of which I had aplenty. "Yes," I answered, willing it to be true.

Henry grunted in reply and stopped. Our targets had halted up ahead. I had been so fixated on them I hadn't noticed where we were going. A mistake I was sure Henry hadn't made. Surveying our surroundings now, I saw that they had led us to the outskirts of Edinburgh, to a depressed area with minimal human activity and several abandoned commercial buildings. Perfect for a fight and well suited to an ambush.

I shot a sideways glance at Henry, but he was completely absorbed in his appraisal of the situation at hand. I did the most helpful thing I could. I remained quiet and let him complete his assessment.

When he did, he moved with lightning speed into the building directly to our left and, without hesitation, I shot after him, intent upon keeping up.

It was a defunct warehouse; its metal racking stood empty. Skeletal towers in front and on all sides of us formed geometric steel spiderwebs stretching to the ceiling. My head swiveled looking high and low for the attack I could feel coming.

Apparently my efforts were unnecessary, I found out thirty seconds later when a heavily accented voice called out to us.

"Hola friends, we do not wish a fight with you." We followed the greeting to a doorway leading into another smaller area within the warehouse. I saw as we entered the space that the ceilings were lower here and it had fewer windows making it darker and more ominous even than the outer ghost town.

A sideways glance at Henry gave me no indication as to how he intended to proceed. I followed him blindly to where the two we had pursued now stood, flanked by two more that I *could* see and who knew how many others nearby. I was afraid to drop my defenses and feel for more in present company.

All appeared to be Hispanic in origin with dark features. The one who spoke sported a mustache that somehow managed to be both neatly trimmed and still the bushiest bit of facial hair I had ever seen.

Henry halted when we were within about ten paces of the four. I followed his lead, stopping beside him. He waited in silence for the other to lead.

"You are not our enemy," the mustachioed leader began. "I see that now. Please forgive my soldiers, one cannot be too cautious these days. We are looking for a specific male, a rebel to be made an example of. He is younger than you, Senor." He inclined his upper half toward Henry in deference to his superior age, although I wasn't sure if it was his physical age or ancient status the mustache referred to. "The young male flaunted our laws and by living outside the rules of our society, he abandoned the protections afforded those within. The youth chose a human mate over one of his own kind." His lip curled when he spoke of the human. These were definitely our guys.

"Upon whose orders do you seek these two, certainly not those of the Court? They sometimes approve matches with humans." Henry's tone was conversational, nothing more.

One of the "soldiers" snorted derisively and Mustache flicked his hand. The soldier was silenced. "The Court does not agree wholeheartedly with these few blasphemous pairings. They are divided on the subject, as the subject itself continues to divide all of our kind. Some among us feel more strongly than others on the issue of purity." He waved to those standing with him. "We endeavor to do our part to keep our society strong that we may survive and live free."

"Your superior must be powerful to go against Court policy. It is a dangerous path to take," Henry challenged.

Now Mustache guffawed. "The Court has grown forgetful that we are stronger than humans. They are not our equals but prey. What species dallies with its food, I ask you?"

It was a rhetorical question, Henry let Mustache go on.

"The ruling Court will not be in power forever. There are others who remember when we were strong, who remember when our teeth had bite." He snapped his own to emphasize his point.

I tried hard to control the stirrings of anger I felt in my mind. These vampires had been sent for James, assuming I was dead. The only ones who would think I was dead are the ones who tried to kill me.

"Do you stand with this Court, or do you wish to see the vampires grow powerful again?" Mustache asked us, his black eyes flicking between Henry and me.

Henry's response was shockingly cold and convincing. "I bear no loyalty to any ruling body. They have become complacent and could do with a shaking up."

Mustache eyed Henry for a long moment, his compatriots were quiet. Everyone waited for Mustache's ruling. Finally, he laughed, nodding. "You are your own man, hmm? Maybe you should come with us to Spain. There could be a place for you in another Court. It promises to bring things back to the way we were when they were newly formed and our purpose was clear."

"I appreciate your confidence. Maybe I will," Henry replied with a considerate tilt of his head.

"They would welcome someone like you. Someone who is not afraid to speak his mind." He nodded toward me, "Someone who understands the value of purity."

Henry nodded, "Indeed, purity has its place. Thank you, I would speak to those who share our philosophy. May I ask when I might seek out this superior of yours? And whom may I say sends me?"

"Forgive me. I am Rafael, my superior is known simply as Miguel." He bowed, adding a flourish with one arm, the other tucked to his stomach. "And you sir?"

"I go by Eliot." Henry bowed back, adding, "And this is my mate Cassandra."

I inclined my head to Rafael, grateful I no longer had a pulse to give me away while I watched to see if he believed Henry.

He appeared to do exactly that. "It was a pleasure to meet with two like minded individuals such as yourselves." He inclined his head toward each of us, "Until next time."

Dismissed, Henry spun on his heel and I followed as gracefully as I could, trying to appear older and more capable than I actually was. I fought the strong urge to look back, feeling one of our new Hispanic friends was behind me, ready to pounce, that this was a trap after all. We reached the street again and I afforded our rear one glance. We were alone. Finally, I let out the breath I had been holding since going into the building.

"Are we safe?" I asked Henry, moving fast to keep pace with his longer legs.

He was staring straight ahead when he answered. "Yes, we will not be followed. Rafael reeks of zealotry. He does not want to consider too deeply the truth of our admissions of sympathy for his cause. To do so might also cause him to scrutinize his own beliefs in greater detail than he is comfortable. One does not look when one does not want to see."

I heard the bitterness in his words and wanted to ask him more about where he came from, what history he had seen that gave him such a jaded view of so many, both human and nonhuman alike.

Instead, I stuck to the safe subjects, happy to have something to talk to him about as we held down our speed on our route home. "Have you heard of Miguel before or the formation of another more puritanical Court?"

"No to both. That gives us all the more reason to go to Spain."

I let this new information roll through my mind for the brief walk back to Henry's flat. The sun burned but as long as I had something thought provoking, it seemed to fade much like a serious headache. There were even a few brief interludes during which I nearly forgot that my skin was on fire.

This new person, Miguel, was most likely a member of Nightshade's hierarchy, I would wager. That would give us two members. I wondered if we could get a picture of him or if we would indeed have to travel to Spain to determine if he was one of the four people in the photograph Indira had uncovered. It might be time to check in with Detective Hanson on the facial recognition. It was hard to contain my excitement. We possibly had half of the bad guys located. Whether we were strong enough to kill them was another question.

Ch. 35

Our arrival at Henry's flat was a surprise to the family. They had not been prepared for our speedy return.

Tonya's face lit up when she saw Henry but she quickly suppressed it. A sideways glance at Troy told me he had seen it as well, yet to his credit, he fought to keep his face neutral. Stephen waved from where he stood by the bookcases, he was laughing into his phone. I couldn't see Tara but heard her, it sounded like she was in the midst of a call as well.

James had been in the kitchen and came out when he heard the door. I felt the burning in my throat as soon as I smelled what he had in his glass. Taking one look at my face, he stepped up and handed it to me. I smiled my gratitude and took it gladly.

When his hand was free, it slid around my waist and he pulled me in close. I found tremendous comfort in his touch and leaned my head against his shoulder as I took a drink to quench my burning throat.

"What were you able to find out? I would assume you discovered something to bring you back so early." James asked me and though I waited for Henry to speak, he did not.

I took another drink and nodded while I swallowed. I could feel the blood flowing through my body, seeing my skin pink up almost immediately. "We did. After we had a little brush with a few of them we followed the rest, except they didn't want to fight as soon as they saw I wasn't a human. They were looking for you and you're right, they assumed I was dead. We met the eldest among them named Rafael. He works for someone named Miguel in Spain. Rafael was talking about this Miguel putting a plan in place to take down the Court and put his own rule into effect. He wants Henry to go to Spain and talk to Miguel, he might have a place for someone like him." James and I both cast our eyes over to Henry.

He was standing in the kitchen, having poured himself a glass of something red. Henry shrugged benignly, "Yes, I do believe I will be going to Spain shortly after we handle Rafael. He is the one responsible for the attack on Tonya, I recognized his smell." He barely paused when the rest of us spoke out in surprise. "I will know for certain when I see him if he matches any of the men in the photograph. It sounds like Miguel might be powerful enough to be at the top level in Nightshade." He took a drink, swirling his glass as if it contained Bordeaux. It was far thicker, sticking to the edges of the glass in a way no grape would.

James looked about at the family around him. "Who will you take against Rafael tonight? Does he have many with him?"

Everyone in the room was listening intently.

"There were four including our target. Two are young and the third will not prove much of a challenge, I think. Rafael should be our initial target, he will be unsuspecting at our initial approach and he is the oldest of them. If it is just you and I we can move quickly and be gone before anyone is the wiser."

Stephen put his hand over the mouthpiece of his phone. "Does this mean I am free this," he glanced at his watch, "evening?"

"Is this the guy you met at the bar last night?" an exasperated Tara asked Stephen.

"Yes, yes it is," he confirmed. "So, am I free?"

Henry nodded, unsmiling, without turning his head from James' face. My body tightened thinking of James walking into odds like that.

As if that was not enough to cause me distress, Henry posed a question to me in the most casual of tones. "I will leave for Spain tomorrow. Claire, would you accompany me? It might be helpful to have someone with me and they already believe you are my mate."

James reacted as expected. "What did you say?" He was completely focused on Henry as he asked.

I put my hand on his arm to stay him. "I was just happy not to have to fight. I would have let them believe anything." And now Henry was leading James right back there into the exact scenario I hoped we could all avoid. It was difficult to fight the urge to scream my frustration. I would have if I thought it could help but I knew from experience Henry was unswayable when his mind was made up.

He grunted, seeing my point though far from happy about it. "Claire, Love, I don't think you should be going to Spain so soon after being turned." He saw my intent to object and hurried to explain. "The sun will be nearly unbearable."

Scanning his eyes, I didn't see any other motivation there or jealousy. "Didn't you say most vampires in hot climates are nocturnal? I might not miss much by doing the same." I really wanted to prove myself and this might be the way to do it. Besides, how often was Henry going to ask *me* for help?

James eyed me, gauging whether or not he should take our conversation private. Right when he was about to "knock," I spoke. "Could you excuse us please?" I asked of no one in particular. Without waiting for an answer, I looked into James' face and raised my eyebrows to indicate I wanted him to follow me. I didn't want him in my head at the moment, it was too confused from everything happening. I wanted privacy although I wasn't sure how to get it.

We went into "our" room and I shut the door behind us. Leaning against it I let my body sag, exhausted. At least if I were human I would have been exhausted. As a vampire I could only feel beat down, which I did.

Closing my eyes, I sighed. His hands were on the sides of my face and I leaned into one, relieved to feel his touch and be alone with him. I missed our house already. Kissing his palm, I opened my eyes.

James looked worried, his eyes were midnight blue.

"What happened out there, Love? You look shaken. There is no need to worry about Henry and me. We've done this sort of thing before, we'll be careful." His eyes roamed my face.

"I'm sure you will." I sighed. "Actually, I'm jealous you have something to do. I'm tired, I wish I could sleep, I don't want to constantly feel like I'm burning somewhere, and I want to be in control of myself. Even for just a few minutes."

James' lips had curved upward with my frustrated explanation until the last. He wrapped his arms around me, knowing what a loss of control meant to me, and I buried my face in his chest taking a deep breath of his scent. It was the relief I had been wanting. I felt comfortable enough to tell him what else was bothering me.

"I killed someone today." I was stroking his arm absently, feeling the strength I once found awe-inspiring to be a comfort.

"When you had your 'brush' with them?"

I nodded my head against him, "I was able to stop short of killing him the first time but then he kept coming and something inside me just snapped." My voice didn't sound like me, it was hollow. "It was awful and Henry was pleased even though he knew I was upset about it."

"Henry is pragmatic. He wants to know he can count on you in a fight. He probably could have helped you, am I right?" He felt my nod again.

"Then he was testing you. It isn't surprising considering what we are probably walking into. We will all have to be able to hold our own, and now that you're no longer human you'll be counted on to fight. We will need every hand we can trust and that will be limited to those in this flat." His hand moved away from mine and wrapped around my back. "We can hope that this will lead to a peace our kind has looked forward to for a very long time."

I puffed up my cheeks and blew out, my new version of a sigh. "Let's just hide in here."

He chuckled, his chest rumbling against me.

"How am I going to be away from you when Henry and I go to Spain?"

"You two aren't going alone. I'm going as a friend of the happy couple. Think of me as a chaperone."

"Are you afraid Henry will steal me away?" I teased.

"No, but I can't let you walk into that snake pit without me. Where you go, I go for as long as we both shall live, remember?" He kissed me. "I made a promise and I take those very seriously."

I fought the urge to remind him that neither of us was living, yet his duty called and I heard Henry's firm knock on the door telling us it was time for James to go.

"We need to be fast, James. They may be on the move already."

With a speedy kiss I let my husband go, though everything in me wished I could call him back to me. I understood the helplessness of the soldier's wife when her husband goes off to war and chose to wait in my room in his absence.

Ch. 36

Somewhere in the middle of the morning, when the human world was waking, I heard the outer door open and footsteps softly padding down the hall, two sets that I recognized. Relieved, I jumped off the bed when James opened the door and walked in.

My eyes ran over every inch of him assessing the damage. He was relatively unscathed. There was no small amount of blood on him, though I could not see any injuries except for a few minor cuts and bruises.

"Did it go alright?" I asked, helping him out of his bloody clothes.

He nodded, his eyes were tired and dark. "Henry was right, they let us come right to them. It was quick and we only had some minor flesh wounds on our parts." He flinched when his shirt sleeve caught in an already healing cut on his upper arm.

He had to reach up and tear the fabric from it when I was unwilling to do it. The wound bled anew for a moment before it started to close back up.

"You need to eat something." I moved to the door to get him a drink and he didn't argue.

"Would you bring it to the bathroom? I need to shower before I do anything else." Eyeing his blood smeared body I had to agree.

Showered and fed, James was nearly back to normal. We were dressing to go out and join the family when I caught James shooting me several curious looks. My hands stopped buttoning my shirt and I asked him, "What?"

"Claire, are you in pain at all?"

218

I glanced down at my body looking for some injury I might have caused myself without knowing. "No. Why, should I be?"

"The sun. Don't you feel the sun?" He moved closer, eyeing me suspiciously.

I focused inward. Right away the sun's burning was apparent. It had, however, lessened considerably. It was endurable. "It isn't as bad as before; maybe it's all we have going on. You have to admit, it's been non stop." I rolled my eyes.

He stared at me and I felt the familiar tickle in my head. *Can you think about becoming a vampire and how it felt?*

Sure. I did and felt him go after it. After perusing that part of my consciousness, James released it and refocused on me.

"Unbelievable," he murmured, "Even after you were turned, we've had crossover between us. We just didn't notice because, like you said, we've been busy." James took my hands looking quite pleased. "No wonder you have been able to handle the transition so well. You have gained some of my tolerance. It will make our upcoming trip to Spain more bearable for you." He squeezed my hands for emphasis. "I cannot make it painless, but at least it will not be unbearable."

I wasn't sure how to answer, so I kissed him before finishing my dressing routine. We went to the fridge for breakfast.

Tara was her usual pleasant self. "Come up for air?" She snorted at her own cleverness.

My first instinct was to lash out at her. It took all of my limited discipline to refrain from reaching out to slap the snide smirk off her face. I wished I'd gotten more of that from James in addition to his sun tolerance.

While I worked to calm myself, James replied diplomatically, "Jealousy doesn't become you, Tara. If you were more pleasant maybe you wouldn't have cause to mock others' happiness. You could find your own."

Tara's sneering mouth snapped shut and her eyes narrowed. The hair on my arms stood as her energy mounted like she was going to change to her cat form.

Henry entered the room from the hall. He was buttoning his suit coat, appearing freshly showered and as unharmed as James. I was buoyant with relief. "That's enough." He did not need to raise his voice; his tone alone quashed any thoughts of disagreement. He continued, "I think we have been cooped up together for long enough. There is a flight on British Air going to Malaga that leaves in a few hours. I have three tickets on hold." Henry looked over my head at James, a knowing smile on his lips. "Am I correct in my assumption?"

"I don't make a habit of sending my wife off alone with another man." James was equally level but I could feel him fighting down his vampire and male predisposition to defend his territory.

James, this is a cover and could help us get another identity on a Nightshade partner. We can't blow it because you can't share.

Share? I thought this was a cover. A soft growl emanated from his chest.

You know what I mean. Nothing is going on and you know it. If we can't make this work Henry will make you stay behind.

His lips tightened against his teeth and his eyes were dangerous when he finally closed them in a long blink. When they opened again, the color had lightened and he forced a smile. *You win. I would rather be uncomfortable*

220

and with *you than worrying that you needed me and I wasn't there.*

Henry's voice drew me back to the present. "If you two are finished with your lovers' quarrel, I would like to know if I am booking two or three tickets."

"Three tickets, Henry." James replied calmly, shifting focus back to his mentor. Without any further comment, Henry left us and returned to his office to book our flights.

Everyone maintained a silent tension while we waited for it to be time to leave. I paid close attention to my reaction to the sun. It had definitely lessened in the past day, which was a huge relief. I still felt it yet it was now more like a sunburn that only rears its head with the occasional chafe of clothing. There were actual minutes that went by without my acute awareness of its presence.

The ride to the airport was equally uncomfortable. Henry had suggested that James and I refrain from any public displays of affection and he had insisted that I leave my wedding ring at home. I had put my foot down at that, compromising by putting it on my right hand instead.

When we landed in Malaga, I was struck by the sparse landscape. My family had lived briefly in Southern California when my dad was stationed in San Diego. We'd made frequent pilgrimages to the desert and this had a very similar feel to it.

Riding in the rental car, I looked out at the hardy scrub bushes and packed sand reminding me of that different lifetime; back when I thought what I was living now was purely legend and Hollywood fiction. Little did I know it would become my reality.

We headed straight to a condo belonging to an associate of Henry's in a resort town called Mijas on the southern coast of Spain known as the "Costa del Sol."

Once the bags were deposited in the unit, we gathered in the open living space where Henry suggested we head to a local vampire hangout at sunset. It would be my inaugural appearance as one of them on their own grounds and I had to admit I would feel far more secure this time now that no one would want to eat me. Until then, we all made busy discussing the details of our pretend lives. We agreed it would be best to stay as true to life as possible, only I would be flip flopping James and Henry.

Our story was that Henry and I had met and he turned me a few years ago. My youth would be difficult to lie about, we had to count on my progress to mark me as older than I was. He and James were from the same coven though Henry was still the leader. There would be no hiding his status as an elder vampire.

Henry was still Eliot, I was Cassandra and James was going to be Philip, it had been his father's name. We were from Michigan. It was a state we were all relatively familiar with and could pass as residents if we were questioned in minor detail.

We dressed up, as all vampire functions tended to be formal. Henry wore a monochromatic chocolate brown suit and shirt and no tie; James the black suit and white shirt combination he knew I found irresistible, and I wore a simple pale blue sundress I had picked up in a hurry on an emergency run just today.

Henry had rented a red BMW, of course. He gravitated to BMW's. I was reaping the benefits of an education in luxury vehicles since meeting my new vampire friends. I had gone from knowing only that they were expensive to now being able to recognize some of the vehicle models on sight.

We drove up into the hills above the town instead of heading to the beach where I had assumed the club would be located.

The scrub became even more sparse as we wound up the narrow, winding roads. I was glad I wasn't driving. The guard rails were all that separated the road from a sudden drop off into the rocky ocean below. The speed Henry was going was making for an unnerving experience. If he were human, I would probably have asked him to pull over and let me out. At least his reflexes were fast enough he most likely wasn't going to crash and even if he did, I would most likely survive unless the car burst into flame or I was decapitated. Oddly, I was not reassured.

Finally, when we reached the top of the tallest hill, a large flat plateau spread out before us. Henry brought the car to a stop. I wasn't sure what I was expecting, but I was surprised when I saw we were in front of a small country church. Its dark wooden roofs were domed in the Moorish style so popular in this region, having been brought up from northern Africa centuries before by the sultans who summered here. The walls were thick stucco and painted white. A simple cross of an unknown metal adorned its central and highest roof.

There were a handful of cars parked in a neat line a short distance from the doors. The church was lit up with lanterns and torches. It didn't shock me that there was no electricity up here considering its remote location.

A large, red haired, brutish vampire dressed in a white suit and tie stood guard at the door. He gave us a visual once over and politely asked our names and current base location. Henry fielded the questions, giving Rafael's name as our reference.

The redhead pressed an earpiece I hadn't notice initially. He mumbled a rapid reiteration of our story and listened for a few seconds.

Simply nodding after his instructions ran through his earpiece, the redhead stepped forward and reached to grasp the round iron handle attached to the thick wooden door. With an effortless tug, the door opened and we were waved inside.

Inside the church, the pews had all been removed while the intricately tiled original floor was still intact and absolutely amazing. The wear from centuries of foot traffic on the orange, blue, white, and green tiles was visible to the naked eye, I was sure even my human eyes would have seen it.

Round, black iron chandeliers hung from chains on the ceiling. White candles filled the cavernous room with an eerie glow.

As it was, I glanced around and saw less than twenty people hovering in several groups and couples scattered about the relatively square room. Either side had a doorway that I was guessing led into the two flanking smaller sections visible by their lower roof lines outside. The wooden doors were closed, lending them an automatic air of mystery.

Once we were inside, each party took the time to stare at us. They didn't bother to hide their curiosity. I did appreciate that no one seemed outwardly unwelcoming. Cautiously, I lowered my shields slightly to do a "sweep" of the room and feel for anything alarming. I figured in a group this size I could risk a fast one.

At once I felt a burst of white hot rage coming from behind the closed wooden door to my left. Its intensity took me by surprise and I staggered when it hit me, recoiling from the force of it. James started to reach for me and as soon as his hand flinched, Henry hissed a warning and reached out instead. He caught my elbow and steered me to an empty alcove directly ahead of us. It was dark and somewhat private.

James was already wrestling with his jealousy and frustration at having Henry take his place, even if it was for show, so when Henry pushed my back up against the wide pillar and put his hands up on either side of my head, bringing his face close to mine, James neared his boiling point.

"What are you doing?" Henry hissed at me. His eyes scanned over my head, watching for any signs of suspicion. "Do you need to feed?"

James answered for me, "She was checking the crowd for danger. She can pick up when someone is hiding a strong emotion like hatred." He had felt it through me which was not helping him deal with his own animosity.

I shot him a look. "I can speak for myself." I turned back to Henry. "I'm not hungry, well maybe a little. But I am not about to lose control of myself." I lifted my chin toward the left door. "Someone is really upset in there."

Henry glanced over at James, his tone forgiving. "We will be required to uphold this charade while we are here. Keep that in mind. Do you remember Russia?"

Something passed between them I didn't fully understand. I watched James closely, I could read him better. James was stoic, his features set firmly before he answered. "Let's hope it doesn't come to that."

Henry's face was equally tight. "I should hope not. But if it does, it may require an equal sacrifice."

What happened in Russia? I tried to keep the panic out of my thoughts.

When I was in the Guard working for the Court I had an assignment that went badly.

Henry was with the Court then. What happened? I repeated the question.

His resolve was palpable. He did not want to disclose the details of the assignment, bringing my anxiety to a new high. *Please,* I asked, coloring my request with a taste of my fears. That we were walking into something more dangerous than I already feared.

He was struggling between holding firm and trying to assuage my nerves. Compassion won out and he relented. *The Russian government had gotten its hands on one of our kind. They were conducting experiments. It was a genetic project and they were hoping to create human vampire hybrids to use as soldiers. There was no feasible way to save her. We were forced to destroy the entire lab and everyone in it. It was a necessary sacrifice to maintain our secrecy.*

I worked hard to control my outward expression should someone be watching. *Is that what Henry meant by sacrifice? That we might have to sacrifice ourselves for the survival of a broken leadership?*

It isn't for any one of the leaders, it's what they represent. Think of the collateral damage if there were to be anarchy. It would start with vampires but cross over to humans and others until we had an interspecies world war. Henry is right, no one of us is worth that.

We tried to blend as we wandered over to a table with full glasses set on it. Each of us took one, I for one was glad to have the sustenance and it put us closer to the mystery door. The table was set up not ten feet from it.

A trio near us consisted of two females and a male, each one especially gorgeous. They were really what humans thought of when they thought of vampires. The leggy blonde female in impossibly high heels was nearly as tall as the male who himself had to be over six feet. The dark haired female had short hair, cut in a straight bob and was shorter, maybe 5'7" and curvy as a 1940's film star.

The male raised his glass, inviting us to join them. Henry again took hold of my elbow guiding me. James followed a step behind, a quick glance showed his face fixed in a serene mask.

The male spoke when we drew near, "Let me introduce myself, I am Diego Garcia. I have not seen you here before. Are you new to the cause?"

Henry took the lead as would be expected of our superior. He said that we were indeed new and repeated our introductions. I watched their faces closely for any hint of doubt, dropping my shields enough to feel anything they might be hiding. The blonde was radiating sex, tossing her long hair over her shoulder and causing endless distraction to several males in the room. She was enjoying the attention.

The male was curious about us but not overly so. He was feeling very amorous toward his clingy blonde companion. The brunette female was also very turned on; unfortunately, it wasn't directed at the male beside her. The object of her desire was my husband.

My first taste of firsthand vampire possessiveness flared at once and my muscles went rigid. Without thinking of the consequences, I lifted up on the balls of my feet and made ready to launch myself at her.

This only took seconds yet Henry was faster, having felt my body tighten, and was prepared. The moment I moved forward, his hand slid up my arm and using my forward impetus to swing me into his body. I smacked hard into his chest, it was sufficient to mold me to him just long enough for him to wrap his other arm around my back. I looked up and saw his intent half a second before he lowered his face and touched his lips to mine.

As soon as we kissed, my passion shifted focus. I tried to jerk my arm loose and pull away, but he was stronger and held me to him for a long, showy kiss before finally loosening his grip.

His eyes were intently focused upon me, sending me a very clear message. I shot a sideways glance at James and he was perfectly still, his expression carefully blank.

Play the part or we're dead. James' voice was in my head and I could feel what he was containing bubbling below the surface, he was trying to keep himself together so that I could. I managed to rub my hand on Henry's chest, all the while attempting to look convincingly turned on.

"Please excuse my mate, she is young and enthusiastic," Henry commented with a wolfish grin at the male. "Her desires sometimes get the best of her."

The blonde ran her hand across the male's broad chest, endeavoring not to be outdone. He slid his hand down her back and grinned back at Henry.

This was getting too strange for me. I liked social boundaries even if some vampires didn't. The fact that this felt like it was moving toward a sex party made my stomach tighten.

The brunette moved toward James at the same time the door we had been curious about was thrown open. Everyone in our little sextet turned to face the sound. Brunette sidled closer to James, I caught her hands wrapping around his upper arm as she leaned into his side and reached her lips closer to his ear to whisper something. I felt my lip curling.

Ch. 37

With great effort, my attention was drawn back to the doorway when out walked a tall, dark male vampire. He was not just slender, he was effeminately so. When he entered the hall, all was silent and still. This was our man, I recognized him from the picture.

Behind him, through the same doorway, a thickset female carried a mangled and bloody body efficiently tucked under her arm, its limbs hanging loosely and drawing patterns in the mess of blood being left behind it. Given that it wasn't ash, it wasn't one of us. She carried it out the way we had come in. No one else appeared to pay it any mind.

"To all who wish to see a return to our former glory, let me reiterate a point." Our man's voice was musical and lilting, a soft Spanish accent giving it flavor. "The reason for our leaders' weakness is because of their lack of strength and purity of purpose. No longer do they rule with the iron fist we saw centuries ago when our kind were strong and had little to fear. The humans knew their place and feared us, as well they should."

A murmur ran through the crowd. Sparing a surreptitious glance around the room, I saw the nods of assent and the recognizable glazed fever of zealots being told exactly what they wanted to hear. Fear settled in my belly and my mind told me to run. I willed myself to stay.

Our guy went on, "Our leaders have grown weak these past centuries, allowing themselves to be swayed by the arguments of those intent upon diluting our power. They demand the inclusion of other beings turned by mistake, matings with humans. All of these are abominations working together to weaken us."

I thought of Lucas, an Elf turned long ago who was a member of the Elite Guard. He was the oldest vampire I knew. I couldn't imagine *anyone* thinking of him as weakening the gene pool.

"We will grow strong again," he continued, his rich timbre conveyed a charisma that was hard to deny. It was an ability that made him a natural choice for the purists' front man. "I propose a new system, ruled by one unswayable leader with a clear vision of the future and our true purpose. As your leader, I will rid us of the parasites who drain our society. I will unify and strengthen us and together we will realize the dream of our originator and eradicate the humans and impure forever." He raised his glass to the mindless followers now whipped into a sufficient frenzy. Their passions were buffeting my senses and I held fast to my protective shields.

The crowd raised their glasses and spoke his name for the first time, "Miguel." Miguel waved benevolently at his followers. I looked around me to see if I could recognize anyone else from our Nightshade group photo but was not so lucky. All I saw were a bunch of vampires who wanted free rein to kill humans and take out their frustrations on anyone different from themselves. Vampire society wasn't that different from ours, I realized sadly. Immortality, it seemed, didn't do a damned thing for tolerance.

This guy is pure poison. I spoke my mind to James without turning to face him.

He didn't answer, his mind blocked from me.

Guessing why, I fought the urge to turn around. I didn't want to see it and have a picture in my head that I wouldn't be able to shake. It would not end well and I tried to concentrate on what they had both told me: sacrifice. I repeated it in my head like a mantra, tying my thoughts up with it to keep me from turning around.

When it was clear Miguel was done with his speech, Henry took my elbow again and steered me toward him. I swallowed my distaste and tried to smooth out my own face to hide anything except serene oblivion. A "yes, I'll drink the kool-aid" kind of look.

"Miguel, I presume." Henry bowed his fingers like iron on my arm pulled me into a curtsy. "Let me introduce myself. My name is Eliot, this is my mate Cassandra. We met your man Rafael in Edinburgh and he suggested we might have some things in common." He waved his hand to encompass the crowd of followers. "It seems you have a way with the masses."

Miguel eyed Henry speculatively, casting only a cursory glance my way. Obviously not interested in a young female, I noted with relief.

"Rafael called after he spoke with you. He was impressed with your ideas," he sniffed at Henry, "and your age." Again, he stared at me with a hint of disdain. "Would you join me to discuss your ideas with me in my office? Alone." He gestured toward the room he had emerged from with the woman and corpse.

Twisting my head back toward the entrance, I saw the thick woman had returned and was standing off to the side, hidden in the shadows. Without a bloody corpse blocking my view, I could see her better. She wore a black pantsuit whose collar didn't completely hide the green serpent tattoo climbing up her neck. Nor did her dishwater blonde hair cut short and spiked on top in a masculine style to compliment her clothing.

I rotated back to Henry for direction. He glanced down at me, "Cassandra, why don't you keep Philip company and try to stay out of trouble?" Not sure at all I wanted to do that right at the moment, I bowed my head in deference to him and then to Miguel before spinning on my heel to return to James.

When I turned, I wished I hadn't. James was trying very hard not to be offensive in his battle with the Brunette over his body. Her hands were very intimately exploring his chest and backside while he remained unresponsive to her advances. Her body clung to his side while she spoke into his ear; I caught a flash of white when she nibbled at his neck.

When he saw me watching, James became more forceful and took both of her wrists in one of his, lithely twisting his body away from her. "Duty calls Brigit, I am under orders to accompany Cassandra in Eliot's absence."

She glared after him as he joined me, I was guessing she was not used to being rejected. Her friends were nearby and she whirled with an angry flourish to return to them. The male put his arm around her and she wiggled into his side, a dog needing reassurance. I stopped myself from thinking the word I preferred to call her, but it was in the same species.

James put his arm out to me and I took it maintaining a friendly distance between our bodies.

"Care for some fresh air?" He sounded as relieved as I felt to be touching.

I nodded an affirmative, embarrassed that I was so distracted by James being come on to by a woman when Henry was meeting behind closed doors with what was potentially a self made king intent upon genocide.

James steered us toward the drink table before walking back out through the entrance doors into the mild night.

Tilting my head back to see the starry sky, I commented casually, "Eventful evening."

"Isn't it though?" James replied equally cool.

We strolled arm in arm around the church, admiring the hills rising around and below us. The starlight was gorgeous, especially up this high and with my new vision. I sighed, trying to clear my head, when he broke in.

Henry will be all right, Miguel isn't nearly as strong as him. I couldn't get more than a rough feel from him. Did you get anything?"

Honestly, I was afraid to sweep him. I don't want him suspicious of us. The first vampire I had used my ability on had caught me doing it and it had turned into a vendetta she carried to her grave.

That's probably a good idea. He definitely had shields up. I would have to touch him to get more.

He was quiet, staring at the clouds starting to roll in. "I don't like seeing you kissing someone else."

"He kissed me," I defended myself.

"I don't like it," he repeated. "If Henry was not my master I would have challenged him right there."

"He saved me from getting us all killed with that move," I reminded him. "What about *Brigit*? How do you think I like seeing her paw you?"

James hadn't said a word when I heard his glass hit the hard, rocky ground, shattering on impact. He grabbed me, one hand on the back of my head, the other on my hips pulling me into him, hard. His kiss was insistent, almost painful, saying "mine" in no uncertain terms. As his lips moved against mine, my new fangs started to vibrate, growing in my excitement.

Ch. 38

The scuffing of a shoe on rock snapped us out of our intimate moment. I stood upright, scooting away from James. A form moving in the darkness directly in front of me caught my eye. It moved closer, becoming clearer. Just as I could make out the female form, her scent came in on the breeze. It was the brunette, Brigit. I recognized her scent immediately, she had rubbed it all over James.

Without realizing I was doing it, I growled at her baring my fangs.

"Well, well, while the cat's away the little mice will play," She purred, her eyes moving from James to me. "Does your friend know this is how you protect his assets?"

James stepped in front of me, sensing my intentions toward her. "Eliot is fully aware of our affections. Is it not a similar situation in your own coven?" He tossed back at her, his hand holding mine tightly behind him.

Control, Claire. We don't want a fight here.

Jealousy was new for me, never having a boyfriend before, and now to have someone blatantly go after someone I loved so much, I was having a hard time stifling the thick shade of green clouding my eyes.

"Does that mean you are open to sharing?" Her fingers ran down the lapel of his suit coat, her eyes boring into mine. I knew she was trying to get me riled. I fought hard to keep my control. Henry was still in with Miguel for all we knew and the results could be disastrous if we fell apart out here.

James' free hand caught hers as it slid inside his coat. "I mean you no offense Brigit, but my loyalties are to the wishes of my superior." Though his words were gentle, his underlying tone was steely.

Brigit was visibly upset, her fangs pressed against her tight lips. Her eyes sparked as she glared at me, "Enjoy your prize." She angrily strode back into the shadows and I thought I heard her mutter, "While you have it."

I started to speak to James, he squeezed my hand and I quieted to wait. Sure enough, Henry approached us seconds later. The ability to track each other by scent, although new to me, was proving handy.

"She will be a problem," Henry stated simply.

James nodded in agreement. "She does not like to be denied. More than that I believe she was sent by her master. I'm concerned they are not completely convinced of our 'purity' of mind. As we suspected, the leaders are not as easily convinced as their followers. Diego Garcia sounds like he is important to Miguel, possibly his second in command."

Henry motioned to the hillside beyond us, "Let's take a walk, shall we?"

We walked for a few minutes before Henry spoke again, his voice so low James and I both had to lean in to hear. "Miguel is delusional. He has swallowed all that he is preaching. He truly believes no one of any worth will stand up to him and that he has this takeover firmly 'in the bag'. He is mobilizing for action soon."

"Did he give you any idea who the other leaders might be? Maybe we could take care of him before he has a chance to set things in motion," I proposed.

Henry shook his head, "No, we can't do that yet. Miguel says there is another meeting he is going to tonight after his cocktail party-turned-rally. He has invited me to go, suggesting I meet some people." Henry was tense, he was worried about who he might be meeting.

"You don't think Anton would be there, would he?" James asked. "It's too risky should word get back to the Court if Anton is supporting the very party trying to overthrow them."

Henry stopped, his head up. "No, he wouldn't risk it. However, I am relatively well known in Europe. My work with the Court and my temporary service might be hard to distance myself from."

"You served over three hundred years ago. How many vampires are that old?" I discounted his concerns.

He shot me a disapproving look. "In this part of the world, three hundred is young. America is home to many younger vampires such as James. You could say there was a 'baby boom' in the mid 1800's with so many immigrants moving between Europe and North America. Vampires wanted to move away from the crowds and persecution as much as the humans did. It was natural that they would also create their own covens."

James gave voice to his thoughts. "You could use your service to your advantage, use it as cause for your discontent. Who better to want to take down the power structure than one who had an insider's perspective?"

Henry eyed James with pride. "You would be a capable politician, James. The Court has suffered a great loss by alienating you."

James ignored the compliment. I knew he quit the Guard for a difference of opinion and he had swallowed that dissatisfaction in trade for my life. He wasn't a willing servant and would break from them if he could. For what it was worth, I agreed with Henry. The Court had lost a great mind and a kind soul when James left them. Though if his former partner, Amani, and the two from the Elite Guard I had met were any indication of what you had to be to succeed in the Guard, I understood why he left. They were all very cold and more than a little cruel. Training the young was more suited to his beliefs.

Deciding it was time to say our farewells and hoping not to be missed, we headed back together. James and Henry thought it best to take Brigit's fire from her so we walked in, me in the middle and the men had their arms around my waist. To any onlookers we appeared the happy ménage-a-trios James had reported us to be.

We made sure Brigit and Diego saw us as we made our final pass through the room. Henry gave a brief bow to Miguel who was holding court with a small group of six or so of his followers outside his office.

No one followed us out and I know *I* breathed a huge sigh of relief when we drove away alone.

Henry had told Miguel he would drop us off and come back later. Miguel had agreed to the plan and Henry shuffled us off at the condo in Mijas. Though we intended to follow Henry at a distance, we assumed Miguel had put eyes on us. We made our preparations accordingly.

Once we parted, James and I went inside to change our clothes to something darker and easy to move in. We had to run back to the church, taking care to stay off the main road to catch up with Henry and follow him to their meeting.

It was fortunate I didn't need sleep or I would be exhausted by now. We made it in barely enough time to see Henry getting into a black sedan. We had a chance to assess what kind of security Miguel brought with him watching them take their places as they made ready to head out.

Miguel knew he was under the Court's radar, judging by his minimal security. He had the spiky haired female and redheaded vampire in the white suit from the front door. That was it. They were in the front seats, Henry rode in the back with Miguel. There were no others with them that I could see, it was just the four.

We ran uphill about a hundred feet, paralleling the road. With the lack of streetlights and our elevation, we remained out of sight for several miles until they stopped on a rocky outcropping overlooking the ocean. A large yacht waited with twin engines running at the dock below.

James and I stopped while we were uphill from the cover a large rock provided. It was too far for us to hear. The four of them descended a flight of stairs out of sight from our vantage point but we saw them again as they boarded the vessel and the crew cast off their lines. Lights inside the cabin revealed at least three other bodies.

Once they headed out to sea, James and I climbed down and ran the seventy feet or so to the water and dove, our splashes drowned out by the drone of the engines.

Ch. 39

The boat continued at a manageable speed several miles out to sea. Stamina aside, we could not match the speed of the boat's enormous engines if the captain pushed them to even half of their maximum capacity.

Eventually, the vessel slowed down to a crawl and James and I caught up. When we reached it, we clung to the edge by the wooden trim bobbing just above the water line. The windows were open in the cabin and we could hear the vampires speaking quite clearly.

"Eliot, why don't you share some of your views with my colleagues?" Miguel's lilting Spanish voice was easily recognizable.

Another voice with a distinct Russian flavor spoke up. "Is that what you are calling yourself these days, Henry? You served that very Court, helping them infect our society with their tolerance of human intrusions. Do you deny this?"

There were a couple of snarls and I felt James ready himself to leap up into the boat should it become necessary. Henry gave his rehearsed statement about his disillusionment and voiced a desire to see the strict adherence to the doctrine from his youth restored. We listened and waited. For several tense moments we heard nothing. Finally, when James and I both were ready to burst, we heard that same unknown Russian speak slowly.

"We have all grown tired of their methods in Edinburgh. You may have some insight we could now find useful." He chuckled. "Having the Henry I once knew on our side would make us unstoppable."

Miguel agreed with the Russian. James and I didn't need to use our bond to understand the relief we both felt.

Several other voices spoke. I listened intently, trying to hear if I recognized any of them. None sounded familiar, only the accents. There was an Englishman, Miguel, a Frenchman and the Russian. Henry knew at least one of them. My fingers were crossed that there would be at least one more from the photograph.

They discussed the inadequacies of the Court, or rather, they all waited patiently for Miguel to run out of steam about how he was tired of the Court and how he could do things better. What we did learn was that Miguel had indeed been put up as the front man due to his innate charisma and that fact that he was clearly being manipulated. The others remained behind the scenes, fanning the flames of dissension, swaying public opinion in their favor, and exaggerating the rift to set the stage for a coup and the resulting war.

The next stage of their plan, I heard with horror, was to assassinate Miranda. They saw her as the biggest threat to their success. That confirmed my hopes that she was indeed innocent of the conspiracy.

"What about Charles or Anton?" Henry asked dully.

"Charles?" The French accent was incredulous. "He is a fool, as long as he is being worshipped by the fawning courtiers, he is content. He will be handled when we take over."

"But what of Anton? Surely you consider him more formidable being by far the eldest and most intelligent." Henry asked again.

His question was met with a weighty silence. After a moment's pause, one said. "His role will become clear in time." They were keeping Anton's involvement under their hats for now.

Henry let the others discuss their ideas for Miranda's execution. Frenchie suggested using a thrall, humans being expendable. "They were unsuccessful against a human. We had to turn one to finally get the result we wanted; thralls could not be expected to fare better against a vampire," he lobbied for a vampire-only operation. The Brit suggested using one of their followers, a vampire, to execute her. That was well received and led to a discussion which excluded any who didn't know the vampire world by name.

Eventually, they settled on a name I *did* recognize. So did James. Amani, his old partner in the Guard and one of the bartenders in the pub above the Court's hall. She had been openly hostile to humans when I was one and James had told me about a time when she had devastated a village of humans for pleasure. He had also told me how he held a secret from their time together. She had killed an important vampire and he could ruin her by telling the Court. I wondered if now would be the time to bring that into play.

Glancing at James, I saw that he was also thinking about revealing Amani's secret.

What should we do?

He agreed we could use that, only he was trying to think on a broader scale. *That is a possibility. Or we could let them think their identities are still safe. We might need to follow them still, see how many are involved. We can't assume the photograph is everyone.*

Good point. What if there are hundreds of them? It could be a war no matter what we do.

Most armies are lost without their leaders. We will use our anonymity for as long as we can to smoke out their leaders. If we need to come back at them in twenty years when they recoup, we will.

The meeting was wrapping up, the engines fired back up and James and I let go of the boat. Pushing off, I let myself sink below the surface. I'd never gone diving before and found the experience of doing it without need for tanks or equipment captivating. James swam on the surface a few feet above me. The water was beautiful, I could see clearly using the small amount of moonlight available.

The fish skittered away when we came near. I remembered what James had said about prey animals fearing our kind and other predators seeing us as a threat. I was pleased to see that once they determined I wasn't a threat they returned and I could see them.

I also found I had a very new fear of sharks. I didn't want to get into a battle for territory with something that had significantly more teeth and moved much faster than me in the water. I increased my speed, James matched me and we reached the shore less than half an hour later.

We ran back to the condo drying with the wind our speed created. By the time we reached our destination, our clothes were only slightly damp although my hair was a mess. I was trying to finger comb it and tame the height when *my* phone rang, the international minutes I had thought to add this time were paying off.

I ran to retrieve it off the kitchen table where I had left it and saw that it was Tonya before I flipped it open. She tried to keep her voice even and hide her anxiety, but I could hear the tension of her voice.

"How did it go tonight?"

"He's fine." I read between the lines. "He should be home any time." I kept walking until I reached the bathroom where I ended the call and set down the phone, stripped off my clothes and got into the hot shower.

The heat was wonderful and I remembered the pleasure I used to feel in breathing the steam into my lungs to feel its weight. I was letting the water run down my face and head, reveling in the feel of it. The briny smell of the salt water and the road dust were mixing in the steam, bringing back an olfactory recollection of all that had happened tonight.

I was so lost in my own head that I had to stifle the startled scream I sounded when the shower door opened. James' arms went around me and he held me tight while the steam clouds billowed out above the shower doors. The water ran over us and I smelled the salt water and dust on him as well.

My thoughts turned to the conspiracy we were now all embroiled in and the potential losses for all sides should things become too much for our little band of rebels to stop. The simplicity of my old life where the only person I could have harmed had been myself suddenly glowed bright, and I wished in that one second that none of this would have happened. As soon as I wished it, I felt James' arms loosen.

Prying my eyes open against the heat and steam I saw the hurt on his face; I'd bled over my misgivings and he'd taken them personally. Not saying anything, he got out, toweled off and went in our room. I opened my mouth to reassure him and shut it. He'd felt it from me, how could I deny what I'd felt? When I ran out of hot water, I too toweled off and went into our room.

James was already sitting in the bed reading. Lying down on my side of the bed I spread my hair out behind me on the pillow to dry. My eyes closed and I willed my mind to slow down. My meditation practices as a human came back to me. Carefully, I simulated breathing slowly and deeply to see if the memory of the act would provide any tranquility. It did not. Again I wished I could cry with frustration. Without a heart beat to concentrate on and breathing to regulate, meditation was pointless. All I could do was try to ignore the non stop running in my head.

This had to be a kind of Hell no one who romanticizes being a vampire considered.

James remained immobile beside me even though I knew he'd been done with his page long before. He was a very fast reader. The lack of page turning was for my benefit. His thoughtfulness pushed me over the edge.

I stood up and changed into jeans instead of my yoga pants. Glancing over, I saw that he was watching me. I answered his unspoken question.

"Out. I have to clear my head." Muttering under my breath when my hand was on the door, "If that's possible."

Ch. 40

Being out on the street was a relief in that there were different things to look at and distract me, though my head swirled no less. The condo was in a trendy part of town, bars and nightclubs surrounded the building resulting in a steady flow of foot and road traffic. The vibrant pulse of the area was electrifying.

I didn't want electrifying. Quiet was what I sought. Recalling the botanical gardens a few miles inland, I changed direction and jogged. Being immortal had one advantage for a young woman traveling alone, I feared no dark street. Despite the need to walk down some very dark roadways that would have had me jumping out of my skin as a human, I glided lightly down them without care.

The extensive gardens were locked off with an easily scaled ten foot high iron gate. Once inside, I felt my thoughts beginning to slow a fraction with the constant sound of gently flowing water. The relief was welcome. I followed the foot paths throughout the gardens, walking all night and letting the serenade of the night insects fill my mind, pushing out the rest of the "noise" that had filled it these past few weeks. Occasionally I would sit on a bench and marvel at the natural beauty surrounding me.

As the dawn approached and I felt the return of the burning on my flesh, stronger now that I was so close to the equator, I stood and made my way back onto the path from the shelter of the Bird of Paradise I had been sitting beside. Watching me from a distance was a young black fellow in his mid twenties. With the breeze going the other direction and the sounds of tinkling fountains in my ears, I had completely missed his approach.

He spoke Spanish at first and I shrugged, indicating I didn't understand. "Hey, you can't be here. How did you get in?" His English was very good.

Thinking fast, I came up with a plausible explanation. "I got locked in last night. I've been waiting for someone to come and let me out." I tried to look appropriately stressed before he came close enough to see me better.

At once he was apologetic, rattling the keys on his large round keychain to find the right one for the gate. "I'm sorry Miss. American, huh? Good thing this place is fenced in, you were safe here." He reached out and put his arm behind me to usher me toward the gate. "You're cold. Let me get you a cup of coffee in the guard house."

"No," I responded too quickly, drawing his curious eye. "I really need to get home. My phone died. My friends will be wondering where I am."

His eyes wandered to my hands, my left finger was bare. "Would you like to call from the guard house? We have a land line in there."

"Really, I'm fine. I just want to get home." Picking up my pace, I forced him to move with me. He reached the gate a step ahead of me and unlocked it, insisting the whole time I let him get me a cup of coffee or a blanket. He felt terrible about what had happened and would make sure the management knew about it, they would speak to the guard who was supposed to check before locking up.

I assured him I was fine and to please not get the night guard in trouble. Really I was off the path, looking at the hibiscus up on a hill, out of sight. It was my own stupid fault I was left in. He grudgingly accepted my story and let me go. I heard the lock turn after the gate clanged shut behind me.

Walking back to the condo, I felt the sun burning into my flesh. The first clear, sunny day in a long time and I had to be a new vampire walking around outside near the equator. James' control or not it still hurt. Yet my flesh was not what burned the most. It was the lack of blood since last night, leading me to stare at the humans around me on the street with a new sort of longing.

There really weren't that many. Most were street sweepers, garbage men and delivery drivers. No one else was up at this hour. The hunter part of my brain told me no one would miss one, there would be no witnesses if I took one right now. Just find a quiet street or business stoop tucked away from prying eyes.

I shook that thought out of my head, fighting with the burning thirst. My counter weapon was to remember the humans I loved and what made them special to me, what made them human. An older man was walking into his house and I saw my dad. A young woman was rolling a dolly full of beer into a bar, I saw my friend Heidi.

It was only *just* sufficient to fight the urge and I was more than a little relieved when our building came into sight. I reached the door and fumbling, had to fish out my key. James opened the door just as my key turned, his face relaxing as he sought to wipe away the worry he didn't intend for me to see.

With a tight smile, I walked right past him and through the empty living room to the fridge trying to regain my peace of mind. After two very full glasses, I could feel some of the burning ease, letting my mind cool and my hands slow their trembling. James wisely remained in the living room while I drank my fill. The sound of him tinkering with the small upright piano in the corner caught my ear. I don't know if it was the overstimulation of digital media but every vampire seemed to have a piano in place of a television.

The melody was a familiar one from when I was a child. My mother used to sing it when I was upset and refused to come out of my room. I had never been able to tell my mother the reason I liked it so much was that it calmed *her* nerves and made it easier to be in the same room with her. She had told me once it was an old song her own mother sang to her and her mother's mother sang to her and so on as far as anyone could remember.

Entering the room, I leaned against the back of the couch to face the piano and James' back. "How do you know that song?" I asked him, thinking it had to be too far back in my head for him to have found it there.

"My mother used to sing it to me when I was a child and couldn't sleep." James continued to play the light melody without turning around.

"So did mine." Forever was a very long time to hold onto resentment and I felt mine easing. "How do you handle it when they're all gone? Everyone you love, I mean."

His hands continued to play. "*Everyone* I love will never be gone."

I knew I owed him an explanation. The emotions in my head were all jumbled up and he wasn't digging so he could not be clear on what it all meant.

"I wasn't sure I wanted this." I watched his shoulders stiffen with the reiteration of his perceived rejection. "Immortality, thirst for blood, forever, the whole package. Not that I hadn't been thinking about it a little since I met you, but I hadn't made up my mind for sure. Then, that night," my voice got thick. "I just wasn't ready to die. I mean, I know humans die but not like that. Not when I was finally starting to live. It didn't seem right, I'd only just found you." I let him feel what that meant.

James stopped playing. "Claire, quite honestly I wasn't ready for this either." He was still staring at the keys, unable to look at me. "Promising to be with you forever was not an issue for me, but to put *this* on someone. It's not something I would ever choose to do. It's a difficult world we live in, physical pains aside. Our future is a long one and what do we hope for? We can only read so many books, learn so many languages, be with so many partners. After that, it is an existence filled with loneliness, burning thirst and pointless tasks meant to occupy our overactive minds for a short while before the inevitable madness of eternity sets in." He plinked a few keys from an unknown song.

I sat next to him on the bench, our hips and shoulders touching. It didn't make everything better although it did bring comfort knowing we weren't alone.

While we sat, James played a few songs. Some I recognized, some I didn't. Neither of us talked. It was mid morning when Henry walked through the door.

"Henry!" I jumped up, more excited to see him than I thought I would be. "Is everything alright? We left you hours ago." James spun around to wait for his report.

"Were you able to follow the yacht?"

James nodded an affirmative. "We were. We heard the meeting in its entirety. It went well."

"That was only part of what happened. We ended up returning to Miguel's office in the church. There were some other lower level members of his organization, no one who seemed overly well connected or even well spoken. I do not believe any of them are those we are looking for."

"What about who you saw on the boat," I asked, curiosity eating at me.

"The French one, Jean Michel was Nightshade, he was in the picture." Henry paused, stared directly at James and dropped a bombshell. "I am considering calling in Lucas and Gabriel now that we have three of the four in the photograph identified and they are planning Miranda's assassination. Do you have any objections?"

Lucas and Gabriel coming could mean only one thing. We were going to move to the next phase. If we were caught, Anton would surely have us killed.

There was no denying I was scared.

James wanted to object but unfortunately, it was a good idea. Lucas and Gabriel were powerful, elders, and cold enough to kill anyone. Never mind Lucas had some sort of power over me. Reluctantly, he agreed. "They would be a great help to us."

Henry looked to me. I shook my head as well, "No objections. How do we tell Miranda?"

"By now Anton has been called and where my loyalty lies is in question. Contact with Miranda is best handled over the telephone as I am not certain what would happen if I were to show up at the Court's hall. Has there been anything yet from our Detective in Minneapolis on the photograph?"

Both of us shook our heads no.

"No matter for now. We will go forward with those we know. I will have to remain out of sight for now. I need both of you to continue to watch Miguel. We might be able to find out more about their plans for Miranda."

We agreed to do so; more night time surveillance I was sure. Henry went in the other room, phone in hand. I heard his voice rumbling through the walls though I didn't hear what he said. After about half an hour he emerged from his bedroom, his face was grave.

"Anton has been a very busy bee. He and his disciples have conveyed my 'intended treachery' to Miranda, advising her that *I* am behind the coup intended to overthrow them and a plot to kill her. She took quite a bit of convincing to believe that that was not the case. Anton apparently told her of my displeasure during my service. However, I have convinced her one of her fellow members of the Court is involved. She is understandably upset and feels she can trust no one, not even Charles." Henry flashed a dark glance at James.

I felt James' mixed reaction and then he tried to shut me out.

My affront was apparent.

Henry caught it and spoke sharply to James. "Can you keep *anything* to yourself?"

James was equally frustrated. "She was perceptive *before*, even more now that she's one of us. We've talked about it, you can trust her," He chided. "The time is coming soon for her to know anyway, if she is to help."

My head was on a swivel going back and forth between them waiting for some indication someone was going to tell me what was going on.

Henry sighed resignedly. "I suppose you are right, the time for action is upon us." He turned to me, "Claire, we have been working with a mole within the Court to monitor the extent of the damage being done from the inside."

I kept my mouth shut and waited, sure I knew where this was going.

"Charles has been monitoring Anton's visitors for some time and Iain has been passing the messages to us. We knew Anton had a partner within the Russian military and they have been discussing an airstrike on Edinburgh because of the high concentration of 'liberals' there. They believe one strong show of force aimed at those who most opposed them would break the back of the other side. Anton and his fellow usurpers would put Miguel up as a mindless puppet and use their agents to hunt down and destroy any vampires not considered 'pure' and allow human slaughter to run rampant."

"It's their very own witch hunt." James added, his displeasure obvious. I was still gaping over the identity of the mole. "Charles? Really?"

"It's an act my dear. Charles is both intelligent and trustworthy." Henry frowned down his nose at me.

I'd never thought Iain capable of espionage nor Charles capable of a complex thought; they were perfectly chosen. My respect for the two of them grew tenfold and I was ashamed to have been so dismissive of Iain in the past. "What can I do to help? I can try to get in with Miguel or Diego," I offered, hoping to prove my worth.

Henry smiled, "Claire, I am afraid James would have better luck 'getting in' with Miguel than you." He put his hand to his chin and ran his eyes slowly up and down my body, appraising me. Involuntarily I twisted to hide part of my body from him. "Diego might be a possibility."

"No one is 'getting in' with anybody Henry," James growled.

A flash of teeth from Henry showed his amusement at James' agitation. "You are right, James. Claire doesn't have what it takes to seduce Diego." He pretended to be thinking hard, "Maybe we could find a way to make it work."

"What do you mean I don't have what it takes? I'm better than Brigit," I shot back indignantly.

Henry laughed and I saw James trying hard not to for my sake. "He means you don't have a partner. Diego likes his girls in teams." James cut a devious look at Henry. "Maybe we could send you in with Tonya."

Henry's amusement disappeared in an instant. "Tonya will not be a part of this."

James was satisfied he'd made his point. "Then we are agreed, seduction is not in the cards for Claire. We will monitor movement of Miguel's inner circle and contact you in Edinburgh if we see any activity. Anything more might raise their suspicions and force their hand before we are ready."

We all agreed with the plan as it was and Henry made ready to fly to Glasgow and make his way back to his flat on foot, where he intended to lay low. The Andrews clan would not be involved just yet but Henry was not ready to send them home until he was absolutely certain we wouldn't need their help. There was a lot at stake if things went badly now.

Ch. 41

Henry's flight left late that afternoon giving James and I some alone time before we had to go on our surveillance assignment for the evening. It was convenient that most vampires this close to the equator didn't become active until nightfall. We wouldn't miss much by staying out of the peak of the day.

We found something to do inside. James helped me to practice my French.

We started with body parts. I pointed to my finger.

"Doigt." His accent was perfect.

I pointed to my lips.

"Levres," he responded, kissing them gently.

I pointed to my nose.

"Nez." He kissed that too, his voice growing husky.

I pointed to something else and he translated, kissing. I only got as far as one more part before we had to take a study break. When I complimented his teaching methods, his laughter rumbled against me and he wrapped his arms around me.

The sun went down and we dressed in our dark clothing from the night before. Momentarily, I was grateful for the lack of sweat my new body afforded me. My black Converse were fine for me. James had some sort of complicated looking running shoes.

I gave him a quizzical glance. "Do you find that kind of shock absorption necessary?"

"Yes, I do." He paused in his lacing to look at me. "Just because we are not easily killed or hurt doesn't mean we can't be uncomfortable. Haven't you been uncomfortable a few times since you've turned?"

"Constantly." I sniggered, "You just never hear about vampires buying two hundred dollar shoes so their backs don't hurt."

He pulled my hood over my head as he walked past. "Let's go."

Miguel's headquarters was not a long run for us. It took less than half an hour this time. Now that we had done it already we were certain of our path. The last few minutes were nearly straight uphill as we went up the backside of the mountain so that we could remain undetected.

When we arrived we assumed our perches downwind from the church, overlooking the entrance so that we could monitor all the comings and goings. Some of the same cars from the night before were present with a few new additions.

Movement by one of the windows caught my eye. I thought I recognized a flash of bright pink. *Amani.*

James craned his neck and, unable to see, jogged in a crouch to where I hunkered. *You're right. They must be giving her the order to kill Miranda tonight.*

Let's get closer, see if we can hear.

He agreed it was worth the risk, the details of the assignment would be highly valuable to us. We carefully picked our way down the hill while moving around to the side of the building, creeping closer to Miguel's office.

We took up our positions near a small tree outside the window, hidden in shadow. We were lucky, Miguel's

255

window was open. Amani stood beside it. Miguel sat behind a large dark wood desk sipping at a crystal goblet.

My throat burned in envy. I pushed the thirst aside for the moment, trying to concentrate on what they were saying. Their words were whispers in the air. I moved closer and glancing over, saw that James was coming around the tree as well.

We were about ten yards apart, he was closer to the front of the building and I was nearer the back. Both of us stopped within a stone's throw of the window.

"I admire your dedication to the cause Amani." Miguel was saying. "That is why I have chosen you for a very important mission."

Amani turned her back to the window and moved closer to the interior of the room. Her voice was harder to hear. I started to creep down closer, avoiding the spill of light from the room shining out onto the ground outside the window.

James was trying to get my attention but I was focusing on the voices just beyond my reach. I was so close I was nearly touching the whitewashed stucco exterior of the church.

"Yes, I'm scheduled to work two days from now. The wine cellar is downstairs, next door to the entrance to the Court's main hall. It would be easy to detour into her quarters. She is usually in there unless they have Court business. Things have been very tense between her and Anton recently."

"Does she suspect anything?" Miguel was on alert, he set down his goblet and braced a hand on the desk.

"No," Amani sneered. "She is far too arrogant. Her love for the humans makes her weak like them. She refuses to see the dissent among her own kind, even when it is right in front of her."

Miguel swept his glass back up for a deep gulp while staring at Amani. I heard the side drawer of his desk open as his free hand disappeared. It came back up with a small black handgun he set upon his desk facing her. "I assume you are proficient?"

"We receive training in the Guard with all human weapons."

Miguel stroked the black metal lovingly. "We have developed a liquid silver bullet. It goes in like a normal bullet and the shell casing shatters upon impact releasing the silver directly into the bloodstream." He pantomimed an explosion with his hand. "This gun is loaded with nine of them. You only need to make one count." He waved dismissively, "After that you may do with the others as you will."

Amani stepped forward and took the gun. "I would be honored." She bowed before slipping the gun into her waistband behind her.

"I know I do not have to remind you that secrecy is of the utmost importance."

"I will speak of it to no one."

Miguel excused her and I heard the door close. I started to walk away from the window and slid on a loose chunk of rocks. I froze and spun my head toward the window. If he looked out, I would be right in his sightline. All I could think to do was to drop into a crouch right where I stood.

Miguel was up and did look out the window, and sure enough, looked right at me. He shouted something very loud and in Spanish, but I got the gist of it. It was something like, "Hey, come kill her."

Dropping my shields, I felt the rush from the guards charging in from the other side of the church. They were coming fast. I got up to run as did James. I heard him hot on my tail.

Unfortunately, the guards heard us as well and were not far behind. We ran up and over the mountain, jumping the washouts and little ravines cutting into the hillside. There was nothing big enough to hide behind or inside within sight and we were quickly approaching the base of the hill that would put us on a roadway with no cover and possibly innocents to be harmed.

What do we do? I asked, not breaking stride.

Hope for a miracle, was his uninspiring reply.

Just then, the ground went out from under my feet. I didn't fall far only a few feet, but it was heading down the hill and the rock jutted over my head, hiding me from sight as I pressed myself back and hunkered in the hollow.

Almost on top of me, James hopped in and saw what I did. We both scuttled up under the rock pulling our legs in and sat perfectly still.

Seconds later, one heavy set of feet was on the rock above our heads before they came crashing down in front of us, the second set right behind him. Their fall took them by surprise as well and James and I were ready.

James lunged at the large one in the white suit from last night. I jumped onto a smaller blonde and knocked him backward just as he was starting to get up. The sounds of James' tussle were peripheral while I struggled with my opponent.

He wasn't more than half a foot taller than I was, although he was much thicker and it was all muscle. But where he was bigger, I was faster and my terror probably added to my speed. His hands closed around my middle and he squeezed me hard. I felt the bones in my back trying to snap and at least one rib did. I put my hands around his throat but the muscles made it too thick for my hands to get a good grip.

The instinct to survive kicked in and my fangs grew. I did the only thing I could and reared back to strike. My teeth went into his throat, tearing it clear. His hands released me and he fell to his knees.

Our heights no longer a factor, I reached out and grasped his head by the chin and back of his skull. In one twist, the job was done and in the length of a human heartbeat there was only ash.

A glance to my side showed me James had also been successful. He came to me and put his arm around me. Catching my wince, he asked, "Are you injured?"

I nodded my head, "Just a rib or two. I'm sure they'll be fine by morning. You?" I scanned him for any obvious injuries.

"No, merely a few bruises. We were lucky."

Suddenly elated, I laughed. "You asked for a miracle." Relieved, we continued home at a much slower pace, certain no one was following us.

Once we were home, James called Henry to tell him what we had learned. The downside of course was that we had been detected and it was unknown if that would change the plan for Miranda's assassination.

Henry said that he would alert Miranda and they would try to take out Amani if she appeared anywhere near the pub. We were told to go ahead and eliminate Miguel. It was time to start taking down their leaders before they could throw the vampires into total chaos by wiping out ours.

"What about the Russian? You knew him," James prompted.

"His name is Gregor and I have put out feelers to locate him if he is still there in Spain or if he has gone back to Russia. I am trying to locate Jean Michel as well. However, I must find Gregor as soon as possible. If you see him with Miguel, you must take care of him but be warned, he is especially lethal." There was strain I hadn't heard in Henry's voice before, "Be careful."

Moving closer to the phone, I asked. "Have you asked the Andrews to help?" I had come to rely on the compulsion between Henry and the werecat family that forced them to come to each others' aid.

"I have asked them to go home to America. This is our war and their Council would never forgive us if we involved their kind. It could lead to a secondary war between our races."

"But I thought they *had* to help you?" I blurted out, growing desperate.

His voice was dark. "I have told Troy I no longer need his help. They are not compelled if I do not call them."

My body froze when I realized things had disintegrated so far that Troy and Henry wanted to break their connection. I was also envious of Henry to know his love would be far away and safe. Mine was going to be fighting beside me and it terrified me. James wrapped his free arm around me, pulling me close.

"We'll start looking for him tonight." He added quickly before hanging up, "I think it would be best to assume that all guns on their side have their new liquid silver."

Henry agreed. "Good luck."

Ch. 42

We were waiting out the peak of the daylight hours, preparing ourselves to brave the last of the sun's rays in an effort to get a jump on those we sought. We were on a near constant stream of blood, James assured me it would make us as strong as possible for our upcoming challenges.

It was a complete shock when we heard a knock at the front door of the unit at half past noon. I looked up from the chessboard but the look of puzzlement in James' eyes matched mine.

"Maybe it's Iain with some last minute information," I suggested.

"It's possible," James said warily.

My spirits lifted when I recognized the voice on the other side. When he walked into the room ahead of James I was already halfway to him.

"Stephen!" I was thrilled to see his face and went to hug him then let my arms drop with a sense of dread. The two beings I loved the most were both going to be fighting some very dangerous characters and I might prove a worse detriment than asset putting them in further danger.

"What?" He was eyeing me curiously. "Aren't you happy to see me? I thought you could use one more."

"I thought Henry told you to go back to America. This is not your fight." James was firm.

"I have my own score to settle with these guys." His jaw was set and expression hard. Stephen didn't put his foot down often and when he did he meant it.

James assessed Stephen's commitment and determined he was not going to budge. He held out his hand, a rarity for a vampire. Stephen took it.

"What about your Council? Henry said they wouldn't like any of you helping." I didn't want him to get out of this only to get in trouble with his own kind.

"I would like to see them try to stop me. This is my battle too and I have every right to be here." Stephen had so perfected his flighty image it was rare to get a glimpse into his strength of character. He was showing it now.

I hugged him again. "Thank you Stephen. We need all the help we can get."

We sat back down to discuss what we knew of our opponents, sharing everything we could think of with Stephen when another knock sounded at the door.

"Are you expecting anyone?" James asked Stephen.

Stephen was genuinely confused. "No, I didn't tell anyone I was coming here."

I went to the door this time. When I opened it, there were two more familiar faces. "Troy, Tonya!" I jumped out to hug them both, my animosity toward Troy forgotten with the gratitude I felt for him at the moment. "We're so glad you're here." Stepping back, I welcomed them inside.

They exchanged a bewildered look and followed me inside. Once we got to the living room, they saw why I hadn't been more surprised at their mysterious appearance.

"Stephen, what are you doing here?" Troy growled angrily.

Stephen stood and I couldn't feel his energy anymore, he'd walled himself off abruptly. I could sense a tingling on the periphery of my mind occupying the space where seconds before, I'd been able to feel the warmth of my friend. Focused on the newcomers, he was angry and raising the energy to change. "Of all of us, I have the best reason to be here. I might ask what brings you two here? I thought you didn't want to have to do this."

Tonya answered quietly, "I *wanted* to come."

I could guess why.

Troy shot her a warning look through narrowed lids, "So I had to. Someone has to try to control the fallout."

Tonya crossed her arms and said nothing. No one else wanted in on that argument and finally James broke the silence. He was stepping into Henry's role, assuming command.

"Now that we have a larger force, this changes our strategy." He directed his attention to Troy, "You can take your family and Claire and I will go together. We will all go to the church first, I think that will be where we have the best chance of finding any or all of our targets."

"Isn't that walking right into the lion's den?" Troy asked.

"That *is* where one usually finds the lions, isn't it?" James responded flatly.

"Yes, it is." A new voice spoke from the entranceway making us all jump.

"Henry? When did you get here?" Tonya sat bolt upright, trying to ignore Troy's protective posturing.

Henry answered her cautiously. "Everyone I was looking for was here so I returned. The better question is what are *you* all doing here? I asked that all of you go back to America.

You do not need to be here." He watched Tonya specifically, ignoring everyone else's reactions but hers.

I watched them feeling every bit a voyeur. I couldn't look away.

You are a hopeless romantic. We are facing devastation of an unprecedented scale and you're worried about whether or not he's going to kiss her?

I don't see anything wrong with hoping for a happy ending. Hope is an important thing for people. If it weren't for hope, they wouldn't rebuild after disaster, no one would get married or have babies.

Troy's sharp tone left no doubt he hadn't changed his mind about his sister's involvement in several things. "*You* don't get to command everything *we* do." He stared at Henry, his jaw clenched.

Stephen lost patience and interjected. "Troy, we all appreciate that you're capable of ordering us around but could you just for once give it a rest? We're all *more* than grown up and can take care of ourselves."

Troy's mouth opened and shut as he stared at Stephen, taken aback by his severity.

"Stephen, I don't think you should step in on something that doesn't affect you." Troy sputtered.

"Au contraire mon fraire this effects all of us, your judgment is compromised. You have become singularly focused. 'Keep Tonya away from the vampires,'" he made a Frankenstein face, "has been your sole objective ever since she was taken in Germany." Stephen gave his words a moment to sink in. "She's a big girl, fully capable of taking care of herself and making her own decisions. So please, stop trying so hard to decide for everyone based on what's best for one member, not the clan."

My eyes roamed Tonya's face. She was staring at Stephen, touched and shocked by his outburst as were the rest of us.

Right then, Henry's phone rang. He had it open and to his ear in a flash. "Gabriel."

He had called in the Elite Guard. They were loyal to all the Court, although Miranda ran the Guard. They would not be able to harm any of the Court or lie outright but if we could keep Anton in the dark for a little longer, it wouldn't matter.

Gabriel and Lucas were some very scary and old vampires. Lucas was an Elf before he was turned and had a different kind of magick than any other I had met. I didn't think anyone could get past those two.

Henry's phone hummed with Gabriel's quiet voice. He said a few words and snapped it shut. "Gabriel and Lucas have located Gregor. They will be here by nightfall and have asked us to meet them at Miguel's church. Jean Michel will be there as well." He muttered quietly to himself, "And so it begins."

For the first time since being turned, I dreaded the setting of the sun.

Ch. 43

An hour before the sun set, we split into two teams. Henry was with Stephen and James, Troy was with Tonya and me. We all had agreed that with James and me split up we could have undetectable contact between the two groups.

With the light still revealing us to the human world, we drove to a turnoff at the backside of the mountain. The only car Miguel's people had seen of ours was Henry's, so the Andrews brought two rentals to the condo. They were perfectly average, nothing that would stand out. We parked and started up the mountain. Once we were high enough up to guarantee there would be no witnesses, the Andrews changed forms. The sun was just beginning to set. Those of us affected watched it go down with relief.

In spite of our predatory predisposition to hate each other, our two species were well suited to work together. The cats nearly matched our speed and agility. Their eyesight was better suited to the dark than our own. We were equally silent.

Both groups went up the backside of the mountain, James' team to the West, mine to the East so that we were essentially facing each other over the top of the church. Lucas and Gabriel were on their way. While we waited, we monitored the area. There were only a few cars in the lot as the last of the sun's rays disappeared.

Do you think we should go in now and pick them off as they come in? I asked James, thinking that might be more advantageous given our small numbers.

I felt his pleasure at my suggestion. *That was my intention. I will take my team down, you keep yours up here as lookout. Let me know when you see Lucas or Gabriel or if any other cars arrive.*

266

I couldn't help grinning at his approval. My pleasure was tainted by fear for him. *Be careful.*

He said he would be and that he would alert me when they had control of the church. We each told our respective teams what the plan was. Tonya was visibly agitated. Her tail flicking a mile a minute while she got up and paced then returned to lay flat, all the while watching the opposite hill. Troy flattened his ears at her, growling repeatedly. The only acknowledgement she gave him was a low hiss. He lay on his belly, sulking.

Watching for movement opposite us, I saw a flash of pale skin in the darkness but couldn't tell if it was Henry or James from that distance. I remained frozen waiting for the next phase to begin.

There was no question when it did. A loud crack shattered the silence as something heavy hit the wooden front doors. I saw one of them fly off its hinges, hitting the ground with a resounding thud.

A pale body I didn't recognize landed on top of it, visible for only seconds before turning to ash.

Growls, scuffles and tearing noises came from inside the building for the longest three minutes of my life. I only knew how much time had elapsed because I had decided if I didn't hear from James in five, I was going down myself and I was counting.

After three minutes, all was silent. It was another forty seconds before James "called" me.

Miguel and his staff have been dispatched. We will take up our positions here and await his visitors.

Is everyone okay? I asked, reaching out to him to feel if he was hiding anything. He was guarding something from me, I couldn't tell what.

Just a few scratches. He announced before he closed off our connection.

I relayed what James had told me. Neither cat relaxed, nor did I. Our attentions turned back to the church. We saw Henry step out to pick up the front door but couldn't see from our angle how he put it back as there was an overhang blocking our view.

Lucas and Gabriel appeared like wraiths from the darkness while we watched Henry below. One second there was nothing, the next, Gabriel spoke beside me.

He had the deepest, most gravelly voice I had ever heard. I jumped when it sounded beside me. "Have they secured the premises?"

I silently praised myself for not screaming. "Yes, they're going to wait down there for the others."

Lucas approached me from the other side. He was a willowy creature with eyes the color of spring grass. The other vampires called him an Enchanter. Apparently it was the name they used for Elves, though Lucas was a one of a kind. It was nearly impossible to sneak up on an Elf and turn him. I was sure there was a story there how Lucas had been caught, not that he would easily share it.

James didn't like him because he had enchanted me upon our first meeting. I had been unable to resist his call in our few meetings since. Now that I had been turned, I hoped that would change.

"So he *has* turned you after all." His melodic voice rumbled next to me as he chuckled. "It suits you. Your magick has turned with you, I smell it." He put his face down next to my hair and sniffed deeply.

"That is interesting," he added, his face nearly on top of my head as he took a few extra sniffs.

Troy gave a chirp I assumed meant we should stay focused. Acting as interpreter, I said the same to the Guard. "We should watch for trouble in case more come than they can handle."

Gabriel laughed for the first time since I had met him. It sounded like boulders slapping together, harsh and not in the least bit pleasant. "I would prefer to wait inside instead of here. Lucas, can you restrain yourself if I leave you alone?"

Lucas' laughter was the opposite of Gabriel's. It chimed like music, tickling along my skin. He frowned at me. "I can no longer call to you." Then his expression lightened, "I *will, however,* always have a hold on you." His hand ran down the side of my face, lifting it up. A distant part of my mind knew I should stop him but another part, the one he had locked into when I was human, held me fast and I trembled eagerly for his touch.

His lips brushed mine softly. Lucas closed his eyes and licked his lips. "I knew you would taste sweet, I only regret not being able to taste your human blood. It would have been delicious."

"Lucas," Gabriel grumbled from my other side. "Another car approaches, let us be on our way."

As silently as they had come, they departed leaving me swaying in place coming back to my senses. Shame flowed through my brain, pushing away the last quiverings Lucas had caused my treasonous body.

I did not see or hear them until I saw a break in the light on our side of the church where they had to cross to get inside. There was a second break as the other stepped through and inside the church. As an afterthought, I called out to James.

Lucas and Gabriel are here. They've just gone through Miguel's window. I tried to keep what had just happened from my mind. James didn't need any distractions right now.

Neither do you. He growled in my head, answering the question of whether I'd kept my thoughts private.

I'm sorry. I ran through all sorts of explanations in my head, except they all felt like excuses and I didn't voice any.

His hold over you has survived your transformation. I see I need to speak to him after all. His animosity prickled through our connection.

Someone else's emotions are always a little disconcerting to experience, which is why I had avoided close contact with others my entire young life. The bond James and I shared had been strong and since I had turned it had grown stronger yet, nearly everything flowed through it now. His emotions colored every word, anything he felt strongly about could not be held back. The effect could be staggering and sometimes contagious.

His rage now ran through our connection filling me with a need to sink my teeth into someone, to feel blood in my hands and taste it on my tongue. My limbs grew electric with the nervous energy I felt surging in my veins. It rolled through me unchecked and without another word I started down the hillside at a full run. Somewhere behind me, I heard cat paws scrabbling along the rocks trying to catch up.

The car Gabriel had seen was nearly to the clearing in front of the church. They were obviously vampires, they didn't use headlights to see in the dark. Smart considering they didn't want humans coming around.

When the car stopped, three vampires stepped out. I smiled, feeling my fangs grow in anticipation, an unfamiliar vicious edge coloring my conscious thoughts. Diego Garcia and his two toys walked around the car to enter the church. I stepped out of the darkness by the driver's side nearest the little brunette Brigit. Perfect.

"Hello," I called out quietly to her.

She whirled, alarmed until she saw me. Her mouth twisted as her eyes narrowed. "Have you come to apologize for your lack of manners?" Her haughty tone pushed me past the breaking point.

I roared and lunged at her. She was not expecting the attack, though her quick reflexes allowed her to dart sideways out of the way just in time. Instead of hitting her, I slammed into the car leaving a me sized dent in the door.

She wanted the fight as much as I did. Her arms spread, she circled back to me, keeping me between the car and herself. Brigit needn't have worried, I was in no mind to run away. Her lunge was fast and direct. She caught me under the arms and slammed me into the metal again. I felt a rib crack. They had just healed. Anger sharpened my mind and quickened my reflexes.

Brigit was only a few inches taller than me and when she pinned me her shoulder dropped, giving me a clear shot at her throat. Her foolish move left her wide open to my attack. My arms were pinned so I pushed off with my toes, mouth open wide, and felt her firm skin break as my fangs sank in.

She screeched and clawed at my shoulders and face trying to get me off. Instinct took over and I wrapped my arms around her, clinging to her. She tore at my face to no avail. When I sensed the fight going out of her, I shoved away from her.

Brigit went down to her knees clutching at her wound. Blood on my face blurred my vision, the haze clouding my mind proved to be the greater obstacle.

I had forgotten about her associates and I was alone for the moment. No one in the church knew I was coming down. I'd felt James block me out before my frenzy and the cats had not yet caught up. It would be a precious few seconds before help would reach me.

Now that I was no longer attached to Brigit, Diego and the blonde who remained nameless were on me. My arms were jerked roughly behind my back, my shoulders threatening to separate as the very tall blonde used them to pull me up to her height. My feet left the ground and my arms screamed their objections.

Diego eyed me, his polite face from last night a memory. "So it seems you are not dead. That you are no longer human did have me fooled for a short time. However, once we knew of Henry's true identity, yours and your mate's were not hard to figure out." He glanced around, I saw his eyes pause as he took in the broken front door hanging slightly ajar. "Are they inside? I know you never go far without your mate and *he* is always with his Master."

His hand flashed out. I felt a searing pain and heard a crack in my shoulder as he slammed a fist into my collarbone, snapping it. "I know he will come to you. Why don't you call him out here?" Diego tipped his head, eyes searching mine. "Now that human blood no longer runs through your veins do you think he would let you die?" His smile was cruel. "Let's see, shall we?"

Again his hand flew and this time I tried to double over except the blonde held me firm. His punch to my stomach was meant only to inflict pain, it could not cause me any actual damage.

I hoped he was still blocking me out. Just in case, I pleaded with him not to come out. He was silent. Diego was more dangerous than Miguel. Where Miguel had been vain and focused only on glory, Diego understood how to manipulate and gain advantage. If James came out, I knew Diego would kill me anyway and who knew how many others. Mentally I cursed myself for being so rash to have run down here.

Try to draw him in to you. James' strained voice finally spoke in my head. I misread his suggestion as wanting me to sacrifice myself. I would have willingly for any one of them, but that *he* was asking knifed through me. *Draw him to you so that you have him within range, then strike. You will have a moment when her arms loosen and you can get free. Use your speed and get away.*

Relieved, I did as I was told. "You're right." I let my head hang forward, peering up at him through my hair feeling the sharp points of my collarbone dig into my skin. Diego was watching me closely. "He doesn't want me." Glancing around us, I whispered and met his suspicious glare, "That's why I'll give him to you."

For a very long couple of seconds he watched me considering my sincerity. Finally, I saw him make up his mind and he stepped forward until he was less than three feet from me. His eyebrows went up and I knew it was expected that I speak.

"James doesn't want me now that I can no longer satisfy his hunger." I let some of the pain and anger I felt at myself for letting Lucas control me flow into my voice, helping me to sound more convincing. "I came here to find you. I can't go back to the Court, and I'm too young to be alone. I need someone strong to protect me, I came to seek a place with you." Shooting a glance at Brigit staring at me with a burning fury, her hand no longer holding the healing wound, I saw a tawny form creeping closer to her nearly within range.

Trying to hold their attention, I dropped my voice and saw Brigit even leaned in to listen. "Henry has gone back to Edinburgh to warn the Court of Miguel's treachery. He was going to speak to Anton as soon as he could gain an audience."

Diego whispered back to me, "Why not Miranda? Is he not closer with her?"

Sensing Diego was fishing and was not entirely convinced of Henry's false allegiance, I gave my most convincing performance as a liar to date. "Miranda is weak. She and Charles are too busy with the humans' affairs. They have not taken the time to ally themselves with powerful vampires as Anton has. He is the most formidable of the three and Henry knows it. I fear he will confess your identities and Anton will send out his Guard to dispatch you."

At that, Diego threw back his head and laughed. "Let him tell Anton. We have nothing to fear from him."

I let my eyes widen in feigned shock. "Is Anton *with* you?"

Diego grew bold in my false naiveté. "Anton, myself and several others have long been working together for our cause. We meet tonight to discuss our plans. If you wish to stay, you may do so in the cellar and we can speak afterward about what use you may have in my service." He raised a hand to move the hair back from my face and I took my chance. I could feel that he had no interest save information. Once that was exhausted, he would kill me no matter what he promised.

The blonde's arms had loosened as we had talked, she apparently didn't see me as a threat any longer. Knowing it was most likely going to dislocate my shoulders, I reared my head back and threw it forward with all my might into Diego's nose.

The resulting crunch of bone and rush of blood was satisfying. Even a vampire who has their nose broken is going to have a hard time seeing through the blood and pain.

Predictably, Diego's hands flew to his face and the blonde dropped me. Instantly, I heard the cat behind Brigit hiss to get her attention. The cat leaped onto her and I heard the sounds of her head being worked free of her body. A rush of movement from the church doorway brought me around to watch.

Gabriel was first out in a burst of speed I hadn't thought possible, even for a vampire. He was on Diego and had his silver stake out in gloved hands before I had taken a step, his trench coat swirling around him like wings. Lucas flew over the car in one bound and spun the blonde's head off like it was a top.

In less than a minute it was over, ash was blowing in the light winter breeze. Once I was free, I tried raising my arms and felt the shoulders go back into their sockets. The left collarbone was going to need more time to mend and unfortunately, my left arm was slower and weaker than I would have wanted.

There was not much time to worry. Gabriel's rough baritone rumbled, "Another car. Everyone inside."

We all did as we were told, Gabriel following suit. He righted the front door so it would not be obvious it was broken until one was right up next to it.

The car pulled up and I heard the engine stop. Several sets of feet crunched on the rough, dry ground. Gabriel stood with his eye against the spy hole in the unbroken side of the door. He held up two fingers to indicate how many were there. As one of the cats gathered to move forward, Gabriel held his hand up to stop them.

We heard another car. This one pulled up closer to the building and I heard more feet and voices. Four fingers went up but that wasn't why my heart was pounding. The voices were speaking Russian. Henry conveyed to us that all must be caught or killed. None of this lot could get away. Lucas, standing beside me, nodded his understanding, his levity gone in a moment as he focused his thoughts toward the attack. And yet, he was beautiful and that tiny part of my brain cried out for him.

Guiltily, I darted my eyes toward James. He was standing on the other side with Troy, his hands clenched at his sides and his black eyes staring straight ahead. His lips were tight over his fangs. I could feel the rage radiating from him like heat. Soon he would have a foe to direct all of that misplaced rage at.

The cats were pressing eagerly against our legs, preparing to leap as soon as the doors opened. The smallest stood closest to me and I looked down into Stephen's hazel eyes. Only the pupil was different when he was in cat form. I reached out and petted his cheek. He rubbed his head into my palm and I thought at least I hadn't managed to make *him* mad at me yet today. He sensed my sadness and leaned into my side where

I could better reach his furry shoulder. I stroked it, enjoying the tactile sensation.

A heavily accented Russian voice called out to someone in the other car, "Is Miguel already here?"

The Frenchman responded and my heart leaped in my chest. This was everyone in the picture but Anton. "We are just arrived. Diego and Miguel are both here. I see their cars."

"It does not feel right; it is too quiet," the Russian spoke softly to one of his companions.

Panicking that they would see the damage to Diego's car or some small amount of ash left near the car and get spooked, I tapped Henry on the arm. When he turned toward me, I pointed and indicated we should go out there. He nodded that he was thinking the same thing.

Everyone seemed to be operating along the same lines. I felt the energy of all the vampires shifting, getting ready, and the cats were nearly humming with excitement. When it seemed our little mob was going to explode, Gabriel gripped the broken door and threw it outward following virtually on top of it.

A general cry of alarm went up amongst those milling about outside. Right away, two of the Russians ran away from the church, angling to move up the mountain. I watched two of the cats go after them. One of the Frenchmen ran the other direction, heading down the mountain and I saw Stephen take up the chase, clearing the car in one jump. He was beautiful as his feline form arced over the nose of the car.

That left two Russians and two Frenchmen in the clearing for the five of us. Lucas went straight for the farther car with the Frenchmen. One was a shorter, heavyset male with the typical dark features of his presumably native land. The other was more slight and short, maybe 5'9" if that.

Lucas' long legs covered a lot of ground. When he reached them, his hands were a blur. Like Gabriel, he had a longer coat which held a silver stake hidden in an inner pocket. Lucas had on gloves and reached inside his coat to pull the stake out as he ran. The heavyset male was the first to be impaled.

The second was the stronger of the two. He was able to land several blows on Lucas, one even made him stumble backward a step. Lucas dropped the stake and exchanged several more blows with the slight fellow. He was taller and had a longer reach and used it to his advantage.

Lucas' right arm shot out and his hand wrapped around the Frenchman's neck. He squeezed and I heard the bones crack before I saw his body go limp. Lucas opened his hand and dropped the body, which fell to the ground without any move to catch himself. Lucas casually walked backward the few yards to his stake and picked it up to finish off his victim.

At the car nearest us, the two Russians proved equally formidable. They both moved with a certainty that comes from military service and being tested in the field. The driver jumped over the car to stand in front of the passenger, solidifying for us who was the boss and who was security.

Driver was tall, over six feet of solid muscle. His neck was as thick as my thigh and biceps strained his suit coat when he was at rest. I was sure that when he fought the jacket would be done.

The boss, Gregor I was guessing, was more normally sized, standing just under six feet and athletically muscled. His icy pale blue eyes stopped me cold. There was nothing human left behind them. James had often talked about how vampires could lose their humanity, especially as they age and lose their ties to their human lives. This man had lost that long ago. The only thing I saw in his eyes was his cold assessment of our threat level, formulating his plan of attack.

I didn't think for a minute he would try to help Driver and I think Driver knew it. He was strictly muscle and was expected to fight and defend; it would not be a two-way street.

Gabriel ran toward Driver and their bodies collided with a bone jarring crash. Driver swung a hand forward, lightning quick, striking Gabriel in the throat. Gabriel flew backward. If he had needed his windpipe, he would be dead. He didn't. He leapt up and wasted no time, in one fluid motion driving the stake through Driver's body as he leaned over him. The ashes were starting to blow when Henry moved forward.

"Henry, old friend, it is good to see you have not entirely lost your teeth." He held up his hands. "So this is how we end? As enemies?" Although his tone was friendly, his cold expression did not change.

"You chose this when you decided to ignore the rules," Henry replied coolly. His hands rested loosely by his sides, though I noticed he stood on the balls of his feet, ready to lunge at a second's notice.

"Rules?" Gregor spat, showing the first hint of emotion. "Living a life of restraint, constantly having to hide what we are, protecting our 'secrecy' from an inferior race?" He sneered. "Those are not rules, those are shackles we put on ourselves and for what purpose, so that *they* do not hunt *us*? I say let them hunt us." His hands slapped and bounced off his chest. "Let them come. Some of us will perish, but many more of *them* will die. We will assume our place as master and they of slave. Their role will be to serve us, to please us and to feed us. Only our *weakest* see it any other way." He had come forward as he spoke and with the last word, he backhanded Henry hard.

I was shocked *anyone* would dare strike Henry. The blow knocked him to the ground. Henry was instantly on his feet, so quickly I wondered if I had really seen it at all.

Thinking of the danger we all faced from this one vampire, I became aware James was nowhere in sight. Somewhere in the midst of the action James had slipped away. Trying to control my rising alarm, I called out to him.

James.

Nothing.

James. I tried to keep the panic out of my mind as I felt nothing but emptiness. I was used to feeling him always somewhere in my mind, but he'd shut me out. It was like not being able to feel my own leg. I was off balance without him.

James! My eyes scanned the darkness, searching for movement while my mind reached for him. I kept bumping into the solid nothingness he was projecting. A sickening sense blossomed in the back of my mind. Had I gone too far with Lucas? Of all people, he knew what was in my mind. What Lucas did was not *me*, it was a spell that I couldn't control yet. I resolved to find a way to get him out of my head for good as soon as we were through this.

Henry and Gregor were getting louder. "Gregor you sound like your puppet, Miguel. Are you the one who has filled his head with such propaganda? Is this entire revolution your doing? You've certainly done it before."

Gregor's eyes widened, his fangs out. "Propaganda? Do you doubt the truth of my words? Do not tell me you do not long for the days when we were free to raid the humans, taking what we wanted, burning the rest. Was it not exhilarating to flex your muscles against the humans, to watch them beg?" His gaze turned inquisitive, "Do not stand there and pretend not to want to again taste the blood of a young maiden, pure and sweet while she struggles against you and you drink her dry."

I was riveted, watching Henry with new eyes as Gregor reminisced about their "good old days." James had said each vampire had his own preferred flavor of human. I guess Henry's was young female virgins. How wrong my first impression of him as a gentle soul had been. Was his real reason for working at the college really a penance? Was he now devoted to protecting the very women he would once have preyed upon?

"I no longer drink from the living Gregor. I have paid dearly for my sins to make amends for the wrongs I have committed." Henry's words were heavy with regret.

Gregor laughed, it was a bitter sound. "Yes, I heard you were caught by the old Court. What was your penalty? Time in a box? *That* was enough to break your spirit?"

Henry's tone was sharper, his emotions starting to bubble up through the cracks in his control. "I spent twenty years in chains, my only reprieve was in a box when the silver cut me deeply enough they worried I would die." He pulled up the cuff of one sleeve to show Gregor his scars.

I gasped in shock. From the back, I could see the top of Henry's wrist. It was silver and shiny with scar tissue. The band was the width of my hand, the scars irregular and patchy. It barely covered his muscles, having the appearance of a burn victim's lumpy and partially healed flesh.

As Gregor studied the damage he stepped forward, closing the gap between them to a mere few feet, I saw James. He was moving slowly, creeping steadily toward Gregor while Henry distracted him.

James was still blocked to me and though I was jubilant that he was okay, seconds later I was again fearful. I prayed he wasn't going to try to grab Gregor. Compared to these two, James was young and inexperienced even if he had been in the Guard.

"Gregor, come with me. We can discuss this with the Court. Certainly there is another way. We do not want a war with humans. Their military alone could destroy us all. It is not worth the price we would pay to destroy their populace." Henry had dropped his hand again and was standing perfectly still, trying to get Gregor to relax his guard. "They will only rebuild as they have done after every other war."

It seemed to be working. Gregor's eyes were cooling, no longer wild with fervor.

All the while, Gabriel had remained motionless, as had Lucas beside the other car. This was Henry's battle and we all knew it. I darted my eyes in James' direction and saw that he was also frozen, waiting.

"My friend, I am tired." He let his exhaustion come through in his features and his voice. "I have been hiding what I am for longer than I can remember. Staying out of sight, moving around when people see that I am not old, only taking enough blood to survive, that is not how I want to spend eternity."

I had never considered it like that. In a way I saw his point and felt sorry for him, for us. That was our lot in this existence. To always be watchful and to always monitor ourselves that we didn't leave the slightest hint of what we truly were and were capable of. How hard would that be after a few centuries, after becoming more powerful than a human feared a vampire could be?

Henry was not to be swayed. "That is exactly how you are asking the humans to live. In constant fear of *us*, of being destroyed if they are discovered. To be hunted for food, to be slaughtered only because of what they are. Is it somehow better if we are the ones wielding the sword if it still slaughters thousands? Is it less morally reprehensible?"

Gregor paused, thoughtful. He considered Henry's face while he pondered this conundrum. Finally, he answered. "If we are doomed to suffer this curse and one *must* be the superior, then I would be among the rulers. It is the way of the world."

"I am sorry to hear that old friend." As he spoke, Henry reached into his pocket and drew a gun.

"Are you going to shoot me?" Gregor gave his friend a patronizing smile.

"Yes, I am." Henry's voice was chilling.

Gregor seemed to realize at the same time as I did that there was something different about this gun. Henry had taken one from inside the church.

My eyes ran to James, wishing I could be holding his hand. Seeing a vampire so old and sad preparing to die was somehow heartbreaking, even though he'd been set to kill us all moments ago.

Henry's hand did not shake or twitch as he raised the gun from his side and leveled it at his old friend's chest.

To his credit, Gregor did not beg or make any false promises. His face merely held a heartrending, resigned sadness and he spoke one final time. "We did have some good times together, my friend."

"Yes, we did." Henry said and shot Gregor three times in the chest.

We all watched Gregor fall, morbidly curious what the silver bullets would do when they pierced a vampire's flesh. He was dead before the last bullet went in. It was not a whole body of flesh and bone that fell, but a cascading waterfall of ash by the time it touched the sand and rock beneath it.

There was no celebration at our victory. No one smiled or cheered at the defeat of several of the masterminds of one of the deadliest and most successful warmongering organizations in the recent history of vampires. Gregor's final speech struck a chord with everyone there, even the cats.

Gregor may have been going about it all wrong but I understood a little better *why* the other side was willing to risk everything and cause so much devastation to both sides. Their unwillingness to live secretly and to hide everything different about themselves was understandable. Being a vampire takes beings who, at their core, are human. It forces them to live separately from the rest of the world, unable to form any meaningful bonds with others who are still in touch with their human side except in rare instances. The end result is the same as a life in solitary confinement. Psychosis, loss of humanity, and perpetual loneliness are all par for the course.

Lucas stood beside me, staring at Gregor's ashes, and I felt him starting to pull at me with his enchantment still imbedded in my brain from when he put it in my human head. There was no question in my mind what he wanted to do. He was hoping to lure me away from here as he had tried to do since we'd met.

Some other woman might have been honored that such an ancient and beautiful vampire wanted her, not me. Here we stood among all of this destruction and I was empathizing with my enemy while Lucas decided he wanted to take me from my chosen mate by messing with my head. It pissed me off.

The answer to my problem came to me in that moment. I could still channel. Claire couldn't refuse Lucas, but James could. Trying hard to battle the effects of Lucas' pull, I looked up to find James. He stood across from me and I called out to him in my head.

When I called, he met my eyes over the ashes. He was no longer angry, he had an expression I hadn't expected. It was a deep sadness. His eyes were so light, they were hard to see in this light and his fangs were retracted, his face was lined with exhaustion. When he felt me call, he merely stared and let me in.

Can you help me?

Why? He was hiding something from me. I thought it might be his reaction to Gregor's words, I could see how they would bother him.

Lucas is calling me. I figured he would understand what I was saying.

He was trying to stay out of my head, I felt him pulling away. *Then go. I will not hold you against your will but don't expect me to give my blessing. I have already given him everything.*

What? Now I understood his mood and attempts to ignore me. *I don't want to go with him. You've never felt his "pull" firsthand have you?*

He met my gaze, his brows furrowing as he thought about what I was saying. *No, he has never cast his enchantment on me.*

James continued to block me. Lucas' hand brushed across my shoulder and his touch strengthened his pull on me. I closed my eyes and clenched my fists, concentrating on fighting his allure working its magick in my head.

You can help me fight this off if you let me tap in to you. My resistance doesn't work against him. To clarify my urgency, I sent him a strong thump instead of my usual gentle tickle.

He jumped and I saw a spark in his eyes. Lucas chose that moment to grab the back of my neck and turn me to face him. He was so bold he was going to try to assert himself by forcing me to look in his eyes not five yards from my husband. As enraged as I was, I was unable to control my body. It leaned in to Lucas as he pulled me up against him.

James' block dropped like an anchor. He knew what I needed and sent me a direct link to a very real and very cold hatred he had been chewing on for a while.

Thank you. The relief I felt at his engagement left me giddy, confident I would finally be able to repel Lucas and his pompous efforts to control me.

I let Lucas bring his face down to me, his eyes locking onto mine to take away the last of my resistance, conscious now of several sets of eyes that had picked up on what Lucas was doing and were watching to see what was going to happen.When Lucas' lips touched mine, I opened my mouth as if to accept his kiss and bit down hard on his lower lip.

Lucas shoved me backward and clamped one hand on his mouth to staunch the flow of blood now streaming down his chin. When he shoved me, Lucas happened to plant his hand on my broken collarbone. The white hot iron of pain that lanced through me when the bones were pushed in was unbearable. I groaned.

James' reaction was instant. He lunged forward to catch me as I fell backward, setting me gently on my butt on the ground. In the next instant, he was up in front of me, guarding me from someone very capable of killing him. I tried to reach up to grab his hand and stop him from getting himself hurt. He let me take his hand yet he did not break eye contact with Lucas.

Lucas' eyes were an intensely bright shade of green and his fangs were out. The blood on his lip had stopped, but not before staining his white chin. I could feel the gathering power like electricity in the air before a lightning storm. Just when it was about to break, Gabriel's voice cracked out.

"Lucas, that is enough."

Lucas broke eye contact with James and stared instead at Gabriel who had moved to stand beside James.

Gabriel was not frightened by his partner's glare. "You know you are not to interfere with these two and yet you continue to do so. Are you so bored that you would like to spend a year in a coffin?"

Lucas' cascading white hair shook with the shudder that ran through his long, willowy body. That subconscious part of my brain Lucas controlled admired the way his body moved when he shook.

A jolt ran through my head like a slap. *I have my limits.*

Sorry, I felt the embarrassment flow through me.

Thank you. His interruption was exactly what I needed to break away from Lucas' spell. Already elated at the return of James to my thoughts, the removal of Lucas' power over me made me a little drunk. It was nearly enough to wipe away the pain radiating outward from my shoulder.

Gabriel had stepped aside to make an opening for me as he extended a hand. I took it and let him pull me up with my good arm. Not one for gushing, Gabriel nodded curtly and turned back to Lucas.

"Our work here is done and Miranda is still in danger. We will return to our duties in Edinburgh." He twisted his head to see Henry and spoke clearly so that all of us could hear. "Our services are required in Edinburgh as are yours. Our

287

last target is not to be discounted because he is only one, he will be backed by more who remain loyal to their cause."

Ch. 45

By the time we got back to the condo, the Andrews clan was exhausted and collapsed to sleep until we needed to make our flight. The only one we could get on, even with Henry's connection with the airlines was not until late that afternoon. It was the beginning of spring break season, the man with the airlines explained. Loads of students and groups are traveling from mid February through mid April.

Although frustrating, we wouldn't be missing a lot. Miranda wasn't going to be at Court until later in the evening. Our reports said Amani had not been seen since Miguel gave her her orders. Maybe she was scared, I hoped. Given what I knew of Amani, I highly doubted that. She was most likely waiting until it was time to make an appearance.

James and I both showered to get all of the dust and ash off of ourselves. The ash was as disturbing to me as being covered in someone's blood, another experience I hadn't had until intertwining my life with James.

When we were dressed and feeling human, well, clean anyway, we both grabbed a drink and sat down in the living room. Henry was in his office, I would guess. He always disappeared in there. I wondered what he did.

Do you remember what Gregor said about Henry's past?

I would never forget. *Yes. It's hard to think of him like that. That he would do those things.*

James stared out the large windows overlooking the city, his face blank. His voice however, was heavy. *Henry is very old. With age, as you might imagine, comes boredom. Some of us do things that we never would have done as human beings just to feel alive, to try to feel* something. *Henry was no different.*

He and Gregor knew each other long ago and wandered throughout Europe and the steppes of Russia, fulfilling their lust for blood and trying to rekindle some sort of joy in their existences. As was to be expected, nothing they tried worked and they continued to escalate until they were out of control. They were brought in for their crimes and somehow Gregor got off. Henry was not so lucky and his punishment was severe. James let what he had said sink in.

From what I had heard, most vampires got a little crazy with being locked in a coffin. That was why a year inside one was considered a terrible punishment. Besides the constant torture of thirst, there was the isolation with no relief. Again, no sleep to give them reprieve, only a constant waking hell to suffer alone. Henry's had been mixed with the pain and paralysis of silver.

Exactly, James answered my thoughts. *Most vampires go crazy from a punishment like that, but not Henry. It turned him around. Instead of coming out more angry and needing to be put down, he came out repentant. Henry has spent the last six hundred years trying to right his wrongs. He has been able to stop a good many of the wars initiated by vampires in the Western world in that time. For that, he has earned the respect of this Court and that is why Miranda looked to him to replace her when she stepped down those three centuries ago. Henry's cool head has made him an anomaly among us.*

No wonder you remain with him. You were lucky to have him as a sire. We both were. That and he's the father you never had. I rubbed the back of his neck, knowing he found comfort in it. His mother had done it when he was a child. *I'm glad he found you.* I thought of him being lost and wild after being turned so horrifically.

James turned back to me, his eyes dark. I could feel his love for me and for Henry. The combination of seeing it and feeling it was amazing. It was rapidly flooding my senses, threatening to overwhelm.

With a creeping sense of dread, I realized this was becoming a repeat of my human life before I knew how to shield myself. Of course James felt it too and the depth of my fear. Wisely, he chose to speak out loud instead of using our suddenly uncomfortable connection. "Claire," he tried to get my attention.

I was busy panicking, trying in vain to throw up shields that were proving ineffective against the bond in our heads.

"Claire," he put his hand on my arm.

This time I heard him and realized it was outside my head, not within. By increments I tried to bring myself back. "It keeps coming back. Every time I think I have it beat, my cursed ability comes back." The fear was starting to build into anger. As a human I had been afraid that I was heading for a lifetime of madness, now I was terrified it was going to be an eternity.

His hand gripped my arm more tightly, the sensation grounding me. "Claire, we work with other newly turned vampires teaching them this very thing. I've done you a disservice by not teaching you sooner and I apologize. We're starting right now."

Hope fluttered in my breast and I remembered he *had* been able to shut me out several times that very night. So busy had I been worrying about him and everyone else as well as fighting bad guys that I hadn't realized what it meant. We *could* block each other out if we needed to.

"When I was trying to reach you last night and you weren't answering, could you hear me?"

James glanced down, hiding his eyes. "Yes, I could." His voice was gentle and I felt an undercurrent of sadness with it. "I could hear everything you were thinking, including your fascination with Lucas."

"Then you could tell I was fighting it." I felt the need to explain myself. "You should have been able to feel how that wasn't really me."

He was shaking his head. "I didn't get that at all. From my side, the part of your mind he enchanted felt exactly like the rest of you." James looked up at me and I saw the anger sparking behind his dark eyes. "It felt like you *wanted* to be with him, it was such a sure feeling. I couldn't hear it anymore and closed my mind to you." His hand slid down to clasp my hand. "After that, when I felt you try to reach me, I couldn't let you in."

I was offended he had thought I would betray him that way. I knew how I would feel if he left me, I imagined it would be much the same for him. At times I even felt it. As much as I struggled against it sometimes, I knew that I would have to learn to accept that I needed him. It helped that I knew he needed me too.

When I was human I used to wonder what made a marriage successful, maybe that was the key; simply to need each other. Not codependence, but an equal partnership. He and I complimented each other well. That had been the very reason our bond had formed in the first place. His ability rounded out mine and when they connected, so had we. My epiphany soothed a part of me that had been struggling with rationalizing his not necessarily unwelcome, but certainly thorough intrusion into my very soul. I leaned forward and kissed him, throwing my arms around his neck. He kissed me back, having felt what I had finally figured out and come to grips with.

"Okay, I'm ready." This was the last piece of the puzzle. Once I could control this last aspect of my world, I knew I would finally be my own person. The anticipation of sure independence made me eager. I felt myself smiling.

James smiled brightly back, lifting his hand from my side to brush back my hair. He kissed me again.

"Don't try to distract me," I teased. "You can't have this constant window into my world forever. You have to help me shut the blinds occasionally."

He affected a very serious, professorial expression.

"Of course. Then let us begin." He twirled his hands, and ducked his head theatrically. We sat beside each other turning to sit face to face on the couch.

"Do you remember when you first learned to shield?" he asked. "You said you pictured shutting a door. You are going to do the same thing now, only you are going to specifically aim for our connection."

He and I had talked about it before. Our connection stemmed from a specific spot in our heads. When I first tried to use it to call him psychically, I had focused on that spot and concentrated on him. Since then it had grown to such an extent that, like my shields, I didn't consciously reach out to it. When I needed it, it was just there.

Nodding, I closed my eyes to help me focus. I found that spot in my head where James "lived" and pictured a door. I tried to close it, but it didn't work. His "spot" was spilling over into so many parts of me it was hard to separate them. He felt me struggling, "Can I try something?" he asked.

"Yes." It was difficult to keep the frustration out of my voice. Even though I knew James was older and more practiced than I was at this psychic stuff, I had a hard time accepting that he was so much better at it.

James stroked my arm before furrowing his brow in concentration. Right away, I felt him in my head. He was being as respectful of my privacy as possible, his presence only moving into the spot that felt like him. He tightened his lips in consternation upon discovering the overflow problem.

I felt him withdraw temporarily while he decided what to do and studied his face while I waited. His ability to remain so emotionally detached from his work was enviable. He treated each newly turned vampire as a puzzle to be solved and my case was no different, wife or not. Because I worked with him now to train the newly turned vampires, I hoped I too would learn to be more scientific about it. Part of my brain was very analytical, I just had a hard time finding it on occasion.

He snorted and I shuffled my feet self-consciously. "You know, the sooner I can get some privacy the better, smarty pants." I was only half kidding.

Not shifting his focus, James flashed a quick and distracted glimpse of teeth at me. "Working on it." He remained introspective for a few more minutes and then I felt him retreat. When he had completely withdrawn from my head, he blinked and turned his attention to me.

"It's pretty simple." James looked right at me and with a straight face said, "You need to work harder."

"What?" Thinking he was kidding, I waited with half a smile on my face for the punch line to come. He wasn't, it didn't.

"You're used to it being easy and this time it isn't. If you work hard, you'll get it."

"You think I'm not trying hard enough?"

"You asked me to take a look. I am and now I'm merely trying to explain that some things require more work than others. This, being one of those things."

Seriously angry with him now, I committed to blocking him out. My eyes narrowed, body tightened and I leaned in to him while concentrating hard on finding him in my head and kicking him out.

My eyes turned inward and glazed over. In my mind I felt my focal point track directly to him. Not only did I find him, I pushed his overflow into only the one central spot. Once I corralled him, I pictured a door and closed it, hearing nothing but blissful silence in his absence.

"Great job!" He practically cheered, leaning forward to touch my leg. No trace of his previous snobbery.

Still upset with him, I strained backward. "I take it you approve of the new work ethic?"

James grinned shamefaced. "I have found anger to be a fantastic motivator. I hope you're not too upset."

"Has anyone ever told you you can be a real jerk?" I couldn't be too mad. He had indeed taught me to block him. My lips curved despite my best intentions.

He gave me his crooked smile, "Forgiven?"

"Forgiven," I admitted.

Ch. 46

By mid afternoon Henry showed his face. He glided down the hall and I watched him glance surreptitiously around the room before greeting us. I shot James a smile and he gave a very un-vampirelike eye roll. Love of my life, yes but not one to play matchmaker with our friends. I really needed a girl friend for these times. I missed Heidi back home.

As if on cue, a door from down the hall closed softly. Tonya padded into the room. Henry's eyes softened as he caught sight of her before continuing into the kitchen.

James noticed me watching them and squeezed my hand. Contrite, I quickly averted my gaze and shifted in my seat on the couch to face James and turn my back to the kitchen where both of them were hovering.

Any worries I had of interfering were void because just then Stephen came shuffling down the hall. His hair was sticking out at a mess of angles, he bore a strange resemblance to a duck who had been electrocuted.

Rubbing his eyes with the heel of his hand, Stephen yawned. "What time is our flight? Do I have time for breakfast?"

"Dinner, Steph." Tonya raised her voice from the kitchen. "And yes, you do." I thought I could hear a new tension in her tone.

Another door opened in the distance which meant everyone was up. "Should I make breakfast?" Stephen asked, stifling another yawn.

"It's dinner," Troy corrected absently, joining the family. He was not his usual pulled together self. His clothes were rumpled. I assumed he had slept in them and his hair was loose around his face, not in its usual ponytail. "Sure Stephen, what did you have in mind?"

Stephen continued his shuffling to stop at the cupboard next to the stove and open the drawer in the lower unit.

I turned to watch him, curious what he would find in Henry's kitchen to suit his needs. I had been through the kitchen and had not noticed anything beyond blood and some local beers.

The crinkle of paper menus drew my eyes. I couldn't hold back the laughter that burbled upward from my throat. "Take out? That's your idea of making dinner?" I teased.

His grin was infectious and in short order Troy and Tonya were joking around while they tried to decide between Chinese and Indian. Tonya won. Indian was on its way five minutes later.

While they were busy joshing back and forth about what they were going to eat and acting the part of a happy family, James' phone rang and he excused himself from the room. Stephen shuffled sleepily until he reached the arm of the couch and then, very agile and catlike, jumped over it and landed easily on the cushion previously occupied by James. He wrapped his arm around me and I leaned into him, enjoying his warmth.

James was gone for a while. I had honestly been having fun relaxing with everyone and didn't hear him say anything when he came in. But, while I was watching Tonya recline and debate with Troy the health benefits of curry versus garlic, I noticed Henry got up and joined James on the edge of the room.

They spoke in low tones, inaudible to me and I would guess the clan as well. I couldn't hear, so I watched their body language. Henry was exceptionally disturbed. James' entire demeanor was tight as he argued his point with Henry.

My radar was up. I'd never seen James argue with Henry before, and it was never a good thing when either of them was upset. Both of them upset at the same time could only mean trouble. I wasn't the only one who had witnessed the exchange.

Troy spoke up, again assuming the role of head of the clan. "What is it?" He sounded calm although he was carefully studying their expressions from his seat on the piano bench, apparently his favorite perch in the condo.

The argument stopped. Henry glanced up, appraising their onlookers. James quieted without altering his posturing. He was steeling himself for an attack, whether physical or verbal I wasn't sure; either one did not bode well. I wondered what he had found out from that phone call. Whatever it was, he was ready to go up against Henry over it. My sense of foreboding grew with each tense second.

"What is going on? Is it Miranda?" Troy pushed.

Everyone in the room was riveted on the source of the drama. Henry had grown still, his quiet stubbornness emanating from him. He was not going to speak. I hung my hopes on my husband.

"James?" I disliked the hesitation I heard in my voice and didn't know how much more danger we could have thrown at us at this point.

He spoke directly to me at first. "I've just gotten a call from Indira's human servant, Kara. She is an interpreter specializing in Farsi. She was following a lead Indira had picked up in her research on Nightshade before she was killed. Kara had gotten herself attached to a delegation from Iraq visiting local energy consultants at the University. They have a few vampires among them and she heard them mentioning one of our legends."

Henry snorted, his lips curled into a sneer. "It is a legend, nothing more."

"Do not discount the legends of your kind. We have many within our own culture and they have often been found to be based in reality," Tonya chastised Henry.

He didn't back down. "Our legends are just that. The Court is responsible for most of them from our very beginning to give us some common beliefs and loyalty to our central government. This one is no different. Lilith has no progeny. She was our originator, she was powerful and she was killed. That is where the story ends." Henry was in rare form. His eyes were black and he was visibly upset.

For as much as he was arguing to the contrary, this legend had him spooked.

James raised his brows at me. "Have you ever heard of Lilith?"

"A little, I don't remember it being bad." I took a guess gauging from Henry's reaction.

Stephen answered from the edge of the kitchen where he was leaning against the pillar between our two rooms. "It's from the Old Testament. Lilith was Adam's first wife. God created her first except she wouldn't let Adam order her around so she was cast out and God created Eve from Adam's rib figuring that would make her subservient."

"She's biblical?" I asked thinking of the ramifications of bible stories being true when Henry cut in rudely.

"Human stories based on fear and local lore written several hundred years after it all allegedly happened does not constitute fact. Most of those stories originated much as your urban legends. A person alleges they knew someone who bore witness to the events. Over time, they were embellished even further and finally were captured in writing. From there, the Catholic Church chose which to canonize, thereby making them 'historical documents.' I find the whole thing laughable."

"How do you know what's true and what isn't?"

Troy interjected making me curious of his religious views. "Archaeologists have found evidence that there was a man named Jesus who lived around the time the biblical texts reference. Maybe he wasn't the son of God as he declared, but he *was* a prophet and people followed him. Lilith might have been a woman from that time."

"You mean a vampire," James stated flatly.

My mouth fell open. "Adam's first wife was a vampire?"

He nodded, "She was the first of our kind. According to legend Adam was the first human, she was the first vampire. When God discovered the two could not live together without one destroying the other, he was faced with a decision. He cared for them both and could not bring himself to destroy either one. Instead, he opted to cast Lilith out of the Garden and forced her to prey upon the lesser creatures. She was displeased with him not only for his rejection, but for making her settle for the blood of animals when she truly craved the human blood she had only tasted once from Adam. *He* was the forbidden fruit, not the apple.

From that time forward she vowed to be a plague upon humanity, preying especially upon the children she was denied. The Jews had talismans they hung on birthing beds and cradles to keep her away. When children woke in the night with nightmares, it was said to be Lilith calling to them."

"She was a boogeyman, meant to explain away humans' fear of the night and why vampires lust for human blood only." Henry dismissed with a wave of his hand, his brows furrowed. As if to explain how ludicrous it all was, he added,

"They even blamed men's nocturnal emissions and adultery upon her, saying she would seduce men in their sleep to get them to impregnate her. Of course they couldn't because our kind cannot produce nor carry children. The whole thing is ridiculous, full of holes."

"What happened to her?" I wanted to hear the rest, legend or not it was fascinating.

"She continued through the ages to kill humans and children indiscriminately until finally the humans captured her around the time of Christ and crucified her." He nodded at my shocked gasp. "Then they staked her. The Inquisition, in the beginning, was all about hunting vampires. Humans wanted to eliminate anything like her. She had put such a fear in them, they went overboard trying to root out any of her children." He paused and let that sink in. "Quite a few of our kind were captured back then. All of those awful tortures the humans associate with the later centuries of the Inquisition, they were all attempts to kill vampires. They weren't happy with just the one option." James' mouth set in a hard line. "They tried to drown us, break our bones on the rack, the Iron Maiden; all failed until finally they found fire. It was more dramatic than staking apparently. Most of the vampires caught thereafter were burned at the stake and the humans were elated.

They thought they had defeated their greatest predator and no longer had to fear the night. They were wrong. Lilith had discovered the way to get a child was not to give birth, but to exchange blood and venom. She had created a son who had gone on to help her create more children and so on until our numbers were many. The legend says he was witness to her death and swore to avenge her against humanity. He went underground after her death and no one has seen him since. There are only the stories," James finished. The room was silent.

Stephen was the first to speak. "So this Kara person heard some Iraqi oilmen telling Lilith stories in a city flush with vampires and you two are ready to tear into each other?"

"No," James answered. "They aren't here for oil, they're here for a figurehead for their movement."

"What? I thought they were going with Miguel the puppet as their fearless leader," Stephen quipped.

"Apparently it was Miguel's idea; sort of an 'I can speak to God' thing," James explained. "He figures it would cement his place so no one could kill him off." He smirked, "Sounds like Miguel wasn't so oblivious after all. So they're trying to find Lilith's son and rumor has it he is in Edinburgh."

"Henry," Tonya spoke softly to him. "Why does it upset you? Even if it's true, wouldn't it be nice to know? So few of our creation myths can be proven or disproven. I would think you would want to know the truth of how you came to be."

Henry was unnecessarily harsh, "I do not need to know where I come from to be content. My burden is one that I will carry forever whether I was created by disease, a slighted son, or God himself." His eyes lightened and he exposed a fleeting glimpse of his softer side. "It does not make torture any less painful if one knows the methods being used. Sometimes it makes it worse." With that, he removed himself from the room, retreating to his office.

We were all quiet and heard his door shut softly. Troy was the first to speak and if I hadn't already been floored by what I had just heard, his words would have done it.

"Tonya, why don't you go see if you can talk to him?" She stared at him, equally shocked.

"We need his political clout and savvy to know how to go on from here." Troy shot an apologetic glance at James. "No offense."

James shrugged his shoulders. "None taken. You're right. My credit with the Court has its limits."

Without further encouragement, Tonya slid off her perch and glided silently down the hall.

The rest of us were left to stare at each other and try to figure out what it meant that now we were facing a myth as well as a coup.

"Hey," I had an idea. "Do we have time to stop at Helios when we get to Edinburgh? He might have books with some more background on the legends. If it's based in reality, maybe there's some truth to some of the literature. We might be able to find out more about him, like how old he is or some hint that could help us to identify him if and when we do meet him."

James was nodding and I saw that Stephen and Troy agreed as well. Stephen growled out, "I would love to get my hands on that daughter of his. She sounds like a real piece of work."

His protectiveness was flattering. James stiffened and I saw him wrestling with himself over his need to be my sole protector.

We've talked about this, you don't have to be so protective now that I am not so breakable.

I know that, but you are mine and I will protect you without his help.

I bristled at his reference to my belonging to him. I tried to appeal to him on another level. *You know he's thinking of*

303

leaving because he doesn't want to watch everyone else being so happy and lovey anymore. He already feels like he's alone.

He is?

Mmm hmm.

He looked pensive when I glanced over at him, his eyes down and brow furrowed. I felt him close the door between us and left him alone in his thoughts.

Ch. 47

The shop was our first stop upon arriving in town. Henry and Tonya went on ahead to the flat. Troy made an excuse for why he needed to take a cab to wherever, leaving the rest of us to go straight to the bookshop.

The golden letters on the bold red paint on the shop's front was so cheery I couldn't help smiling. I went in first, James and Stephen both flanking me. I had an image of them elbowing each other, jockeying for position and had to choke back a giggle.

When the little bell above the door chimed, Alan popped up from behind the counter.

"Claire, James! How are you? I hear congratulations are in order." He came around to shake James' hand. His grey hair was in its usual disheveled state and he was again wearing his trademark rumpled green turtleneck. What was different were his eyes, there were bags under them and he was pale and drawn like he hadn't slept in days or he'd been sick.

Remembering myself, I introduced Stephen quickly and then asked him what was on my mind. "Alan, are you doing okay?" Leaving out the fact that he looked like absolute hell.

His eyes grew watery, "Davina is missing. She disappeared right after I spoke with you last." Alan's chin quivered and I felt my heart wrench.

He led us into the café at the back of the store. They specialized in vegan foods and had great coffee as I recalled. Davina had run the café when I'd been there last.

"Who's working in the café with her gone?" I didn't see any other employees last time I was here.

Alan was a witch and very active in the magical circles here in Scotland and the UK. James and the other vampires had been aware of his presence and he of theirs though they hadn't officially met until I happened into Alan's shop by coincidence.

It was interesting to me that Alan had not been able to sense Davina's treachery but maybe his divination didn't work that way. Maybe he could only see the end, not the middle.

Either way, now it was up to us to tell him what Davina was up to and I did not look forward to it.

Alan's voice was flat when he answered. "My sister's girl, Fiona." As he said it, we reached the café and I saw Fiona. "Four coffees please, Fiona," he ordered, leading us to the largest of the five tables in the back.

Fiona smiled a sweet smile at Alan and I took the opportunity to size her up. She was a plain girl. Dishwater blonde hair, grey eyes and nondescript features that weren't altogether attractive nor less so either. She was perfectly uneventful. Dropping my shields I felt nothing either, which was strange. Everybody had a feel, even if they were blocking as well, I could always feel *something*. She was watching me closely so I turned away from her with a polite smile, hiding my confusion.

We all sat down at the table and made small talk until Fiona delivered our coffees. We each had a cup in front of us but only two of us were drinking.

"I'm sorry. I didn't think about your, ah, aversion to coffee." Alan stuttered, trying to speak in code.

I glanced quickly at Fiona. She was wiping down the counter, not interested in us at all. "Does she know?"

"No, she knows nothing about any of this," Alan said quickly. "She lives with my sister in a little town north of here with the rest of the family." He stared down into his cup like it was an oracle full of answers for him. "None of them know."

Stephen got right to it. "So, your daughter disappeared, huh?" His voice and posture confrontational. It was odd coming from him. "Was she into anything suspicious?" He stared right at Alan, taking a cautious sip of the steaming coffee.

Alan was silently shaking his head, his eyes tearing up again. I shot a warning look at Stephen, mouthing "be nice" at him. It wasn't Alan's fault his daughter had gone to the dark side and I highly doubted he was in on it unless he was an amazing actor.

James stared at Stephen who arched an eyebrow at him, matching his stern glare. Exasperated, I threw up my hands.

"Oh fine, I'll tell him." I turned to face Alan beside me and started to put a hand on his arm then stopped short not wanting to shock him, he would know soon enough what I was. "Alan, I don't know how to tell you this, but Davina is, um, she's ah." My words failed me after my blustering.

James saved me as usual. "Davina had Claire killed in Minneapolis. She set her up for a meeting with some unfriendlies." He saw Alan catch the hint that his daughter was involved with non-humans, watching him grow pale. James' voice changed, growing deadly calm. "I cannot forgive that easily."

Alan gasped in horror, staring at me. This time I saw the clues add up in his head. I was cool to the touch, pale, not drinking my coffee and I had avoided contact with him when I had hugged him at our last meeting. Most likely I was breathing but I couldn't be sure. I was trying to remember to do that although sometimes I forgot. "Claire, you're a..." He let his words trail off, unable to voice them.

He grudgingly accepted James as an exception to the rule on vampires. He'd been involved with some messy "cleanups" over the years resulting from clashes between vampires and humans that weren't easily forgotten.

Unable to say it out loud, I nodded my head. It struck me this must be what some people felt like when they tell people they're gay. The not knowing how it would be received by someone who professed to care about me was difficult. People can say they are accepting of something until it noses its way into *their* lives. Then, the truth can be painful. I had seen it and felt it a thousand times when I couldn't block out what people around me were feeling. I could hear what they said about being cool with something then I would feel their distaste or discomfort.

Alan reached out, cautiously this time and his fingers hovered over my hand. He met my eyes, hesitant.

"It's okay," I said softly, suddenly afraid he would find me frightening. The courage to experience what he really thought escaped me and I kept my shields up tight for the moment.

His hand slowly lowered. I saw a slight tremor just before his fingers touched the back of my hand.

"Ah." He half sighed, half gasped as my cold skin registered with him. It was cold, not cool because I hadn't eaten since we left Spain. He turned, eyes scanning my face for any changes. "It isn't that obvious," he said in wonder. "You are so beautiful now, but it is still you underneath it."

Alan's words gave me comfort. I felt a tremendous relief that my changed nature didn't immediately stand out to a human who knew me. It gave me hope that I could keep in contact, albeit minimally, with my parents and friends.

All of a sudden it struck me. I was this close to a human and I wasn't thirsting for him, even when I was starving like now. My chest swelled at the prospect. I was already gaining control. I shot an excited smile at James. He didn't seem surprised and grinned back.

When I turned back to Alan, his hand was up near my cheek, fingers outstretched. He was frozen as if caught in the act of doing something wrong. He asked embarrassed, "May I?"

I didn't see why not and said, "Okay."

Alan softly laid his fingers on my cheekbone, stroking down toward my chin. "Fascinating." He mumbled to no one. Becoming aware he had an audience, he grew self-conscious. "Your skin isn't just cold, it is firmer as well. It's human, yet not."

I nodded. It was the same way I had felt about James' skin when I had first touched it. I had found it mesmerizing and could completely understand Alan's interest.

Stephen could not. "Are you not even a little surprised that your daughter forced this upon us? You don't seem even the slightest bit upset." He shot me an apologetic look. "Sorry Claire." He stared at Alan. "We're lucky it's turned out okay but that doesn't undo what *she* did."

Alan stared down dejectedly at his coffee, swirling his cup and watching the brown liquid spin.

"It's okay, Alan. I don't blame you, but we do need to find her before she causes any more damage. Do you have any ideas where she might have gone?"

Alan stared down dejectedly, studying his cup. "I'm sorry, I wish I could help. My daughter has been missing for days and I don't know where she might have gone." He closed his eyes letting his stress thinned shoulders slump.

"What about that boyfriend you were talking about last time we were here?"

"I never met the boy. She only rarely talked about him with me and after I told her not to hang out with him anymore... I know she was with him when she told me she was at a girlfriend's house." Alan's voice shook. "I should have said something, I should have been..." He put a hand over his eyes.

I reached out and stroked his shoulder, watching James and Stephen closely. Stephen's thoughts were obvious. He was thinking he wanted to find Davina and it wasn't going to end well for her. James was more contemplative, maybe he had some ideas as to where a young woman with a penchant for vampires might hang out.

Eager to change the subject, I patted Alan's upper arm.

"Alan, I could really use your help with something. I was hoping to borrow your library."
"Yes, of course." He lowered his hand, wiping at his eyes. "What do you need?"

"I'm looking into a legend. A vampire legend about a woman named Lilith and her son."

Alan blanched and, trying to hide it, took a gulp of his cooling coffee. He took another gulp, buying time. "Let me see what I can find." He pushed back his chair and excused himself. "I'll be right back."

I watched him go, hiding my suspicions until he was out of sight. Stephen was staring intently at Fiona who was busily cleaning a coffee maker, blissfully unaware of our existence by the look of her.

"What are you doing?" I whispered harshly at him.

"What do you mean, what am I doing? I'm trying to figure out what's going on here."

I looked at James for his opinion. He shrugged his shoulders, "I agree with Stephen. Something is not right with her."

"What do you mean?" I looked over my shoulder at Fiona again. She was setting up the now clean coffee pot, contentedly humming softly to herself.

"Her?" I shook my head at him. "Alan's the one holding something back. Did you see him when I mentioned Lilith?"

"He's definitely hiding something," James agreed, also keeping his eyes on the girl behind the counter.

"But something is amiss with her as well."

"You're right on both counts. This guy is broken up for sure and yet he hasn't been looking for her." Stephen raised his eyebrows and put his hands up, questioning. "What girlfriends did he talk to about the phantom boyfriend? Has he tried to call her cell phone? We know she has it on her. Why wouldn't he involve the police? I'm not sure he's telling us everything he knows." He pointed his thumb at Fiona and lowered his voice. "As for her? Your cousin is missing and a group of super hot strangers comes in to talk to her father and you aren't even remotely curious about what they're saying?"

James was watching Stephen, and aside from a snort and a smile at the mention of being hot, was otherwise impressed with Stephen's observations. "You have to admit it makes sense, Claire. Her disappearance was odd but the lack of curiosity here is even weirder."

When they put it like that, I did see their point. There was no *one* thing that jumped out as being wrong, yet I agreed something was definitely wrong. Something none of us could quite put our fingers on.

We didn't have any more time to discuss it, Alan was back. Rather quickly, I thought in passing.

"I believe I've found what you're looking for." Alan held up a large, red leather book triumphantly over his head.

Ch. 48

"Ah, here it is." Alan had his head down over the open book, leafing carefully through its worn pages. He gripped the book gently, lovingly even. It was apparent in the way he handled it and refused to hand it over that he knew it well. He assured us he needed to handle the ancient text and went about searching for what he wanted. Meanwhile, I heard his heart rate increase and I could smell his fear.

"Lilith is rumored to be the first vampire according to legend," Alan summarized. "She was said to be Adam's first wife and grew angry with God, taking out her wrath on humankind when he chose them over vampires to populate this planet." He made a show of scanning the materials with his finger, flipping the page backward and forward before announcing, "I don't see mention of a son or any sort of lineage." Alan closed the book gently and laid his hands on top craning his neck back to look at me, being careful not to look directly into my eyes. He assumed I was far more powerful than I really was but his action, though false, was telling.

"Sorry Claire. I don't think I have what you're looking for in here. Maybe I could check around and find another source. If I do, would you like me to call you?" He raised his eyebrows, trying to be ever so helpful.

"Sure Alan. That would be great," I agreed, straightening up and taking a step back.

Alan used the space to stand up, his hand still on top of the book. "Well, is that all that you needed?" He glanced at his watch. "I do apologize, I have an appointment in an hour."

Recognizing our dismissal, our little group made our way back through the shop. Alan filled the silence by mentioning a book signing he would be having there tomorrow night with a local author and wouldn't we come by. Stephen assured Alan we would *definitely* be back. I fought the urge to smack Stephen.

Alan ushered us out the door, saying his rapid good-byes. We followed his example and the door shut with a faint tinkling of the bell behind us.

As soon as it did, we walked down the sidewalk and turned the corner at the first street a few storefronts up. Stephen was the first to say it aloud, "We have to get back in there. There's something he's hiding and I think it's in that book."

"I know. His heart was pounding, did you hear it?" I asked them both. "Why didn't he just tell us he didn't have anything and send us away? Why show us that book?"

"He knew we weren't leaving without something so he manipulated what we got. It's smart." James tapped a finger against his temple, thinking. "Claire do you remember the door straight through the back of the café? That should lead out the back of the store. One of us needs to get in there and check things out. There's more in there, I'm sure of it."

"I can go back and distract him while one of you runs in. I have a valid excuse, I want to see if he wants that anti-vampire amulet back." I laughed at myself. "I certainly can't wear it now." Fiona would hopefully stay out of the way long enough for one of them to run past her into the shelves of the store.

"Don't hurt Fiona," I cautioned, backtracking to the sidewalk toward the shop. However suspect she might be, she didn't need to get hurt.

James and Stephen both watched me go. Stephen was ready for a fight. I hoped he would not be the one going inside. James was more capable of keeping a level head and taking the situation seriously.

Before I could finish tying myself in complete knots over what might happen, I was at the front door. Pushing it open, I heard the bell and saw Alan's retreating back meandering slowly in the direction of the café.

"Alan," I cried out, stopping him in his tracks.

His body stiffened as though he'd been shot. He turned very slowly, fixing a dull stare on me. His uncharacteristic lack of a spark twisted at my insides. Normally just being in his presence was enough to bring a smile to my face. The man behind these dull eyes bore no resemblance to the man I knew. His heart skipped a beat at the sight of me.

Walking slowly up to him, I held out my hand to touch his arm. "Alan," I spoke hesitantly. "Is there anything you want to tell me? Is there something going on, do you know why Davina disappeared?"

My keen ears picked up the sound of a door closing accompanied by the flash of someone behind Alan going into the shelves.

"Claire," he replied hoarse and defeated. "Claire you need to go home. It isn't safe for you here." He caught my eyes, "Even now."

"Alan, they did this to me at *home*. Do you really think I'm safer there?"

His skin turned grey and he looked like he was going to be sick. I took heart in the fact that it bothered him. I couldn't be that wrong in my prior judgment of his character. His strange behavior was due to something else. It had to be.

His eyes darted around searching for watching stares and he shook his head the tiniest bit. Taking a leap, I lowered my shields enough to feel what was really going on. As I suspected, he was not afraid where his daughter was, only what was going to happen to her. He felt me reach out to him and tried to push me out.

"What are you supposed to do for them to let her go?" I took a guess.

He started to deny it and stopped himself when he saw that it was no use. I had felt his choice and the costly toll it was taking. "That's the problem. She *wants* to be with them. She doesn't see the danger she's in." He was barely whispering.

Leaning in, I whispered back. "Who is 'them' and why are we whispering?" I searched the shop. There weren't any customers nor did I hear anyone except Fiona rattling around in the back.

Alan flicked his eyes her direction.

"Fiona?" I mouthed, eyes open in surprise.

He nodded, frowning. "I don't have a sister. She was left here to wait for you."

I felt that familiar feeling of dread. "By 'them'?"

Again his head moved in confirmation of my question.

"Who are *they*? Have you seen them?" I spoke so quietly he had to lean in. Our heads were less than a foot apart.

"I'm not sure who they are, I haven't seen them because they pass messages through her." He thumbed at the café. "They're your kind, Davina's been following them around since last fall. It was just before you came by with yours. I warned her to stay away from them, but she only hid it from me."

Ignoring the rude reference to James being "mine" I reminded him of something. "Was it about the time that man came in asking about the book you were getting for us? You said he wasn't a vampire, he was maybe a servant."

"Yes, it was about that time." He rolled his head toward the back of the store. "This one is the same. Nothing stands out, you'd forget her in a minute only something isn't quite right. I don't know what she is but she has no destiny, no future. She's blank." He was deeply troubled by that.

I realized *that* was what bothered me about Fiona. She was human, only she wasn't. The nothingness of her was artificial. It was as if who she was had been erased. She was an empty vessel. The vampire who made her had turned her into a virtual robot. The depravity of some of us boggled the mind. I shook my head in disgust.

As if by summons, Fiona walked up behind Alan. When I saw her, a flash of color popped out of the book racks and ran behind them to the back of the store.

"Fiona, hi." I smacked my forehead with the heel of my hand. "I forgot to ask Alan about a chain for something I bought last time I was here." I glanced back at Alan, "So when you can get that chain in, could you call me?" I wrote down my number on a paper bookmark with the store's name out of a basket on the front counter.

"I'll do that, Claire. Thank you for stopping back. It was good to see you again." He leaned in to give me a hug. It was tighter than it needed to be. I thought about asking him what he saw of my destiny, and if it had changed since his last prediction had passed.

Afraid what he might say, I let it go. Better to walk into disaster blind than with false confidence.

I whispered in his ear, "We'll bring her back." He swallowed hard, giving no other outward evidence that he heard me.

"You take care, Alan." I stopped at the door to wave at him. He held up his hand, Fiona staring stiffly from behind him.

Walking out of the store, my legs felt heavy. I reached the alley where we had split up and found James and Stephen waiting impatiently.

Stephen was staring expectantly at me, a book hanging loosely in his hands.

"I think we should get out of here before we say anything else." I glanced around us and up, expecting vampires to drop off the rooftops at any moment.

Catching on to my paranoia, James and Stephen both cast their eyes around, searching. Seeing nothing of any immediate threat, I stepped out onto the street. No taxis were anywhere to be seen.

James stepped up beside me, one arm snaking around my waist and his lips flicked against my ear through my hair. "What are we running from?" It would look like a purely romantic gesture to any onlookers and no one but us could hear.

Stephen scooted up and put in an arm from the other side. "What the hell is going on?"

I kept my head down to hide my face should anyone be looking. My skin was crawling with the feeling that any minute we were going to be set upon.

"Vampires have Davina. Alan's scared and Fiona's not his niece." I felt both bodies react.

James moved out from under me. "Taxi!" He called, raising his hand.

The little blue Renault stopped and James waved me in first, then hopped in quickly behind me. The cabbie twisted his head and gave us a long look. His eyes lingered on me, raking over my body and leaving a filthy stain behind.

James saw it too and angled himself so that his body blocked the cabbie's view of all but my legs, easy in a car that size. Thankfully it was cold and I was wearing jeans. He gave the driver Henry's address and a cold stare.

Cabbie smiled, winking knowingly at Stephen. "All three of you going there?"

Stephen playfully winked at our dirty minded driver who had probably seen us all cuddling close on the sidewalk, giving him fodder for his fantasies. "Yes we are, and boy are we happy we found *her*." He reached around James' back and put a hand on my knee, his other went to James' shoulder. "She's going to work the camera and record our love."

Stephen gave a flirtatious smile to the driver who was so morally offended he didn't look at us or talk to us the rest of the way.

I felt James' body rumbling beside me and feared he was angry but a quick glance at his ducked face gave me a view of crinkled eyes and his face split in laughter. Thank goodness for the driver's radio.

Stephen was just sitting back, looking every bit the cat that ate the canary.

Ch. 49

The shower in the flat was running and Henry was standing in the kitchen, a towel around his waist and a glass in his hand.

Stephen's expression was hard despite his teasing tone. "Finally closed the deal, hey Henry?" Only Stephen could get away with saying that to Henry.

James walked over to the player on the shelf behind the piano digging through the music library without saying a word.

I stood stunned, staring at Henry. He was long and lean, his form as perfect as any Greek statue. His wet brown hair was mussed, I'd only ever seen it slicked neatly back. An easy smile twisted his full lips. The combination was worth a second look.

His physical perfection lay in direct contrast to the network of pale scars crisscrossing his body and I couldn't help staring. His wrists were matched, thinly covered in mottled and uneven skin. There were countless smaller scars marring his chest and what I had seen of his back. They could be from bullets or even knives for all I knew. They all told a story of a violent life, whether that was before turning or after I couldn't know.

Returning from a fruitless music run, James was behind me growling softly in my ear, his arms wrapping around my waist. I saw Henry's smile broaden before I got the hint and blinked, averting my eyes.

"We have an appointment with Miranda at midnight. She has some other business to attend before she can slip away and meet us here. I trust you can take care of yourselves until then." Henry finished his drink and set his glass in the sink before striding back down the hall. The sound of the shower got louder for a matter of seconds when he opened the door then was muffled again when it closed.

James moved back to the piano to plink at it. I tried to focus on the notes he was playing and couldn't. Stephen opened the fridge, in search of leftovers most likely.

"Am I the only one uncomfortable being here right now?" I asked, trying hard to ignore what was happening behind closed doors. I could smell that Troy wasn't here. Maybe that was why he went off by himself when we arrived. I wish he would have told me, I might have gone with him.

Stephen's acerbic reply came as a shock. "Some of us have had to get used to it. We live in a virtual commune."

"Stephen, I'm so sorry. I never thought..." No wonder he stayed out whenever possible.

He shot me a look of disbelief, "You really never thought about that one?" He rolled his eyes, shook his head and stuck it back in the fridge.

James started playing the piano. I recognized the tune "Crack the Shutters." Despite my rising irritation with Stephen, I felt a smile twitching at the corner of my mouth. A disgusted sound emanated from the kitchen and some glass jars clinked together hard while he rummaged. The song was about a couple. In bed.

"Does anyone know what happened to Troy? He was in a big hurry to get going after we landed," James asked, having stopped playing and spun to face us. "He might want to be around when we meet with Miranda."

Stephen stood up, having found success in the form of pizza in the freezer. Thoughtful for a moment, pizza still in hand, he finally shook his head and shrugged his shoulders. "No. I don't think so."

"I assume it has something to do with this." I gestured with a thumb back down the hall toward the source of noises our hearing couldn't miss. "Maybe he knew once he gave Tonya a green light, this would happen."

"He's known it was coming to this for a while now whether he blessed it or not." Stephen turned back from starting the oven. "It was merely a matter of time. The only reason it's taken this long is Henry and Troy have a mutual respect for each other and Tonya couldn't defy Troy without punishment."

I watched him, waiting for him to go on. When he didn't, I prompted him. "Why would Troy need to punish her?"

"Clan rules. The Clan's success depends upon a hierarchy like a lion pride. We are a different cat but the rules are the same for us." He poured himself a glass of water and took a drink before continuing. "The Council encourages it so that we can keep each other in check and they have fewer incidences of rogue weres they have to handle. They're pretty hands off in case you haven't noticed."

I had indeed noticed that. Whereas the vampire's Court was involved in a number of their activities, the wereanimal Council was only involved when absolutely necessary.

"Stephen, why don't you call Troy and let him know Miranda will be here around midnight," James requested.

He pulled his phone from his pocket and dialed without comment. I recognized Troy's recorded voice on the other end before Stephen left him a message. Stephen hung up and flicked his eyes up at James. "Done."

"Now what do we do for the next," I glanced at the clock, "four hours or so?" Feeling incredibly sensitive to Stephen, I decided against my first idea for killing time with James.

322

"We could go out looking for Davina," James suggested. "It's dark. Stephen could certainly lend a paw if he wanted." They made eye contact and held it briefly before James looked to me. "Or we could take a look at that." He pointed at the book we had taken from Alan lying on the kitchen counter.

"I like the idea of staying in," I affirmed. "I don't think we should do anything right now with the city overrun with conspiracy and evil ancients possibly out there somewhere." My nerves were already frazzled, I didn't think I could handle another night of tracking bad guys.

"That sounds good to me." James rose and glided across the room to retrieve the book, returning to sit beside me on the couch. He slid the book over onto my lap. I cracked it and started perusing the contents. Alan would have known he had this book and it was far more thorough than the one he'd shown us. According to the index there were quite a few pages on Lilith; her legendary son was mentioned in a number of places as well.

Turning to the first mention, I started to read about him. There was some confusion in the stories between Lilith and her son and which one exactly terrorized which population during different periods, though it was clear they were both excessively cruel.

No one knew exactly when or where he was "born" although his insane rage at humankind had been seen throughout the world since his mother's death. He had hunted extensively in the Middle East, causing the nomadic tribesmen in several regions to go to war with their neighbors for fear the son was among them.

In Europe, he was credited with causing several revolutions, bringing down two empires and being the cause of a number of mass emigrations. Operating mostly at night, he had inspired many popular stories told through the ages for the express purpose of keeping people inside during the dangerous hours of darkness. Characters such as wolves, witches, and goblins were said to have arisen out of humankind's collective subconscious fear of the night and the unknown. Seeing the evidence of Lilith's son's atrocities, I could see why we all had the same basic fears regardless of where or how we were raised.

I became aware of Stephen chewing a piece of pizza over my shoulder as I neared the end of the section.

"Wow," he said around a mouthful of food. "This guy and his mom were the original nightmare."

"Mm hmm," I agreed absentmindedly. Alan's unwillingness to share what he certainly had known and Davina's disappearance came together in my head. "Oh my gosh! What if Anton knows him? What if he knows Lilith's son and this is all for him? The war and everything?" I waited to hear their thoughts. Personally, I was terrified at the prospect that we had wiped out most of his middle management, leaving us a clear path between him and us.

Stephen's eyes grew wide and I heard his heart slam in his chest, moving back into the kitchen to grab a beer from the fridge. He wasn't a big drinker, although given the circumstances I envied him a little buzz. Maybe I could convince him to get drunk and I could just take a little taste. That was a small detail I had learned by accident once when James needed an emergency transfusion after I had imbibed.

Left alone, I watched James. He was staring right through me. His thoughts turned inward and face blank. I was guessing he was running the evidence through his own mind, checking to see if he could come up with anything different. I hoped he would.

When he reanimated, James glanced over toward the hall and stood without a word.

I heard a soft knock on the bathroom door and James and Henry mumble a quick exchange. The door closed again and I heard the rumblings of a second exchange before the water shut off. The ramifications of this possibility were stupefying. If we were right, Miranda was in worse danger than we'd thought. I wondered if Miguel's people had passed along their realization that I was not dead. If they really still wanted me, I could use that to draw them out.

Quickly, before he could detect my thought train, I sealed up the door between James and I in my head. He felt it, as always. Any time either of us "touched" the bond, it was similar to a fish tugging on a line. There was no stealthy way around it. However, if it was sealed, nothing else could come through.

He eyed me suspiciously when he re-entered the room, we lacked the privacy he wanted to discuss it. I averted my gaze from him and settled into the couch, crossing my legs and leaving no question that here I would remain. I imagined I felt his displeasure emanating from him. Not certain how I was going to do it, I was determined not to be alone with James before Miranda's arrival. I was trying to look anywhere except at him when the buzzer from downstairs made me jump.

I looked up to see Stephen moving toward the intercom on the wall. It buzzed again, twice in rapid succession. Stephen jogged the last few feet and hit the button.

"Hello?" He was calmer than I would have been.

"Let me in, Stephen." Troy was breathless and something else that heightened the strain in the room; Troy was scared.

Stephen hurriedly buzzed him in and ran out the door while the rest of us waited. There was a flurry of doors opening and closing down the hall and I knew Henry and Tonya were

325

getting dressed in a hurry. They must have heard Troy and it sped them along.

Taking a chance, I gazed up at James. He was visibly agitated. At first I thought it was due to Troy's arrival but from the way he was staring at me, brow furrowed and eyes dark as midnight I knew it was because I wouldn't "talk" to him. I disengaged without saying anything. He knew I was up to something and he didn't like it.

The front door opened and Troy staggered in, exhausted and naked. He must have run in his cat form. Stephen was right behind him carrying a bag in his hand and a pained expression on his face.

Henry walked in from the other direction just after the front door closed. Even disheveled as he was, with wet hair and a sweatshirt and jeans, he controlled the room upon entry.

"Troy, what's happened?"

Troy stood, wobbly legged, and Stephen streaked past us down the hall, presumably to fetch Troy something to wear. It was hard to ignore Troy's naked form standing less than ten feet from me. Instead, I tried to focus on his face. The wear I saw there astounded me. We had parted ways only hours ago and he was as fresh as any of us. Now he looked years older and his eyes were drooping with a need for sleep.

Stephen returned with sport shorts and a long sleeved tee. Not a bit self-conscious, Troy dressed on the spot. I, at least, felt some relief having his body covered. There were very few unattractive supernatural beings in my world, though I had met some. These few I had seen naked were not among them, except one. Shuddering, I quashed the memory of Gaston before it could fully surface.

Once dressed, Troy sank down in the chair, closing his eyes with an exhausted sigh. I had grown used to the silence when finally he spoke.

"I was going to meet an old friend in Glasgow. She had some information for me and I didn't want to wait until she brought it over in the morning. The timing seemed fortuitous." Troy kept his eyes closed and his voice was soft. "It was dark when we got in so I changed and ran, figuring it would be faster than a car. It didn't take me long to get there at all." Troy opened his haunted eyes. "Someone had beaten me there. She was still warm to the touch. I had only just started to sniff around, looking for what they wanted, when I heard them and followed their voice; they were speaking some language I didn't recognize." Troy stared up at the ceiling. "I saw them sitting at her computer; on the screen was the research she was doing for me. She had Henry's address in her email and her phone was next to the computer." His voice was pained. "I had to assume they'd found my text. It wouldn't be hard for her to find us here." Troy finally looked down, choosing to focus on Tonya standing at the edge of the room. "They could have been the Iraqi contingent Kara told you about, one was a vampire. I couldn't risk it, so I took care of all three. I don't know if they were the only ones or if they had friends outside."

Tonya crossed the room to sit on the arm of the chair. Her voice was soothing as she stroked his hair. I had a flash of a cat grooming her young to comfort him. "Was it Rachel?" She kissed his head when he let out a ragged groan and leaned forward to put his head in his hands.

By way of explanation, she spoke to us for Troy. "Rachel was someone from our past. She loved Troy and would have done anything for him." Tonya leaned in toward Troy, still cradling his head. "What did she have for you? What was she working on?"

"Talking about legends got me thinking. I had her looking into a legend of ours. It originated with the Winnebago tribe. The legend describes a young boy who befriends a cougar that helps him in battle and blesses his life so long as he says a prayer and calls on the cougar before going forth into battle. The only thing the cougar asks is that he can feast upon the flesh of the fallen. When the boy grows up he marries and the wife is stolen and ends up falling in love with her captor. The boy eventually finds her and waits for dusk to fight. While he is waiting, *they* attack. Because they surprise him, the boy cannot pray to the cougar first and he cannot help him. The boy is killed but the cougar was watching him and makes a deal with a demon to bring him back to life. The demon makes the boy a demon like him and returns him to the cougar to seek his revenge."

"It is rumored among the weres that this is a story of a cat and vampire working together. The boy heals after being killed, his bones come back together and he rises again. Together he and the cougar slaughter the village, consuming those they destroy." Troy watched us to see if we were understanding the relevance of the story.

"The legends about Lilith's son speak of him being kept by those loyal to her after her capture. They hid him and nourished him, keeping him safe until the Inquisition was over and the humans were satisfied they'd found the only vampire. Because there were no other vampires, her followers had to be something else. A number of clans' lore tell of young men with enchanted lives being cared for by our kind. I thought I could find him by tracing our stories." He stared at Tonya, his face stricken. "Instead, I might've led them right to us and told them everything we know in the process."

Ch. 50

I stood by the piano watching the cats care for their leader. Tonya showed her softer side, stroking his hair, rubbing his shoulders and speaking softly to him, reassuring him. Stephen called for Troy's favorite, Chinese, and ran out to pick it up.

The division in the room was obvious. The cats had taken over the living room and kitchen leaving the vampires the den with the piano and bookcases. I tried to be discreet as I watched their interplay, while Henry was more obvious. His eyes followed Tonya as she comforted her sire. He was like James, Tonya was his now and he was possessive as his nature would dictate.

James did not watch any of it beyond an occasional cursory glance to confirm they were still in the room. For the most part, he perused the backs of Henry's books. Sometimes he would open one and read a section, seemingly unconcerned over any of it. I knew he was suspicious of my closed link, waiting to get me alone. Before I knew it, the buzzer sounded. We had agreed to stay put for now. Meeting Miranda trumped fearing an attack from a few vampires. We were five strong and had some pretty powerful beings in our family.

Henry flicked his calm eyes at the clock, confirming it was slightly past midnight as he strode to the front door and call box. Depressing the button, he spoke into it. "Hello?"

Miranda's voice was clear. "It's me."

He buzzed her in and waited by the door for the few seconds it took her to arrive on the fourth floor.

Hearing her steps, Henry opened the door and closed it immediately after her, knowing she would be alone.

"I trust you were not followed." Henry's somewhat disrespectful tone caught me by surprise. I hadn't heard him address her outside of the Court's hall. Maybe his stint on the Court made them peers or something.

She shot him a withering glance, "This is not my first time slipping away for you."

He nodded curtly. "Has Amani shown herself yet?"

The cold smile that twisted Miranda's lips hinted at a vindictive streak I hadn't suspected. She'd been only kind, albeit harsh, in our dealings.

"Yes, thank you for the warning about the silver bullets. She did kill one of my guards but Iain and I waited for her in my quarters. We watched her sneak in expecting to find me unaware. Instead she found herself staked before we tried out the new weaponry against her. Those bullets are remarkable, I intend to have some made for our Guard."

While she was talking, Miranda glanced over at me and actually did a double take, I saw her nostrils twitch. That was a first for me to see, a vampire doing a double take. Her black eyes were wide with fascination. "It's been done? Did it survive?"

She had been exhaustingly curious about our bond. It had been Miranda who had been the one to warn us not to let me remain mortal for fear of losing me, for fear of losing our bond. She wished for us to remain together, no matter the potential loss to the Court should the bond be destroyed with my turning. In her case, the loss of her mate had been far greater than the bond itself. I nearly didn't have the heart to tell her ours had grown stronger, worried she would take the news hard.

Fortunately, she didn't ask me. She had asked James. He was forthright with her, for once not trying to hide anything from her. "Yes. It has changed, for the better." His gaze was intimate and I was self-conscious.

Upon hearing James' report her eyes closed and her chin dipped to her chest. Watching her mourn felt voyeuristic and intrusive, I had to look away. Turning away, I plucked a book from the shelf and tried to concentrate on the words inside the front cover.

Miranda recovered herself. "What is it you needed to share with me, Henry? Amani is dead. Who is really behind the attack and are there to be more?" She was very matter of fact for someone who'd just survived an attempt on her life hours before. Maybe that came with age or maybe it wasn't the first time. I didn't want to know.

Henry filled her in on what had transpired in Spain, including our damage control, as I liked to think of it. She was impressed that we had been able to defeat several older vampires. Her eyes darted to me and James caught it.

"Yes, Claire is coming along nicely. Her training has been erratic but seems effective. Soon she will be a great asset." James and his clinical assessment had endeared me to Miranda, thereby securing my future protection by the Court. He really was good at political maneuvering.

"If you have taken care of everyone at that meeting then who is left to pose a threat to me?"

Henry produced a copy of James' email from Indira. It was the picture, I recognized it at once. He held it out to her and she approached it slowly. "This is the only known picture of Nightshade Holdings."

Her lips tightened and I saw her fangs straining against them, eyes black with rage at being betrayed. If we didn't kill Anton, she definitely would as soon as she saw him again. I nearly felt bad for him. Nearly. "And these others, were they killed in Spain?"

"Some." Henry's tone turned grave. "Miranda, there are more." He let that sink in. "And I think we know whom they are using to rally individuals to their cause."

She eyed him suspiciously. Her inert chest gave the false impression she was holding her breath. "Go on," she urged, preparing herself for the worst.

"You are familiar with the legend of Lilith and tales of a son?" He asked it knowing someone at her level would be familiar with all of vampire lore.

Her initial response was the same as Henry's had been. She tried to dismiss it, only he wasn't playing this off as a fairy tale now. The mounting evidence was becoming hard to deny.

Henry laid it all out for her including Troy's discovery at Rachel's house tonight.

"I can believe this Kara heard them speaking of the legend, however, it is doubtful it really is him. Why would an ancient such as he trouble himself with our doings? More likely, someone has tried to revive the myth so that he can use it to his advantage."

No one tried to argue; it was likely Henry was thinking that very thing. "Even so, by invoking the legend, this vampire has excited a following with numbers possibly large enough to make a difference. If they are successful against us, it does not matter whether he is the rightful son or not. The damage will be just as great, the impact of their rule disastrous."

Seeing the truth in his words, Miranda did not waste time arguing the facts any further. She saw the need for an immediate plan of action and that was where we focused our energy. It was agreed that we needed to capture Anton and present him to the Elite Guard for trial and possible execution for treason. As Miranda coldly pointed out, if he was killed during the attempt to capture him there would be no risk of escape. She and Henry were both very comfortable with that option. To my amazement, James encouraged it. Occasionally, his violent side surprised me. Upon seeing my reaction he defended his position.

"Claire, have you forgotten so easily who was behind your and Stephen's captures? And who most likely pulled the strings that led to the damage in Germany?" His eyes were alight with passionate anger.

Thinking about the way he had been abused, as well as the rest of our family under orders descending from Anton, I had a much more personal motivation for catching him than just trying to head off vampiric global domination and total war between the races. However, I realized if we went public with our efforts and failed, we would be left hanging out in the open, exposed to any and all of his allies. We would end up running the rest of our days. We had to be sure we would succeed.

Miranda stood and announced she had to get back. Conveniently enough, Lucas and Gabriel were staying close to her on the heels of the assassination attempt and she was going to see them yet tonight.

"What time is your appointment with the Elite?" James asked her.

Miranda checked her watch. "One thirty, I really must be going." She smoothed her charcoal skirt needlessly, her silver silk blouse showed not the slightest wrinkle in it. She buttoned her suit coat and prepared to leave.

Moving toward the door to open it for her, Henry bowed his head adding innocently, "We will be seeing you soon then."

She placed her hand on his arm, stopping briefly in the doorway. "Be careful." Miranda cast her gaze about the room, letting her eyes rest on me. "All of you."

Her caution made our plans for this evening real to me. I felt my nerves starting to hum as the tension began to flow through my body. As a human, an adrenaline rush had made my body feel alive. As a vampire, it was an entirely different ball of wax. Every nerve ending was alive; each whisper of a breeze, each tingle of contact, everything that touched me was a thousand times more intense with the enhancement of my senses.

James appeared beside me. "Settle yourself Claire or you won't be any good tonight." He laid his hand on my arm. Looking at it, I shifted the direction of my thoughts. It was easier to think of just the here and now.

Stephen cleared his throat. "Don't you two have a massive assault to prepare for?"

Unable to resist his charm even when he was being difficult, I smiled affectionately at him. "We do." Feeling exceptionally giddy as the tension heightened my senses, I scooted in front of James and grabbed on to his shirtfront, pulling him into me for a light kiss.

I was just thinking about how much time we actually had when Henry's small cough interrupted us and he pointed out we were on a tight schedule and needed to dress for the evening. James and I grabbed some of the things we might need, storing them carefully inside our clothing, taking care to keep them from touching our flesh.

Ch. 51

At one fifteen on the nose we walked into Frankenstein's Pub, the human establishment that sat directly over the seat of the vampire Court in Old Towne Edinburgh. The bartender, the large black man with equally dark eyes whom I had met on my first visit was tending bar. Not surprising considering they were down a bartender turned wannabe assassin.

I'd sensed something different about him when I'd been a human. Now that I was not, I knew immediately what it was. "He's a human servant."

"We can't have *only* vampires working here. We have humans in the mix to keep the crowd interested without being suspicious." James explained without taking his eyes from the other customers. Frankenstein's played up their name with monster themes and every night was a different sort of spin on that, leading to some interesting crowd mixes. Mixes that easily lent themselves to accepting the real monsters.

An advantage to going with Henry was that we apparently didn't need to wait for an invitation to descend to the hall. Upon arriving in the stone foyer where I had always had to wait for Rose, the pale escort, Henry knocked one time and the door immediately opened.

A tall, lean to the point of emaciated dark haired vampire opened the door and assessed our group. Though male, he was femininely built with delicate features and barely any visible facial hair; his starved form lent him a sad beauty. He wrinkled his nose at the cats. Vampires did not like other top predators and this one was no exception. His lips pulled back in a sneer and he looked like he wanted to say something. Henry's sharp voice checked him before he uttered a word.

"You are here to allow us entrance, now stand aside and do your job. You would do well to remember your place." Henry's stern tone garnered no protest from the glorified doorman.

The skinny beauty stepped back, dipped his head in a subdued bow and waved us inside. The six of us tried to remain unobtrusive on the long walk across the gymnasium sized hall to the front of the room where the three tall chairs sat. I could see as we crossed the halfway mark that the three members of the Court were not in the room. Luck was with us so far, there was still a possibility of keeping the advantage of surprise on our side.

James tickled our connection and I opened the door to him, having tucked away my intent to give my all if need be tonight. Though it took some time and some serious effort, I was learning how to compartmentalize just like him.

Can you scan and tell where they're meeting?

Letting down my shields, I cast out my feelers to see if I could sense Miranda or Lucas. Because I was most familiar with those two, I would have the best chance of touching upon their emotional energy.

I ignored the general buzz of those around me. We were near the front of the hall and I could feel most of the "noise" was behind me. Filtering through the unfamiliar humming, I zeroed in on those I recognized. *They are in Miranda's sitting room.*

James sidled over to Henry and murmured quietly, "They are with Miranda." The rest of us moved in to hear.

"We don't know how long we have before they come out. Lucas and Gabriel will not be able to help us to apprehend him. They cannot act against the members of the Court, only prisoners, so getting him to them is our problem." Henry said, looking at each of us. "No one knows what we have done to this point. If any of you want to walk out, now is your last opportunity to do so." His expression was somber as he waited for our responses.

No one spoke and I saw resolve on each face. Each of us had a personal reason to be here and each one of us was going to see this through.

Tonya laid her hand on Henry's arm and spoke softly. She spoke for all of us. "Tell us how to get this son of a bitch."

With a final appraising glance, Henry went ahead and began laying out his strategy. "We have two choices. We can walk in the front way or the back way."

"There's a back way?"

Henry gave me a look and I felt embarrassed. Of course for security reasons, they would never have just one exit to their quarters.

James excused himself and my eyes followed him into a crowd of nondescript young vampires, emerging seconds later with Iain in tow. Iain's hair was still purple, his black leather pants adorned with a silver studded black leather belt, and today's concert shirt paid homage to My Chemical Romance.

"Hey," Iain nodded, glancing around our little circle. His eyes stopped on me, his nostrils flared and he looked not at James, but at Henry. "Really?"

"How does he know...?" I started, astonished.

"It's the blood exchange." James explained distracted. "His smell will wear off in a few months." He wheeled on his assistant. "Iain, we need to go in the back way to Miranda's quarters. While we do so, we will need a distraction should Anton decide to leave."

Iain was a different vampire, serious and capable.

"Consider it done." He started to walk away and stopped himself. "Miranda changed her locks on the back door. You'll need this." He handed James a very normal looking key. "Oh, and this might come in handy." He slipped something quickly into James' hand which he slid in the back of his waistband before I could see what it had been.

"Thank you, Iain."

Iain flashed a smile and saluted loosely before he strode away without looking back. No one around us seemed to be paying us any attention though there was no telling whether that was feigned or real. With as much as they could hear and sense otherwise, I found it hard to believe we were really slipping anything past them.

The audience of hangers on may have typically presented themselves as mindless beings interested only in Court politics, but that didn't preclude certain members from being loyal to Anton or possibly even having their own devious interests at heart. It was possible some were going to wait to see how the drama played out, not wanting to pick the losing side.

"What did he give you?" Troy asked.

James flashed his teeth grimly. "Amani's gun."

We tried to maintain any semblance of secrecy we might still have and we followed Henry and James as silently as possible toward the side of the hall nearest the coat closet. There we halted and split into two groups. James, Tonya and Troy in one, Henry, Stephen and me in the other.

James looked to me though his words were for the group. "We'll be at the back door guarding until you are inside. Once you are in, try to keep Anton from becoming too suspicious." Then, just for me, he continued. *It will take a few minutes to get to the door. If you keep our connection open, I will be able to figure out the best time for us to enter without turning it into more of a struggle than absolutely necessary. We might be able to keep our casualties lower that way.*

Got it.

Do you still have the gloves and handcuffs?

He stepped forward, bringing us so close we were nearly touching. The effect of his proximity mixed with my inability to touch him was a heady experience. I felt him reacting to my thoughts with some of his own.

My lips curved into a slow smile. I smoothed a hand over the top of my skirt where my shirt hem hung loose, hiding my last line of defense. *Be careful, I have plans for you after we're done here.*

His thoughts were in line with my own and I saw the beginnings of a picture in his head making it *very* hard for me to concentrate. *Hey.*

Sorry. It's hard to control with you bleeding over like that.

He did refocus on our surroundings but it tickled me that it was not without some significant effort. Having this new level of insight into each other's minds presented some unique challenges.

We parted ways, but not before I caught sight of Tonya's hand brush across Henry's back as they separated. James took his team to the left side of the hall and disappeared behind a tapestry partially obstructed by a broad stone column.

Go ahead and knock. Keep them busy while we come around to the back hall.

Okay. I started to move to the right side of the hall and found the door to Miranda's private room where she went between Court obligations.

Henry, Stephen, and I walked straight up to Miranda's door without interference from the guard standing nearby. He was hard to see because he was partially hidden by another stone column. My guess was that his obstruction was by design, not wanting to be highly visible to any possible wrongdoer from across the room. His loyalty was not in question, Miranda would have been diligent in replacing his murdered predecessor. Henry was on the approved list, we were given a nod in response to our silent request.

We arrived at Miranda's door and I heard their conversation, it had grown louder. Gabriel's insanely deep baritone ground out low, trying to bring the volume back down. It seemed to be working, their tones backing off in volume, not in tension.

Without thinking about the repercussions, I cast out my ability to pick up the emotional energies in her quarters. I was leaning in, concentrating on the building anger, frustration and fear I felt emanating from the room. Who would be that afraid? I worried Miranda was in trouble and thought about telling James when my thoughts were brought to a screeching halt.

Ch. 52

Henry's hand clamped down on my shoulder at the same time the door flew open and Lucas stood in front of me. His lips were stretched tight, his eyes a deep jade green. At once I felt his undeniable pull except this time James was already in my head and let me tap into his resilience, lending me the ability to resist.

He smiled, revealing perfectly even teeth. He had significant self control to be that angry and not have his fangs grow on him. Hopefully that came with age, mine really needed work.

"My dear, I heard you knock." Lucas threw a dark look over my shoulder and the pressure on my shoulder was gone. Elven heritage gave him the advantage of magick over Henry's age. "Won't you come in?" Stepping back, he waved us inside.

Once I stepped past Lucas and could see the room, I understood the feelings I'd been picking up. On the chaise, shoulders slumped around a face chalky white and streaked with tears, sat Davina Brightmore.

When she saw me, Davina sat bolt upright and stared, her mouth falling open in shock. "You're supposed to be dead," she sputtered.

I, on the other hand, felt the raw burning rage so easily brought on with my impulsive nature well up and had the urge to tear her apart with my bare hands. She had caused her father tremendous heartache and had just confirmed that she'd been the one responsible for forcing my turning before I was ready. Dropping into a crouch, I readied to launch myself at her when a long white arm reached out encircling my waist.

Respecting the tight hold Lucas had on me, I continued to glare at her. In my head I pictured the damage I wanted to do to her body. I could feel her bones breaking under my hands. If only I could get my hands on her, I wouldn't stop until there was nothing left.

James tried to calm me through the distance except my rage had a firm hold and I didn't want to be calmed. Instead I pushed against him, channeling some of my rage down our connection and into him. With a sadistic glee, I felt him struggle to contain it.

Gradually I started to regain control of myself. The fiery rage slowly banking inside me, allowed me to tuck it away so that I could think straight. Gradually I became aware my back was warm where it was pressed against Lucas. Spinning around in Lucas' arm I put my hands against the exposed flesh of his chest above his shirt.

"You're warm!" I exclaimed, staring at my hands where they were touching him.

He smiled, putting his other arm around my back. "I told you when we met that your magick calls to me. Now that you are like me you feel it, too."

"How does magick make you warm? Why am I not warm?" I was puzzled.

"Aren't you?" Lucas raised an eyebrow and raised my hand, showing my flesh pinking up with the warmth coming from where our bodies touched.

"Why are *you* here?" Anton glared at us.

I stopped struggling against Lucas whose arm clamped me tightly against him. James had asked me to distract them. I had to say I'd done a bang up job of that so far.

Henry had done nothing to stop me, most likely seeing my antics as a useful distraction as well. He continued to look peaceful, making no attempt to intercede or answer Anton and leaving it to me.

I couldn't bow with Lucas holding me so tight. Instead I opted for a deep head bob, my chin touching my chest in the process. "I apologize for our intrusion. I wanted to discuss some matters with Miranda and in my eagerness I forgot myself." Ducking my eyes, I attempted to appear contrite and guardedly surveyed the other parties in the room.

Charles hovered behind Anton, watching Henry for a signal of some sort. He must have seen or sensed something because he subtly shifted himself away from Anton. Miranda gave an exasperated sigh covering her relocation to a chair several feet away. Gabriel had his arms crossed watching things from the back of the room near her dressing screen.

Sensing now was our opportunity to take Anton, I called to James. His reply was biting. *We'll be there in less than a minute. I'm sure you can keep things* warm *until we get there. Try not to hurt the human, we promised her father we would return her.*

His rebuke stung. Anton spoke before I could defend myself. "Your sire is shirking his responsibility." Anton advanced on me shooting Henry a hate filled glare. "It is a good thing you do not often sire children Henry, you do a poor job teaching them to bite their tongues." I had only enough time to close my eyes before the blow landed.

I would have thought it would hurt less to be struck by him as a vampire. It didn't. My lip split on my teeth and the taste of blood ignited my thirst. Eyes going straight to Davina, I felt the familiar vibration of growing fangs in my gums and fought down my urge out of desperation. Lucas tightened his hold for which I was suddenly grateful. If I lost it now I could get lots of people I cared about hurt and by what I was sensing in my head, one of them was close to blowing up already.

I kept repeating "be still, be calm" as a sort of mantra trying to distract myself and him. I could take a little punishment. My ability to heal was far superior to Davina's. So far it was working. The second blow was harder and clearly intended to push me over the edge.

"You will respect your superiors," Anton hissed.

The room swirled past me in a rush as I was swung around and away from Anton. Lucas apparently did not like the handling of my education and passed me to Henry before he stepped between Anton and my bleeding face.

"She acknowledges her misstep and has paid you proper respect already. I believe it is her Sire's responsibility to dole out her punishment from here."

Gabriel reinforced Lucas' ruling. "It is my duty to enforce the laws and to keep the members of the Court from abuse of their power." He stared evenly at Anton, no hint of fear in his expression.

Seeing that avenue closed to him, Anton let it go for the time being.

"Where is your mate?" Anton eyed me suspiciously. "Where one is, the other is never far away."

Making a show of sucking on my bleeding lip, I shrugged.

Henry lied effortlessly. "James had a stop to make, he will be joining us shortly. He asked me to stay with Claire. You might have noticed she remains sensitive."

Anton turned his glare to Stephen who had been silent this entire time. His nostrils flared. "Why did you bring one of

344

your pets? This is not a menagerie. You bring in your cats and humans as though this is some sort of circus sideshow. I assure you it is not. You..."

Anton's resentment seemed to encompass all forms except his own. I had not yet seen a group he didn't regard as beneath him. Humans, weres, human-loving vampires, newly turned vampires he didn't like as humans; it didn't seem to matter. It crossed my mind he could be the very vampire we were searching for and then rapidly discounted it. Anton was powerful but he was not older than Henry. I didn't think anyone in this room was older than Henry.

"Anton, I am beginning to tire of your ranting this evening. You decry the *entire* human race yet here you have brought an unapproved human into our inner sanctum yourself. What is *your* excuse?" Charles gave us a glimpse into his real intelligence.

"I am fully aware the cost to her for her presence and I am willing for her to pay the price." For her part Davina had glazed over, she knew she would die here. "Suffice it to say she is here to serve me tonight."

A metallic click at the back of the room behind the dressing screen halted Anton's speech. Three heads popped into view floating above the screen as they walked around to stand beside Gabriel.

At once Anton sensed the trap we'd sprung and he glared not at James or Henry, but at me. He pointed an accusatory finger my direction. "You are a plague on us all. Your presence, whether as a human or vampire, brings nothing but absolute chaos and you continue to disrespect this Court." Sneering at the weres flanking my husband and me, he went on. "You and your mate bring these *creatures* into our private chambers, unwelcome, and reveal to them our private escape routes, putting our safety at risk." Straightening out his features, he lifted his nose. "By the laws of our society I am allowed to demand satisfaction. Will it be from you or will you be hiding behind your sire? He can stand up for you if he deems you worth the risk." His haughty demeanor was threatening my fragile self-control.

Don't Claire. He is baiting you.

I know, but I can't ask Henry to fight for me. Besides, I can distract him long enough for you to sneak up on him.

Like it or not, he couldn't argue with my logic. We still needed to get Anton wrapped up and carted out of here without setting off the group outside the door.

Let me figure something out. Don't move.

Knowing James' plan would involve someone else taking a risk for me, I stepped around Lucas and approached Anton boldly.

He smiled victoriously. "I see you have stepped forward. By accepting my challenge you agree to face me. You may choose a Second to assist you in understanding the rules but Seconds cannot fight with you and the terms of the contest are mine." His eyes narrowed. "The first term is that you cannot choose a member of this Court as your Second."

My stomach twisted. Unwittingly, I had accepted his challenge. Helpless, I looked over at my allies for some clue that there was another way.

Stephen was the same color as the vampires and James was in a mental frenzy attempting to figure out how he could take my place. The rest of them were more successful at hiding their reactions outwardly though I could feel their upset. I had messed this one up huge and there was nothing anyone could do to help me.

"Anton really, she is barely turned. Do not waste your time on her." Charles waved a hand in the air, brushing away the conflict as a point of mild annoyance.

Lucas offered, "I will be her Second."

James growled, moving closer. "That will not be necessary." He turned to face Anton. "I will act as her Second."

Although I was annoyed at their attitudes, I didn't want to get James hurt by any more accidental missteps on my part nor did I want Lucas to misconstrue an acceptance as anything more that it was.

Making what I thought was my smartest choice I looked to Gabriel. He had always been fair and I respected his insightful and well thought out opinions. Plus, he had the authority to rein in Anton should things get crazy. "Gabriel, would you act as my Second?"

Lucas chuckled, genuinely amused by my choice.

James, however, tried to hide his hurt through indifference. I saw the look in his eyes and felt how deeply my rejection cut him despite the blank expression he kept for appearances. He would have closed the door between us were it not for its situational necessity. I was torn between sparing his feelings and sticking to my guns. Anton took the decision from me.

"Seconds have been chosen. There will be no further delay." He moved toward the back door.

"Wait, who is your Second?"

Anton answered me without turning around, "I choose Davina of course."

Stunned, I shifted to see her reaction. She was staring at his back, eyes and mouth wide in horror.

"I await you in my quarters." Anton opened the back door and Davina slowly rose to follow, powerless to refuse.

I watched them go. The implications of what I had done were starting to sink in and I began to tremble.

Stephen's warm hand went around my shoulders and he pulled me in close, putting his lips to my ear. "If you want to run, we can. This feels like a setup." Stephen's gift for reading intentions was a very reliable lie detector. "He's up to something but he's shifting all the time. I can't read him clearly." Stephen paused and I craned my neck to see his face. His brows were furrowed in concentration. Shaking his head he said, "His mind isn't right. I can only read him in flashes. It's like a cell phone cutting out at all the important places."

Henry walked up behind us. "If you run, you have to run forever. Once a challenge is agreed upon, it has no statute of limitations."

I saw Henry as a life raft in this sea of confusion. "What did I agree to?"

His voice was the warm fatherly one I used to find so comforting. I took it as a bad sign that he used it now. If it was meant to reassure me, it wasn't working. Knowing its purpose lent it the opposite effect.

"You have accepted a challenge from a member of the Court. It is a duel of sorts. He has chosen the grounds so you can be certain he will use it to his advantage. He will also choose the challenge. It can be mental, physical, a task or combat. The choice is his." Henry patted my arm as he moved past me. "We need to go. You do not want him to be more angry than he already is."

"Henry," I whispered catching his arm and closing the door to James for a few precious seconds. "If this ends badly,

348

promise me you will get James out of here safely before he does something stupid."

His eyes went dark and he nodded once before he walked out, Tonya and Troy following behind. Stephen took his place and caught my hands.

"Don't do this," he pleaded.

I answered logically. "I have to. You heard Henry, if I run I'll always be running. I can't do that forever." I glanced past him and stared at the face of my husband. "I can't ask my family to do that." My false smile was directed back to Stephen. "Besides, we needed a distraction. I think I've done my part on those tonight. Hopefully, I can pull this last one off and you can take him." I squeezed his hands and gestured toward the door with my head. "Go ahead, I'll be there in a minute." I tapped my temple. "Need to put my game face on."

Stephen shot a look at James, clearly blaming him for this. "This is my fault. I never should have sent you to them."

I touched his arm and he faced me again. Putting my hands on either side of his face to force him to meet my eyes, I spoke firmly. "Stephen, my life has been infinitely better because you introduced me to him. I should be thanking you." Kissing his cheek, I gently pushed him away. He only glanced back once to give me a small smile before following the others.

Heading him off, I met Lucas' eyes and was stern. "I don't know what the magick is that I feel but it's not going to change anything. And certainly not now, so please stop trying to pick a fight with him, it's making it hard to concentrate. For both of us."

"My dear, your magick is a part of you. It is an earth magick like my own and it calls to me. I cannot deny my nature." He

349

bowed slightly, "Nor can you." Lucas glanced at James and back at me, winking. "Forever is a long time to be with only one. I can wait for you to grow bored." With that, he strode out leaving me with James and Gabriel.

"Gabriel, would it be possible to meet you outside? I would like to have a minute alone with my husband." It occurred to me I might be saying that for the last time.

He regarded me steadily. "It is good to say your good-byes. Your mind will not be busy with unnecessary distractions." Gabriel left as well and James and I were alone.

Before I could say anything James spoke, his voice low and hoarse. "Don't say good-bye to me. You aren't going to die, I won't let you. I promised."

His speaking the word aloud made it real and I wished I could find a release for the grief I was feeling through tears. "If things go badly," I forged ahead needing to ease the concerns I could, "I want you to know I love you. *Only* you." My eyes met his and our minds touched, giving the words added weight.

More than anything I wanted to touch him yet I knew that my strength would evaporate if I did. Instead, I moved past him and closed the door between us. I could hold back my terror no longer and he didn't need to feel that too, nor did he need to experience my death with me if it came to that.

Gulping nervously, I turned the corner and entered the back hall where Gabriel waited.

Ch. 53

The back hall was just that. It was a narrow passageway that was drier than my imagination had painted it. In my mind it was cold and dank, complete with wet walls and torches. I was right about the torches, yet was surprised to find the space dry and dusty with only a few spider webs. There were no adornments, doors or passageways. The hall was for function only and was too narrow for Gabriel's broad shoulders and mine to walk side by side. He naturally took the lead, walking ahead so that we could speak easily.

"This contest will most likely be a physical one given Anton's affinity for weapons." Gabriel was matter of fact, not being at all moved by the fact that I was shaking uncontrollably by now. I wondered if he was cold as a human or if it was an age thing. I would most likely never get old enough to try it out personally.

Gulp.

He went on, "He is older and stronger so you will have to use your wits." Gabriel paused and glanced back over his shoulder to study my face before moving on with a shrug. "He probably has an advantage there as well."

Considering I would most likely die in the next few minutes, I did not want to go to my grave having him think I was a halfwit. "You know, I'm not stupid."

Gabriel stopped and turned around. I didn't stop in time and ran smack into his chest. It was exactly like hitting a bus. He didn't move a muscle. "You will excuse my lack of confidence, but you are less than a quarter century old. Your opponent has had centuries to perfect his skills."

I had resigned myself to death by the time we reached a door on our left. Walking through, I saw that either Anton had been busy rearranging or he had planned this in advance.

351

The furniture had all been moved to the sides making a long, wide open clearing in the center of the room.

I noticed the wall above the fireplace was missing two important pieces. They were sitting on the small table in front of the hearth. The two swords lay beside each other, both easily the length of my arm, their hilts wrapped in leather.

"I am a gentleman," Anton spoke clearly from my left where he stood with Davina. "You have first choice of weapons." He motioned with his hand.

Fingering the weapons, I tried to figure out which one might be easier to hold. The leather on the brown hilted sword felt tackier, easier to grip. I hefted it in an effort to get a feel for its weight. It was awkward to balance and I nearly dropped it, needing to grab it with the second hand before it slammed down into the tabletop. Relieved I hadn't broken anything, I readjusted my grip and swung the blade in an arc.

The weight of the sword proved itself harder to control than I had thought on my initial appraisal. Unable to stop its swing, it spun me in a half circle until I was facing the door at the back of the room. James was there, staring at me. Any color he had drained from his face as he took in the sight of me holding the sword clumsily in front of me.

Anton's laughter tore my attention from James. He had picked up his sword and was wielding it with the skill of a buccaneer in an old Errol Flynn movie. My heart sank. He glided to Davina's side and I watched his expression change like the flip of a switch. His face went scary, his fangs grew and he didn't stop until his body nearly touched Davina's. He grabbed her by the back of the neck, pushing her face into his. Anton's lips moved and his eyes held hers, entrancing her.

Seeing Davina's terror and helplessness before her face went slack inspired a wave of sympathy for her despite my animosity. I'd had my share of mind tricks used against me and understood the frustration of not being in control of my own actions. Maybe she had been under their control this whole time. Maybe she hadn't been behind my assassination attempt on purpose.

Watching Davina, I thought of Alan. He was so scared for her. He would never know what had become of her if I didn't make it out of here and if Henry didn't stop James from avenging me. I held no illusions for her future should I die here today. Anton had already expressed his intent to kill her. Of course he would drain her before discarding her like a piece of garbage, I thought bitterly.

The thought of her being drained of her blood ignited the ever present burning thirst in the back of my throat. I hadn't had anything to drink in hours. I heard the rush of blood in her veins and smelled her from across the room. My mouth nearly watered in want of her. I started toward her until Anton heard me and stepped in front of her.

"To the victor go the spoils, Claire. All you have to do is defeat me." His mocking denial served only to twist my blood lust into rage.

Anton walked away from me, giving me his back to show how unthreatened he truly was by me. He took a spot in the middle of the clearing before turning around and Gabriel stepped out, a sword length in front of him. Gabriel gestured for me to join him, stepping out of the way for me to take his place.

In a surprisingly warm gesture, Gabriel took hold of me by my upper arms and kissed both of my cheeks. Wordlessly, he walked away and took his place beside Davina. Arms crossed as usual, Gabriel kept his watchful gaze on us.

I turned my focus back to Anton staring intently at me, all pretenses of teasing now gone. He raised the tip of his blade and lowered it in a form of salute. I tried to do the same only it didn't have quite the same effect. The three feet of steel wobbled when I raised it. Anton refrained from mockery. All seriousness now, he monitored my every move, gauging my competency. I kicked off my black heels just as Gabriel's rough voice ground out,

"Allez," and the duel began.

Anton started by swinging his sword one handed at mine and I skittered backward, only by some miracle staying on my feet with the blade out in front of me. On his backswing Anton's blade nearly struck my midsection only my blade slid sideways as I tried to gain my feet against the force of his blows. By pure luck I deflected his effort, tearing my skirt up the sides in the process, freeing my legs for better movement.

Standing, I tried to take a swipe at Anton and failed to lift the blade all the way up. Instead only striking at his lower legs. He easily jumped over it.

In my head I felt a familiar tickle and I kept it closed off, I especially couldn't let him in now. The pain of us parting would be enough without him feeling as though he were the one dying. Instead, I pushed against him to be sure he could gain no foothold in my mind.

The thought of losing James and being killed before I was ready combined with my blood lust. A surge of power rushed through my limbs, a veil of red descending over my eyes blocked out everything else. My fangs grew with the heat of my fury.

Rushing forward, I wildly slapped my sword against Anton's with a flat metallic clang. He pushed against me and I fell back only to rush him again. Each time he pushed me away, my rage was nothing against his greater skill and battle knowledge.

Vampires do not physically fatigue, although we do mentally. After being beaten back enough times, I felt my concentration slipping and I faltered. Anton took advantage of my misstep and was on me at once. Fangs snapping at my neck, he pressed me up against the side of the couch, our swords crossed between us. In a movie, this would have been the part where I pushed him away in a surge of adrenaline. However, this was not a movie and as Gabriel had pointed out, I was no match for Anton.

The edge of Anton' blade slid into the side of my neck. Fortunately the blades were too sharp to cause much pain. I felt the blood running down into my top, adhering the silky fabric to my chest. Feeling my death was near, my survival instinct reared up and I struggled against him while he easily held me down, slowly letting the blade slip into my flesh.

Again I felt James trying to open the door between us. I was too exhausted to shut him down this time and felt the door swing wide open.

Claire, let me help you, he pleaded. Desperation was surging through him and jolted into me.

No, you can't interfere. He'll kill you, too. I worried Henry's promise would be pointless because James wasn't going to wait until this was over before he did something stupid.

No one has to know.

It was genius. He meant for me to channel him. I had done it before in a physical fight and it had saved me then, maybe it would now. Focusing on our connection, I zeroed in on James' physical capabilities and found what I needed. As a member of the Guard he had been trained in human weaponry and was pushing his memories and how it felt to wield a blade as well as the strategies involved.

My eyes bored into Anton's. I watched confusion set in as my new strength poured through me and I was able to push him off of me. When there was enough room, I rolled out from underneath him. He fell forward onto his hands and I used the few seconds' reprieve to stand and reposition myself. Now that my muscles accepted James' ability to balance the blade, maneuvering my sword was much easier.

As Anton stood, I raised my blade and stabbed it straight into his shoulder. Shocked, he fell back a few steps, holding a hand to his wound. I kept up my momentum, pursuing him to swing again, except this time he was ready for my newfound speed and parried my attack. It was far more difficult for him now as we traded blows and his frustration fed his anger.

We were more closely matched this round and the attacks intensified. We each bled from superficial wounds that quickly healed. Anton's frustration-fueled fury grew and he took on an entirely different persona. His attacks became more frenzied and erratic, the style switching from fencing to barbarian style hack and slash fighting. In a flurry of punishing strokes, he drove me back toward where Gabriel stood beside Davina.

Just as I was sure I was going to be trapped against the wall, Anton stepped back and stopped his sword mid swing by his shoulder. Confused, I halted my own and started to turn my head to check behind me when I felt a searing pain in my back and instantly lost control of my body. Paralyzed, I fell limply to the ground.

Ch. 54

While I lay frozen on my side, I could see the reason for my paralysis. The point of a wooden stake protruded from below my ribs. Fortunately she had used wood, if it had been silver I would be dead.

Unable to do anything to defend myself, I watched helplessly as Anton came at me again with his sword raised for a final blow to my neck. His arm back he started to lunge when he was blindsided by a dark blurred form. I wouldn't have known who it was if I hadn't "heard" his intent before James moved. He was the only one who could have gotten there in time. Gabriel had moved out of the way, in keeping with his role as an uninvolved Second, I assumed, and no one else could have known what happened. James, however, had felt it with me and knew instantly what Davina had done. He had guessed the rest and started to move the instant we felt the wood pierce my flesh.

A scuffling behind me told me someone else had taken custody of Davina as well. The threat neutralized, Stephen was at my side in a heartbeat assessing the damage. "That bastard's a cheat. I knew we couldn't trust him."

"Does this mean I win by default?" I jokingly whispered, trying to take my mind off of the agonizing pain my unresponsive body was experiencing.

Stephen's head peeked over and I saw his features upside down in front of my face. "I think it's safe to say Anton's done fighting for today." I saw the pulse pounding in Stephen's throat when he glanced up to where I would guess James had tackled Anton.

"Did James get the chain on him? Did we do it?"

"Yes. We did it." His voice was soft and he bent down to kiss my temple. Stephen's lips tightened and his brow furrowed, "I have to get this out. Are you ready?"

"Yeah," I replied, steeling myself for the pain I knew was coming.

Stephen put one hand firmly against my back and in the next instant the stake slid out, taking my immobility with it. Rolling forward, I instinctively curled up in a protective ball.

Able to move again, I craned my neck to see what had happened. Anton was lying on his side tied in a silver chain. Henry stopped to remove the gloves and cuffs from my skirt on his way to tighten them on Anton's wrists. James had not had time to put on his gloves and he had some amount of "rope burn" on his palms where it appeared he had tried to balance the chain on his cuff to keep it from touching him, temporarily paralyzing himself in the process.

Lucas came to my side and Stephen remained where he was behind me, his heat radiating through my skin where his legs touched me.

"Can you move?" his voice chimed, his white hair falling around me in a veil. His pale hand touched my chin and his long fingers cradled my face.

"Yes, I can." To prove it, I pulled my face back, away from his hand before I felt my resolve completely desert me.

Lucas smiled at my move, not upset in the least. As persistent as he was I had to give him credit, he was not overly possessive like other vampires I knew.

As if on cue, a familiar growl sounded from above the white veil blocking my view. "If you don't mind Lucas, I would like to check on my wife." James' tone was polite enough but just barely.

"Of course," Lucas replied lightly, replacing his hand briefly to stroke the side of my face before standing and stepping aside.

The light from beyond us was again blocked as James knelt down in front of me. Concern lined his features as he stared down at me. "The pain will fade soon. It will be faster if you feed." He didn't have to ask how I felt, he knew.

James' reminder brought my thirst back full force. All at once I was consumed by it. I became very aware that Davina was somewhere close behind me.

Wiggling, I tried to sit up except the stake had torn through my abdominal muscles and they were slow to reattach. I struggled to roll onto my stomach, attempting to rise on my hands and knees. The wound continued to bleed and was undeniably painful.

Stephen's warm hand and James' cool one both touched me. "She didn't do it of her own will, Claire. You know she was under Anton's control." James' voice was cautionary, "She doesn't deserve to die for that."

I was only half listening to him. Most of my mind was occupied with trying to find a way to get up and taste her blood.

"Let her have a little, James. Claire has to *walk* out or Anton's people are going to suspect something's up and follow us," Stephen argued. "She needs blood and we have only one human here."

Grasping hungrily to his reasoning, I agreed with Stephen. "He's right." I nearly whined, "I won't kill her, I just need a little." My throat ached with need.

Miranda weighed in with the final word. "Let her feed, the human owes at least that much." With the struggle against

Anton over with, Miranda and Charles were no longer bound by compulsion not to interfere. Miranda sounded tense, she was probably worried about any suspicion that might fall on her.

Ch. 55

James and Stephen helped me to my feet, one on each arm. When I stood I saw that Tonya had Davina restrained, easily holding her hands behind her back. From Davina's pained expression I gathered Tonya was being a little overzealous.

My eyes went straight to Davina's throat where I watched the thrum of her pulse. The rush of the blood in her veins filled my ears until it was all I could hear. Davina paled at my staggering approach.

James spoke softly to Tonya, "Let her have one of her wrists. It will be easier to stop her from going too far."

Tonya didn't seem too concerned either way about Davina's welfare. The cats' satisfaction for justice seemed to be wanting. She released one of Davina's arms and Davina immediately tried to put it back behind her again, but James' hand shot out and grabbed it. In an act of compassion, he met Davina's eyes and I knew he was using a trick to make it more pleasant for her when I did feed. Without it, I knew firsthand how unbearable it could be.

She did not fight when James raised her hand to my face. "Drink, but not too much or you will have to tell Alan you killed his daughter."

That cooled my thirst slightly and I looked up at him. James' expression was grave. "This is a live feed, Claire and you have all the components right now of not being able to stop. Remember who she is and what she means to Alan and you might be able to control yourself."

I stared at him for a minute before my need got the better of me and my nose captured Davina's heady scent. The smell of blood just under her skin was intoxicating. Without any further consideration, I brought her wrist to my mouth and sunk my fangs into her flesh. Instantly I was rewarded by the warm blood I so desperately needed. Each beat of her heart pushed another mouthful down my greedy throat.

All too soon the beats became more labored as did the flow. My mind was focused on only one thing, feeding. Everything else fell away until I became aware of James speaking to me.

Claire, you need to stop. She will die soon, she is already weak.

I tried to ignore him.

No one here would blame you if you killed her. Half of them would do the same solely for the blood. His tone softened. *But you will not forgive yourself if you kill the one thing that means the world to your friend.*

I saw Alan so heartbroken for his daughter, weeping for her return. With great effort, I removed my mouth from Davina's wrist and with a flick of the tongue, healed the wound. When I raised my head, James was watching me, his eyes midnight. He nodded his approval.

Charles spoke up, no hint of the airy, nasal voice I'd come to associate with him. Revealing how much of an act his persona had been, he called out in a clear voice that commanded respect. It was not just me who was amazed at the transformation, I saw the shock in Anton's eyes. "Lucas or Gabriel will have to carry out the trial on a neutral ground of their choosing. The rest must leave through the main hall." He looked at Henry, "They saw you come in and they must see you go out."

Henry agreed.

Troy raised his voice in question. "Where are you going to try him? Can't you do it here? This place is considered neutral and we have plenty of witnesses, right?"

"It makes sense," Miranda said nodding.

"It is Lucas and Gabriel's decision," Charles said, watching them for any signs of disagreement.

Lucas spoke first, his tone grave with the responsibility of his office. "Anton will be tried for his treasonous acts here, this is neutral ground."

Gabriel replied, in some ceremonial context, I could only assume, "I agree to hear the case."

With that, Anton was dragged into the middle of his pre-cleared dueling field and set on his knees, his hands were bound in front of him and he fell forward into a hunker. I flashed back to Bradley's trial. He was one of Anton's underlings who had caused so much pain and trouble for us when I first met all of them. He had died screaming that none of us would survive. It still gave me chills to think about. Ironically, these were *his* silver trappings being used against his kinsman.

"Anton Richelieu," Gabriel's voice rang out clear and commanding. "You stand accused of conspiring against the high Court in an act of treason as well as performing and orchestrating acts so public they threatened the secrecy our laws hold sacred above all else. How do you plead?"

Anton glared at all of us.

"You must speak for yourself or we will make our decision based upon the evidence given by these witnesses to your acts," Lucas reminded Anton, who surely knew the rules of trial.

Anton's face was frozen while his eyes rolled erratically in his head. Could a vampire have a fit, I wondered?

Gabriel considered him for a long moment before turning his attention toward us. "Who speaks against this being?"

Henry stepped forward, "I do. I bore witness to his orders to execute the other two members of the Court."

"I do. I heard his men give the order for assassination," James echoed.

Lucas glanced about the room. "Are there any other witnesses to these charges?" His eyes stopped at me.

Getting the hint, I stepped forward. "I heard the same."

Tonya no longer needed to hold Davina who was lying across the top of a console table temporarily pushed up against the wall. "I also was witness to Anton's treachery." Her voice was venomous in her anger, likely remembering his thralls' violence only a few days ago. "By his actions, he risked a war between our species."

Each of our six stepped forward. Miranda and Charles did as well, able to speak out against another member of the Court within the confines of a trial under a compulsion of honesty their offices required. The evidence was tremendous. Anton had committed treason against the vampires' ruling body and was in violation of our highest law, secrecy. His life was forfeit.

Gabriel and Lucas moved closer together, a brief mumbled conversation ensued. Shortly, Gabriel spoke out again. "Anton we find you guilty of both charges. How do you plead?"

He maintained his silence. Watching Anton closely I thought I saw a flash of fear cross his face and his eyes were continuing to fly about in their sockets. It couldn't be the silver, something was keeping him from speaking and clearly he wanted to.

Gloves on his hands, Gabriel reached into the inside pocket of his long black coat and I knew what he was grabbing. The silver flashed in his hands and he proclaimed as he raised the stake high, "You are hereby sentenced to death." The stake swung down and Anton fell backward without a sound.

I had seen quite a few vampires die in my few short time among them. Anton's death was nothing like the others. Instead of turning straight to ash, Anton's mouth fell open and a grey mist streamed forth as if Anton was breathing out his last breath.

Spellbound, I watched the mist swirl above his head and gather into a mass above us. Everyone in the room watched this strange phenomenon equally perplexed. The mist formed a large ring over our heads and foolishly I clapped my hands over my mouth and nose. A ghostly chuckle rang out; I couldn't tell if it was out loud or in my head. It seemed to be everywhere.

"You have succeeded only in the slaying of a vessel. I will have my war and the humans *will* die. You cannot defeat me."

I heard fear in Miranda's voice for the first time.

"Lillith would be proud of you, Daemon." She gave him a name I didn't known he had. "Your hatred of humans matches hers."

The eerie voice did not deny it. "I watched them torture and kill my mother. I will have my vengeance."

Henry tried to reason with him. "That was long ago. You cannot hold their kind accountable for the wrongs of their ancestors."

Daemon's laughter was a bitter staccato prickling down my spine. "Can you show me that they have changed? That they are any less fearful of what they do not know? That they do not destroy for their own gain? I think not. They are guilty of the same trespasses for which they accuse our kind and for which they condemned my mother to death. God made the wrong choice thinking them the superior beings."

I heard James' gentle voice, "What of their good? You can't deny that there are many who do kindnesses, selfless acts for others." His eyes rested on me. "Some make sacrifices that are truly extraordinary."

The mist swirled above us and I craned my face upward to see it massing above me. "Yours was not such a special human, even *she* felt the pull to become one of us. They are never happy with their lot, always seeking more. That is the only reason they do not attempt to destroy us entirely with their weapons. More power, longer life, endless wealth, they keep us around in hopes of becoming like us. That is the true irony in all of this. Left to their own devices they would eventually destroy themselves. I intend to beat them to it and have my satisfaction." With that, the mist moved to the door, slipped underneath and out into the main hall.

Charles ran to the door, whipping it open to reveal a hall filled with no less than one hundred vampires all milling about and talking amongst themselves. No hints of disruption from what had occurred within these back rooms nor from the mist, which certainly had to have gone right past them. No one in the hall was acting any differently, though if anyone had been newly possessed, I doubted anyone here knew what that would look like. Daemon was gone. Charles stepped back inside and closed the door.

"What the hell." Stephen was blinking, gaping at the door with hands on his hips.

Miranda answered, back in control. "That was Daemon." Mumbling, she added, "I have never seen him, I thought it

366

was only legend. Priests in the fifteenth century named him after the terror he inspired."

Charles stroked his doughy neck pensively. "Only the very ancient among us are powerful enough to transfigure. Mist is the hardest to achieve. I've never seen it done before."

"Let's not push our luck, the natives don't seem to know what we've done. Let's get back to Miranda's quarters and get out of here," Stephen wisely suggested, moving toward the back door.

All were in agreement and moved to follow. We walked in silence until we reached Miranda's rooms where Troy asked, "When are you going to announce it?"

"Lucas and Gabriel will announce it with us tonight, after you leave." She stopped and raised her voice, "Anton's position will need to be filled at once, Daemon *will* try again. Henry, do you have any desire to return to us?"

Henry answered without hesitation. "Thank you for your consideration." He shook his head. "I have no desire to be tied to Edinburgh at present."

Tonya hid her pleased smile behind the back of a sun kissed hand. Troy refrained from grumbling, which I took to be an improvement. Stephen rolled his eyes and walked out the door; Troy followed close behind. Next went Henry and Tonya walking side by side.

James and I were turning to leave when Miranda asked, "When will you be returning for the girl?"

"Oh my gosh, I forgot all about her!" It wasn't every day that I met the oldest vampire in the world. Davina had completely slipped my mind.

James squeezed my hand, telling me it was okay. "We will call a car for her in the morning when there are fewer people here and the announcement has been made. I don't want her linked in any way to this or her life will never be safe."

Miranda cocked her head and eyed James speculatively. "James, have you ever considered a career in politics?"

Without a moment's hesitation, James replied with a certain "No."

"You know being a member of the Court is far different than life in the Guard. You have the power to forward your *own* agendas." Miranda tried pressing his buttons. "You could do much to change the way humans are regarded by our kind."

James shook his head. "I appreciate your consideration Miranda but I have no desire to become involved in the Court's business beyond what I already am. My skills are better suited to helping the newly turned. We can teach regard for humans one vampire at a time."

"Very well. I will have Iain bring the human what she needs for the night and arrange a car when it is safe." She changed the subject gracefully, conceding defeat for the moment, although I didn't get the impression she was giving up. "We will leave her in Anton's quarters. No one will enter before morning." She looked meaningfully at me. "Claire, I suggest after returning the human to her father, you go home." She grew serious and explained to us both, "His allies will not retaliate here however I can make no guarantees beyond these walls."

"I agree. We will take care of this and be on the next flight out." James put his arm out and I took it, grateful for the support.

No one followed us out of the hall or onto the street but I swore I heard that eerie laughter in my head several times. Shuddering, I leaned further into James.

Ch. 56

When we returned to Henry's flat he buzzed us in and met us at the door in his coat. "We are going home tonight. I trust you have made plans to leave the country as well?"

James answered that we had. They shook hands, an exceedingly rare occurrence among vampires. Then again, these two were unusual vampires. "Thank you Henry. We'll see you back home," James said solemnly.

Henry released his hand as Tonya walked out of the back hall carrying her bag. "Ready?" she asked, her eyes only for Henry.

I watched him hold out his hand for her to take before they left together. After James closed the door behind them, I felt the toll of the night coming to roost. Mentally fatigued, I sagged and felt James scoop me up and carry me to the couch, setting me down gently and kissing my forehead before returning to the kitchen to pour us drinks. We sat quietly on the couch for a while. I had three drinks to his one and he very kindly continued to pour them for me, allowing me to rest. In a few hours I was feeling better. James booked us on a ten o'clock flight giving us plenty of time to recuperate.

After eight Iain called to tell us Davina was capable of walking though she was still weak. He was putting her in a car and would escort her to Alan's door. James called Alan to tell him Davina was on her way. Alan wept his gratitude.

James warned him to watch for unusual characters and to shake the hand of everyone new. If he sensed anything amiss he was to call Iain, he would know what to do. "She is your responsibility, you must make sure she tells no one about us." He cautioned him. As a witch in training Davina could technically know of our existence without facing termination yet the same rules for sharing the secret applied.

"Take care of her Alan, and keep her close."

Next James called the car and unusually subdued, we packed and locked up to head to the airport. In the cab James put an arm around me and told me to rest. Gladly I did as I was told, closing my eyes for the blissfully uneventful ride to the airport and I got as close to sleeping as a vampire could during the long flight home. When we pulled into the garage, I was so happy to be home I jumped out of the car and winked at James before racing around the front of the car and running inside.

Inside the kitchen I turned around grinning at him. "We can finally have a moment's peace!"

James laughed with me, my enthusiasm contagious. We had been constantly on guard, waiting for the powder keg to explode and war to break out at any given time since we had met. While Daemon remained on the loose, we had decapitated his movement for the time being. It would take years, maybe even decades, for them to rebuild their leadership.

That gave us a long time of just being a normal couple. With no more "what if's" surrounding us, I felt far more secure with our future. The idea of no more drama for a while gave me an idea. There was something I really wanted to do.

"Do you think we could go out with Heidi and Troy like we talked about before? You know, something normal?"

"I think Troy could be convinced you can control yourself now that he's seen you in action." He set me up on the counter and pulled out his phone. After a brief call to Troy, we were on for a double date for Thursday night. We were going to try drinks and a movie, James and I would have an easier time faking drinking than a full fledged meal.

"I should check in with the school and see if I can still do a class or two this semester." Studying the calendar, I saw that I wasn't quite at the deadline yet. "Maybe they still have some slots open for some of the classes I want."

"Where did you put your course guide?" I pointed and he went to get it.

We stood in the kitchen, making a list of classes. Talking about the different subjects and classes made for very interesting conversation with my one hundred, fifty some odd year old vampire husband. We ended with a short list of a few classes I wanted and were going to unpack our bags when my phone rang.

I didn't recognize the number. "Hello?"

"Are you back yet?" It was Aunt Sandi.

I tried not to groan out loud. "Yes, we just got home." My mood brightened when I realized I had some good news for her. "We caught Bradley's boss. You can tell the Detective."

She was silent for several heartbeats. "Is he coming back here?"

"No."

I let her make her own assumptions.

"Well, Detective Hanson will be pleased to hear it." Sandi's voice became hesitant, "I know it's last minute, but I was wondering if you two would like to join us for dinner tonight at my house. I've invited your parents."

I didn't know if I was ready to see my parents just yet but supposed now was as good a time as any and saying no might do more harm than good. My Dad was of concern, we would have to avoid him for a while after this. "Um, okay. What time?" I swallowed my doubt.

We agreed on seven o'clock and I hung up. James lifted an eyebrow at me. "What do you suppose she's up to?"

"I don't know. I don't think she's had dinner with my parents since Uncle Jim died." Thinking through the possibilities, I was sure she wasn't going to let an important cat out of the bag. "You know with the detective there she won't be giving up our secret. She said she doesn't want him to know about the existence of vampires, remember?"

"Yes, but she doesn't know about you yet. That might change her mind."

"You have a point."

In truth, I had worried about the same thing. Sandi was upset when she saw what he was and was really mad when she thought he was going to *try* to turn me. Now that I *had* been turned, she would probably consider her initial opinion of James as correct. Hopefully that didn't mean she would endanger herself and my family by outing us in front of them. Dad already had his reservations about James, he needed no encouragement.

"Vous souhaitez pratiquer votre Français?" James asked me, trying very hard to look serious.

I giggled, his distraction worked. "Yes, I would love to practice."

We had another practice session and it had some very exciting results. Eventually when we needed to clean up for dinner, I suggested we practice some more when we got home. My tutor agreed that practice made perfect.

Ch. 57

We were the last to arrive a few minutes after seven. My parents' minivan sat in the driveway as well as the familiar silver Toyota.

Sandi answered the door, I could hear the others talking in the other room. She took one look at me and she went ashen. Before she could raise a fuss I whispered swiftly and forcefully, hurrying to get the words out while she might still listen.

"Aunt Sandi, listen to me. I was dying. I asked for this. Please don't freak out." My eyes ran to the empty hall behind her hoping to get this out of the way before anyone else came to investigate.

The look she gave him made it clear she assumed James had been the one. I had suspected she would.

"It wasn't him." It was important to me that she knew that. It gave me some small amount of pleasure to see her mentally reassessing my husband.

I pressed on. "You should know Dad already suspects something is different about James." Placing a hand on her arm, I added, "We could use your help with this." My eyes pleaded with her for her cooperation.

She frowned thoughtfully, putting a hand over mine. "You're cool, not cold. Will you warm up any more when you've been inside for a while?" She stepped aside to allow us entrance as she asked. James started to walk in and stopped when he felt my resistance.

It wasn't intentional. Physically I could not walk through the doorway. It was as if some invisible door had closed. My feet could not cross the threshold.

James whispered to Sandi, "You've consecrated the house, you have to invite her in."

Her eyes widened. "You can sense my protections?" She mumbled curiously to herself. "I run salt around the property every year and say a few words a woman taught me once, I wasn't sure they worked." She eyed James curiously, "Did I invite you in before?"

He nodded, "You said please come in."

Sandi turned back to me, "Claire, won't you please come in?"

Just like that the barrier was removed and I easily stepped across the threshold. I heard my mother's voice call out from the kitchen.

"Claire, honey is that you?" She came through the doorway and her eyes found me. She gasped when she saw me and I worried for the worst. Smiling broadly, Mom opened up her arms and wrapped me in a tight hug. Pulling back to examine me like only a mom could, she shook her head grinning. "Marriage agrees with you honey. You're absolutely radiant!" She hugged me back to her and I relaxed in to it feeling relieved. If only Dad could be so easy.

Releasing me, Mom turned to James and hugged him as well. "James, we had such a wonderful time in France. We've brought our pictures, we were just showing them to Sandi and Earl." She started to walk away and waved us to follow back in to the kitchen. "You two come in here and warm up. You're cold."

I shot James a look, only to see that he remained serene.

You'll get used to it. Most of us try to avoid letting humans touch us. For now, we can blame it on winter.

But they're my parents.

Then you will just have to develop a circulation problem.

I said something snide in reply that got me a little jolt just as we entered the kitchen. Detective Earl Hanson was standing at the center island, a half empty glass of scotch in front of him as well as a pile of loose photographs. Next to him was my Dad, a bottle of beer on his side of the center island.

Mom had fluttered back in and had a glass of wine sitting next to the stove where she landed to briefly stir something that smelled a lot like marinara sauce. The basil was dizzying. Everything smelled so different I had to *re*figure out what everything was.

Dad stared straight at me and gaped. His eyes shifted to James who possessively wrapped an arm around my waist, pulling me closer to his body. I reached up and rubbed his chest reassuringly. My dad wouldn't hurt me no matter what I was. James didn't necessarily agree.

"Hi Dad." I smiled brightly at him, ignoring his scrutiny and acknowledged the Detective as well, "Earl."

My mom turned around and swept her glass up in her hand. Taking a quick sip, she moved to stand behind my dad. "Doesn't she look radiant, Doug? I've never seen Claire so beautiful."

Dad continued to stare, barely giving Mom's question a half hearted, "Uh, huh."

Mom gave his shoulder a little push, "Doug, you are such a *man*." Giving up on him, she took another sip of wine and asked Earl the same. "What do you think Earl? Doesn't my little girl make a beautiful wife?"

My heart sank. Mom was nervous and had obviously been drinking fast. She was headed toward drunk by the sound and smell of her. She had been doing so well these past few months. She must have been more nervous than I had thought about having dinner with Sandi.

Earl indulged her, smiling and agreeing with my mom, even though he wasn't so sure the source of the change in my appearance. I didn't like having attention called to the very thing I'd hoped to keep on the down low.

"Mom, I have to give credit where credit is due. I *am* a happy bride," I leaned into James for emphasis, "but Tonya shared some beauty secrets and makeup with me after the wedding. Not all of this is natural." I circled my face with my finger. *That* was certainly true.

The men still looked unconvinced and Mom was only half listening as she started to page through the photos. Sandi had returned to the stove and was diligently stirring and seasoning.

"Claire, come over here and see our pictures." Mom beckoned with the hand holding her glass over Dad's shoulder. I spared a look at him and saw the old lines of exhaustion around his eyes had returned. This was obviously not the first hint that she was backsliding. Damn. I guess it wouldn't be such a bad idea to give them some distance after all.

James' arm tightened and he leaned down to kiss the top of my head. I craned my neck to see him. He smiled at me and kissed my nose. I did my best to return the smile though it was strained.

"Oh, aren't they cute," Mom gushed.

"Let me see those pictures." I pulled away from James enough to stand opposite my parents and far enough away that Earl and I wouldn't touch. James stood behind me, his hands on the counter around me, still protecting.

Mom reveled in the retelling of their time in France and she had to have thanked James about a hundred times. Even Dad's mood lightened while they relived their trip. Their exchanges were playful and I was glad that they'd had a great time there.

We were nearly done with the second set of photos when Sandi asked for help setting the table. Mom took napkins and silverware, I did plates and glasses. Sandi's assignment of breakables to me didn't escape my notice, though I did appreciate her subtlety. She was cooler than I had thought.

Mom hummed to herself, concentrating on folding the linen napkins and arranging the full compliment of silverware Sandi had given her. I took the stack of plates and bowls in one pile without thinking anything of it. When Mom saw my stack of china balanced in one arm her eyes bulged.

"Wow Claire, you must be stronger than you look." Hurriedly I shifted to put my other hand under the stack.

"It's nothing Mom, I have them rested against me so it isn't that heavy." I distracted her, asking her more questions about her newest pursuits; she was always into some new hobby every few months. I was rewarded for my curiosity.

"Well, I don't know if I told you but I joined the gym. I started swimming again, you know I used to be quite a swimmer when I was younger. Well, I saw that there is an adult swim club and we have meets and everything. I signed up last week. Our first meet is in a few weeks."

I listened to the men in the other room as Mom prattled on about a swim meet I would be shocked if she ever attended. James was quiet while my dad and Earl discussed tools. Dad was more of a hand tool kind of guy, preferring them for his woodworking and Earl sounded like a power tool sort of fellow. He was about efficiency, Dad was a craftsman.

Earl asked James his opinion and he diplomatically answered, "I like both. When I need to do repair work around the house, I like power but when it's something more artistic like the wood craft Doug has been teaching me, I prefer hand tools. It lets me feel what I'm doing and I can watch it cut. I like to have more control."

Dad was quiet, I imagined he was impressed. That sounded like something he would say. Whether he wanted to admit it or not, Dad and James had a lot in common.

Finishing setting the last of the glasses in record time, I tried not to make it obvious I was hurrying as I joined the men in the living room. Mom was chatting up Sandi exhaustively while she finished the last of the meal preparation.

Earl excused himself to assist in the kitchen, giving the three of us some nice awkward family time.

"I'm glad you enjoyed yourselves in France. We did too." I tried to bridge the distance I felt growing between my dad and me.

Without speaking, Dad stood up and walked around the coffee table to stand close to me. He studied me intently making me very uncomfortable. It was like he was trying to see some hidden drug problem or something. I didn't know what he expected to find. I didn't really think he would figure out the real reason I was different all of a sudden or that James was different from other people, yet I didn't want him asking questions, either, on the off chance he might hit on the truth.

"What's going on with you two?" Dad shifted his gaze between us.

"Nothing Dad." I tried to laugh it off. "We've been traveling a lot and eating on the road. I know I'm just tired."

He shook his head. "Claire, don't lie to me. I can tell there's something physically different about you and it isn't makeup and it isn't diet or sleep." He stared at James, his eyes narrowed in suspicion. "I saw it in *you* the night of the wedding." A light went on in his eyes. Dad's body tensed, he drew closer to James' face. "Is it a disease? Do you have something? Something you've given to my daughter?" His voice dropped to a menacing hiss, "So help me if you did I..."

James hid the impact of the shock I felt run through him at Dad's nearly accurate guess. His voice grew rich with influence as he spoke to Dad. "Doug, you ought to know by now I would never harm Claire. I assure you I have not given her anything. She is perfectly fine."

I broke in, consciously fighting the impulse to touch him. "Dad, I'm fine. I'm healthy and happy. I've been so busy with school and work that I haven't been able to get out much so I'm a little paler and I've been wearing more makeup to cover it up. I like how it makes me look." Winking at him, I tried to lift the mood. "Now that I'm a grown woman I have to start looking like one."

He did smile at that. "Don't change because you feel like you have to." His eyes flicked to James with a warning, he wasn't entirely convinced.

My nostrils flared and I rose to his challenge. "Dad, is this because you don't think I'm old enough to get married? What happened to 'It doesn't always take a long time to realize you love someone?' Were you lying when you said that? I hope not, because your time to object has passed." I fought to keep my voice down and the hurt out of it.

James put his hand over mine and squeezed. I knew I needed to keep myself reasonably sedate. Being "young" I could lose control easily and I was in a house full of humans. Good thing the smell of their blood was being dulled by the odors coming from the kitchen.

Dad saw James' gesture and I thought he might have softened a little. Either way, he put his hands up in surrender and told me, "I wasn't lying. I also hadn't considered how hard it would be to think of my only little girl all grown up and married already. *You* may have been ready but I wasn't." He flashed his teeth in a brief smile.

Ch. 58

Sandi's call to dinner interrupted any further discussion, or, I could say, *saved* us from it. We were seated opposite my parents and Sandi and Earl sat at either end of the long table.

The dual purpose of acting the part of a gentleman, James showed me how he dished as little as politely possible on both of our plates. James had laid the bread diagonal across the pasta bowl so it covered a big corner of the meal. I could see how I would be able to hide quite a bit of the food if I was careful.

Just before the last portion was dished by my Dad, Earl cleared his throat and stood. As expected, we all looked up and waited. Holding his glass aloft, Earl smiled at Sandi and my hand flew to my mouth. *This* was the reason for their dinner party. I hadn't sensed it with my defenses in lock down.

"We wanted to congratulate James and Claire on their recent good fortune of finding each other." He bowed his head at us and we lifted our glasses back.

"And, as you know Sandi's family is gone and she's always considered you family even after Jim's death." He cast a warm look at her, her eyes twinkled damp in the light, "She wanted you to be the first in the family to share in our happy news. Sandi has agreed to become my wife." My aunt beamed happily at Earl and I lifted my glass high before putting it to my lips. I got up and hugged her, as did everyone else in turn, sharing our well wishes at the news.

Sandi was visibly relieved to have her news received so well by my dad, her deceased husband's brother.

Dinner conversation was lively as we discussed the upcoming wedding. They were going to keep it small and hoped we all would attend. All present assured the happy couple we would indeed be overjoyed to share their day with them. I picked at my bread and pushed my food around so that it looked properly disturbed and nibbled at by the time we were done. I did catch the Detective watching us both more than I was comfortable. James and I offered to clear the table and when my mom started to object, Sandi piped up.

"Jeanette let them, they're the youngest and we cooked. Sit back and reap the rewards of your age."

It worked. Mom didn't object any further and James and I were able to clear and scrape plates burying the evidence under the soiled napkins.

Shortly after dinner Mom started to fade, the effects of stress, alcohol, and food exacting their price. Dad ushered her out and we all said good-bye. I followed him outside, helping him with Mom. She gave me a wet kiss on my cheek to accompany the less than firm hug before we poured her into the front seat. When he hugged me, he rubbed my arm and told me to go inside.

"You're freezing, go on in." He kissed my cheek and jerked his head toward the house. "You did all right with him. He'll take care of you." Dad gave me an appraising look, "Not that you need that anymore. You've changed in a good way, honey. I'm proud of you."

"Thanks Dad." I got a little choked up and was grateful I couldn't cry.

We agreed to get together again soon and Dad left, Mom already sound asleep in the passenger seat.

I walked back up to the house and James was waiting for me. Smiling at him, I passed on Dad's ruling on him. He snorted, "He liked me better when I was just the boyfriend."

"He'll get over it," I gave his chest a consoling pat.

When we returned, Earl was waiting calmly at the table and asked before we could even sit down, "Sandi tells me you caught the guy, is that true?" He was wearing his cop face, blank.

"Yes," I answered. "We did. We found him in the UK." I decided to keep it general. "We turned him over to local authorities and they took care of him."

"They took care of him? How so?"

James took over. "Things got ugly and our guy ended up being shot during the pursuit. He's dead, there won't be any more murders."

He nodded, eyes appraising us the whole time. "Uh huh." He didn't sound convinced. "What town did you say that was in?" Earl took another drink of his scotch.

James answered without hesitation, "Edinburgh."

Earl nodded without saying more. Sandi said she was going to get coffee.

"Let me help." Earl rose and joined Sandi in the kitchen giving James and I a chance to talk.

"What do you think he's fishing for?" I whispered to James.

He was watching the kitchen doorway looking contemplative. "I'm not sure. Edinburgh is a large city. We should be okay. If he pushes we can get someone official to back up our story."

"I hope so." I mumbled as Sandi came back in carrying a tray with four china cups, cream and sugar. Earl followed behind with a coffee pot.

Sandi set up the four cups and Earl started pouring. Something had happened in the kitchen, I wasn't sure what, only that Sandi was tense and Earl's jaw was set. I hoped it was a lovers' quarrel.

James and I graciously accepted our cups and our hosts sat back down in my parents' seats across from us.

Earl sipped at his coffee, his eyes never leaving us. Sandi had her hands in her lap looking incredibly unhappy. I didn't need to use any additional skills to read that.

"Sandi makes good coffee." He took another sip before setting his cup back down on its saucer. "Not like that cheap crap you get at coffee shops now where they charge you an arm and a leg and dump a ton of shit in it to hide the fact that it's cheap coffee."

Sandi fidgeted nervously. She wasn't the only one. I was developing an urgent need to get out of there.

"Go on, try it," Earl prodded.

James maintained eye contact with Earl, accepting his challenge. Threading his top two fingers through the handle he took a small sip. "Yes," he shifted his gaze to Sandi. "It is a good cup of coffee. My mother used to make coffee like this. I remember the smell."

"Your parents died, right?" Earl was on a scent.

"Yes, when I was young." He remained outwardly calm, his voice steady though I could feel his anger starting to mount. James was not happy with Earl's aggressive line of questioning.

"That's right. You were raised by some relatives, right?" Earl took another sip of coffee. Pretending to be distracted by something in his cup, he stared into the dark liquid while he waited for James' answer. "In Canada?"

"Some friends of the family in Quebec."

"Where was that?" He shifted to me, "Claire, you haven't touched yours. Try it."

"I'm full, and besides, I don't want to be up all night." I put him off gently. "It smells great, Sandi," I offered weakly.

"I don't know how you can be full, you didn't touch your dinner." He leveled a steady gaze at me.

I froze, not sure how to respond. This was not a conversation I was prepared to have tonight.

Yawn. I heard his command in my head. I did so immediately.

James took one more sip and glanced at his watch. He stood abruptly placing his cup on the table. "Sandi, Earl it has been a pleasure." He half bowed to them both. "If you don't mind we did just fly back today and I'm afraid it's catching up with us."

He pulled my chair out and I got up. Sandi and Earl walked with us to the coat closet. No one spoke beyond Sandi thanking us for coming even though we had only just gotten in.

Earl remained silent, the weight of what he was not saying hung over us all. He suspected something. I wondered if Sandi said something to him despite her assurances she wouldn't. Maybe her anger over my turning was stronger than her fear that Detective Earl Hanson would consider her crazy.

"Claire, James, please do come back soon." Sandi hugged James, then me. She held on to me and spoke softly in my ear. "So much has changed for you. Please let me know if I can be of any help. I might be able to help you more than your mother on some things." When she pulled back, she kept her hands on my shoulders, her eyes tearing up. "You can tell me anything, I promise I can keep a secret."

I wanted to believe her. "Thanks Sandi, I appreciate that." I gave a little wave and faked another yawn, my hand covering my mouth halfway through.

James had the door open and half bowed from the waist. "It was good to see you again, Earl."

"I'm sure we'll be seeing each other again soon," Earl said, waving from beside Sandi as James and I stepped out the door.

It was hard to hold to a walk when we were finally clear of the door, I wanted to flee yet I knew they were watching. James wrapped his arm around me in a public show of support, keeping my pace painfully slow.

Ch. 59

James opened my door and I slid down into the comfortable leather, breathing out a huge sigh of relief when he closed it. As soon as his door shut and the car roared to life, we were finally able to speak unguarded.

"What did he mean, 'he's going to be seeing us soon'?"

"I don't know," he frowned at the dashboard, his pale features taking on a demonic mien in the green glow. "Do you think Sandi would have said anything? If they're lovers it would be difficult for her to keep all she knows secret."

I was shaking my head before he finished. "I don't think she told. That's what she was trying to tell me at the door. He's working independently here." The night's events gave me some hope. "If he loves her, won't he be more trusting of her? He is going to be more likely to believe her when she tells him we aren't hiding anything."

"I like the way you think, although that is only part of the reason I let you seduce me," he teased, the corner of his mouth twitching.

I snorted. "Me seduce you? Right. Aren't a vampire's abilities to seduce young virgins legendary, not the other way around?"

"If you recall you *did* kiss me first."

"I wasn't in control of my faculties. Besides, if you had wanted to stop me you could have."

James turned to watch me, a curious expression twisting his features. "*If* I had wanted to stop you, I would have. Things might have been very different."

388

I reached out to grab his hand off the steering wheel. Kissing his knuckles softly, I stared at his hand, tracing the lines on his palm with my finger. These hands knew my body as well as my own. The thought of never having experienced that was awful.

"I wouldn't want it any other way. You and me is all that I need. It doesn't matter the where and how."

His foot pressed down on the accelerator and the German engineering answered his call eagerly, its longer strokes growling through the gears, our speed climbed steadily. I watched the scenery and other cars fly past us.

We spent the rest of the night talking, and not talking. I'd always found James fascinating and now I understood a little better some of his perspectives. Some of the things he talked about made far more sense when you factored in how our thirst feels or how the sun affects our bodies. He could have described it before, only I wouldn't have understood like I did now.

And when I heard his references to time, they took on a whole new meaning. I was going to be around forever. Just a week ago a century had seemed like a lifetime, now it was nothing. Instead of counting my time in years, I would soon be recording it in decades. It was a lot to wrap my head around.

Ch. 60

No one called or came over all day Wednesday. It was heaven. We had no obligations. I wandered over to the computer to make a request for classes and James emailed his editor to tell him he was back in town and open to assignment ideas for the paper's newest husband and wife writing team. Some time late in the afternoon, a fruit basket arrived with a congratulations card from the writing staff at the Star Tribune. I suggested sending it to one of the Andrews so it didn't go to waste.

Later, when the phone rang. It was not the voice we wanted to hear.

"This is Detective Hanson, Mr. Thomas." He sounded official, that couldn't be good. James flicked his gaze to me. We watched each other while he spoke to the Detective.

"What can I do for you, Detective?" He was painfully polite.

"You and I need to meet. I will be off duty in a few hours and wanted to talk to you. Can you both meet me at the Mall of America at six? In front of The Rainforest Café?" The Detective was establishing dominance, picking the time and place. I felt my nerves beginning to hum.

"That would be fine, Detective. Will you be bringing Sandi?"

Detective Hanson growled, "This is business." The line went dead.

"What do you think?" I asked, fearing the Detective was too smart for his own good. What did we do if he figured it out?

"Hope that he doesn't," James declared bleakly in answer to my thoughts. I glanced at the clock.

Almost two hours to fret. Great.

Ch. 61

We arrived early and James and I walked around the Mall trying to ascertain if this was a solo operation or if the police department sanctioned it. There were no other officers in the area so we assumed this was off the record. The only reason I could think he would want to meet us alone filled me with dread.

James and I stood on the second level overlooking the rotunda in front of the restaurant below. At a few minutes to six, Detective Earl Hanson strode up to the open area in front of the restaurant, ignoring the fake alligator roaring in the fountain behind him. Earl crossed his arms, every inch a cop.

"Well," James pushed off the railing looking grim. "Let's go see what he knows."

I followed him down the escalator to meet my future uncle and possible wrench in the works, hoping against hope that only one of those things proved true.

Detective Hanson saw us come down the escalator and walked away from the tourist trap, leading us closer to the more isolated bistro tables in the open mall. He motioned for us to take our seats.

"What brings us here today, Detective?" James gave him the respect of his rank.

Lowering his voice, the detective glanced over both shoulders and mostly stared around our heads instead of making eye contact. "I don't want Sandi involved in this. I don't know if she can handle anything like this, she's pretty sensitive."

I snorted, choking back a laugh. The detective shot me a nasty look. "Sorry."

"I know there are things in this world we can't always explain by logic. I'm not a believer in magic or hocus pocus, but there is something going on here that isn't normal."

"I don't know what you're talking about." James' voice was dead calm.

Its effect on the detective was telling. Hanson feared him, I could feel it when I did a quick sweep. Thankfully, he also did not have intentions of turning us in. His emotions were locked away other than that. I understood how Stephen had a hard time using *his* ability on the detective. He was skilled at locking himself down.

Swallowing his nerves he went on. "Mr. Thomas, I have been trying to figure you out since I met you. There's something not right about you. When I was trying to find a match on that old photograph you asked about with Interpol, I made a few new friends. I had one call over to the station in Edinburgh looking for your guy." He watched us closely. James didn't react but I had to concentrate on making myself breathe so he wouldn't think I was holding my breath. "They don't know anything about a guy turned over by a couple of Americans. There isn't anyone there implicated in any American crimes." He continued to watch the tourists swirling in commercialism's mecca. "I wanted to know more about you, Mr. Thomas. After all, we are going to be family. I checked up on your story, there isn't anything backing it up. A buddy of mine works over in the County Records office and I talked to him last night. Would you like to know something interesting? You don't exist. How do you get a job, a house, and a driver's license if you don't exist? What are you hiding from and what have you gotten Claire into?" He risked a glance at James' face and quickly averted his gaze. "Doug doesn't like you, and I'm starting to think he's onto something."

He stared directly at me, not afraid in the least. "And you, Claire. You're a different person from when I saw you last."

393

Detective Hanson cocked his head, "Or is person the wrong word."

James' temper flared and I felt my eyes go wide.

He knows. What do we do if Sandi told him? What if he's told his partner? How many people are we dealing with?

"What *was* that?" The detective's sharp question cut into our conversation.

"I'm sorry?" James remained nonreactive.

The detective was chancing fleeting glimpses between both our faces. "That thing you do." He was pointing at us, waggling his finger from one to the other. "Your pupils start dilating and constricting, like someone's flashing lights in them."

James' voice was deadly quiet and my veins were vibrating with our combined apprehension.

"Detective, I don't think this is the best place to have this discussion. Can we go somewhere more private?"

"Do you mean somewhere with fewer witnesses?" He was equally subdued.

Trying to avoid an immediate crisis, I interjected. "What if we go somewhere we can be seen *and* not heard?"

Both men watched me expectantly. "Do you have somewhere in mind?" James kept his internal comments shut off.

"They have glass elevators in the parking garage. We can stop one between floors and that will give us a few minutes before the alarms sound. We can have privacy there and anyone in the skyway or in the parkway can see in, everybody's happy."

I liked the surprised approval I saw from both of them. It was funny how men generally didn't think a young woman capable of strategy. Give me a few more centuries and I would be amazing. James chuckled in my head before he stopped himself abruptly and found some lint on his sleeve to focus his eyes on.

We walked inside the mall to the parking ramp attached by skyway, nearly empty this time of day. The day shoppers were gone, the evening diners and after work crowd was just starting to shuffle in.

Fortunately most of the locals who didn't have strollers used the stairs so the elevators didn't get used very often during the week. We walked right in to one and Detective Hanson pushed the button for four. Halfway between three and four, I pushed the stop button.

"Okay, which one of you wants to tell me what is going on?" The detective watched us closely.

James answered first, watching the people below us. "I am sorry, Detective, I can't tell you what you want to know."

He threw up his hands, "Typical blood sucker, you're all alike. None of you wants to talk until your life is on the line."

"I don't know what you're talking about." The elevator was quickly becoming claustrophobic.

It didn't work. "Cut the crap, Thomas. Your kind has bothered this town for long enough. My partner was cut down in cold blood by your lot and I intend to see his murderer punished." Hanson's nostrils were flaring and his face was going red.

"Did Sandi tell you?" I asked hesitantly.

"Sandi? No, she doesn't know any of this. I figured out you're the walking dead on my own. I'm a detective, it's what I do." He gave me a disappointed look. "A lot has been happening in this town and our outlying counties that can't be explained by logic. We've had enough help from 'alternative' consultants over the years that seem to know a lot more than they let on. I followed a few of them and saw some freaky stuff." He paused, frowning when he stared out the glass at the sidewalk below. "What I have the hardest time stomaching is not what you do, although that's disgusting too, but that you're real. I don't dare say anything to Williams. He would have me up for mental leave as soon as look at me, the man's got the imagination of a flea."

"You can't know this, Earl," James stated flatly. "It puts you and Sandi in danger. Only a very few are approved, anyone else must guard their knowledge as though their lives depend on it. It does."

Earl was shaking his head, his eyes closed. "I don't want to know. I want you to help me take down the network responsible for Jim's murder. We got some of them, but people are still disappearing. There are more out there." He finally gave James a long look. "I know you can take the memory away. After we solve Jim's murder, I don't care what I remember of you all. But please, let me put this to bed."

I felt a visceral pulling at my insides and it felt so real, like someone was pulling out my guts that I wrapped my arms around myself.

James nodded slowly. "I'll help you. Remember, if anyone knows about this both of our lives are in danger."

"I'll help, too." With the verbalization of my offer the feeling that I was being eviscerated disappeared.

"No," James whipped around. Earl was forgotten for the moment.

"I want to help. He was *my* uncle."

"Claire," James pleaded, gripping my upper arms tightly. If I was human it would have given me bruises. "They'll kill you."

My chin jutted out obstinately. "They'll kill you too. Do you think that is somehow easier for *me* to take? Especially now." I let that hang and knew he knew exactly what I wasn't saying. Forever alone with half of me gone.

Earl cleared his throat, reminding us he was still with us. "I think our time is up."

We followed the direction of his gaze and saw a mall security guard pointing up at us. James hit the stop button again and the elevator started moving up to the fourth level at once. When it stopped we flowed out, Earl leaning close to James. He extended his hand. When James took it, Earl's "tough as nails" detective attitude came back out. "I'll bring you what I have later tonight and leave it for you to examine. I expect your full cooperation on this."

"I said I would help." James meant what he said and didn't like his integrity being questioned.

The detective studied him a moment longer. "Good."

James nodded and released Earl's grip. Earl turned to me and shook my hand as well, only pausing a moment at my cold hand before he caught himself.

"What do you do in the summer?"
"Air conditioning," James replied, deadpan.

Earl shot him a look to see if he was kidding. He wasn't.

We parted and James and I went straight to our car.

I could barely wait until the door closed before I asked what had been troubling me. "What was that feeling? I felt like my guts were being torn out. Did you feel it too?"

"*That* is a compulsion," he stated flatly, staring out the windshield. Savagely, he punched the ignition button.

"You mean your compulsion to help? *That* compulsion?" At the sight of his clenched jaw, I tried to reassure him he didn't have anything to feel guilty about.

"It wasn't me that I felt. It was you, I felt it *through* you."

My hand went limp on his arm.

Lips pulled tight in a grimace, his pale face cast in that eerie green dashboard glow. James pulled out of his parking spot, the engine roared and we drove home, the door between us locked up tight.

Ch. 62

As promised, Earl dropped off a manila envelope about a half an inch thick with no outside markings.

"It's a personal file," Earl said simply, handing it to James before turning. "Call as soon as you have something." He started to walk away and paused to call over his shoulder, "Please."

James closed the door and looked at the folder in his hand. "If you're in, I guess you're all in." Brushing past me he nodded at the dining room table. "Let's take a look, shall we?"

I fell in step behind him and took a seat.

The contents of the folder slid out in a pile of neatly paper clipped sections, each labeled with a name. Not surprisingly, I saw Jim Martin, my uncle, on top. Brian Peterson was second. I wondered if he suspected anything about Stephen or if he just figured he hung out with vampires. There were seven files total inside the folder.

Sifting through them, I scanned the top sheet of each giving a color copy of driver's license photos and basic information about the victims. "They don't have anything in common." I touched each one, "This woman was in her forties, these two are in their twenties, this guy was a commercial plumber on a job in the city and this guy was in advertising."

James was scanning the plumber's file, flipping through the pages. "This man was last seen leaving for work. He lived in Hutchinson and his van was found in La Crosse, Wisconsin. He wasn't found for a few weeks and when they did find him, animals had done a lot of damage." Our eyes met over the file.

That sounded familiar. We both dug through the other files and each one had a similar description of the body; animals had damaged the remains to the point the cause of death was unknown. "These aren't all vampire attacks are they? Some of these seem like they've been eaten and hidden, like an animal kill. It was like it was coming back to feed on them."

James was impressed. "Nice catch, Claire."

I used to watch tons of Animal Planet.

We flipped through the rest looking for more similarities a human might miss.

From there we started to look at the locations of the victims' homes and offices as well as where they were found. James went upstairs and got an Atlas so that we could mark them for a visual. We used blue dots for homes, green for work and red for where they were found.

James was staring at our mapping when he smacked a hand on the atlas. "Brian is an outlier. He doesn't fit." He removed each of the pins for Brian and we stared at the remaining dots. We had been staring at the pins for a few minutes when James exclaimed, "It's all the *same* animal."

Surprised, I jumped. "What do you mean?" Except I was afraid I knew exactly what he meant. A *true* animal wasn't going to come down into the city to take victims. It had to be a were.

He pointed at the circles. "They're random. Too random." His fingers traced the circles one by one. I hadn't seen it at first but when he pointed it out, I saw that two of the circles were equidistant from each other. The victims worked in pretty much the same general vicinity and were hidden in the same areas.

"What does it mean?"

James stared at the map, intentionally avoiding my scrutiny. "The police know hunters, but humans only. They don't understand a were's mind. The beast in him pushes him to return to successful grounds, usually somewhere he's been initiated. Someone has brought him to that place and now he keeps coming back. The human side, or what remains of it, needs to keep the hunting grounds away from home. He tries to hide it with the intelligence of a man." He continued to study the map, his fingers absently tapping his temple.

I watched his profile, "Have you ever hunted a were?"

"Yes," he confirmed flatly. "I had to hunt rogues when I was in the Guard. It was one of the reasons I quit my post."

"Why? Weren't you any good at it?" The were's ruling Council contracted vampires to hunt down renegades who were not in control of their beast or chose not to adhere to their laws.

James avoided my eyes and his response held no hint of pride. "I was *very* good at it."

My James wasn't a cold contract killer and I refused to see him that way. I watched him flip through the files, his head bent over the table. A brown chunk of hair fell into his face while he concentrated. Kind and thoughtful, *my* James only fought to defend those he loved. I heard his words in my head, "It was one of the reasons I quit," and I believed it.

"There we go." He pulled the map over and pointed at a spot in downtown Minneapolis.

"What happens at 6th and Marquette?" It was the intersection his finger marked.

"The abductions have all centered around this spot. I think this is where we need to start. I can go in the morning with the commuters."

"Let's check it out now." I moved eagerly to get my coat.

He smiled and shook his head. "The area is commercial. It's long since closed down. We don't want to break in and scare it off, it would be best to wait."

"Okay, we'll wait until morning then."

"Claire, the area will be packed with humans at that time of day. The streets and office buildings will be full of them. We will be listening to their hearts beat, smelling their blood. I respect your self-control but even some older vampires find this type of situation difficult. It might prove too much for a young vampire. It would be safer for me to go alone."

He was right and I had to concede the point. "Fine, I'll just wait here." My shoulders slumped.

James chuckled and my head shot back up. He was grinning his charming little grin at me. "I've never seen you pout before. It's kind of cute."

I shot him a look and stood up to refill my glass, grumbling about "vampires are not cute." He came up behind me, putting his arms around my waist.

"Mad?" he asked softly.

"No, not really. I have a hard time thinking of you doing something dangerous without me." I answered honestly, choosing to leave out my feelings of inadequacy for now.

"You know I've done a reasonably good job of defending myself for over one hundred and fifty years. I'm relatively sure I can do this safely." The levity in his tone softened the blow, though it hit home regardless. He didn't need me. That was difficult to admit since I undeniably needed him.

He continued to study the files all night and I moved on to read a book. When it was time for him to leave, I saw he had a messenger bag strap slung crosswise over his chest. In answer to my query, he patted the bulge in the bag behind him and offered cryptically. "Tools of the trade."

Of course he would need silver to hold and possibly destroy the were should he find it. "Be safe," I cautioned.

His response, "Naturally," was all I got. He'd walled me off from reading more into it than that.

Waiting was awful. None of the magazines or books held my interest for long. Finally, after several hours, I heard the door and hopped up to meet him in the kitchen.

Arms around him, I felt my anxiety fading. "Did you see anyone suspicious?"

"No, no one suspicious although I did see a few vampires and asked them to keep an eye out. The building is nothing special and the top few floors are under construction. I put in a call to the city offices to find out who both owns the building and who is renovating and I hit a dead end. I'm going to have to try another approach."

"What about the Council, can they help? Won't they know who of theirs is in the area?"

"The Council won't have anything, they never hunt their own. They leave that to us and they'll know we're on it by now; they have an amazing network of eyes and ears." He tapped the pile of folders. "Its organization will tell us some things about the animal, like a human murderer, each animal has its own style of hunting and killing."

"What's this one's style?" My eyes roamed over the files trying desperately to make connections.

He shook his head, pushing the pictures away in frustration, "I'm not sure. Something isn't adding up. We're missing something big."

Ch. 64

We had plans with Troy and Heidi that night, but invited Detective Hanson to stop by after work that evening for a quick meeting of the minds. He arrived promptly at half past five, his face grave.

He was barely inside when he made the announcement. "Another woman has gone missing."

I felt all of our disappointment as the Detective filled us in on what he knew. "Monica Hauser. She's twenty-four and works as an accounting temp at a small marketing firm in the US Bank Tower. A co-worker reported seeing her car in the ramp running this morning with the door open and her purse on the ground."

James called our attention to the map we had laid out on the table with the files.

Earl studied the map and colored circles. "Yeah, I've plotted it all out too. What do *you* make of it?"

James shrugged. "They all work in this area." He pointed to the intersection except he didn't mention the building.

Earl was nodding. "We're focusing on the work angle too. They've all been in their positions for less than a year and all work within a six block radius.

"Did you interview their employers?"

"We did. No one had any stalkers and they all came from different companies in different industries. Some drive to work, some take the bus and we have one with a work van who carpooled. That's the best I've been able to do to connect them." He sighed, rubbing the back of his neck staring at the information in front of us. Clearly he was at his wit's end.

405

I felt bad for him. I was frustrated after just one day and he had been at this for years. Now another woman was out there, possibly dead already. He had to be going crazy.

"It's the building, I know it," James mumbled to himself. He went for his phone and dialed, still staring at the table. I heard the other party answer with a gruff, "Yes?"

"I need a favor."

"What?" he growled in annoyance.

Apparently the grouchy party on the other end of the call was a man of few words. Catching myself, I realized "man" was probably the wrong word.

"I need the owner of a building on 6th and Marquette as well as who is behind a renovation project on the upper floors."

"It'll cost."

James' eyes narrowed and lips tightened. He growled, "It always does."

"I'll get back to you." Click.

Earl was eyeing him, head at an angle. "Who was that?" His human ears had only caught the one side.

"A guy."

"One of mine or one of yours?"

"One of mine."

What will it cost? I wanted to know.

Usually a favor.

"You're doing it again." Earl slammed his fist down. "What the hell is that?"

I had forgotten he could tell when we were communicating. We were going to have to do it in the mirror so that I could see what he was talking about.

"I told you we felt connected from the very start. I wasn't kidding," James reminded Earl, tapping his temple for emphasis.

Realization dawned in Earl's widening eyes. "You two can talk to each other in your heads?"

James answered in the affirmative, going on to clarify. "I tell you this knowing that you will not divulge it or use it against us. Remember it can work against *you* as well." He let Earl make what he wanted of the threat. Two vampires who could communicate silently and were nearly impossible to kill could be a formidable enemy. I was pretty sure Earl could figure that one out. He *was* a detective.

James aimed a pointed glance at his watch and Earl got the hint.

"I'd better get going. Sandi's making Pad Thai. It's one of my favorites." His expression lightened at the thought of her.

"We have plans, too. We're meeting some friends for a movie and drinks," I offered cheerily.

Earl glanced nervously from James to me. "Is that a vampire joke? What are you drinking?"

"No, they aren't like us. I would imagine drinks would be of the fizzy variety since only one is of us is of age and un-vampy enough to consume."

"I notice you didn't say human. Would this be some other form of monster I don't know about?" Earl couldn't *not* be a cop for one minute, could he? I cursed my loose lips.

James gave him a stern warning. "There are many things you don't know about, Detective. If you go looking for monsters, I can't guarantee you won't find them. You are in enough danger as is. Leave it at that," his tone softened, "please."

Earl was visibly affected by James' strong caution, nevertheless he had to push. "Is your friend Stephen one of those 'others'? I never did get him in the same room as Sandi, but I got a funny feeling from him. He wasn't one of yours though. He's warm and I saw him eat a sandwich."

"You should be on your way, Detective." I could hear the growing menace underlying James' words. So could Earl.

"I have to be going then."

Troy called as I was making sure I was sated for the evening. One more screw up by me and Troy would never let me near Heidi again.

"How do you two feel about going dancing instead of a movie? The Killer Hayseeds are at the Medina and Heidi loves them."

I was nodding vigorously, welcoming the chance to dance with my husband again. James watched me, I felt him searching in my head to test my control. At Troy's prompting, he answered reservedly, "Sure, we will meet you there about seven then?"

"Great, we will meet you outside the front doors. We are pulling tickets off the printer now." I caught Troy's enthusiasm cooling at James' hesitation.

After James hung up, I shrugged at him. "I have to brave the big bad world eventually. There *are* people out there."

He intentionally ignored my sarcasm. "Are you sure you want to try *dancing* so soon?"

"Why is dancing so much harder than a packed theater?" Both scenarios had me elbow to elbow with humans. Proximity was going to be an issue no matter what we did short of a polar expedition.

"The movement, the touching, the scents are stirred up." He clarified. "Their blood pumps more vigorously and their sweat carries the smell to a whole other level." Staring into my eyes and trying to open the door between us, James asked me again, "Are you sure?"

Thus far I'd been relatively good at controlling my urges, if not my temper. Should things get difficult, I trusted James and Troy to end the night before anything too telling happened. I couldn't face a lonely eternity. "I'm sure."

"Okay, if you want to try it we can." He frowned down at me, "I find it scandalous I haven't taken you out yet. Every man should take his wife dancing."

I giggled. "I like the sound of that." My arms slid around his neck and I reached up to kiss him.

He kissed me back with such vigor I seriously considered canceling our plans and staying in. With a reluctant groan, I withdrew from his embrace.

"We should get ready. I need an opinion on what to wear." I pulled him playfully by the hand.

"My choice?" He made his voice husky and seductive.

My determination wavered, I had to turn away and start heading up the stairs so I didn't call off the entire night, opting instead for pure physical pleasure.

We had fun getting dressed, both making promises of things we were going to do to each other when we got home. In fine spirits and well clothed we pulled up to the Medina Ballroom several minutes early.

James had chosen a little silver dress he had bought for me in Paris. I loved the way the silver played in the light and the pale ivory wrap I wore with it offset my light skin perfectly. James had faded jeans and lightly striped blue shirt with some sort of gray design on it that suited his sculpted body perfectly.

I was very aware of the women around us staring at James and put my arm possessively through his. Playing into our earlier promises, my husband knocked and I opened the door.

I have just as much competition as you do, Love.

Glancing around us, I saw a few men cast some glances my way though I argued it was nothing compared to what the women were doing. Several were blatantly ogling.

He chuckled. *You don't see it like I do. Men see other men on the prowl, women don't.*

Yeah, men are more out there with it but I would argue that they're less likely to do anything. If a woman is being obvious, she's going to go for it. I'm not leaving your side tonight.

You have nothing to worry about, Claire. I'm very loyal.

Tilting my head back to see him, I sniggered at his efforts to look wide eyed and worshipful. The thought of him being that gaga was ridiculous.

A man can be just as "gaga" as a woman. We just don't show it like you do.

You show me lots of things, I flirted.

Not everything. I have to dole my tricks out slowly to keep you interested.

I was still laughing when we saw Troy and Heidi standing by the doors. Troy had his black leather jacket open over his black shirt and faded jeans. Heidi was wearing a tiny denim skirt with a fitted red top matching her red tipped Pat Benetar shag. For the evening she had replaced her nose stud with a small ring. I envied Heidi for her ability to carry off the look complete with red high top converse. If I'd tried it, I would have looked like an idiot.

"Hey!" Heidi threw her arms around me. "Where's your coat? Aren't you freezing?" She looked me up and down.

"Not yet," I fibbed. "But if we don't go in soon I will be." I faked a little shiver and rubbed my arms for emphasis.

We ducked inside and Troy gave our tickets to the man standing guard. Due to some "unknown" luck Heidi couldn't get over, we were able to get a table next to the dance floor in perfect view of the stage despite the throng jockeying for position. The couple there got up as soon as we approached and they made eye contact. James winked at me and I thought I saw Troy hide a smile.

I chalked our incredible drink service up to the waitress's undeniable lust, yes I felt it, for my husband and Troy. Heidi had her hackles up right away. Troy kissed her and rubbed her back, reassuring her of his disinterest in anyone else.

Shortly after we all got drinks, the lights went down and the packed house went wild. The band opened with a cover of "Squeeze Box," one of their more popular tunes. People immediately began streaming out onto the dance floor in a wild stampede.

Heidi, a devoted follower of the band, shouted to be heard. "It's always like this for the first few songs. In a few more they'll play something slow and then it will settle down to just plain busy."

Reassured this wasn't going to be the worst idea ever, I settled in to people watch and enjoy the music. Troy had pushed back from the table, turning his chair to face the stage directly and Heidi had shifted so she could lean back on him. James and I scooted our chairs together so when we leaned our bodies touched. As the sweat started, I leaned in closer and put my nose into his shoulder.

Ch. 65

As predicted, when the band played "Somewhere Between I Love You and I'm Leaving," the crowd thinned and the wildest of them stepped out. Heidi jumped up and grabbed Troy's hand. Winking at me, she dragged him out onto the dance floor.

James touched my shoulder and I lifted my head. "Are you doing all right?"

I smiled nervously. "I think so. It's gotten easier now that I've adjusted."

He stood up and offered his hand. "Then may I have this dance, Mrs. Thomas?" His lips curved and a lock of his wavy brown hair spilled onto his forehead.

Taking his hand I rose and pushed his hair back affectionately. "I do believe you owe me one, Mr. Thomas."

We danced, lost in our own bliss for the first song. The next was also slow and the third started to speed up. I was a decent dancer but James was great and a strong lead, which made me appear far better than I deserved credit for. The smell of those around me was made manageable by holding my breath and taking a few sniffs from James' collar when I needed air to talk.

Eventually the house lights flashed on and the band announced they were taking a short break. James and I made our way back to our table and found Troy and Heidi were already seated, both their faces shining with sweat. Heidi had a glass of water in her hand and an empty in front of her. Troy had a cocktail and water in front of him.

James and I joined them, Heidi was grinning broadly. "You two sure can dance. Don't you get tired?" She made a show of fanning herself with her napkin. "It is so hot out there.

Especially if you get near the stage, those lights must add another twenty degrees."

I waved it off, "I steered clear of most of the people and the stage so it wasn't that bad."

Heidi gave the universal girl signal she had to go to the bathroom and that it would require an escort. I squeezed James' hand and kissed his cheek as I stood. I watched Heidi give Troy a lingering brush on the lips and I caught the look that passed between them. What they had was real, I had to be happy for them both. Heidi hadn't had great luck with men thus far. She deserved some happiness, as did Troy. He had tons of responsibility being the head of his clan. It would be a change for him to have someone to help make his burden more bearable, even if he couldn't share all of it.

Heidi and I made our way through the throng to the restrooms by the bar. Mostly out of fear, I tried to hold my breath without making it too obvious. When we got into the restroom, there were a ton of women in there doing various things to their clothes, lips, cleavage and hair. Few were actually using the facilities, so Heidi went right in. I was wearing the lightest of makeup now that I didn't really need it, I took the opportunity to touch up my lip gloss.

When Heidi emerged, she was so excited she was ready to burst. Jokingly I pointed at the stall she'd just exited, "Do you need to go again? You look like you need to go."

She elbowed me, reaching for the soap in front of us and spoke to my reflection. "Troy said he has something important he wants to tell me tonight." She squealed in girlie anticipation, "We've been spending so much time together, I think he's going to ask me to move in. What else could it be?" She wiggled back and forth, rinsing her hands.

I knew another thing it could be. He hadn't told her about his dual nature, the family would have told us. It would be a big

414

deal when he told her. I just wasn't sure she would be as excited about it.

Faking a happy response, I grinned right back at her, "That's great Heidi! I'm so happy for you." We fought through the line of women waiting to have a turn in front of the mirror and returned to the club.

Chattering happily amongst ourselves, we didn't notice the bodies blocking us until Heidi bumped into one, I barely stopped in time. My senses were more of a hindrance than a help in this crowded, noisy scene. I had been assured over time I would develop the ability to sift through the "noise," although right now I was probably more blind than a human keeping myself in mental lockdown.

"Hey," said the large, immovable body Heidi had run into. She looked up and the smile she'd been sporting was gone. I watched her features crumble as she recognized the olive skinned blockade.

"Vince, what are you doing here?" Her voice trembled in fear and she caught it, straightening her shoulders and sticking out her chin in a mask of defiance. "Don't you have a gas station to rob or something?"

The giant of a man towering over my friend laughed harshly, "I just came with some of the guys. You remember Clay." He gestured to the mass in front of me. "And Pete's over there getting us another round."

"It smells like you've had enough already. Besides, I thought the coach didn't let you guys drink."

"I forgot you were the morality police," Vince sneered, his expression darkening. He had those chronic dark circles under his eyes that gave him a perpetually stoned flavor and the booze was making him sweat. The combination of sight and smell was less than flattering. "Oh that's right, you don't have any, you just like to preach 'em." Plus he was a prick.

I could just about smell the testosterone on them which was hard to do over the alcohol. Vince especially was in a state, his heart rate was coming up fast. I imagined he was planning on doing something. "Come on Heidi, the guys are waiting." I tugged at her arm.

She stared up at the square, black stubbled jaw for a few feet as she sidestepped to give him a wide berth. When she was going around him, Vince stage whispered to his teammate.

"Of course there's a guy waiting." He raised his voice, this time for Heidi's ears and to her humiliation, a number of people nearby. "I told her if she charged she could make some good money with her numbers."

Heidi's body jerked like she'd been physically struck and instead of the sharp retort I would have expected, she seemed to shrink in upon herself. Rage, not my own, danced across my flesh leaving a lingering trail of electricity in its wake. Feeling it secondhand was strangely hollow, it left me unsatisfied like a stale piece of cake.

The hair on my arms jumped to attention, warning me of his arrival a fraction of a second before Troy arrived on the scene. He was close to changing. *I* could feel it but a glance at Heidi showed she was clueless how close she was standing to ground zero of a potential bloodbath.

Troy's voice was choked with righteous fury as he stepped into Vince's face and stuck a hand up in his chest, checking him hard enough the larger man had to windmill to keep his footing, colliding with a man behind him. "Why don't you two leave the lady alone? You have had a bit too much to drink tonight." Falling back, Troy's hand slid into Heidi's. She blinked and I saw tears sparkle in her dark lashes.

Vince's face turned purple before he reined himself in and laughed. It was harsh and forced. He could sense something dangerous in Troy and was trying to find a way out without losing face in front of his friend and the small crowd who was gathering sensing something was afoot.

I felt another familiar form materialize beside me. "Is there a problem here gentlemen?"

I didn't need to see James' face. His voice and the new shade of pale the linebackers modeled told me enough. They were in over their heads and they knew it. Just when I worried we had something ugly on our hands, the very large aforementioned Pete showed up, three drinks balanced in his enormous hands. The towhead had a formidable frame, standing at least six foot three, and had shoulders that would make a coach cry. His large body carried some extra weight though he was by no means soft. Unlike his teammates, the large blonde had a friendly smile and kind blue eyes.

"Hey guys, what's up?" He staggered into Vince, spilling a little on his front.

Handed the distraction he needed, Vince overreacted, jumping back and sweeping the liquid from his shirt. "Christ, Pete. Watch yourself, man," he mumbled, "Damn drunk," wiping his shoe on the back of a pant leg.

Pete laughed uncowed through a sloppy grin and foggy eyes, "I've had just as much as you."

"You're a lightweight." Vince took his drink, Clay also, and Pete, chore now finished, finally noticed us.

"Hey Heidi!" He leaned in and kissed her cheek messily, easily sweeping her off of her feet and into a big one armed hug.

Troy bristled until Heidi smiled warmly and hugged him back. "Hey Petey, how've you been?"

He shrugged and set her down, "Can't complain. You still singing in that band? You were good, I missed you after you left the club." Pete's compliments had Heidi blushing.

Heidi and Troy had given us an impromptu concert of carols at our Christmas party.

"No, we lost our bassist and drummer. They transferred up to Duluth. It got too hard to practice. Do you still play bass?"

My opinion of Pete was definitely rising. He was a decent guy. One out of three wasn't bad.

Pete laughed. "Yeah, but I'm nowhere near good enough to play with you guys."

Heidi stepped into Troy's side, he put his arm around her waist, still keeping an eye on the other two. "Troy plays a mean guitar. If we practiced a little and got a drummer, we might be able to have something."

Pete and Heidi hugged again, agreeing to keep talking about practice if he could fit it around bouncing at the club, a perfect career choice for the big man.

Pete's companions had moved a few feet away and were making a conscious effort to appear uninterested, hoping to be forgotten. When Heidi said good-bye to Pete our party moved back toward the table.

The houselights flashed again and the bar went dark. Heidi tapped Troy. Without a word, he put his arm around her and passed her his drink. She tipped it back and took a big mouthful. Before anyone could say anything, the band was back on stage and another fast song I didn't recognize broke out.

Troy stood up holding out his arm and Heidi took it, happy again. James and I opted to sit for another song, watching to make sure there wasn't any sort of trouble being planned by the two chuckleheads we had just had the displeasure of meeting.

Nothing presented itself by the next song and James and I joined the thinning masses on the dance floor. I wasn't having a hard time with the humans around me. James was right about their smells being stronger, though I found it relatively easy to neutralize the desire for their blood when I focused on the sour smell of sweat surrounding them. He saw that I was coping and I felt his approval. Not just approval, he was impressed. I gave him a little extra pat where our hands touched.

Eventually the show ended and we stayed while we waited for the crowd to clear. Heidi's acquaintances were not mentioned again, all of us glad to have her over her embarrassment.

When the lights were all the way on again and we had reached a lull in our conversation. Troy noticed the bartender and even the waitress previously impressed by us was growing impatient.

"We should get going before we're kicked out," Troy suggested. "We're the only ones left who don't work here."

Troy helped Heidi into her coat before sliding his on and we all walked out into the nearly abandoned parking lot. The only cars to be seen were ours and one or two others in the main part of the lot. I was willing to bet the line of six or seven cars on the far end belonged to the employees inside.

"What do you say we go to the coffee shop over there?" Heidi pointed to the building with the neon cup of steaming coffee half a block up. "I'm not ready to call it a night. You aren't tired are you?" Her brows peaked hopefully.

I was having a good time and felt James' concurrence. "We're not tired, let's go."

Our chatter was light matching our moods as we all made our way across the now deserted lot. The area wasn't well lit and Heidi had to hold onto Troy to help her navigate. We were halfway across, Heidi and James laughing at something Troy said, when I got a flash of intense emotion that was gone as fast as it had come. It felt like anger, only it was fuzzy and hard to understand. Blindingly intense it flashed into my waiting head again before disappearing. Just as I was about to mention it to James, a shot rang out, piercing the relative stillness of the night. All of us reacted instinctively in very different ways. Troy pushed Heidi behind himself and dropped into a sideways crouch, James stepped back to me as both of us turned toward the source of the sound, behind the building across the street.

Ch. 66

"Get her out of here, Troy," James barked.

Normally Troy might have objected, however, given that his love was in danger and not a fast healer, he didn't argue. He started to move away, keeping her tucked securely behind him. Heidi saw that I was staying and started to object, digging her heels in literally and figuratively.

"No, Claire you can't stay here. Come with me." Her voice was rising, panic evident in her face and tone. "James, don't be stupid we can call the cops. Let's go!"

She couldn't see the physical changes James and I had undergone in just a few seconds or that we were both at the ready for whatever the shooter might do next. The precise reason the shooter had chosen his position was going to be his downfall. In the darkness of the street we could take him out with no witnesses or injury of innocents.

"Heidi, go with Troy. I'll be fine." I tried to influence her with my voice. It didn't work.

She pulled away from Troy, he evidently thought holding her too tight would hurt. Unfortunately, it also meant it was ineffective. Heidi stepped around Troy and another shot rang out.

This time *I* stepped between her and the shooter and when the third shot sounded, I felt the impact of the bullet when it hit the ball of my shoulder. Standing mere feet in front of her and twisted as I was, I couldn't hide the injury.

She was hit by a small splatter of blood, staining the front of her coat and neck red.

Her hand flew to her neck and came away wet and slick. She started to hyperventilate, "Am I shot? Where am I hit?" Her hands were roaming her body, searching for a wound that didn't exist, smearing the blood now on her hands everywhere she touched.

Troy put his hands on her shoulders and tried to soothe her, "Heidi you're okay, please come with me." He was trying to hide the anxiety in his voice from her as he took her arm again, pulling her backward to get her out of danger.

James had stepped in as soon as the bullet hit me. He smelled the blood and roared. Heidi stood paralyzed, her eyes and mouth open in shock. My arm was useless for the time being while I wheeled with him and we darted across the street.

Their smell gave them away. I had smelled them before and the alcohol thinning their blood emphasized their scents like a bullhorn does a voice. James went for the shooter, Vince who was hiding behind a dumpster. He got one more shot off before James pulled the gun out of his hand and slammed it into his head. His skull made a wet crunching noise and Vince sank like a stone, unconscious before he even had a chance to see us.

I smelled Clay as he wedged himself into a doorway behind me hoping to avoid detection. I could feel his fear and resistance. I opened up, feeling that he was only here because he couldn't stand up to Vince, he was afraid. Instead of killing him, I reached in and grabbed him by the throat with my good hand. In a low voice, I called to James. He was with me at once.

"He won't hurt Heidi without Vince to push him," I explained, saving him.

James took over while I monitored him closely to feel how he used his influence to erase part of Clay's memory. As far as he would know tomorrow, he drank too much and lost track of Vince some time after the concert.

After his memory was altered, James hit Clay on the head just hard enough to incapacitate him and I caught and lowered him so he didn't scrape himself up. We started to walk back when James caught my good arm. He stopped me and pointed at my wound.

"Let me see it." With the thin straps on the dress, it was easy to see the entrance wound.

He hissed through clenched teeth, "It's still in there. I have to get it out for you to heal right." He was apologetic.

I gritted my teeth and nodded. "Then do it." I'd had to do the same for James once and remembered it had been horrible to know I was causing such pain to a loved one. I wasn't sure which one of us was going to hate this next part more.

As gently as one can possibly dig into another's joint and extract a smashed ball of lead, James pushed his fingers in and did what he needed to do. Hard as I tried, I couldn't swallow all the screams that resulted from his efforts. Right on top of the pain from the gunshot and the ensuing removal, I felt my throat catch fire with the need to feed and replenish my body with all the blood it was losing.

Running footsteps were echoing toward me and too late I realized they belonged to Heidi. My heart went into my throat, I didn't want Heidi to be the person I saw first when I was so thirsty.

James thought faster than I did. He jogged over to where Vince lay dying and tossed him the rest of the way behind the dumpster. I didn't need to be told what I needed to do. The key was not to think about it. Feeding on a dead man was not something I relished the thought of, though it was preferable to eating my friend.

I trotted over and grabbed a hold of Vince's shoulders, biting into his neck to get the fastest flow possible. Meanwhile, I heard Heidi coming closer and I sucked as hard as I could, feeding hurriedly, spilling on myself a few times when my mouth was too full to swallow all of it.

"James, where's Claire?" Heidi's small, frightened voice reached my ears.

"She's okay. She got scared and got sick, just give her a minute." He tried to buy me time.

I heard Troy apologizing. "There was no getting her out of here without Claire." I didn't envy him the position he was in. If he had physically dragged her away, she would never have understood and would have held it against him thinking him a coward to leave James and me to face the gunman alone. He had to let her stay. I knew he was thinking of telling her about himself tonight but not like this. I didn't want her to find out about me like this. She didn't have to know about us. She *shouldn't* know about us. Too many did already.

My thirst quenched, I felt my face for blood and wiped it on my hand which didn't help, covered as it was with my own blood. I was sure I was a fright. There was no way I could step out now even if I could get my fangs under control, they were not going back in yet. I felt like a teenage boy who couldn't turn away from the blackboard.
James heard my distress, "Heidi, you should get home. The police will be coming and we don't want to be here when they do. I'll get Claire home."

"Why?" She was so scared and small sounding. I wished I could help her but feared if she saw me, the damage would be irreparable. "What don't you want me to see?" She was scared and now her brain was starting to work, filling in some blanks. "Where's the guy with the gun?"

She was sturdy stock to keep herself together even if it was only just. I felt her "shorting out" as her brain wrestled with itself. Part of it wanted to shut down in shock, the other part wasn't going to let up until she saw me.

"James, I want to see what's behind that dumpster." She sounded a little more sure of herself.

He laughed, "What's to see? Claire is throwing up and you can't really see anyway, the nearest light is probably fifty feet away and everything throws a shadow."

"If she's so scared she's puking, why aren't you with her? You don't let her out of your sight under normal circumstances," she accused accurately. "Now you want me to believe you let her go down a dark street with a gunman and puke her guts out and you aren't even holding her hair? No way." She listened. "I don't hear her puking. Is she hurt?" Heidi's voice went up three octaves. "Claire?"

Sirens sounded in the distance. Someone had dutifully called about the gunshots and screaming. We needed to go.

Troy tried reasoning with her. "Heidi, James is not the bad guy. He protected you, they didn't do anything wrong. Claire just needs a moment to compose herself. *We* need to go or we're going to be involved with the police." Troy could smell the blood. He knew what was happening.

"No," she was still arguing, trying to make sense of it all. "I'm not moving unless Claire comes with me and she is in one piece. Friends look out for each other, even when their husbands don't want them to." Her tone was biting.

Hearing the sirens grow louder, I made my decision. Smoothing my bloodied dress and hair in a vain attempt to appear less like a walking nightmare, I stood and stepped around the dumpster and into the faint light coming from the distant streetlights. "I'm fine Heidi. We need to go now."

Heidi took one look at me and fainted dead away.

Troy caught her and swinging her lightly up into his arms said grimly, "Let's go."

We moved fast, getting to our cars and out of the lot before the police turned the corner. None of us sensed anyone out on the street, gunshots tended to clear a street fast. But just in case, we drove the first few blocks without lights. Since I needed to clean up, we went to our house.

I hurriedly took a shower and dressed in clean jeans and a sweater, James had to change as well. He had gotten blood on himself digging my bullet out. Troy borrowed some sweats to replace Heidi's bloodied party clothes. When Heidi woke we were presentable and looking as normal as inhumanly possible.

Ch. 67

Heidi woke gradually, turning her head slowly to take in her surroundings and figure out where she was. She saw Troy sitting at her feet on the couch with her but sat bolt upright when she saw me sitting in the chair across from her, James standing behind me. A sense of calm was emanating from someone. I had felt it before, long ago. My eyes slid over to Troy's face and I saw the ghost of a smile before it disappeared again. My attention shifted back to our guest.

She scrambled backward as deeply into the corner of the couch as she could, drawing her legs up into a protective ball, pausing only briefly when she saw she was wearing my clothes. Her eyes were wildly searching us both, trying to justify what she was seeing with the bloodied figures she'd seen in the alley.

"How come we aren't at the hospital? You were hurt, I saw it."

I worked hard to remain calm. "A lot was happening and it was really scary but I didn't get hurt. See, look at me." My hands spread to show her I had no outward signs of injury, I was careful not to move my shoulder. That would take another day to repair itself, bones and joints were more dense than flesh and only time could heal that.

For the first time, I saw doubt creep into her eyes. A quick scan assured me we were on our way to convincing her though we weren't there yet. The comforting "purr" Troy was sending out kept her mind listening instead of going into panic mode. "You were covered in blood, Claire. How do you explain all that blood? I had it on me, too." She looked down at herself. Her clothes were changed and skin cleaned up, but she was still seeing the blood in her mind's eye.

My answer wasn't a total lie. "It wasn't my blood. James got into a scuffle with the gunman and the gun went off. I was standing nearby and some of it got on me." I let it sink in for a minute. "When you fainted, James helped Troy carry you to the car and you got some blood on you. I loaned you some clean clothes."

"He's dead? Who was it? Was it someone we knew? Is that why they were shooting at us?"

"It was Vince."

Heidi thought quietly about that for a minute, staring at her knees held tight against her chest. I withdrew from her, giving her privacy.

Troy touched her foot and she scooted over, a scared child seeking comfort. I could only imagine what it did to you when you lost both of your parents young like she did. She was probably even more insecure than I was.

Not anymore you're not.

You'd be surprised.

James gave a little cough, his version of clearing his throat. I agreed they should have some privacy and we soundlessly exited the room, going into the kitchen to speak softly among ourselves.

"Do you think she's buying it?" I asked hopefully.

He considered it before he answered, "I think so. If we can cast enough doubt, her mind will do the rest. No one wants to believe the unbelievable, even if they think they do."

"You mean like is there a God?" I agreed with him. No one wanted to really know that.

He nodded, "Right. If there was undeniable proof that would mean people would have to believe in heaven, hell and being

428

held accountable. It would change how people live, don't you think?"

"Maybe it would make us better."

"I don't know. I think human nature is hard to deny, even when the consequences are right in front of you. How many kids lie even when their parents have the evidence right in front of them? I can remember taking a piece of cake before supper once when I was very small." He grinned boyishly, "I had so much in my mouth I had to finish chewing to tell my mother I hadn't taken it."

Laughing at the image, I reached into the fridge for a drink. My shoulder knitting was taking plenty of energy and I would have to feed even more heavily for the next day or so to make up for it.

"Be quick," James cautioned.

"I know." I poured the glass and drained it fast, washing it right away.

A quick scan told me Heidi was calmer even with Troy no longer "purring" and it would be okay to return. James and I walked in holding hands. She wasn't the only one who needed a little extra strength at the moment. It wasn't every day I bald faced lied to a friend.

Heidi was smiling nervously when she glanced up at me. "I guess I kind of freaked, huh? It's been a really weird night."

I widened my eyes. "It was scary for all of us. It was a good thing Vince was a bad shot."

"I swore I saw blood when I heard the shot," she mumbled to herself. "I felt it splash me."

"There was a little snow melting off of the lights, maybe some splashed you. I think we were near one when he fired on us," James offered.

He was right, she *was* trying to tie it together and make another reality she could live with in her head.

"Can I get you a cup of coffee or something?" I asked her, trying to catch Troy's eye over her head.

"You could use something warm." Troy kissed her cheek tenderly. "I'm going to help," he said, starting to separate himself from her. At Heidi's look of alarm, he smiled disarmingly, "I know how you like it."

She returned his smile uncertainly. "Thanks."

Vulnerable Heidi was new to me. I was finding it disheartening to be part of the cause.

Troy and I headed into the kitchen and I heard James making small talk with Heidi about the show. She sounded happy to be discussing something other than the tragedy that had ended our night.

Instead of taking the time to put the kettle on, I nuked enough water in a Pyrex measuring cup to make a Starbuck's single. We'd started keeping them around, not enough coffee drinkers led to a lot of wasted beans.

"Heidi told me you were going to tell her something tonight," I started, staring at the twirling measuring cup as heat bubbles began to form on the sides.

"She thinks you want her to move in with you." Turning, I leaned against the stove behind me. "You weren't going to tell her anything else were you?"

"I was going to tell her something entirely different." Crossing his arms he leaned back against the counter. "In light of this evening's events I think we should let time blur some of this before we go down that road." His forehead wrinkled in thought. "It hadn't been my intention, but I like the idea of asking her to move in."

My face split into a huge grin. "That's great, Troy. Congratulations in advance."

The microwave dinged and I got a mug while Troy grabbed the coffee. He knew the kitchen as well as I did so I sat back and watched while he added the right amount of sugar to Heidi's coffee. No cream, I noted. A good hostess should know these things.

We returned to the living room and a far more relaxed Heidi. She wasn't back to her normal self, though I didn't really know which of her selves was the real her. She seemed to have a different persona for every situation. A defense mechanism I was guessing. I genuinely hoped Troy could give her the stability she so desperately needed. Her grandmother who raised her was probably a nice lady, although I didn't think they were very close; Heidi never mentioned her.

She gratefully took the coffee mug and sipped on it while James, Troy, and I tried to appear normal and relaxed. We talked about someone who worked for Troy at his computer repair shop. His employee, it turned out, was a demoralizing influence on the other employees and Troy was thinking of firing him but he wanted it to be for legal reasons so as not to open himself up to a lawsuit. James and I gave our two cents and just generally filled the silence with unimportant talk.

The secretive glances I snuck at Heidi revealed her introspectively sipping at her coffee while she leaned against

Troy. Sometimes I thought I saw her steal a quick glance at me, though I couldn't be sure without staring.

After a while, Heidi's coffee was gone and we had all run out of unimportant things to say. Heidi announced she was tired and wanted to go home. Troy offered for her to stay with him saying she shouldn't be alone tonight.

Heidi brightened, she didn't want to be alone either. I ducked my head so she couldn't see me smile when I thought of how happy she would be when he asked her to live with him. He had a secret, sure. Even then, she could do a lot worse than him. He sure beat Vince. I snorted at the thought.

"What?" Heidi had heard me.

Embarrassed, I laughed at myself. "Nothing, just some dust I think." Lame excuse, I thought to myself and James agreed, stifling a laugh.

Heidi thanked us at the door for an interesting evening. "Sorry it got weird and I freaked. I guess I'm a little higher strung than I thought. We should try again soon, I'm pretty sure *that* won't happen again."

"You're right. It isn't something that happens to normal people," I admitted. Too bad I wasn't normal. I was almost getting used to being shot at and ambushed. Poor Heidi was self conscious thinking *she* was the odd one reacting inappropriately. It wasn't her fault she was surrounded by violent creatures.

Troy nodded his head at James knowing he would prefer not to shake his hand. I was watching them when Heidi, acting on an impulse I didn't catch in time to intercept, threw herself at me for a sudden hug.

On instinct, I threw my arms up to catch her and winced when my shoulder took the full impact of her body. Startled, she immediately jumped back and searched me for injury. Boldly she grabbed the loose collar of my v-neck sweater and pulled it off my shoulder.

"Oh my God!" Her hand flew to her mouth as she stared at the freshly healing red scar. Releasing my sweater roughly she pushed herself away from me and I watched her helplessly as she felt our unified betrayal tear a hole through her insides.

"Heidi, it isn't what you think," I started, not sure what else to say.

"What?" Her voice shook with the anger and hurt inside her. "You didn't get shot tonight? You didn't lie about it? You didn't miraculously heal in a few hours?" Troy put his hand on her back, projecting his calming "purr" and she whirled on him. "You knew! How could you let me think I was the one with something wrong with *me*? *She's* not normal."

"Heidi, look at me," James commanded.

Wheeling, she glared at James, staring at him angrily. She blinked a few times and repeated her question sharply. "What?"

Ignoring her now, he spoke anxiously in my head.

She's immune, I can't erase her memory.

We have to tell her.

Too many humans know already, it would put her in danger and us as well.

Do we let her freak out and run out of here tonight to tell someone what happened? Put that together with the bodies and it won't matter what the Court wants to do, the humans will lock us up or try to kill us. I shot back at him. *I won't*

433

hurt her. You can't ask me to do that. My venom gave way to pain. *She's my only real friend who isn't one of* us. *That's important to me.*

He wrestled with our choices. Meanwhile, Heidi had placed her focus solely on Troy. He was trying hard to placate her but she was in a fit driven by a deep agony and fear of abandonment that hurt even through my shields.

There was no way out of this without telling her. The damage it would do if she didn't know was far greater than risking her being let in on our secret. I turned and stared at James. His eyes were calm and his expression blank. *There is a loophole but it's up to Troy.*

You mean if he tells, we don't get in trouble?

Right. Because our kind sometimes overlaps with theirs our governing bodies accept each other's decisions. If Troy tells her, he has to get her approved somewhat similarly to how you were, and she won't be in danger.

Thank you. "Heidi." I spoke softly.

She was still smacking at Troy's shoulders and head while he took it. He wouldn't raise a hand against her even to stop her from striking him, so frightened was he that he would hurt her by accident.

When I was with James as a human, I knew he held back physically when we were together and he had warned me of the dangers, though he'd always tried to block that worry from me. Feeling it from Troy now, I got a taste for what it must have felt like for James when we were together. No wonder he had been so much happier once I was turned and he had come to terms with it. What a relief it must have been for him to be rid of that burden of fear. I felt his gentle push in my head.

I told you it was complicated.

I guess. Do you think he would ever change her?

That is a lot to ask of either of them, Claire.

Regardless of anyone being changed, tonight had to be dealt with. "Heidi, I think you should sit down." I tried to influence her with my voice. It didn't work, it only served to catch her attention.

"Why?" Her face was wet and her chin quivered.

"Please," I pleaded. "Listen to Troy." Flicking my eyes to his, I got confirmation of what I'd felt. He had already decided to tell her.

I think the only reason she listened to me was because I wasn't Troy. His betrayal had cut the deepest. She consented silently and perched on the arm of the couch nearest the door, he sat on the far end with his hands nervously clenching on his thighs. James hovered over the chair where I sat.

Troy began and she locked her eyes on him. "Heidi, you were right about what you saw tonight." We all watched her for a reaction. Outwardly, she stayed calm. Even inside she was frozen, waiting for what was coming next. Troy continued, "Vince did shoot Claire." He nodded at me and I pulled down my sweater. I showed her my scar which was already less pink than it had been minutes before. "You've noticed that my family, James, and Claire are different from other people."

She nodded. I saw her thinking about that nagging feeling there was something unusual about us she couldn't put her finger on. Had she ever said anything or had he merely picked up on it?

Troy's trepidation was clear, he took a deep breath. "What do you know about the paranormal?"

Nervously I shuffled my feet as he said the same thing he had said to me that night. Heidi shot him a dubious glance. She still wasn't sure if we were putting her on.

"I don't know. I don't believe in God but I believe in ghosts." Her voice was small and uncertain. "I used to think I saw my parents when I was little."

"Well, there are things in this world that people are afraid of or can't explain so they tell us they don't exist, but they do." He wasn't sure how to make the leap, how to say the words that would change her life, and how she would see him forever. "Do you understand?"

Heidi frowned in confusion. "No, I don't. All I know is that Claire got shot and now she's healing all in the same night. James killed a man and I'm the only one upset about it. Maybe we should have waited for the police and let them sort it out."

Troy shook his head. "The police don't know about us."

Her eyes widened and then narrowed. "Is this a cult thing? Or a gang?" She looked accusatorially at me. "Are you in this too now? Is that why you're different all of a sudden?"

I closed my eyes, not sure I wanted him to proceed, and hating the fear I saw on her face. Troy bravely pressed on.

"Heidi, my family is different." He didn't move any closer to her, fearing she would run.

"You've said that," she snapped.

"We have what you could call a genetic anomaly. It gives us certain abilities that most people don't have." He watched her closely, we all did.

Her head cocked to the side, she was listening. "We are stronger, faster and can change what we are."

"What do you mean you can change what you are?"

I interjected, "Troy you could show her. That worked best for me."

Heidi's posture tightened and she readied to defend herself. I tried to reassure her. "Heidi, no one here is ever going to hurt you. He's just going to show you. It's one of those things you need to see."

Troy did much the same thing Stephen had when he showed me. He walked into the kitchen; seeing the change itself would be too shocking. After a short time when he was removing his clothes, I felt the hair rise on my arms. I watched Heidi to see if she could feel the energy build. She shivered and rubbed her arms. She *was* sensitive after all.

Heidi wasn't a screamer, I had to give her credit. Still, she hopped up and jumped over the arm of the couch she had been sitting on to hide behind it when the large mountain lion padded carefully out of the kitchen, his hazel eyes only for her.

The rest of us watched her, curious to see how she would take this news before deciding what else to tell her. Troy had been willing to tell her about himself. This was as good a place as any to start, I thought.

Ch. 68

After the initial shock wore off, Heidi rose to a half crouch peeking anxiously over at the cat. "Troy?"

He blinked and gave the soft mew I had heard the cats utter among themselves. It was a loving sound. Slowly he approached her, one paw at a time. She stood and actually took a step forward around the front of the couch.

They met in the middle, his nose touching her extended hand, their eyes focused on each other. She held her breath as she stroked the fur on his cheek cautiously. He purred and rolled his head into it.

We gave them a minute while they wordlessly reconnected. I felt her accepting his dual nature, putting together clues she had seen and felt during their time together.

She turned slowly to face me. "Are you a cat, too?"

Reluctantly I shook my head, what I was didn't have fur and didn't purr. "Not exactly. Why don't you come back and sit down?"

Obediently she eased herself back onto the couch, this time sitting on the seat. Her hand never came off of Troy's fur and when she sat down, he hopped up next to her.

"Watch the claws, Troy," James warned. Troy gave a low growl and shot him a disdainful look, laying his head in Heidi's lap. I laughed at their familial exchange. Heidi only looked bewildered.

"We're another sort of creature," I put my hand on James' arm beside me. "We don't turn into anything soft and fuzzy. We're more cold and pale." It was hard to say the word. I was waiting to see if she would make the connection herself.

She didn't, she was watching me expectantly. This was going to be hard. I decided to just blurt it out. "Heidi, we're vampires." Her reaction was unexpected. She laughed. "Are you kidding?"

Incredulous, I pointed out the obvious. "How can you not believe me? You're sitting there petting your boyfriend. Can you not believe that there are other creatures out there?"

"Sure, but vampires are scary and drink blood and you aren't." She was in denial. Somehow a soft cat was more palatable than the walking dead. Go figure, I thought with a weird jealous twinge.

"Show her," James repeated my words back to me. "It worked for Troy."

Fear glimmered in Heidi's eyes as she grew wary. The distrust I saw growing there upset me. Despite her misgivings about *our* natures, I wanted to show her we were not scary, only there was no way to do that. No one wanted to pet a vampire. Sighing in regret, I made up my mind. I put my faith in our history and hoped what she knew of human me would be enough to keep her from fearing me forever.

I didn't want to induce any sort of bloodlust bringing out the vampire the usual way, with anger or thirst, so instead I concentrated on the fear I saw in her to bring on the change. The thought of frightened prey excited the animal instinct underlying a vampire's nature. We were baser creatures which was why the two needs we had that typically drove us were sex and food. At once, I felt the vibration starting in my mouth and my fangs grew, pushing their way to peek out from under my lip.

Her eyes widened and I knew my own had grown black. The combination of dark eyes and extended fangs gave the appearance of whiter flesh and more prominent bones, more of the skeletal profile the legends reported only that was all it was, an optical illusion. As soon as I saw her reaction, I worked to cool the emotions I'd used to bring out my monster, and returned my face to its human façade.

Heidi's hand tightened, clutching a chunk of Troy's fur. To avoid upsetting her he bit back his yelp, keeping up his purring for her benefit. "How did this happen? Did he do this to you when you got married, is that why you're different? Did you know before?"

"I knew from the moment Stephen introduced us. We hadn't really planned on this except something happened, kind of like tonight. I would have died if it weren't for Henry."

"Henry? My boss, the librarian, is a vampire?" she tittered nervously.

I nodded. "He saved me. It isn't easy, but it let me stay with the people I love." I spoke from the heart and I felt it strike a chord with her.

Her eyes welled up. "How nice for you." She was thinking of her parents. She would have preferred the change to the loss.

"It isn't for everyone, Heidi," I assured her. "It isn't all romance and awesome power. There's a cost too and I see why James didn't want me to turn for him."

"Really? I've always seen it either as super scary like Nosferatu or just about the awesome sexiness of it."

"It's more like being an insomniac who's so hungry it hurts and always feels like she's on fire."

"That sounds like it sucks," she conceded.

"Parts of it do," I rolled my shoulders. "It's worth it for me."

Heidi petted Troy, choosing to stare at the trails her fingers made in his golden fur. I felt her attempting to come to terms with it.

"Heidi, there's one more thing."

Her hand froze on Troy's coat. "There's more? What, is our mailman a troll?"

I fought the urge to laugh in spite of what I was about to tell her. She needed to know how dead serious this next part was. "You have to keep the truth about us secret. You can't tell anyone or there are parties on both sides who will hunt you down and kill you. We only told you because we didn't want you telling the wrong person and risking us all."

Her throat moved convulsively to swallow.

Good. I hoped I conveyed the seriousness of our need for secrecy. All of our lives depended on it.

The ringing of James' phone broke the silence.

"Detective, I thought you might be calling." Speak of the devil, although *that* human could have his memory erased, unlike Heidi.

We should have called Detective Hanson about tonight. That was foolish of us not to.

James walked away, I could hear him explaining what had happened. This death was not related to the others we were investigating and if he needed to, James would be happy to "lose" the body. The Detective stiffly told him that wouldn't be necessary. Something had nearly taken the head off and combined with the blood, head trauma and rough tearing at the neck wound, he could pass it off as a jumper whose neck hit the metal edge of the dumpster on the way down.

By the time James returned Troy had changed back, dressed, and he and Heidi were making ready to leave. This time, she didn't try to hug me though I took heart in her smile. It might be okay in the end but it would take time.

Ch. 69

Our crazy night behind us, James and I redoubled our efforts to find the mystery killer.

"What if it's not a were working alone?" Seeing Troy had brought another type of hunter to mind.

"It's possible. What were you thinking?" he tossed back.

"Well, you said it kills like a were except there's something else strange about it, right? What if it's one of us working with a were? You said maybe something got it started on that territory, right?"

"You might be on to something." He started to roll it around his brain. "You might indeed." He started to sift through the files, looking for something in particular.

It was the forty something woman. "Here, see how she was found next to a tree and mauled severely?"

My stomach would have turned if it could have. Hers was a particularly gruesome find. "Yes, I remember."

"Something about it has been bothering me only I didn't know what. Now I think I get it." He pointed to the branches of the oak tree above where the body was found. He pointed at one particular branch that was isolated from the others, there being significant clearance for someone to sit on. "There are some big cats that drag their kill up and hide it in a tree. They wedge it so they can return and eat from it often."

"How long had she been missing before they found her?" I tried to see the file. He tipped it toward me so I could see where he pointed. "Five months," I read out loud. "It was late winter. Lots of weather and mush that time of year, she could have easily come loose and fallen out of the tree." I forced myself to look closely at the picture of her body again and saw what James was thinking. "She has bite marks from fangs at her neck but other than a claw scratch trying to hide them, her neck is not disturbed. The were went after her like meat." I was referring to the damage it had done to her stomach and limbs. It had been eating on her for a while after she was killed. A were kill is more damaging; if it had bitten the neck, it would have taken more with it.

He was nodding agreement. "I think you're right. The killer is vampire and the were gets the bodies afterward." James was hesitating, thinking, before he added thoughtfully, "That idea fits perfectly until the last body they found." He grabbed the file for the younger man.

The body was more difficult to examine this one being found in the summer near water. However, it was less likely a vampire had made this kill. This one did not have the same bite and claw combination as the others. This one had a broken spine in two places with scrapes from teeth going down to the vertebra and the body had been well eaten. "The pattern changed with this one. It's more violent, like the cat was controlled at first and now it's not."

"Do you have any ideas on what kind of cat?"

"I'm thinking leopard," he said grimly.

We waited until morning before we called Troy. He sounded sleepy even though we had given him until well after ten.

"We were up late," he mumbled sleepily. Poor Heidi, I *bet* she had trouble sleeping. It had been a busy night.

"Troy, we need your help." James declared. He explained we had been tasked by the local police to check into some murders that were pointing toward a were, one of which was Brian's murder.

"I can be over in a few minutes. Let me get dressed."

He was fast, Troy and Heidi came knocking less than half an hour later. They hadn't been able to eat yet so I enlisted her help in the kitchen, thinking that would keep her from those pictures. I could hear their conversation and followed along while we chopped vegetables and grated cheese for omelets.

"You're right. It's a were." I heard the shuffling of pages while they flipped through the files again.

"Do you see the very edges of the claw marks under that goring? Those gouges are post mortem, see how they didn't raise any blood?" He paused and I heard him breathe out low. "This guy is not killing them. He's eating them. He's not in control of his beast at all. Is he working with someone?"

James muttered an oath under his breath. "We think he was with a vampire. At least until this last one. Are there any clans working in this area? Any others friendly with vampires?"

"No, leopards are solitary. They don't operate in family groups." He paused and I heard more shuffling. "This one is different, he's in a frenzy. Out of control. He's going to be incredibly dangerous."

More paper. "What do we know?" James asked rhetorically. "We know he's a leopard which tells us he's solitary. He's not in control of his beast so he's not going to have a steady job or humans in his life. Is it safe to assume he's going to have a violent record? Maybe work in a menial job?"

Troy agreed, "Right. He won't be able to function in a normal social structure. He's going to be a loner and I am guessing he will be newly changed. He'll be a young cat. Anything like this that threatens our own secrecy is put down before long." More flipping paper, "We may be in luck. Given his time pattern, I would guess he's due to kill again soon."

"He took another woman yesterday. Any chance she's still alive?"

"Maybe. Cats like to play with their prey."

Our omelet project was complete. I clattered the plates to let them know we were coming out. The hope was they would clean up the pictures before Heidi saw them. It might complicate things for them if so soon after learning about Troy's dual nature, she saw the ugly side of what sometimes came of a change.

While Troy and Heidi ate, conversation was minimal. I could feel Heidi's apprehension when we had been in the kitchen and she was still nervous about being with James and I. Afterward, their meal finished, Heidi offered to do the dishes and let me join the meeting.

"It's okay, I can stay with you," I offered.

She smiled knowingly and teased me. "Why, so you can ignore me while you listen to them in the other room?"

I ducked my head, embarrassed to be caught but happy to see a glimmer of her acceptance. "I'm sorry Heidi. I should be in here with you being supportive, not letting myself be so distracted."

"I'm fine. Don't worry about me, I've been through worse. This is just a complete resetting of my understanding of reality. What's to support?"

"Really, I can stay here. We can hang out. They can take this." As much as I felt like I needed to be with them, I really didn't. There was nothing I couldn't discuss with them later.

The ray of hope in Heidi's face made my decision for me. "What do you want to do? What would make you happy?"

"Serious?" Her joy was my reward. "I wanted to go down to Electric Fetus. They have a vintage collection I heard is colossal. Troy and I were going to go today."

"Let me grab my purse." Pleased to have some sense of our former camaraderie I went upstairs to retrieve my purse, ducked into the kitchen for my keys and met Heidi back at the door. No need to tell anyone where we were going, they heard everything.

"Ready?" I asked her, feeling light and happy for once to be doing a purely human thing. She nodded, guardedly excited.

"Then let's go." Today I would show Heidi there was no reason to fear me. I was the same old Claire who used to work with her stocking books.

It was a Friday, barely after noon; downtown was bustling, though not for shopping. The only people in town were the working set and they were worrying about lunch. The skies were grey so I didn't need shades but thought about wearing some anyway so I could hide my stolen glances from Heidi.

The store we were going to was a music shop dedicated to new and old cd's, albums, and the occasional bong. The people inside liked their ipods in addition to owning the vinyl their downloads originated from. I had always liked the smells of incense, mildewed album covers and clove cigarettes. Now that there was no smoking in the state, there was no clove smell anymore although the rest was the same as it had been when I was 13 and my dad used to bring me to shops like this looking for old classics for the turntable.

Heidi went straight to 80's punk and I moved toward alternative rock, my preferred flavor as of late. We clicked through the used cd's for a solid hour, sometimes raising a

447

special find to get each others' attention and share, otherwise we were lost in our own searches. The steady click, click, click, click of people snapping through the cd cases as they scanned covers or contents filled my head allowing me to focus on nothing at all. It was phenomenal; it was close to the release of sleep. Funny, I had never loved sleep as a human. However, I hadn't realized how important being able to escape my thoughts for a while was until I believed I had lost it.

She bought a Pogues cd and I grabbed the latest Rise Against. Out on the street, Heidi said she wanted to go to a coffee shop up on Nicollet. It wasn't a chain and she preferred it, saying the quality was better. I laughed and told her she sounded like my soon to be uncle Earl.

She laughed lightly back before asking me my preference. "Do you want a coffee?"

"I'm fine," I answered politely.

She stopped walking and put her hand on my forearm. "I'm sorry. I forgot. Does that bother you?"

I shook my head. "I'm getting used to it."

We took the car since it was a little cold for Heidi to walk so far. Fortune was with us and we found a good spot on 5th and Nicollet. I couldn't help noticing we were within blocks of the building James and I were interested in.

Heidi got out and stood on the sidewalk to wait for me while I gathered my things and locked up. We turned the corner and even from a few yards away, I could smell the coffee beans. When we reached the door and Heidi opened it, the scent was overpowering. Heidi saw my reaction and asked what was wrong.

Pointing to the door, I asked, "Do you mind getting a take away coffee instead of sitting inside?" Seeing her confusion, I added, "The smell is a bit strong. I'll wait here for you."

Somewhat sheepishly, she made a show of tiptoeing in to the shop, making me laugh in the process. Waiting patiently, I looked in at the store windows around me. This one was for a high end purse shop and was hung floor to ceiling with a quilt comprised entirely out of every shape and size of purse imaginable. The sun was low and I could smell snow coming. The cold didn't bother me but I had never liked wet, clingy clothes and wished Heidi would hurry up so we could get back inside.

The hair on my arms started to rise under my coat. Visually scanning around me I didn't see anyone who stood out as a were, yet nothing else had ever done that to me in the same way. A were had to be nearby and close to changing, his excitement was palpable. Then I smelled the blood. It was faint but definite.

Heidi finally came out holding a small bag and a mid sized fancy coffee smelling of vanilla. She took one look at my frozen face and started swinging her head around, trying in vain to see what had me spooked.

Pointing at her arms, I asked her, "Did you get a chill a few minutes ago?"

She held out her hand, indicating the world around us. "It *is* the end of January, of course I felt a chill."

"I mean the kind of chill you felt last night when Troy changed," I said point blank. "It tingles and your hair stands straight up; it has nothing to do with cold."

Heidi's body stiffened. "What do you mean? I don't remember feeling anything but shock at the time. My boyfriend changed into a..." She looked around us before

449

ducking in close, "You know what. So you'll forgive me a slight relapse in memory on the small details.

Rolling my eyes, I tried to explain. "When they change there is an energy they put off. Some people who are sensitive can react to that energy. My arm hair has always lifted. I saw you rub your arms to warm them."

"I really don't remember." She pursed her lips thinking.

While we stood wondering, I felt the tingle again and saw Heidi shiver and rub her arms without thinking. Midway through the motion, she stopped herself dead and stared at me, mouth open in astonishment.

"Oh my God, Claire. Does this mean one is here?" She tried to look around without being too obvious and was wildly unsuccessful.

Any supernatural being with half of a brain would have laughed out loud at Heidi's attempt to be sneaky. I didn't have the heart to tell her. Instead, I tucked my arm in hers and guided her away from the middle of the sidewalk and back to the car.

There was no point hiding; if someone was looking for us, they would find us easily enough. My concern was in protecting Heidi and giving her means of escape if it came to that. Some creatures were less concerned about publicity than others.

The were I felt was disguising himself well but he was near. He was close to changing.

James.

Claire? I just got a call from my guy. The building, it's owned by Nightshade. The renovation upstairs is a little cloudier but he's working on it. Nightshade or what's left of it has gone to the winds so it looks like we were right and the vampire that had been controlling this thing left it without any sort of a Master.

We just found him. Where are you?

His alarm bleeding over jabbed straight into me.

I tried to push it back so I could still function. *The car is on 5th and Nicollet. Heidi's locked inside. I'm going to follow him.*

No! Stay where you are. We can be there in a few minutes.

James, I can feel him changing and I can smell blood. It's human. He's getting ready to start.

He was warring with himself over helping the innocent and protecting me. I felt his compulsion twisting my gut and knew the decision he had to make. I wasn't sure which of us it came from but I too wanted to go to the aid of the victim. She couldn't end up like one of those butchered corpses stashed for leftovers until someone found them. The pictures flashed through my mind.

I pushed the keys into her limp hand. "James and Troy are on their way. I have to go now. If anyone approaches you that isn't one of us three, leave." She sat heavily in the seat, staring out the windshield.

Thankfully she didn't ask how I knew that. Maybe she figured I called when she was in the shop. "Um, okay."

"It's going to be okay, Heidi. I promise, just sit tight and lock the doors." Gently closing the door, I walked briskly toward the source of fresh blood.

My hair was standing straight up all over my body, the scent of blood sharpening all of my senses.

The trail led, unsurprisingly to 6th and Marquette. I passed the shops below and following the scent trail behind the building where I saw the steel door slightly ajar and a tiny smear of blood on the stoop a human would have missed. Without hesitation I walked in. I kept my body sideways and low to minimize the target. There was nothing in the main area and I let my nose guide me into the stairwell and up to the eleventh floor.

When I opened the door, I was greeted by the sight of open walls, revealing the infrastructure of metal beams strung with electrical wires, plywood, and covered with a skin of plastic sheeting. Each step I took was ninja quiet to a human's ears. To mine, it was clumsy shuffling anyone could hear in the echoing space.

The smell was heady when I emerged from the stairwell. My fangs grew of their own accord and I felt the familiar burn in my throat responding to the metallic taste on my tongue from the very air I "breathed" in to smell.

The soon-to-be officespace was a large "L" shape with the door being in the short leg. What I was looking for was just a few feet in, lying on the floor unconscious. Her hands and legs were not bound.

She had been struck on the head which explained the blood but a perfunctory examination revealed she was in fine health otherwise. As a matter of fact, the second, faint heartbeat I heard within her told me something she might not even know yet. She *had* to be saved.

Ch. 70

I stood from my crouch and continued to sweep the area visually to no avail. My mental sweep told me there was another being in here and I was right, he was definitely male. I couldn't make sense of his mind, it was too animal which made his thoughts fleeting. All I could read from it was that he was excited and had tasted her blood.

His excitement started to bleed over to me and my throat blazed with thirst. I fought it. She was a living being and had a child inside her. My job was to protect, not take her life. I felt the fire flaring, growing stronger as he drew nearer. Spinning around, I looked behind me. I couldn't see him.

Too late, I thought of the exposed floor joists and ductwork above me. Just as I craned my neck to see, his heavy body crashed into me from above. My head slammed into the concrete floor. The world spun while I tried to shake off the haze resulting from my certain concussion.

His body moved off of me once I was down, the light sound of his pads on the floors told me he had moved toward his prey. Battling the confusion and dizziness, I pushed myself back up on my feet and staggered toward her and the dark, partially human form lowering itself down to her. The profile of an oddly shaped human head was silhouetted against the prone woman's and he moved to scoop her up and bring her to his face, I swore I saw spots in the low light.

I knew I couldn't sneak up on him and I abandoned the pretense of stealth, opting for a more direct approach.

My ability to run in a straight line was severely hampered by my temporarily concussed brain.

"Hey!" I shouted, trying to get his attention. He snarled, still in human form but just barely, if the energy he was creating and the odd way he was crouching were any indication.

"Hey, you bastard, this is *my* territory. That is *my* kill," I bluffed.

That got his attention. "Mine. I caught her." He snuffled the air as he turned to face me.

I startled at the sight of his catlike irises and amber eyes, there was little human left to his mind. His body, though somewhat hidden by his hunkering posture was obviously large and muscular. The animal in him twisted his features until they were nearly unrecognizable as human and spots patterned his face and neck like giant brown freckles. When he snarled, his teeth were pointed like those of a cat, not a human. He had spent a lot of time in his animal form.

The mind I was dealing with was more animal than human, I didn't hold out much hope for reasoning with it. It didn't matter, I still had to try, anything to get him away from the woman.

I growled low in my throat, fighting animal with animal. Moving slowly, I started to circle to the other side of her. If I leaped our momentum would push him away from her, giving me a chance to save her.

His eyes followed me as I came around, his body slowly wheeling with me, mimicking my arc. When I stood directly across from him, I started to close the gap to be sure I could make the jump and not hit her. Sensing my plan when I took a step forward, he leaned over her possessively, his weight supported by one arm, the rest of him forming a bridge over her.

Assessing my options, I flashed on an aspect of my ability that I hoped would work on an animal; otherwise I was low on ideas. I'd channeled emotions into others before but only humans and vampires, never an animal or were. If this had a chance to work, I was going to have to tie in to one of his animal needs and those were few.

I chose one quickly and thought of my home and my need to protect it. Hoping to excite his need to protect his territory, I stepped toward him and channeled my attack. He snarled at me, stepping all the way over his prey but nothing more. My efforts had been too weak; maybe due to the fact that I had moved so much as a kid, I wasn't tied to any one place. The concept of territory was not personal for me.

I was gauging the intelligence of just ramming into him and hoping for the best in an all out physical fight when James called to me, trying to find me.

The connection was strong and I could feel him close by. The thought of my lover so close and the stress of the situation excited my senses and my body reacted unconsciously. I sent him a picture in my head of my path, eagerly anticipating his arrival.

The leopard raised his head again, sniffing. His growl was lower this time, less aggressive. Taking advantage of his curiosity and needing to keep him interested, I brought up some memories my feelings for my husband.

My emotional and physical response to that stimulus was much stronger than my previous attempt to inflame him. I sent out a feeler and found the hunter's mind. It was changing over to animal fast, his body appeared to be following suit and my skin was prickling with the energy. Holding on to the feeling, I sent my need through to him. The reaction was instantaneous.

He leaped the rest of the way across the woman and stalked toward me, his eyes never leaving my face. In the several paces it took for him to reach me, I stood mesmerized by his change. With each crouching step, I watched his body morph from human to leopard until he halted a hands breadth from my face, a low rattle emanating from his deep chest. He was taller than anything I'd ever seen on four paws, his shoulder was even with mine. When he reached his head up, sniffing the air with his jaws slightly open to taste the air around me, our mouths were inches apart.

I fought the panic rising within me. He was so large compared to the Andrews, I doubted I could beat him in a straight fight. Still, he was away from the woman and at least I knew James and possibly Troy were nearby. My job was solely to buy time at this point and that, I could do.

Sensing another predator so close, he dropped into a defensive posture, snarling in my face to show me a full set of razor sharp teeth. Standing firm I growled back, not expecting much. The cat brushed past pushing me with a shoulder, testing me. Regardless of fear and reservations that I couldn't beat him in a fight, my nature rose to the challenge and I hissed, pushing with both hands on his rib cage, knocking him aside and taking him off of his feet.

The moment his paws left the ground he was already twisting in midair to right himself, landing gracefully on all four. As they hit the ground, I heard his nails dig into the thin gray and blue commercial carpet. Sparing a glance at the gigantic claws, I saw they were each as big as my thumb. He growled low and menacing before he charged. I had only enough time to brace for the impact as the huge beast leaped and crashed into me, a mass of claws and teeth biting and tearing as we landed rolling on the ground.

My hands went up to guard my face out of instinct. His powerful teeth sank into my forearm holding it tight. I used the other to punch at his head. One blow landed solidly below his ear, stunning him for a few precious seconds. I pulled my feet up into my chest and got them under him, pushing with all of my strength. He flew backward across the room, sliding several yards across the floor. I smiled in satisfaction as I heard a crunch upon impact. He was slower to regain his feet, favoring a back leg. Yet still he ran at me, crouching low as I scrambled backward, hurriedly pulling myself up with a metal rail that presented itself behind me.

This time he lunged at me, like a man, wrapping his paws around my waist using his greater weight to his advantage. Again we went down. My hands, pushing against his throat to keep his snapping jaws from me, were too small to wrap around his neck and break it.

From where the woman lay on the ground, I heard a moan as she began to regain consciousness mere feet from where we snarled and struggled. I didn't have watch her to know when she saw us. Her gasp and racing heart clued me in.

The leopard dug his good back leg into the wood floor and pushed, spinning me around while he got a claw of his obviously not quite useless leg, hooked into the back of mine. I felt the limb go limp as my hamstring snapped with a sound of wet meat.

Pain temporarily shaking my focus, I watched the human woman clumsily trying to get to her feet.

The light coming in through the windows above glinted on something around her neck. Eyes zeroing in on it, I made out the shape of a small silver cross hanging from a delicate chain. The sight gave me an idea, the only problem was that I needed to bring her to me. My body could not carry me to her.

Calling upon the vampire nature fully aroused in me, I called to her. All I needed was to make eye contact, I hoped I could do it. "Hey!" She didn't turn, my call only served to cause her to redouble her efforts to escape. She had gotten to her feet and stumbled forward, frantically searching for an exit.

I concentrated hard on how it had felt when I had experienced commanding through James. Hands braced against the leopard's neck I held on to that and raised my voice, "Help me." It was not a shout, though it resounded through the large, open space.

So intently was I watching her, waiting to see if she would turn around, another set of claws gouged my side without me even trying to block them. My body was weakening from blood loss. Soon, I would have trouble controlling *my* urge to sink my fangs into the woman I'd come to save.

Then, she turned! Her eyes focused on mine and I locked onto her. The leopard was oblivious to her movements, so intent had he become with me. It was hard to tell, my psychic defenses were getting harder to hold as I lost strength, and I felt his excitement at tasting my blood in his mouth. My elbows were threatening to give. Sensing it, he pushed harder.

The woman crawled across the few feet separating us and I commanded her again. "Give me your necklace." Her hands automatically reached behind her neck to release the clasp and she held the tiny cross cupped in her hand. She started to step closer to hand it to me and I realized her danger. If she accidentally got bitten or scratched she might be turned and who knew what that might do to her unborn child.

Trying to spare her, I commanded her to toss it to me. She did so and it landed just beside me, easily within my reach. It had worked, she was free.

"Now run. Leave here and forget tonight. You were attacked by a man on the street, you hit your head, you remember nothing."

She nodded mutely and unsteadily turned on her heel. Once our eye contact was broken, she regained control of her body and followed the command now rooted in her brain. Her legs moved her out of range and rapidly out of sight. I heard the steel fire door close on the stairway and she was gone.

I was able to return my full attention to the leopard rapidly gaining ground in our deadlock. Precious blood was leaking from my mounting collection of scratches and bites. Having to use both hands to keep his mouth from tearing into me, I realized I couldn't grab the necklace to put it on him. I was going to have to release his hissing, snarling mouth and take what damage I must when I grabbed it. And I would have to be careful or if I touched it I would be paralyzed and he could take his time eating me until help came.

Steadying myself, I made ready to push him up hard and buy myself a precious few seconds before he came back down and possibly bit through my neck. He would know to decapitate a vampire from being around them. When I pushed and tore him off, his claws raked my ribs, grabbing for a hold as his body lifted off of me. I pulled my sleeve down to cover my hand, scooped the necklace by the chain and brought it back just before his teeth closed on my throat.

The were came down, mouth wide, aiming for my neck and my arm moved from an instinct as old as life itself. My hand swung and when it struck the side of his face to push him away, the weight of the cross and trajectory of my swing carried the tiny ornament directly from my palm into the snarling mouth above me.

The body of the leopard changed at once from a twisting, writhing shifting mass to a dead, crushing weight as he froze. I pushed his mouth shut to seal in the silver so it didn't fall on me and pushed with what was left of my strength to roll him off of me.

Faintly, I heard the fire door whip open, slamming with a bang into the concrete walls of the stairwell. James' familiar footsteps brought him to me in two breaths and he dropped down to run his hands over me, taking stock of my numerous injuries, most of which I hoped were superficial though I suspected a few were more worrisome. I turned my head, or rather, let it fall in his direction, to see him. He was sniffing at the leopard.

"He has silver stuck in his mouth. Careful if you move him."

James' expression was pained. "You did great, Claire. I couldn't have done better."

Bet you wouldn't have gotten shredded in the process. It was easier not to have to move my jaw to talk.

Where did you get silver?

The woman, she had a cross. I got her to bring it to me.

You commanded a human?

I had to.

James' attention was back to my physical needs as he smelled all the blood and recognized a good amount was mine. "I'll have Troy bring the car around. We'll get you home." His eyes hardened as he looked across me to the huge body beside me. "I'll be happy to hand him over."

On cue Troy jogged in to view. He quickly took in the scene and nodded approvingly. "Nicely done, Claire."

If I had the energy I would have laughed. How could anyone looking at my body say this was nicely done? Troy had low expectations. James growled in my head and I felt his anger with the leopard mixing with his pride.

A young vampire taking on an out of control were twice her size and *commanding a human is impressive. You will recover from your injuries. That is a success to me.*

I didn't answer the compliment that seemed so poorly deserved. He chuckled, taking my stubbornness as a good sign.

Troy spoke up. "The car is outside. If you can give me a moment, I can get rid of the street light out back. We can get them out that way."

My mouth tried to move and, feeling too tired to make it work, I gave up. *Did he bring Heidi? I don't want her to see me like this.*

James translated. "Did you tell Heidi to stay in the car? She doesn't need to see this."

"Yes," he responded. "She is scared but," he paused and his voice grew strained, "she was *supposed* to be waiting in the car."

A shoe scuffed by the door, "I couldn't just wait while who knows what happened in here." She approached and I watched her reaction as she took in the bloody scene including the giant frozen leopard. Troy grabbed her by the shoulders and tried to turn her into his chest. She balked, shrugging him off. Heidi came up beside where James knelt and sunk down in a pool of blood.

"Claire, are you dying?"

I blinked and tried to speak. One word was a lot, "No."

Her hand found mine and she squeezed. I weakly returned the gesture and curved one corner of my mouth. Her hand was warm on mine and I felt her pulse in her fingers. My hand tightened in a surprising strength borne of need.

Misreading it, Heidi brightened and looked up at Troy and James. "Hey, she just squeezed." She glanced back at me. "That's kind of hard, Claire. Can you loosen the grip a little?" she joked.

Doing as she asked for my own reasons I released her hand to grab her arm and started to pull.

"Hey, Claire, what are you doing?" Heidi's eyes opened wide and her smile faded when she began to realize my intention.

James intervened grabbing my wrist and squeezing, easily breaking my hold on her. Heidi scooted back, slipping in the blood beneath her and Troy helped her to her feet. Her jeans were covered in the dark liquid and she was rubbing her arm. This time she let Troy hold her and hide her face.

"Troy," James reminded him softly, "the car?"

Without a word, Troy left us with Heidi still clinging to him.

"Soon, Claire. Just hold on until we get you home. It'll hurt a lot less once you feed." He leaned in to kiss me around my fangs.

When Troy came back he was alone. "Light's out. I'll get the leopard. He can go in the trunk." He eyed me warily. "You ride in the back and make sure Claire's okay." A fool could read his true meaning. James was to restrain me if I tried to eat Heidi again.

James nodded and scooped me up in his arms. Troy grabbed the leopard, taking off his belt first to secure the mouth closed.

The vampire version of passing out is more of a zoning out. I was distantly aware of the noises around me, though it just sounded like there was a tv on in the other room. The only thing I could *not* zone out was the smell of the human in the front seat. Friend or not, my reserves were about used up and I wanted her desperately. I tried closing my eyes but that made it worse, giving me nothing else to distract me. Instead, I opened my eyes and stared up at James. He knew the battle I was fighting and talked to me in my head the whole ride. I didn't answer. I just listened, concentrating on his low, comforting voice as he sang my mother's song to me.

Finally we were home. Troy parked in the garage and before the engine was off, Heidi shot out of her seat. Troy backed

462

his own car up to nearly touch ours so he and James could throw the leopard into his trunk. I heard both trunks slam and Troy drove away without so much as a good-bye.

James closed the garage door, went in the house, and came out carrying a covered mug and a blanket to wrap me in. Even vampires don't want blood all over their houses. He carried me directly into the bathroom all the while I was busily sucking down the contents of the mug. Stripping us both, I heard his clothes sink softly to the floor and my own wetter garments smack against the tile.

He lifted me over the tub wall and held me while he washed the blood away. My wounds were already healing on the surface. The muscle and tendon injuries would take a few more hours and a lot more blood. Already I was able to take some of my own weight on my good leg as I felt the blood flowing through my vascular system.

My body cleaned and hair washed of gore and blood, James helped me to dry and dress myself. For once I didn't mind being taken care of. In bed, he lay with me and gave me a choice of books.

We lay together, me drinking a steady supply of blood and he read me two books for the next forty-eight hours. During that time, Detective Hanson called and James filled him in on what had transpired. We didn't know for sure, but believed the were had been working with a vampire. We would question him if we could before handing him over to the "authorities." This time the detective didn't question that term further. He wanted to thank us for catching the bad guy and was pleased to hear that, unlike our human system, this rogue were would be executed. There were no last minute save in his future.

"For us everything rests on being invisible. We don't have such indulgences as pardons and parole." James was unusually bitter. "We have to make harsh decisions, unlike humans who give endless chances to their own monsters."

The detective didn't argue. "You're right, we do give too many chances to the monsters. But wouldn't you welcome the option of a second chance for a mistake?"

I felt him thinking about those of his kind and those like the leopard he'd hunted over the decades. All damned for mistakes they were not allowed to repent. "Yes, Detective, but that is a luxury we just don't have."

Ch. 71

On the third day, we were invited to the were's trial and inevitable execution. As much as I didn't want to attend, I felt I owed it to the victims' families who would never know their loved ones had been avenged. That the killer had been stopped and they no longer had to fear anyone else suffering by his hand.

Much like the vampire Bradley's trial had been, it was outside, in a remote part of a wildlife reserve in the Minnesota River Valley. We drove to a trailhead where I recognized Henry's BMW already parked. I voiced my surprise.

"He's here with Tonya." James squeezed my hand.

Of course the clan would be here. These events were open to all weres and they treated them like reunions. The Weres' Council was not as involved as the vampires' so they didn't find as much cause to gather as we did. Aside from the occasional clan to clan get together, they pretty much lived their own lives.

And so it was a virtual party atmosphere I encountered when I reached the glade near the river where the others were gathered. Several normal looking "families" mingled and talked amongst themselves. Several had physical similarities like the Andrews had, though not all.

Tonya and Henry approached us, carefully avoiding any physical displays in front of the other weres. Tonya saw me examining the crowd.

"The clans are usually the same animals, like us. They look alike because the more time they spend in their animal forms, the more they take on the characteristics of that animal and obviously most animals in a species have strong resemblances." She gestured with her head toward a group that was very diverse from hair color to skin color. "Some who don't have any of their own kind in the area and are compatible form their own clans."

"Compatible?" I eyed them wondering if she meant as humans or as animals.

"Yes, usually the prey animals such as rabbits and mice. Predators can't be with prey for long. As you can well imagine, that wouldn't last beyond their first changing."

"Oh."

Stephen came striding up, giving me a huge hug. "Hey stranger, nice work." He winked.

I smiled and was ready to downplay the congratulations when a tall, dark haired woman with a body so muscular it was no longer feminine, stepped into the glade from the trees. A hush fell over the crowd and I gathered this was the emissary of the Council. Tonya told me she was a bear, that explained her shape. Stephen gave my arm a squeeze.

"Welcome fellow weres. We gather to hear the case against one of our own. Bring him," she called in the direction of the trees.

Two short, stocky men who could have been twins walked with the leopard in human form. At first I didn't understand what kept him from running. There were no shackles on him and he moved under his own power, so I knew he was not being touched by silver. Then I saw the sun peek through the clouds and reflect on the silver tips of the short spears each of the twin guards carried. The spear tips were inches from the prisoner's sides. Though not touching, they could be brought into play well before he would be able to escape, no matter how fast he was.

The prisoner and guards came to a halt in front of the woman. The weres gathered to hear her. She spoke only to the accused.

"You have allowed your beast to freely roam these cities. Your behavior has put us all in danger. This is not acceptable by our laws." She turned to the crowd and raised her voice. "Those among us have been witness to these transgressions."

As if it had been prearranged, I watched the crowd move aside to allow the woman an unobstructed view of Troy and our party. She lifted her head and sniffed, recognizing the scent of vampires in their midst. James and Stephen both closed until they had me sandwiched between them.

"Speak" she commanded him.

Troy raised his voice for all to hear. "A human police detective was aware of animal killings and enlisted the help of my associates." He indicated James and I.

I watched for her disapproval but if she had any she kept it hidden very well both outside and inside, I realized with frustration, unable to read her.

"They found him attempting another killing. The female was able to capture him."

She watched us for a moment longer before turning back to the prisoner. "Is this true?" Everyone watched him, curious to hear his defense.

He looked around himself and down at the silver on either side of him, trapping him. "Master wanted them. He gave them to me. He died. I wanted them." He snarled in frustration for having been denied his kill.

I was easily able to find his mind, having touched on it before. He was growing excited thinking of his kills, the

467

vampire had allowed him to take the bodies once they were dispatched, only insisting that they be hidden well away from there. Once his master had left, he was free to kill and eat at his leisure in the same place. That was why the last victim had so much more damage.

Who was his Master? Did you find out?

Troy tried to get it out of him before he handed him over but his mind is too far gone. All he could get was that his Master was strong, male and a vampire. I think it was Gaston or Bradley given the times with which we are working. This Master disappeared about the time they did and he has been operating on his own since.

Desperately, I hoped he was right.

The Bear woman's loud, rough voice raked over my ears.

"You have no control over your beast and are a danger to the rest of us. By order of the Council, your life is forfeit." She nodded to the twins and in perfect unison, stemming from an amount of practice that made me shudder, they pushed their spears toward each other through the beast and pulled them back out.

When the silver pierced the leopard's skin, his face froze in a permanently snarling death mask and he fell in a heap. I watched for signs he would turn to ash or somehow magically disappear. Nothing. Just like that, the killer was dead.

Confused, I turned to Troy, "Don't you disintegrate or something?"

Without looking away from the heap of spotted man he answered wryly, "No, we aren't as theatrical as your kind. We just die."

Stephen snorted.

Once the execution was over, the twins cut off the head, putting it neatly into a bag before they picked up the body and threw it without ceremony into the river to be washed downstream and cleaned of evidence. The weres resumed mingling and a surreal atmosphere of a reception descended.

Our presence was not necessary and our mixed clan made to leave until a rough voice beside Troy stopped us.

"May I speak with you?" the bear-woman asked. Now that she was closer, I could see that her eyes were the color of cinnamon and her hair was dark but there was a lot of auburn to it.

"It would be our pleasure, Madam," James answered first, bowing in a show of respect.

She was pleased with his manner and bowed her head in return. "We owe you thanks for your help once again. Our races have worked well together this time." She glanced over at Henry and Tonya. They didn't have to touch for her to see what was between them. "I will not interfere with that which benefits us." With that, she bowed again, turned and walked away.

"What did that mean?" Stephen watched the woman's masculine back disappear behind a clan of short chubby men whose animal counterpart escaped me.

Tonya was watching the woman go as well. "I think we're good for now." She spared a sideways glance at her little brother. "I'm still staying off the grid for the time being."

"That would be best for both of us," Henry seconded.

Before we could become any more involved in politics or draw more attention to ourselves, we melted back into the woods and left as fast as we could without running.

Ch. 72

I sat in the office finishing up a paper to email my professor before leaving for Utah. Apparently someone had turned a vampire there and she needed guidance through her transition. James and I were excited to go and get away from everyone for a while. When we got back, we had an assignment for our other employer, the paper. We had sold Phil, the editor, on sending us to Greece for a week.

My parents had only had us over for dinner once in the past month since the execution of the wereleopard. My dad was uncomfortable with the changes he saw in me and remained suspicious of James. Dad was ex-military and a perceptive man. He would prove to be a challenge to fool forever, though we hopefully had more time before we had to decide on a more permanent separation between us.

Henry and Tonya had been keeping a low profile and I was happy for them. Last I had heard, they were somewhere in Asia. They'd had so many roadblocks to their relationship for so long it was good to see them find happiness together. The thought of forever alone would be awful in my opinion.

As if I'd called him, a floorboard squeaked and James stepped into the room. Without turning, I put my arms up and he stepped in behind me, leaning down to kiss my head. I wrapped my arms around his neck and held him while I tipped my head back and kissed him upside down.

"Are you nearly done?" James asked, playfully nipping my nose.

"I just sent it. I am officially done until next week." The every other week format of Weekend College was working well and let me juggle work and school for now.

"We should get going soon," James reminded me.

He was referring to the reception my parents were holding for us today. They had rented out a ballroom at the Sheraton. It was a nice hotel and large enough to hold the hundred or so people coming for the event.

I was excited to have my family meet James again and introduce him as my husband. But what I was the most eager about tonight was meeting Stephen's new boyfriend. He'd decided to stay and was dating someone new. They had only been together for a week or so although I hoped for his sake that it turned into something. Even if this guy wasn't the love of his life, it would be nice for him to have someone he could open his heart to again. I was sure if he would forgive himself and allow it, he would find someone he could love.

Now that everything was calmer and there weren't any conspiracies running rampant, we didn't see the clan every day like we used to. It was good to be alone but sometimes I missed them.

I was nervous to see Heidi again. We hadn't seen each other since we had solved Earl's murder case. Troy said she was coming around as it all settled in to her brain, that we could still be friends given time.

Earl and Sandi were going to be there tonight as well, their wedding was just a few weeks away. Earl was almost as nervous to meet the entire family as James and I were to have Sandi meet Stephen. She would figure out he was "something" but the what, she would have to figure out herself. She could keep a secret provided we didn't do anything she deemed unreasonable.

That was why we had decided against wiping Earl's memory for the time being. He could help us to manage Sandi as well as be our resource within the police department. Miranda had tentatively approved him as someone who could act as an ally when one of ours, or even a were, showed up in their investigations.

"What should I wear?" I asked James.

"How about that red dress Miranda sent," he suggested jokingly.

Miranda was still sending things and trying to sell James on taking Anton's place with the Court, at first I'd thought that was why she let us keep Earl. The competition for the vacant seat was heated and there had been a few deaths already, which was inevitable considering the seat hadn't been empty for centuries and there was no election process. A member had to be killed and the party who killed him or her usually took the position. It was not a perfect system but when you considered how hard it could be to kill a vampire, even for another vampire to do so, it was more obvious why it didn't happen very often. It seemed a lot like natural selection to me. Only the smartest and strongest could rule.

I playfully swatted his rear and he growled. "This is our reception, not a dance club," I reminded him.

"Well," he stood up and spun my chair to face him. He lowered himself down to crouch in front of me. His kiss this time was slower and more suggestive. "The first step in getting dressed, is getting *un*dressed."

I threw back my head and laughed. He took the opportunity to nibble my throat and I growled back at him.

"I can do fashionably late," I giggled.

Acknowledgements

A huge thank you to every reader who has shown support for this series and helped to make it the absolute joy it has been to write and share. Although I don't get the opportunity to speak to every reader personally, if I could, I would tell you from the bottom of my heart, "Thank you."
To follow the works and adventures of this author, go to her website: www.hksavage.com
or visit her Facebook page under HK Savage or follow her on Twitter: @HKSavage